THE CRIME-SOLVING
COUSINS MYSTERIES

THE CRIME-SOLVING COUSINS MYSTERIES

BOOKS 1, 2, & 3

SHANNON L. BROWN

SIENNA BAY PRESS

Bundle:

Cover Illustration Tima Ghuloom

Cover designed by Najla Qamber Designs

Bundle ISBN: 978-1-945527-33-3

The Feather Chase:

Copyright © 2014 Shannon L. Brown

The Feather Chase Cover Illustration and Lettering © 2014 Jeanine Henderson

ISBN: 978-0-9898438-0-5

The Treasure Key:

Copyright © 2016 Shannon L. Brown

ISBN: 978-0-9898438-5-0

The Chocolate Spy:

Copyright © 2017 Shannon L. Brown

ISBN: 978-1-945527-12-8

❀ Created with Vellum

Sophie, Jessica, and their friend Tony never dreamed that they'd be in the middle of so many mysteries. They're glad you're here to join them!

THE FEATHER CHASE

THE CRIME-SOLVING COUSINS MYSTERIES

1 MAYBE A MYSTERY

"We've been going uphill for ages. This was a dumb idea." Jessica stumbled on the uneven dirt path. Her cousin Sophie had brought her to the middle of nowhere to torment her.

"It wouldn't be dumb if you'd worn sneakers instead of those fancy sandals." Sophie glared at Jessica's feet. Looking up, she pointed to the right. "Check out Pine Lake. The water's sparkling in the sun."

Jessica glanced in that direction, then sat down on a boulder. What good was a lake in the distance? She tucked her hair behind her ears, pulled a bottle of fingernail polish out of her purse, and started painting her thumbnail her favorite shade of pink.

Out of the corner of her eye, she saw Sophie lower her arm. "I'm not going to let you make me miserable. Follow me—or stay here with the wild animals."

Wild animals? Jessica's gaze darted around the thick pine trees surrounding her. Then she leaped to her feet, knocking the open bottle onto a rock.

Sophie stood with her hands on her hips and looked at her with disgust. "Pick it up, or the woodsy police will give you a ticket."

Jessica grabbed it, then tried to wipe off the dirt that had stuck to the oozing fingernail polish, but there was no saving the bottle. She held it up in the air. "It's all your fault."

"My fault? I didn't ask for you to spend the summer at my house. You staying with us while your mom and dad are gone was our mothers' idea. We haven't seen each other since we were little kids, but they thought you should stay at my house for the summer?"

"I know." Jessica stared at the bottle in her hand and felt tears welling up in her eyes. She *wouldn't* cry in front of Sophie.

"Here." Sophie pulled a plastic bag out of her pocket and handed it to her. "This is left over from a snack the other day. Put the bottle in it. There's a trash can at the end of the trail."

Jessica carefully dropped the sticky bottle and brush into the bag and put it in her shorts pocket.

"Flip that rock over too. Pink nail polish doesn't belong in a forest." Sophie glared at her partially painted fingernails.

When Sophie continued up the hill, Jessica walked beside her but kept her eyes open for those wild animals. When a bush rubbed against her legs and a small leaf stuck to her shorts, she quickly brushed it off. "Can you tell me what the purpose of this walk is?"

"Didn't you think the lake was beautiful? Isn't it great just being in this forest?"

Jessica looked around and yawned, covering her mouth with her hand. "I don't like forests. I like shopping. I prefer city things." For probably the tenth time today, she wondered why her parents had sent her to a town in a forest. She liked living in London, England. Her house there overlooked a nicely groomed park. She didn't have to walk around in all this nature.

"Maybe the outdoors will grow on you. Pretend we're on a great adventure."

"I think twelve's a little too old for that."

"I'm twelve too, and I don't think so. My dad says you're never too old to use your imagination."

"Okay. We're on a great adventure." Jessica lowered her voice to a whisper. "We're going to find a bunch of spies around that bend in the path."

Sophie seemed startled, then grinned. She must not have known Jessica had a sense of humor.

As they rounded the next bend, Jessica pointed to the ground. "Look. There's a briefcase."

Sophie giggled. "You're really getting into this."

"No, I mean there *really* is a briefcase."

Sophie looked in the direction Jessica pointed. "There is!"

A black leather briefcase, something like her dad used to carry papers to meetings, lay on its side, next to a big pine tree. Jessica knelt beside it.

"No!" Sophie shouted when her cousin reached for it. "Don't you watch all those spy movies? The briefcase is booby-trapped."

"You must be kidding." Jessica poked at it with her finger. Then she picked it up off the ground. "Gee. Nothing happened." Setting it on a boulder, she pushed on the latches. "It's locked up tight."

"We'd better take it to the sheriff's office."

"Good idea. Maybe they'll give us a reward for bringing it to them."

"Don't count on it. It's *more* likely that my mom will let us have something sweet for dessert."

Jessica laughed. "What is it with your mom and sweets? Last night's dessert was a bowl of apples, so I had to cut mine up to eat it with these." She tapped a finger on her braces.

"She's sure sugar will kill us all. I hadn't thought about your braces. Let Mom know, and she'll get other kinds of fruit." Sophie bent over their discovery. "Now, let's see this thing. Seems like an ordinary briefcase to me."

"How many briefcases have you seen?"

Sophie stood. "Lots."

Jessica stared at her in disbelief.

"Well, lots on TV."

Jessica rolled her eyes.

Sophie walked around the area, checking under bushes and pushing aside pine branches.

"What are you doing?"

"I'm making sure nothing else is hiding here."

"It's just bushes and bugs." An insect flew around her a couple of times.

Sophie stopped and pursed her lips in an annoyed way. "There might be a tent or sleeping bag. This could be from a camper."

"You think someone went camping and took along something people carry to a business meeting?"

Sophie circled a tree. "People do strange things."

Yes, like this.

Sophie stood and brushed her hands off on her jeans. "Let's get this to the sheriff so we can see what's inside." She grabbed the briefcase and started walking down the trail. "I'm glad we're getting out of here long before it's dark. I don't want to have to wonder about whatever bad guy dropped this thing when owls are hooting and bats are flying."

Jessica glanced around the forest nervously. "Owls and bats? If they're out at night, where are they during the day?"

"They must be asleep."

Jessica stared up at the treetops. "What if someone wakes them up—by accident?"

"I don't think that can happen." Sophie checked her watch. "This is taking longer than I want it to. Follow me." She took off running down the path they'd come on, veering to the right, then down a steep, narrower path.

Jessica ran as fast as she could in her sandals. Her feet started to hurt, and the pain inched its way up her legs until they turned to Jell-O. Gasping for breath, she made a mental note to use her mom's exercise equipment when she got home and kept her focus on Sophie. Her sandal strap caught on a root in the path, but she jerked it free and stayed on her feet. A tiny image of long, brown hair in a ponytail, faded blue jeans, and a white T-shirt leaped over a small stream. Sophie hit the ground on the other side with both feet and kept running.

"Wait," Jessica yelled as loud as she could.

Sophie ground in her heels and came to a full stop as Jessica hurtled down the hill toward her, her arms flailing at her sides. As she got closer, Jessica decided not to jump the stream—she knew she couldn't make it—so she held her arms straight out and stepped from one rock to another.

About halfway across, Jessica asked, "Why didn't we come back over the bridge like when we left?"

"This way is faster. I usually run all the way home and jump over this stream in my backyard. I forgot about your sandals."

"They're fine where I'm from. We have sidewalks. There is no stream in my backyard. And you must admit the shoes look pretty good." She paused, thinking about which of two rocks to step on next. Only one more rock to go and she was over.

"I'm more of a sneaker kind of girl." Out of the corner of her eye, Jessica saw Sophie lift up her right foot. "See?"

"Can't look now." Jessica carefully stepped on the last rock she needed to cross the stream. When it shifted from side to side, she flapped her arms to keep her balance, then jumped to land. "Made it."

Sophie was standing in front of her with her eyes closed. She'd probably been waiting for a splash. She opened one eye slowly before opening the other. Yep, she had. "Let's get this to the sheriff." Sophie held up the briefcase.

"Slowly this time."

Sophie shrugged and said, "If we're going to walk slowly, let's at least take the shortcut through the woods into town."

"No problem."

They walked past Sophie's big white house, then through the woods. Jessica asked, "Do you know your sheriff?"

"Yeah, I've spent some time in the sheriff's office."

Jessica stopped. "Were you arrested?"

Sophie stopped beside her. "No. When I think I've found a mystery, I drop in and talk to her about it. Besides, her office is the most exciting place in town." She took a step and waved her on.

Jessica stepped beside her. "The sheriff's a woman?"

"Yep."

She thought about the hard-as-nails sheriffs and police officers she'd seen on TV and in the movies. "Is she tough—like a human bulldog?"

"Of course not," Sophie replied. "She's normal." She seemed to be thinking about her for a moment. "Sheriff Valeska is tall and has brown hair, but you usually can't see it because she has a sheriff's hat on top of it." Sophie turned to Jessica and looked her over. "I don't think she wears makeup or fingernail polish."

Jessica grimaced. She wouldn't leave the house without perfect makeup and hair.

"Sheriff Valeska is really nice, but she says my love of mysteries tries her patience sometimes." Sophie grinned.

Jessica laughed. Then she pictured her cousin's description of the sheriff and grimaced again.

When they got to town, they walked several blocks, past businesses and houses. Then Sophie led her through the door of the sheriff's office. It surprised her when they walked inside that a pretty woman in a uniform sat at a desk, and Sophie said, "Hi, Sheriff."

"Hi, Sophie." The sheriff smiled.

"Sheriff Valeska, this is my cousin Jessica Ballow."

"Pleased to meet you, Jessica. Sophie's mom told me you were arriving yesterday." Glancing from one to the other, she said, "Other than being about the same height, you're strikingly different."

Standing still while someone scrutinized her wasn't easy, but Jessica did her best to be polite. "Our moms are almost identical, but Sophie has her dad's brown hair and brown eyes, and I have my mom's blonde hair and green eyes."

"I think you'll enjoy your summer in Pine Hill, Jessica." The sheriff pushed back from her desk and smiled broadly. "Now, Sophie, I know from experience that you came here with a mystery. What's up?"

Sophie set the briefcase on the sheriff's desk and sat down on one of the avocado green plastic chairs in front of it. Jessica stayed out of the way and stood off to the side. After describing where they'd found the briefcase, Sophie asked, "So, do you think it belongs to a spy?"

Sheriff Valeska laughed. "I doubt that." She picked up the briefcase and examined it. "The bus stops at McGuire's Motel just outside of town. Nellie McGuire rarely remembers to turn on her No Vacancy sign when the motel's full. My guess is that someone got off the bus thinking they could get a room there but couldn't. The sign for Cutoff Trail is across the street from the motel, so they took it, hoping it was a shortcut to Pine Hill and another hotel. But it's a steep hill—"

"No kidding." Jessica sighed. "When we ran home, I was so out of breath I didn't think I'd ever catch up with Sophie."

"You aren't the first person who's gotten tired on one of Sophie's treks through the woods."

Jessica relaxed. Maybe she didn't need to work out.

"Go on, Sheriff," Sophie begged.

"Oh yes. The briefcase owner probably got tired when he or she neared the top of the hill and set down their luggage." Leaning back in her chair, she added, "My guess is that there's a suitcase near the place you found this briefcase."

Sophie's brown eyes sparkled. "Ooh, we'll have to search again."

The sheriff shook her head and grinned.

Sophie scooted to the front of the seat. "Come on, Sheriff, Let's see what's inside."

"Please open it!" Jessica urged the sheriff.

Jessica watched her push on the latches, then push again. When they didn't budge, the sheriff reached for the phone. "Homer, this is Mandy Valeska. I've got a locked briefcase here that needs to be opened. Okay. Sure." She hung up the phone.

"Is he coming now?" Sophie leaned forward in her chair, nearly tipping it over.

"No."

"What?" both girls said at the same time.

"He's got a woman up at the resort that accidentally locked her baby in the car. He'll be here in about a half hour. I need you two to be very quiet while you wait. I have a lot of work to do." She faced her computer and started typing.

Jessica sat in the chair next to Sophie, tapping her fingers on the arm of the chair until the sheriff stopped typing and frowned. She tucked her hand into her pocket and glanced around the room, her gaze coming back to the big clock on the wall every few minutes. A half hour with nothing to do was a very long time.

Finally, when she didn't think she could sit still a minute longer, a small man wearing worn jeans, a red flannel shirt, and wire-rimmed glasses that sat on the end of his nose entered the sheriff's office.

"Mr. Winston!" Sophie called out and turned toward Jessica. "He's our locksmith, so now we get to see what's in the briefcase. This is it."

Sheriff Valeska moved the briefcase to a table in the middle of the room. "Here you go, Homer."

He set a small leather satchel on the table, then picked up the briefcase and turned it from side to side, carefully examining the two locks. Then he reached into the satchel and took out a tool. "This will only," Mr. Winston said as he put it into one of the locks, "take a minute."

Jessica heard a small click.

He repeated the process on the other lock.

"There you go."

He put his tool back in his open bag, closed it, then picked up the bag and practically ran to the door.

"Thanks for coming, Homer," the sheriff called after him, "but don't you want to see what's in the briefcase?"

"No time." He gave a quick smile and waved as he went out the door. "Got to get over to Simpson's Shoes . . ." His voice faded away as the door closed behind him.

Sheriff Valeska turned toward Jessica and Sophie. "Are you girls ready for the big reveal?"

They crowded next to the sheriff as she popped the briefcase open.

2 FLYING FLUFF

Poof! White things flew into the air.

Sophie grabbed a handful, then opened her hand to see what they were. "It's raining feathers." Opening the briefcase was better than she'd imagined.

"Catch them, girls. We need to get these back in the briefcase." Sheriff Valeska rushed into a back room and returned with a white trash bag.

The three of them grabbed feathers out of the air and dropped them into the bag. When a deputy walked in the door, he stopped and stared wide-eyed at them until the sheriff said, "Hank, help us clean this up." Moving into action, he picked feathers up off the floor, adding them to the plastic bag.

A few minutes later, Jessica looked up and around. "There aren't any more feathers floating in the air."

The sheriff said, "I'll clear them off this table and we'll be done."

Sophie turned toward Jessica and giggled. "No, we won't. Jessica's covered. She must have been right in front of the briefcase when it opened." Sophie started plucking the feathers off her, then paused and studied a handful of them.

"Hurry up." Jessica shifted from one foot to the other.

Sophie turned the feathers over in her hand. "You know, there are little bits of white, fluffy stuff mixed in with the feathers."

Jessica lifted a feather off her wrist and dropped it in Sophie's hand.

"Okay, I get the message." Sophie dropped them in the bag, then walked around Jessica, looking her over. "She's clean."

Sophie peered into the open briefcase, then picked up two feathers that had stuck to the side and dropped them in the bag. "All the feathers are in the bag now."

Sheriff Valeska scowled. As she put a tie around the top of the plastic bag, she said, "But you added another set of fingerprints to the inside of the briefcase. Yours." She shook her head. "While there isn't anything illegal about feathers, I can't think of any reason someone would carry them around in a briefcase. I'm going to have a deputy dust this for fingerprints. And I'll have to get your fingerprints, Sophie, so he'll know to ignore them."

"My fingerprints!" Sophie said excitedly.

The sheriff laughed. "Someone else might be annoyed at having their fingerprints taken, but Sophie's excited."

"I'm learning that she's one of a kind," Jessica said.

Sheriff Valeska got out the fingerprinting materials, took all ten fingerprints, then pulled out a wipe and handed it to Sophie.

Sophie stared first at the wipe then at the black ink on her fingertips. Having the ink on her fingers might be fun. Then she could show people and tell them what had happened.

Jessica rolled her eyes. "Wipe it off, Sophie. It *won't* be fun to walk around with ink on your fingers."

Yeah, it probably would have been. Sophie gave in and took the wipe. "Other than when we first opened the briefcase and, of course, when I got fingerprinted, this wasn't as exciting as I'd hoped."

"Nope," Jessica said. "Not much excitement here. A pillow fight would have given us feathers—and fun."

"I'm not sure I agree." As Sheriff Valeska walked toward the back room with the briefcase and bag of feathers, she said, "I don't want to get you girls going again, but it's a bigger mystery than *I* expected. A briefcase full of feathers?" She vanished out of sight through a doorway.

"Now what?" asked Jessica.

Something at the edge of Sophie's vision caught her attention. She squinted and peered out of the corner of her eye. Almost cross-eyed, she reached up and plucked a feather out of her hair. "I guess all the feathers didn't land on you." Sophie held it up. The sheriff thought they had a mystery. Solving it would be much easier with their own feather. "This can be our first clue."

"Actually, it's Sheriff Valeska's clue. It's now property of the sheriff's office."

"Sheriff?" Sophie called out.

"Yes, Sophie?" the sheriff answered from the storeroom.

"Can we borrow the feather I just found in my hair?"

After what seemed like a long pause, she said, "Well, since you found the briefcase and there are so many feathers, go ahead. But remember you're just borrowing it and have to bring it back."

"Gotcha." Sophie rushed over and opened the door with one hand, clutching the feather in the other. She said to Jessica in a low voice, "Let's get out of here before she changes her mind."

"Absolutely."

Once out the door, Sophie went straight to a bench on the sidewalk and motioned for Jessica to sit next to her. When Jessica was seated, Sophie covered her mouth with her hand and said, "See that man?"

Jessica leaned closer. "I can barely hear you."

"I said, 'See that man?'" Sophie replied in a slightly louder voice and gestured to the right with her thumb.

Jessica started to turn that way.

"No! Be subtle. Don't let him know you're watching him."

Jessica hummed softly, and with an almost believable casual

look, turned that direction. "I see a man in a brown suit and a rust-colored tie."

"That's him."

"That's who?"

"That's the man who stole the money from the bank and left it in the briefcase in the woods."

"You've lost it. By the way, I thought the briefcase belonged to a spy."

"Spy, bank robber, it could be either one."

"And don't you always have strangers in this town?"

"Well . . . there are always tourists at the resort—but look at that guy."

"I can't."

"Why?"

"He's gone."

Sophie whipped around. "He was wearing a suit. Almost no one wears a suit in Pine Hill. Even the tourists. They dress in brand-new, relaxed-type clothes. Sometimes I think I could find a price tag hanging off them if I got close."

Jessica giggled. "They can't be that bad."

"The clothes are. But the people are usually okay. They just want to relax. As the ads say, 'Come to Pine Hill in the mountains to unwind. Let clean air and sparkling water revive you.'"

"You're kidding."

"Nope. Men leave their suits behind. From what I can tell, it's tough to relax in a suit and tie." Sophie pulled her shirt tightly around her neck like she was wearing a tie. Her breathing cut off and she let it go, gasping for air. "Whew. I can see why."

Jessica settled down next to her on the bench. "Let's work out a plan of action."

"Agreed. First we need to find out all we can about this feather."

"Good plan. Let's get on your computer and Google 'feathers.'" Jessica started to stand.

Sophie grabbed her arm and pulled her back down. "It isn't that easy."

"Huh?"

"I'm surprised you haven't asked about a computer before. Or cell phone access."

"Mom said she'd text me when she arrived in the Middle East where Dad's working, and I knew that wouldn't be until later today. I'd just assumed you hadn't needed to text or call anyone on your phone."

"I don't have a cell phone. It wouldn't matter much if I did anyway. The reception in town is okay but not great, and almost zero outside of town."

Jessica pulled her phone out of her bag. "Nothing."

"Told you. You might have service a block away. They say it's because of the mountains."

Jessica tucked her phone back into her purse. "Well, it's easier to use a computer with a larger screen for something like this anyway."

"Um . . ." Sophie looked down. This felt more than a little embarrassing.

"Is your computer broken?"

"That's just it. Mom likes things that are old, and doesn't like things that are new. She also thinks I'd find a way to get in trouble on the Internet."

Jessica sprang to her feet. "You don't mean—"

Sophie sighed. "Yep. We don't have a computer. Well, other than the one Dad has in his office since he works at home, but that's only for his business."

"How do you do projects for school?"

"I go to the library."

"Great. I like libraries." Jessica sounded kind of nervous when she quickly said, "Is it a brick building like all of these?"

Sophie nodded, then stood. "We do seem to like brick here. The library's only a few blocks from here. I go there a lot."

On the way there, Jessica stopped in front of a drugstore.

"Let's run in here, Sophie. I want to replace the fingernail polish I dropped."

"Sure." Sophie followed Jessica through the cosmetics section to an area with dozens of bottles of nail polish. "So many colors."

"The choice isn't just about color. There's frosted or not, and other things, too." Jessica scanned the shelves, searching through lots of polish. "I found it! It's the perfect pink." She held up a bottle of nail polish.

Sophie shrugged. One pink looked pretty much like another.

"It's the same as the one that got ruined. It was my favorite." She clutched it to her chest and rushed to the cash register.

When they were standing in line, Sophie felt like a jerk. "Um, I think that was my fault." She tapped the top of the bottle in Jessica's hand. "You know, that it fell. I think I should pay for it."

"How 'bout we split the cost? It was stupid of me to be doing my nails in the middle of a hike."

Sophie pulled money out of her back pocket, gave it to her, and Jessica took the rest out of her purse.

———

Stepping into the library made Jessica feel at home for the first time since she'd arrived in Pine Hill. She had to play it cool, though, because if Sophie knew she spent a lot of time in libraries, her cousin might figure out that she was the extra-smart type. Then she might not fit in here, just like she didn't seem to fit in anywhere else.

Sophie typed "birds" in the online catalog. A long list of books flashed onto the screen. "Wow. Twenty-two books. Something in here should solve the mystery."

Jessica peered over Sophie's shoulder and laughed. "The first two are books for little kids, and the third one is a turkey cookbook."

Sophie paged through the list. "Here's one that sounds good.

Birds of North America. And here's another one that might help. *Raising Ducks and Geese for Fun and Profit.* Maybe the feather is from a duck or a goose." She checked through the rest of the list and sighed. "Only two useful books out of twenty-two."

After writing down the two call numbers, she tore the paper in half. "I'll find this one and you find the other one," she said as she handed Jessica the bottom half of the paper. "Let's meet"— she looked around the room, then pointed at a couple of chairs —"there."

Jessica loved wandering through the stacks, seeing what this library had to offer. It took her longer than she'd expected to return with the book she'd been assigned. Sophie was already flipping through her book, so Jessica sat and started checking hers out.

A minute later, Sophie sighed as she closed the book and set it on the table next to her chair. "Is yours useless, too?"

"It's only helpful if you want to buy a few ducks or geese and stick them in your backyard."

Sophie grinned. "Interesting thought, but I don't think Mom and Dad would go for it. Mine showed pictures of birds, but no up-close feather photos."

"We'll have to find another way to get answers." Placing her hand on her stomach, Jessica said, "I'm starving. Do you know when we're having dinner?"

"Mom can't leave her antique shop until the last customer leaves. Then she comes home to cook dinner. Dad *isn't* good in the kitchen." Sophie shuddered.

"Let's hurry to your house. Maybe the customers left early."

Sophie patted her pocket. "I'll be happy to have the feather in a safe place at home."

As they walked, Jessica thought about the briefcase full of feathers. They could just leave the whole thing to the sheriff, but Jessica already knew Sophie well enough to be sure she wouldn't like that idea. She figured Sophie must be thinking about the feathers too, because she hadn't seen her stay quiet this long.

When they turned onto the shortcut through the woods to Sophie's house, her cousin finally broke her silence. "We should be working on our mystery."

"Cousin, we just *found* a briefcase. I admit that having feathers inside it is strange, but we don't know for sure that there is a mystery."

"The sheriff said it was a mystery. I think bad guys chased a criminal through the woods, and the criminal dropped the briefcase."

"And the guy chasing him didn't notice when he tripped over it?" Jessica shook her head.

"It was off to the side of the trail, so he wouldn't have tripped. Anyway, think about the mystery."

Trying to appear very serious, Jessica said, "I'll give it my deepest thought."

Sophie rolled her eyes. "Why don't I believe you? The big question is: why did someone leave the briefcase out in the open on the path, where anyone could see it, and why was it filled with feathers?"

"That's two questions."

"Whatever. Do you ever get that funny feeling that someone's watching you?" Sophie asked as she glanced around.

Jessica shrugged. "Sometimes. Why?"

"How about now?" Sophie stopped and glanced over her shoulder.

"Nothing." Jessica stared up into the tall trees, then around to the path behind them. "Everything seems normal, at least as normal as a forest ever seems to me."

"I keep getting the feeling that someone's watching." Sophie snapped her fingers. "I know. It's the guy in the brown suit."

Jessica studied the ground. Pushing a rock to the side with her foot, she studied it. Then she raked a pile of leaves aside.

"What are you doing?"

"I'm looking for your mind. You must have lost it around here because you seemed intelligent just a short time ago."

"Funny. Let's be quiet and see if we hear anything."

A loud cracking sound made them both jump.

3 HIDING SECRETS

Jessica whispered, "What was that?"

"A branch breaking."

The girls looked at each other and Sophie whispered, "It could be just an animal."

A chill went through Jessica. "You're telling me it's either a wild animal or a criminal?"

"That does sound bad." Sophie peered over her shoulder one last time, then whispered, "I'll beat you home."

"No, you won't," Jessica whispered back.

A second later, Sophie took off running, and Jessica chased after her. When the heel on Jessica's sandal caught on a tree root, she grabbed the tree's trunk and swung around it, barely stopping herself from falling. Her shoes seemed to catch on everything in her path. If running from spies and thieves was going to be part of her life in Pine Hill, she would, unfortunately, have to wear sneakers.

Sophie's big, old, white house came into view around a bend in the path. They ran up the steps, pulled open the wooden screen door, and skidded to a stop.

"We're home," Sophie called out.

Jessica's racing heart started to beat a little more normally when her aunt April answered from the kitchen, "Dinner in twenty, girls."

They fell onto the sofa, panting. Sophie set the feather on the coffee table and between breaths said, "Let's examine the evidence."

Jessica picked up the feather and studied it. "Remember the fluffy white things that were with the feathers?"

"Yes, but I don't know what they were."

"That's another piece of the puzzle that's missing."

"You know, it's complicated enough just finding out about this feather." Sophie tapped her chin with her finger. "We should ignore the fluffy stuff for now."

"Good idea. I've thought about feathers enough. Let's hide this and take a feather break."

"Agreed. For now." Sophie grabbed it out of Jessica's hand and walked into her bedroom.

Jessica followed her. "Where can we keep the feather that's safe?" Jessica glanced around the room. Under the lamp? No, it might blow out if someone opened the window. In the drawer in the nightstand? No, too obvious. Maybe . . . she noticed Sophie kneeling in her closet.

"What are you doing?" Jessica pushed clothes on hangers out of the way and knelt beside her. "Do you have some kind of secret hiding place?"

"The best." Sophie used a bent hanger to pry up one of the floorboards, then reached in and pulled a metal box the size of a big paperback book out of the hole.

"That's great! Did you make this hole?"

"No. The board's been loose all my life. But I was reading a book where a loose board in a closet hid a treasure."

"So you threw down the book and ran to the closet."

Sophie nodded her head. "You can't imagine how excited I was when I pried up the board, and inside I found a metal box."

"And?"

"And it was empty." She sighed. "Too bad, but it makes a

great hiding place." Sophie dropped the feather in the box, fit it back in the hole, and replaced the board.

———

After dinner, Sophie, Jessica, and Sophie's dad, Lucas Sandoval, waited for Sophie's mom to bring the bowl of fruit, but she came through the kitchen door carrying a yellow box instead.

"Dessert?" Her mom hadn't given them an actual dessert in months.

"I knew you girls would be hungry after wandering around in the woods all morning, so I bought you a surprise at Bananas." When she set the open box on the table, they leaned over to peer inside.

"I see slices of cake and a plastic container with," Sophie picked it up, "strawberries in it. Wow! Strawberry shortcake." She set it down and licked her lips.

"Correction," Mrs. Sandoval said. "Strawberries on banana shortcake. You know how Abigail Bowman is about bananas."

Sophie laughed and turned to Jessica. "She puts them in everything in her bakery, but the weird thing is that it's all good. I guess you could say she's bananas about bananas."

Jessica groaned.

"She was trying out a chocolate chip cookie when I stopped in today."

"With bananas?" Jessica grimaced.

"No. She wanted to see if other people liked things without bananas."

They all laughed.

Mrs. Sandoval snapped her fingers. "I almost forgot. I bought some cream for you." She went back into the kitchen and returned with two cans of whipped cream. "I've got some paper-work to do, so I'll leave you guys to it."

Mr. Sandoval said, "Dessert is a special occasion for us. You need to visit more often, Jessica." He put strawberries on cake, covered it with whipped cream after reading the directions on the can, then put a spoonful of his dessert in his mouth. "Mmmm."

Jessica and Sophie made their shortcake. Then each grabbed a can of whipped cream. Sophie stopped to read the directions on the can.

As Jessica squirted hers, she said, "Uncle Lucas, you and Sophie act like you've never seen a can of whipped cream before."

"We haven't." He put the can down and took a bite of shortcake.

"What? Really?"

Sophie said, "Well, we've never seen a can of whipped cream in this house." Slowly eating a bite, she enjoyed the thrill of having dessert. "Yum."

"Now I understand why you had to read the directions and you have two cans for three people. You've got enough here for you and your closest friends."

Mr. Sandoval laughed. "None of us knew we had too much. Oh, this is so good."

Jessica tasted hers. "It is. And the banana shortcake is delicious." She wiped off some cream that splashed on the table, then asked, "This table is big and heavy. It seems old, so I wondered, is it an antique?"

"Almost everything in our house is an antique. Mom loves them, and she doesn't like much that's new." As Sophie took another bite, her mind shifted to the mystery, and she pictured a man running with a briefcase through the woods. "You know, Jessica, I like my theory about spies in Pine Hill."

Mr. Sandoval made choking sounds.

Sophie ran into the kitchen, coming back with a glass of water. Her dad took a sip. "Spies?" he croaked, then took a long drink of water.

"Sure, Dad." Sophie explained what had happened that day.

He sat back and laughed. "I know I've told you over and

over to use your imagination, but you might be overdoing it, Soph."

"You wait and see." Sophie knew they'd stumbled upon something exciting. She knew a mystery was waiting to be solved.

4 A CREAMY MESS

Jessica stretched and watched the pattern of morning sunlight on the wall as it filtered through the trees outside her window. Morning. Worse yet, morning a long way from home. She'd spent every other summer with her mother and brother somewhere in Europe, her dad joining them when he could get away from work. Except for when they'd all gone to Thailand the summer Dad worked there.

Rolling over, she squinted at her cousin.

"Good morning," Sophie said, radiating happiness.

Jessica grunted. Mornings were, well . . . early in the day. And there wasn't a reason to be happy.

Sophie added, "Isn't this a beautiful day?"

Jessica squinted again, then blinked a few times.

"See the sunshine coming through the window?"

Jessica blinked then grunted again. No matter how hard she'd tried in the past, she'd never been able to make complete sentences first thing in the morning.

Sophie rolled over, turning her back to her. "Maybe you should just get out of here and go take your shower."

Jessica stared at Sophie's back, wishing her parents were

here. They'd sent her to this strange place where she didn't know anyone. And now her cousin was being mean to her again. Jessica got up, grabbed her robe off the end of the bed, and trudged into the bathroom.

"Hurry up," Sophie shouted. "You don't need six pounds of makeup here."

Jessica bit her tongue to hold back the tears. That horrible person wasn't going to make her cry. She hurried into the shower, feeling better the longer she was awake.

After her shower, Jessica opened the drawer in Sophie's dresser that she'd been given along with half the closet. She chose hot pink shorts with flowers on them and a matching pink T-shirt. Then she dried her hair, deciding to leave it straight, only touching it up with a flat iron. Blush, lip gloss, and mascara— and a quick repair of her less-than-perfect fingernail polish— completed her look.

She wandered around the house for a few minutes. Hearing noises, she pushed open the kitchen door. Sophie, Miss Sunshine, stood at the counter, wearing an old white T-shirt and the usual faded jeans. Jessica didn't think she'd bought the jeans faded either because they looked like they'd been around a long time. Instead of fixing her hair differently today, she'd pulled it into another ponytail.

"I'm having strawberry shortcake for breakfast." Sophie glared at her in a way that said, *Do you have a problem with that?*

"Sounds great." Jessica smiled, trying to be cheerful as she put some of the leftover cake in a bowl and spooned strawberries over it. But Sophie continued being nasty.

"Here." Sophie slammed a can of whipped cream in front of her, then got the other one out of the fridge. When she squirted the cream in her bowl, it splattered onto Jessica's arm.

Jessica stared at her arm. She just knew Sophie had done that on purpose. Pointing her can at her cousin, she pushed the top. Whipped cream flew onto Sophie's chin and splashed her hair.

Sophie blinked, then reached up and touched her chin.

Uh-oh, Jessica thought, *I definitely should not have done that.*

Sophie pointed her can at her and squirted it. Jessica could feel the whipped cream covering her hair.

She pushed on her can's nozzle and sprayed Sophie with all her might, covering her from head to toe. Her cousin just stood there, stunned. Finally, when Jessica's can sputtered, spit, and stopped, Sophie turned on her, letting her cream fly. Jessica put up her hands to block the flow, but she could feel the gloppy cream hitting her head, her feet, and everything in between.

When that can made sputtering sounds, Sophie glanced down at it, then around the kitchen. "Oh, no!"

Jessica followed her gaze. Whipped cream had splashed onto the cupboards, countertops, and fridge. "We're in trouble now."

"Maybe not. If we can get this cleaned up before Mom or Dad sees it . . ."

Jessica grabbed the dishrag and started wiping the front of a cupboard. "Do you think the whipped cream will hurt the wood the cupboards and floor are made of?"

"No. They're even older than Mom and Dad. They've seen it all." Sophie pulled out a mop, got it wet, and wiped the floor.

A short time later, Sophie leaned the mop against the counter, then slowly turned in a full circle. "Whew. I think that's it."

Jessica threw her rag in the sink. "Finally. When I wiped off the full coffeepot, I realized your dad might come in to get some before we finished. But we made it."

Now that they had the kitchen clean, Jessica really looked at Sophie for the first time. She was leaning against the cupboards and covered in whipped cream from her hair to her knees. Jessica giggled. When Sophie seemed puzzled, she pointed at her.

Sophie looked down at herself, then at Jessica. For a few seconds Jessica thought she would yell at her, but instead she burst out laughing.

That made Jessica start laughing. She laughed so hard that she crumpled to the ground, holding her aching middle.

Sophie slowly slid down the cupboards and landed on the floor beside her. "I didn't know you knew how to laugh," she gasped between words.

"You were so mean that I thought you never laughed."

"I wasn't mean. You were. You were nice after we found the briefcase, so I thought you were a nice person."

Jessica stopped laughing. "Me mean? What about this morning? You yelled at me about my makeup."

Sophie wrinkled her brow. "That's because you were nasty right away. You got out of bed and didn't say a word."

"I never talk in the morning."

"Never?"

"Never. Mom says I'm the worst person in the morning that she's ever seen or heard of."

Sophie stared at her in disbelief. "I didn't notice it yesterday morning."

"I'd traveled the day before, so I slept in. You were already up and didn't see me until after my shower."

"I'll remember not to talk to you when you first wake up. Your photo is next to the word grumpy in the dictionary." Sophie leaned over and hugged her. "I'm sorry, Jessica."

Jessica hugged her back. "Me too."

The kitchen door swung open, and Sophie's dad walked in carrying a mug. Jessica held her breath, hoping he'd be thinking about something else, get his coffee, and not notice his cream-covered daughter and niece on the floor. Instead, he poured a cup of coffee, then reached down to swipe his finger through the whipped cream on Sophie's cheek before turning and walking toward the door, licking it off. "Soph, you'd better replace the whipped cream before your mom knows it's gone."

Jessica watched him walk out the door. "He didn't yell," she said in amazement.

"I knew I had a great dad, but he's even greater than I

thought." Sophie looked at the empty cans of whipped cream on the counter. "But he's right. Mom sees food as something that's not to be played with." Sophie stood. "Let's finish with this mess, then wash our clothes and us. We can go to the grocery store for whipped cream this afternoon—after we've done some sleuthing." She had that excited *I love a mystery expression* again.

5 SHOES AND CLUES

Jessica dreaded the next thing she needed to do. "Before we leave, I have to get something."

"Huh?"

Jessica held up her right foot. "Shoes."

"You'll have to excuse me for saying this, but you have a lot of shoes."

"Yes," Jessica said, "but not shoes I can run in."

"Now you're talking. Let's go get some at Simpson's Shoes."

"Not necessary." Jessica furrowed her brow as she thought. "But why does that name sound familiar?"

"Mr. Winston was on his way there after he opened the briefcase."

"Ah, yes. No, I just need my suitcase." She just didn't see any other choice.

"You said 'shoes' and now you want your suitcase? Are you leaving?"

Where would she go? "No. I didn't unpack everything."

Sophie waved her on.

They went outside and through the side door of a separate garage, where Sophie pointed to a suitcase leaning against the back wall. Jessica exhaled deeply and opened it. Then she reached into the side pocket.

Sophie bent over her. "Do you have shoes in there?"

As Jessica pulled out first one shoe and then the other, Sophie exclaimed, "Sneakers! You have sneakers, but you've been hiking in sandals?"

"Mom made me pack them. I've only worn them in gym class and didn't want them this summer."

"Your mom's smart."

Jessica held up the white, slightly worn shoes. She sighed. "I guess so." After slipping them on, she walked around the room. They would work. But they weren't cute.

"You seem sad, cousin. How 'bout if I treat you to lunch at Donadio's Deli?"

"I am hungry." Jessica tried hard to smile. "At least I can run now. Of course, I hope I don't *need* to run."

———

When they got to town, Jessica read the signs as they walked by stores. Walking past the window of the shoe store the locksmith had mentioned, she said, "Ooh, love those blue flats. We'll have to come back here." Still reading store signs, she ran into Sophie's back. *Whap.*

Sophie caught her before she fell. "We're here." She pushed Jessica upright and held open the glass door.

When Jessica looked up, a dark-haired boy behind the deli counter was staring at them and laughing. "You didn't tell me a cute boy worked here. And he saw clumsy me run into you," she whispered to her cousin as they walked inside.

"Who?" Sophie followed Jessica's gaze. "Oh, you mean Tony. His parents own this place."

Tony made their sandwiches. Jessica had a veggie on whole wheat with chips, Sophie had roast beef on white with potato salad. He didn't say much but seemed to be nice. And oh, so cute.

When they sat down, Sophie whispered to her, "You think Tony's cute?"

"Yeesss." Jessica took a bite of her sandwich. He'd put on just the right amount of mustard.

Sophie shrugged. "I never thought much about him. He sometimes hangs out with me and my friend Megan." She started eating her sandwich. "He's really brainy."

Jessica's heart started beating faster. Maybe if she hung out with smart people this summer, she would get used to it. Then she might be able to relax and be herself when she got home. "What subjects is he good at?"

"Science and math. I think." Just then, several more customers walked in the door. "But he's probably going to be too busy here this summer to even learn your name."

Jessica sighed. "It doesn't matter, because we have to solve this mystery. Besides, he may not like girls with braces." Jessica clamped her mouth shut over the braces she'd gotten last March —the braces she tried to pretend weren't there and weren't reflecting light that blinded everyone in the room. Her mom would tell her that no one noticed them, that she was exaggerating. She knew better.

"I've known Tony for a long time, and I doubt he cares if you have braces." Sophie finished her sandwich, then sat back with her soda in her hand.

Jessica popped a chip in her mouth, crunched it, then started coughing when Tony spoke from behind her. Taking a big drink of her soda, she looked up at him.

"Hi, Sophie. Having a good summer?"

"Good so far. This is my cousin, Jessica."

"I heard you were visiting."

Jessica's face went hot, but she hoped not red, when Tony smiled at her.

Turning to Sophie, he asked, "Did you hear that someone unlocked the doors at Simpson's Shoes during the night?"

Sophie wrinkled her brow. "Just unlocked? They didn't steal anything?"

"That's what my dad said." He shrugged. "They're open today, so they couldn't have taken much. Heard from Megan?"

"I got a postcard from her." Sophie grinned at him. "She commented on the cute guys in Florida."

He burst out laughing. "Sounds like Megan." A group walked in the door, and he started for the counter, saying over his shoulder, "Back to work."

After he left, Jessica asked, "I haven't met Megan, right?"

"Nope. Her family is spending the summer at a beach near her grandmother's house."

"Ah. I wondered why you didn't have any friends." As soon as she'd said it, Jessica cringed, wondering if she'd offended her cousin.

Sophie laughed and poked Jessica in the arm. "I have friends. But they're either helping at a family business or out of town." She grabbed a chip off Jessica's plate. "We do need to find out more about the feather. That should lead us to why someone filled a briefcase with them."

Jessica looked down at the remaining bite of her sandwich. "This is so good."

"Everything here is great." Sophie stared off into space. "I wonder if the unlocked doors at Simpson's Shoes are a clue."

"A shoe store has nothing in common with feathers."

"You're right about the lack of a connection with a shoe store. But mysteries can be mysterious."

Jessica rolled her eyes. "I can't believe you said that."

6 DANGER RUN

Outside the deli, Sophie started to turn right, then stopped. She had a better idea. "How about a milkshake?"

"Seriously?" Jessica said. "After what we just ate?"

"The resort—the big building up the hill—makes the best shakes. They also have a big display of wildlife from this area in the lobby. Maybe they'll have info about our feather." They started in that direction. "Besides, I've got room for a shake."

"I'm surprised, but so do I. It must be all this exercise."

As they climbed the hill, Sophie checked out the sky in all directions. "It's getting gray and cloudy. But I don't think it looks like rain."

"I hope not. It wouldn't be fun getting caught in it this far from your house."

Sophie shrugged. They'd dry off if they did. Jessica might think it was a big deal though.

Toward the top of the hill, Jessica stopped. "Sophie, this place is like a mansion, and I'm just wearing shorts and a T-shirt. You're in jeans."

"We're fine. Remember, people come here to relax."

As they neared the building and a limousine pulled up to the door, Jessica nervously touched the front of her shirt and ran her fingers through her hair. When they walked in the door, she let out a giant sigh of relief. "It's really elegant in here. Chandeliers. Tables with white tablecloths. But everyone *is* dressed like us." Jessica nodded toward a group of men in suits. "Except for them."

"Suits, huh?"

"Maybe the guy in the suit is staying here with that group."

"That's possible." She wouldn't give up on any clue though. Not yet.

Jessica turned in a full circle. "This lobby is gorgeous. There's even a huge waterfall so it sounds like I'm outside, but I didn't have to run up the side of a mountain to see it."

Sophie laughed. "I'll have you loving the outdoors soon. Just as in mysteries, the waterfall isn't as simple as it seems. It has a secret."

Jessica eyed her suspiciously. "How can it have a secret?"

Sophie glanced around the room. No one seemed to be watching them. Around to the side of the falls, she opened a shorter-than-normal door. "This passage goes right through, but they don't tell visitors to the resort. Probably because you get really wet."

"Makeup running down my face and hair hanging wet doesn't sound good to me." Jessica stepped back.

"The display about birds is over here." Sophie motioned for Jessica to follow her across the room.

A glassed-in display had photos of the birds in Pine Hill. But no pictures of feathers. "I thought we'd get *something* from this."

Jessica pointed at a brass engraved plaque on the wall. "This says, 'State Fish and Game assistance on this display gratefully acknowledged.' Maybe they could help us."

"Fish and Game. Why didn't I think of that? We can call them first thing Monday." Sophie turned toward Jessica. "I feel like we got some help with the mystery. Ready for pure deliciousness?"

"Always."

They chose one of the small tables scattered throughout the lobby and ordered shakes, Jessica's chocolate and Sophie's filled with tropical fruit.

As soon as the server left, Jessica asked, "Did I really hear you order something with fruit?"

"Mom makes me eat it so much that I know I should hate it, but I love it."

"I like chocolate." Jessica licked her lips.

Sophie grimaced. "I'll work on the outdoors with you, and you can work on chocolate with me."

Jessica shook her head. "I think it will be easier for you to love chocolate than it will be for me to love the outdoors."

When their shakes came, Jessica did a happy dance in her chair. "Ooh, a chocolate milkshake that's topped with whipped cream, chocolate chips, and white chocolate shavings. Perfect for a chocolate connoisseur like myself."

Sophie stared at her. "There you go again. Sometimes you don't sound like a kid. Must come from living all over the world."

"Maybe." Jessica seemed almost guilty about something. She turned in her chair and looked around the lobby. "Sophie, there's a man in a brown suit over there." She gestured with her head toward the front door.

Sophie turned that direction. "There is. He's probably with the other men in suits."

"I don't think so. I can tell that his suit doesn't fit well. The other men are wearing suits that appear tailored to fit." Jessica smiled. "Spending time shopping pays off."

Suddenly, a man Sophie had never seen before pulled out a chair and sat down at their table. "I'm interested in the feathers you found."

"Feathers?" Sophie asked innocently. He was wearing a gray suit, not brown, so maybe the criminal, maybe not. A man could own more than one suit.

"I know about them." He reached into his suit coat pocket.

Before he could pull out a gun, Sophie grabbed Jessica by the hand and pulled her to her feet. They had to get out of here to protect themselves and all of the people around them.

"We're leaving. Don't follow us. There are a lot of people here watching you." She swept her hand through the air toward other tables. "If you don't want me to scream, don't try to come after us."

They backed away for a few feet. Then Sophie pulled Jessica along and they half walked, half ran through the lobby.

"What are you doing?" Jessica tried to skid to a stop, but Sophie tugged her forward.

Sophie said, "He must be the man who owns the briefcase. And he might have been pulling a gun out of his pocket."

"Maybe not. He might be with the police."

"Not a chance. I know all the deputies."

Jessica asked in a high-pitched voice, "What if we *are* being followed by a criminal?" She turned to see if he was there and stumbled, but Sophie kept her on her feet. "He's following us."

Sophie tore through the lobby toward the waterfall. "Here. He can't see us from where he is." Pulling open the door, she pushed Jessica through it and they huddled near the floor. Peering out one of the holes that let in light, she didn't see anyone suspicious. When she glanced over at Jessica, she found her cousin crouched next to her with a stupid expression on her face, staring at a blank wall.

Sophie nudged her. "Jessica?"

Jessica blinked and water ran down her face.

"You okay?"

Jessica nodded slowly. "Are we safe?"

Sophie checked the peephole again. "He's gone." She carefully surveyed the lobby from one side to the other. "I don't see the man in the brown suit either."

"I'm sorry I seemed to freeze, but considering the stress of the moment, it's understandable," Jessica said as she studied the room.

Sophie stared at her. "What?"

Jessica sounded nervous as she said, "I read something about it."

Sophie shook her head, spraying water everywhere like a wet dog. Then she stepped out of the door and started back toward their table, checking the other tables and the rest of the room to make sure the men had left. "I know we're a little wet, but it was the only place I could think of in a hurry."

Jessica wiped water off her arms. "I'd rather be wet and safe." She picked up her half-melted milkshake. "My hair's flat, my makeup must be a mess, and this doesn't look as good as it did before. You want to stay?"

"Actually, I've been thinking about how no one knows we're here, so let's go *after* I call home to check in."

They checked Jessica's phone—no bars—so Sophie used a hotel phone against the wall, and they put her call through.

When they reached the edge of town walking home, it started to sprinkle.

"Yikes. More water." Jessica swiped at her cheek and picked up speed. She could really move when she had to.

As they turned onto the driveway, big drops of rain plopped down. Darting up the driveway, they took the porch steps two at a time.

Inside, Jessica followed Sophie into her room. "I'm cold and wet." She shivered. "I'm going to put on a sweater and jeans."

Sophie whirled around. "You own jeans?"

"Of course." She pulled them and a sweater out of her dresser drawer, then changed her clothes and dropped her wet clothes over the side of the bathtub.

"Why haven't I seen your jeans before?"

"Because," she turned in the mirror to check out the outfit, nodding with approval, "I don't wear jeans very often."

"What about school?"

"Uniform."

Sometimes Sophie felt like her cousin lived on another

planet. Then again, a uniform would make it easy to get dressed in the morning. "Since we hurried home, I think we have time to call Fish and Game before they close. Otherwise we have to wait all weekend." She left to find the number in a phone book, then came back. "Why don't you listen and remind me if I forget to tell them something."

Sophie told the person on the other end of the line what they needed, then hung up.

"That was too fast. What happened?" Jessica asked.

"The waterfowl biologist just left for a two-week vacation."

Jessica groaned. "Well, it was a good idea. I guess we won't be able to see the sheriff about the mystery any more until Monday, since her office will be closed. We have the weekend off."

"She's usually there on Saturdays."

Jessica sighed. "Only you would know that. Then let's not talk about the mystery anymore tonight."

Sophie started to argue, then realized that Jessica didn't love mysteries and they'd had quite a mysterious day. She picked up her book and sat down to read. Her cousin got a call from her parents, and she grinned from ear to ear the rest of the night.

When Sophie went to bed, she was glad to be in a safe place. Her eyes started to close; then she blinked. Were they really safe here, though? Was someone trying to get to them to find out about the feathers?

———

Sophie sat on the end of her cousin's bed, a few feet from where Jessica had set up her hair care and makeup products in front of her dresser mirror last night, what her cousin had called her "beauty station." Jessica had scowled as she'd walked to the shower, but Sophie thought she'd be okay by the time she started to dry her hair.

"Jessica, it's sunny outside," Sophie shouted over the hair

dryer. "Let's walk to the sheriff's office and see if she's learned anything new about the feathers."

Jessica turned off the dryer and smoothed her hair in the mirror. "We could call and find that out."

Whew. She had timed it right. "I thought she might tell us more if we were in front of her."

Jessica picked up a tube of something and smeared it on her face. "You're probably right."

"Maybe she'll have something new to help us solve the mystery."

Putting in her earrings, Jessica said, "I'll keep getting ready while you talk. Makeup and mysteries go well together." She reached for the tube of what Sophie now knew was mascara.

When Jessica said she'd finished, her blonde hair was perfectly styled and her makeup was perfect for, well, shopping at the mall. She and her cousin didn't have much in common, but at least they had the mystery to work on together. "Let's go see the sheriff."

Jessica got dressed, and then they had a quick breakfast of cold cereal before leaving. Sophie closed the front door and shouted, "Race you."

Jessica, a few feet in front of her, took off running. She seemed to be moving faster now that she had her sneakers, but it only took a minute to pass her.

In front of the sheriff's office, they found a deputy directing traffic around a four-car accident, and the sheriff appeared to be interviewing the drivers.

Jessica cocked her head to the side. "Doesn't seem like anyone was hurt."

"Nope, and the cars only have little dents. I wonder why?"

Sheriff Valeska picked something up off the sidewalk, then walked up the nearby alley.

Jessica said, "I'm guessing that the sheriff will be a while longer. Maybe we should go inside and wait."

"Good idea."

As soon as they'd stepped inside, Sophie pointed and said, "Look!" then ran through the building and out the back door.

"Sophie!" Jessica hurried after her.

7 CLUE TWO

"Hey!" Sophie yelled at the man sprinting down the alley.

He held a brown jacket over the side of his head, making it impossible to see his face, and glanced over his shoulder.

"Stop!"

When he glanced back again, he stumbled, and white things dropped out of the jacket as he fell forward and caught himself with his arms. Then kneeling, he pushed and pulled on something before glancing back at her. Tugging sideways at it, he fell over, then shoved his hand into his pocket, climbed to his feet, and took off running again.

Sophie chased him down the alley to the street, where Jessica caught up with her. "Rats. He vanished."

"Who?"

"A man. He acted suspicious when he ran out of the sheriff's office."

"You're making a mystery again. Maybe he ran because a crazy girl shouting at him and chasing him made him really nervous."

"No. He had a brown jacket. It's him. Let's go see if he left some evidence in the alley."

They walked up and down the alley, but as far as Sophie

could tell, nothing appeared suspicious. "He fell about here, behind either Kendall's Jewelers or Pine Hill Gifts." She studied the ground.

Jessica stood in place, watching her. "No Wanted poster or timetable for a robbery lying on the ground?"

"Give me a minute." Sophie pictured him running. Snapping her fingers, she said, "When he slipped, I saw something fall. He pushed and pulled at what must be that pile of wood." She pointed to the side of the alley. "They're remodeling inside the jewelry store, so I guess this is the wood and other building supplies that are left over."

They ran over to a stack of scrap plywood and two-by-fours, the same things her parents had used when they did some work on the garage.

Jessica crouched beside the pile. "Hey Sophie, there're some torn-edged papers sticking out from under this board. But it's probably just trash."

Sophie crouched. "No. This makes sense. He must have dropped papers as he tripped. Then they got wedged between pieces of wood when he landed against the pile. He was pushing hard on the stack of wood, but he couldn't seem to shift it. Then it tore." Sophie put her hands on the pile. "Here, help me push against it with all our might."

Jessica crossed her arms and stared at her. "Why would you think a man who must be bigger than us couldn't move it, but we can?"

"He didn't have time to do much." Sophie put her hands on the side of the stack. "Push."

Jessica touched the stack and grimaced. "Yuck. If there's only trash under this sawdust-covered, splinter-filled pile, you owe me a chocolate milkshake."

"Deal. Ready?"

Jessica put her hands against the pile. "Okay."

"Push."

Groaning, they pushed as hard as they could. Nothing

happened. "Again." Sophie stood ready. Jessica stepped into position and they pushed. This time, the top of the stack rolled backward, freeing the papers.

Sophie reached down and slid them out from under a board. "Yes! Yes! Yes! Here's the clue we've been waiting for." She waved a stack of papers in the air.

"What's the clue?"

Sophie thumbed through them. "We have a corner of most pages, almost a half page of a couple. They're typed, official-looking papers and newspaper articles." She studied the wood-pile, then sighed. "I guess we'd better stack this up like we found it."

A short time later, Sophie stood back and surveyed the stacked pile of scrap lumber. "I think it's neater than when we got here."

Jessica brushed off the front of her shorts. "But we definitely are not."

Walking back to the sheriff's office, Sophie flipped through the papers. "There are ten pieces of paper."

"Can I see?" Jessica leaned over. "Did you actually find a big clue for a real mystery?" When Sophie handed them to her, she stopped to study them. "The typed pages look like official documents. There are words like *wherefore* and *whereas*."

"I know I've heard those words on TV shows and movies with lawyers."

"I don't know if you noticed, but some are from the bottom of a page and some are from the top. And a couple are just small corners." She flipped through them. "You know, Sophie, these might have been stuck between those boards for a week or two."

"Nope." Sophie smiled confidently. "Remember getting soaked yesterday?"

Jessica rocked back on her heels. "Oh yeah. This paper has never been wet." She flipped through them again. "There's only a paragraph or so of each of the two newspaper articles. If we had the whole articles, we might know a great deal about this mystery."

"So you finally admit we've found a mystery."

Jessica pursed her lips. "I don't think I have a choice. If that man was innocent, I don't think he would have run away from a twelve-year-old girl *and* abandoned these papers."

Sophie fingered the pages. This definitely wasn't another feather. "I wonder if there's more than one mystery. Let's see what's going on with the accident in front of the sheriff's office."

A man in a brown suit came around the corner of the next block, walking toward them. Jessica said, "Hey, look at him."

"Who?"

"That man. It's kind of crazy, but I'm getting suspicious of all men in brown suits."

As soon as Sophie focused on him, he did a one-eighty and went back around the corner.

"He's carrying a briefcase like the one we found."

Hurrying after him, they watched him slowly amble past the sheriff's office. Then he abruptly tucked the briefcase under his arm.

"After him!" Sophie called over her shoulder as she raced down the sidewalk with Jessica on her heels. The man darted around the next corner with both girls close behind. Rounding the corner onto Dogwood Street, they came to a stop and found an empty street. "There isn't anyone in sight."

"If we were in the city, there'd be plenty of people to question. We should solve a mystery there."

Sophie could tell that Jessica was starting to enjoy crime solving. "Maybe we'll go to the city for our *next* mystery."

Jessica groaned. "Oh no. What have I said?"

Sophie smiled. "Admit it. You're hooked on mysteries."

Jessica pressed her lips together.

"Not talking, huh?"

Jessica shook her head.

8 MISSING EVIDENCE

The cars from the accident were driving away when Jessica and Sophie walked into the sheriff's office. Jessica had already been in this office more times than she'd expected to be in any law enforcement office in her whole life.

Sheriff Valeska entered right after them, took off her hat, threw it onto her desk, and sat down. Leaning back in her chair, she rubbed her eyes, "That was an odd accident."

Sophie sat forward. "Why?"

"The drivers said they saw something go across the street. They swerved to avoid it and hit each other." She pulled a small toy car out of her coat pocket. "When we searched, we found this wind-up car on the sidewalk."

"Diversion," Sophie said with certainty.

Sheriff Valeska laughed. "It's more likely that a child was playing with this toy, and when it went the wrong way and caused an accident, he or she ran away."

Sophie crossed her arms. "We got here just after the accident. I saw a suspicious man go out the back door and down the alley."

"You followed a man?"

Jessica added, "And just now we saw a man in a brown suit

carrying a briefcase that looked like the one we found. We followed him too, but he vanished on Dogwood Street."

Sheriff Valeska stood. "I'll see if anything is out of order."

After checking around the office, she said, "Everything seems fine here." Then she went into the room where she'd taken the briefcase the other day. "It's gone!"

"See? I told you, Jessica." Sophie sat proudly, with a smug expression on her face.

"What's gone?" Jessica asked.

"The briefcase." Sophie smiled in a superior manner. "Right, Sheriff?"

The sheriff dropped onto her chair and faced her computer. "It's hard to believe, but our usually overly dramatic Sophie was right." She clicked the mouse a couple of times, then said, "Sophie, tell me every detail you can remember about both incidents. And carefully describe the suspects."

Sophie bounced all over her seat. "I'm part of a crime scene. Let me think. The suspect who went out the back door was wearing a cream-colored dress shirt and . . ." She stopped for a minute. Then her face grew red and she buried her face in her hands. Jessica could barely hear her muffled voice. "I've seen this happen in movies and read about it in books. I thought I'd have a fabulous description, but all I remember is he had on a light-colored dress shirt."

The sheriff encouraged her. "That is a clue. You're sure it was a man?"

"Absolutely." She tapped her foot, then jumped up. "I couldn't see more than his back or side because he held a brown jacket up near his face. I'll bet he did that so I couldn't see him." Placing her hands on the sheriff's desk, she leaned forward. "I do know he had short hair, dark brown or black. What do you think, Jessica?"

The sheriff turned toward Jessica. "You saw him too?"

"Only from a distance when I ran after Sophie. She was chasing him, so she got much closer."

"Sophie chased him?"

Jessica smiled. "A possible villain on the run? What do you think?"

Sophie said, "Yes, I'm sure now. He did have short, dark hair. And then we found the bits of paper that were wedged in the lumber behind Kendall's Jewelers."

"Bits of paper? Did he drop them?"

"I think so."

"Let me see them."

Sophie pulled them out of her pocket and handed them to Sheriff Valeska.

She flipped through the pages. "This looks like trash."

Jessica said, "That's what I thought at first."

The sheriff handed them back to Sophie. "You can keep these."

This surprised Jessica, because even she knew they were important. But Sophie had seen them fall, not the sheriff, and it must be difficult for a sheriff to build a crime around what a kid says. Sophie quickly stuffed them back in her pocket.

Jessica added, "We only caught a glimpse of the man with the briefcase a few minutes ago and could really only see that he was wearing a brown suit."

The sheriff kept working. "We'd dusted the briefcase for fingerprints, then put the feathers back inside. I was going to take it to the crime lab tomorrow when I went to the county seat for a meeting so they could go over it with a fine-tooth comb." She leaned to the right and pulled a file folder out of her drawer, checked something, then continued working at the computer. "On Monday morning I'll need you to bring in the feather you took. It's the only one we have now." She clicked the mouse before adding, "You girls should probably go now. "

Sophie patted the pocket with the pieces of paper. "Sure. We'll let you know if we find any other clues."

"Oh, and girls, please don't chase any other strangers."

Sophie stood. "We'll be careful."

When they were walking out the door, Jessica asked Sophie, "Did you call her and tell her about the man at the resort?"

Sophie glared at her.

Uh-oh. I guess not.

The sheriff stopped working and focused on the girls. "What man?"

"The one who asked us about the feathers and chased us through the resort," Jessica answered.

The sheriff pointed at the chairs in front of her desk. "Sit, ladies. Tell me what happened."

Jessica went step-by-step through the incident. "Then we hid in the tunnel behind the waterfall."

"You girls be careful. I don't know what's going on yet, but this feather mystery is one of the strangest things I've ever heard of."

Jessica said, "Don't worry. We will, Sheriff."

As they left, Sophie muttered, "Feather Mystery. So it has a name now." She turned left, so Jessica figured she was headed toward her bench. "Let's solve this mystery."

Jessica laughed. "We haven't even figured out what kind of bird the feather is from. And we don't know if both the feathers and the papers are connected. Sheriff Valeska didn't think so."

Sophie didn't seem to be paying any attention. "I know!" She pointed a finger in the air. "Our mystery is like the last book I read. No, the book before that."

"Hurry up and tell me."

"Something happened, and it seemed like it didn't have anything to do with the mystery, but it turned out to be very important. I really think we need to consider what's going on at Simpson's Shoes. That's the only other mysterious happening in Pine Hill."

"No way. Your mystery thinking is off this time. Like I said before, unlocked doors in a shoe store and a briefcase full of feathers don't have anything in common. We have three things that might not go together at all—feathers, papers, and unlocked doors."

"You'll see." Sophie glanced over at her bench but kept walking. "It's probably time to go home."

When they were at the edge of town, Jessica swatted at a fly buzzing around her head and caught a glimpse of a man behind them. "Ooh, Sophie. A little while ago I looked back and saw a man behind us. He's still there and looks like a suspicious type. Do you think he's following us?"

Sophie started to turn around, but Jessica put out her arm to stop her. "Hey, you're the one who said you have to be casual."

"I'll tie my shoe." She bent over, retied her old sneakers, and glanced behind them.

"What's he wearing?"

"Green shirt. Blue jeans."

"He's the minister from our church. You'll see him again at church tomorrow morning." Sophie grinned and stood. "I think he's okay."

"Whew. I'm glad we're going to be out in the open today. We find a briefcase in the woods and all of a sudden, I'm seeing a bad guy when there's a good guy. This could be a long, long summer."

"You'll love solving mysteries soon."

Jessica didn't say anything to Sophie, but her stay in Pine Hill *had* been exciting.

9 WHAT'S UP WITH DOWN?

Jessica opened her eyes and blinked a few times. Her cousin's pale pink walls with a painted border of little purple flowers came into focus. She knew Sophie well enough now to be certain she hadn't chosen the pink or the flowers. But the forest green fleece blankets that covered the beds were pure Sophie.

When she rolled over, she found her cousin's bed empty. Jessica walked to the bathroom door and heard the shower running, so she lay back down and picked up her book. The girl in it always got straight A's. What would it be like if people knew she was brainy too? That she easily got straight A's?

Sophie came out of the bathroom wearing a robe, and a towel wrapped around her head.

Jessica said, "Morning, Cousin."

Sophie stared silently at her.

Jessica flipped back her covers. "I think I've been awake long enough that I'm in a good mood, but I'll take a shower before you say anything to me."

Sophie nodded.

As hot water sprayed down on her, Jessica felt more and more awake. By the time she walked back into Sophie's room, she was humming her favorite song. Sophie sat on the end of her bed, already dressed, this time in a less faded pair of jeans and a green T-shirt instead of the usual white. Jessica flipped through her clothes hanging in the closet. Would people at Sophie's church dress the same as they did at hers? She started to ask, then immediately realized that wouldn't work. Sophie wouldn't notice clothes. Jessica settled on a white skirt and a pale pink top.

Jessica stepped over to her beauty station, carefully did her eye makeup, then added blush.

"Do you miss your parents?" Sophie asked.

"Yeah." She chose a soft pink lip gloss.

"I see my dad every day. It must be strange to have your dad gone for months at a time because he's working in a country that's far away."

Jessica pictured running to her dad in the airport the last time he'd come home. "It is. And now Mom's visiting him, so they're both gone." As tears filled her eyes, she sat on her bed with her back to Sophie.

"I have to admit, I didn't want you here and I didn't like you much at first, but you're growing on me."

"Thanks. I think." Jessica smiled at Sophie's awkward way of saying she was starting to like her. She blinked the tears away and sniffed. "I even miss my little brother."

"Do you like him? I've always wanted a brother."

"He's constantly in the way, but I guess I'm used to having Frog Boy around."

"Frog Boy?"

"Yeah, when he was a baby, Dad called him 'our tadpole.' I knew a tadpole was a frog, so I called him Frog." Feeling a little less sad, Jessica turned to Sophie and smiled. "I'm the only one who's allowed to call him that."

Sophie grinned. "Even you might not get away with it when he's our age."

Jessica went over to the closet, chose a pair of white sandals from her shoes on the floor, and slipped them on. "I'm ready for church. Do you have any ideas for afterward?"

"I'd love to get out in the woods again. How about another hike on Cutoff Trail?" Sophie practically bounced, she was so excited.

Jessica cringed. She still had an image in her mind of owls and bats hovering overhead, ready to swoop down. "Can we go somewhere that's not so filled with nature?"

"Well, getting in the middle of nature is usually my first choice, but . . . deal." Sophie sat silently. "It's so sunny and beautiful today that we should go somewhere outside. I know. I could give you a tour of Pine Hill. We might see a person or place that helps us solve The Feather Mystery." Sophie's eyes lit up whenever she talked about the mystery. She made it difficult to *not* be excited about it. "Maybe later we could study the papers for clues."

"Since I didn't want to study them last night, today works." Jessica flopped back on her bed. "We're going to end up using all of our summer vacation to solve this."

Sophie laughed. "Sounds like fun to me." She put her feet into her usual sneakers. "We'd better grab some breakfast so we'll be ready to go."

Sophie's dad stepped into the kitchen a little later. "Ready, girls?"

"Ready," Sophie answered.

A short drive took them to a brick church—what else?—on the other side of town that, other than the bricks, reminded Jessica of her own church. It was hard not to miss her family on Sunday morning. They would go to church together every week, her dad joining them when he was in town. Not a single part of her normal life existed here. Jessica bit her cheek so she wouldn't cry.

As the minister stepped up to the pulpit, she scooted closer to Sophie and whispered, "Please *do not* tell him I thought he looked like a criminal." That humiliation would be too much to take today.

Sophie hesitated, then nodded.

Halfway through the service, a boy a few rows up turned his head to the side, and Jessica's heart caught in her throat. *Tony comes here!* She liked knowing he believed the same things she did.

After church, Aunt April and Uncle Lucas dropped the girls off in front of Great Finds, her aunt's antique shop, because it was, her aunt said, "centrally located." The shop was closed for the day, but Jessica looked in the window and saw a room filled with furniture and small things—she guessed all old things, like those in Sophie's house.

"Okay. Tour time," Sophie said.

They went over to Sophie's school, a building less than half the size of her own, and they peered into the windows of Sophie's science classroom (she'd had a fun teacher last year), the cafeteria, and the library. Walking through town after that, Sophie turned a corner, onto a street Jessica hadn't seen before.

Jessica glanced into the shop windows as they walked by, stopping in front of a flower shop called Buds & Blooms. She peered into the window. "Mom loves flowers."

Sophie said, "Mine too. I haven't been around here in a while." She turned in a circle, scanning the stores. "Hey, that's Mrs. Bowman from Bananas." She pointed to a woman standing by the front door of a shop across the street. "It's funny that she's here, because she's blocks from her business and even farther from her house. I guess she went shopping in that store."

"She isn't carrying anything."

"True. And she seems to be in a hurry."

The older woman crossed the street and quickly moved out of sight.

"I don't remember what used to be in that store, but I know it's different now. The sign above the door says, 'The Down Shoppe.' Down what?"

Jessica shrugged. "Probably like a fluffy down comforter or down coat that keeps you warm in the winter."

"Fluffy?"

"You know. They're filled with feathers."

"Feathers!" both girls shouted.

———

They hurried across the street, and Sophie and Jessica stared into the store window.

"'The Down Shoppe' is such a perfect clue." Sophie craned her neck, trying to see inside. They may have made the breakthrough in the mystery that she needed.

"The window display is empty. And more than a little dusty. I wouldn't shop here unless they cleaned the place up."

Sophie cupped her hands and held them against the glass. "I can see farther into the store now."

Jessica copied her. "There isn't anything in there. You know, Sophie, the Down Shoppe might only have feathers *in* things. Not loose feathers, like in the briefcase."

"Maybe." Sophie walked over to the glass front door, then muttered, "Still nothing. And a sign says they don't open for another three weeks." She banged on the door.

Jessica jumped. "Hey!"

"I see a woman in there."

A woman with long brown hair crept slowly toward the door. Dressed in worn overalls and a yellow T-shirt with a huge flower pin on the shoulder strap, she would be hard to miss in a crowd. Keeping her head down, the woman pointed at the sign on the door and stopped when she was about five feet away.

"We need to talk to you," Sophie called out.

"We?" the woman said loudly from behind the closed door. She wasn't making sense.

Then Jessica said, "*Parlez-vous anglais?*"

The woman shook her head from side to side.

"Thank you. *Merci.*"

She raced to the back of the room and out of sight.

As Sophie started to speak, Jessica said, "'We' is actually *o-u-i* and means 'yes' in French. I asked her if she spoke English."

Sophie's brow wrinkled. "I guess that means you speak French?"

"We lived in the south of France during some of those years you and I didn't see each other."

Sophie hit her forehead with the palm of her hand. "Yeah, now I remember Christmas cards coming from a cousin I didn't know who lived far away."

"Yep. That was me." She cocked her head to the side and tapped her foot on the ground. "There was something odd about that woman . . . I just can't figure out what."

"I know I couldn't identify her later. Her hair almost covered her face."

"True," Jessica muttered.

Sophie pushed on Jessica's arm. "What do you want to do now?"

Jessica shrugged. "Now I would like to do something that is absolutely not related to this mystery. You're from here, Miss Pine Hill. What would be fun?"

Fun would be camping, or a hike in the woods, but Sophie knew Jessica would not like those ideas. What would be outside that Jessica wouldn't mind? "Let's walk down to the lake."

They went down a slight hill on a paved path that wove through pine trees. Then they stepped out of the trees, and the lake sat in front of them. Sophie never got tired of seeing it. A bright, sunny Sunday had brought out boats of all sizes.

"Wow! This lake is beautiful. And enormous. With an awesome sandy beach." Jessica turned first to the right, then to the left. "Hey, Cousin, why haven't you taken me to this un-woodsy place before?"

"I showed you Pine Lake your first day here. Remember? From Cutoff Trail?"

Jessica winced. "Guess I didn't pay attention to the lake."

A boat roared by, pulling someone on water skis.

Turning to Sophie, Jessica said, "We have to come back to this beach when we're wearing bathing suits."

"Sounds good. Um, you know, Jessica, I've been thinking. We have to investigate the Down Shoppe."

"Not the mystery again. You won't relax until we solve this." Jessica took a few steps toward the water, then turned to Sophie. "Okay, I'll be the voice of reason again. You're pulling in unrelated things and calling them clues. The Down Shoppe might have nothing to do with the briefcase."

"But they have feathers in there."

Jessica raised one eyebrow. "Would a jewelry store automatically be part of a crime if someone had found a briefcase full of gold?"

"Maybe." Sophie grinned.

Jessica grinned back. "We'll see. What was it about that woman?" She stared out at the lake. "Where to now, Cousin?"

"I'm hungry. Let's go home and help Mom make dinner." Sophie took a couple of steps, then let out a little whoop. "I just remembered that I recorded an old detective movie the other day. It might give us some mystery-solving ideas."

10 OUCH!

After they'd done some chores the next morning, including vacuuming and dusting—the dusting an extra Sophie said she hoped would earn points with her mom—Jessica sat down on the couch in the living room. She hoped, but it was probably too much to ask, that they wouldn't do something mystery-related today.

Sophie plopped onto the couch. "What would a world-famous detective do right now?"

Yes, it was too much to ask.

Sophie sprang to her feet. "Read through the papers. There *must* be clues hiding in them."

Sophie hurried into her bedroom, Jessica following, since she knew Sophie wouldn't let it go. When she'd removed the metal box from its hiding place, she took the papers out and placed them on her bed in a single layer.

They both sat on the edge of the bed and went through them one by one.

Jessica didn't find the few sentences from the newspaper articles very useful. "One talks about coats and sleeping bags and another about tourism. And we only have a little more of the official-looking papers, which, like you said earlier, use words lawyers use, like *whereas*. We can't even tell if any of these have something to do with Pine Hill. Maybe they are just trash." She flopped back on the bed. "We don't know a whole lot more than we did a half hour ago. This is just like the feathers."

Sophie picked up the ten pieces of paper and slowly went through them. "Since we're losing the feather, maybe there's a way to learn more about the papers. I understand the words in the newspaper articles, but the typed, official-looking pages are different. Not only are there words I don't know, there are long strings of numbers and letters too. Trying to read these is worse than reading something for language arts class. In fact, it's even worse than social studies." She threw the papers down on the bed.

Jessica picked them up. She might not be able to figure out what each page was about, and she sure didn't understand the letters and numbers together, but she did know almost all of the words. They didn't come together to mean anything though.

"You seem to understand what you're reading," Sophie exclaimed.

"What?" Jessica looked up from the last page, blinked, and paused. Had she given herself away? "Um, you can read all the words. It's a matter of understanding them."

"You're right. There for a minute, I thought you really understood what you were reading." Sophie took the papers out of Jessica's hand. "I wanted to solve this myself, but my dad usually has good ideas about these things. Let's take the official-looking pages to him." She headed down the hall to his office, then paused. "The door's closed." She shifted from foot to foot.

"Are you allowed to knock?"

After a few seconds, Sophie reached up and gently tapped on the door. Jessica hoped she wouldn't get in trouble.

"Yes?" Uncle Lucas called.

"We have a question for you."

"Come on in."

"Whew." Sophie said as she reached for the doorknob.

"Does he usually get mad if you knock?"

"I *usually* leave him alone to work. He's an accountant, so he has to keep track of a lot of numbers." Sophie started to push the door open. "He says the only way to focus on his work in the summer with a chatterbox like me around is to close the door."

Jessica grinned as they walked inside. Sophie handed the papers to her dad and told him how they'd found them—minus the part about chasing the guy.

"They're pages from a legal document," Uncle Lucas said as soon as he'd paged through them.

Sophie wrinkled her forehead. "We noticed the words lawyers use."

"Don't ask me any more than that. You need to talk to a lawyer." He reached for the phone and dialed, then said, "Sara Samuels, please."

Jessica tapped her foot and checked out her uncle's office. He had a nice computer. Too bad Sophie couldn't use it.

"Sara? Lucas Sandoval here. My daughter and niece found some pages from a legal document and want to know more about them. Could they bring them in for a quick legal review? I'm sure two o'clock will be fine. Thanks."

Sophie kissed her father on the cheek as he was hanging up the phone. "Thanks, Dad."

"The office is at Oak Street and Acadia Avenue, on the other side of town." He got one of those stern parent looks. "The two of you need to be on time."

"We will, Uncle Lucas. Um, I know Sophie doesn't use your computer, but could I use it morning or night to send a message to Mom and Dad? We were going to text, but you can't do that here. Then they said they'd call every few days instead, but—"

"Of course. Come in tonight and write to them."

"Thank you." Jessica closed the door and sighed. Being able to communicate with her mom every day would make a summer in Pine Hill *much* easier to survive.

After a quick sandwich, the girls headed to Sophie's room.

Jessica studied her clothes in the closet, pulling out a couple of outfits and laying them on the bed. "You know, Sophie, I think you're supposed to dress nicely when you go to see a lawyer."

"Hmm. Like a fancy restaurant?"

"Something like that."

"I've only been to a couple fancy restaurants. Mostly the resort." Sophie flipped through her smaller amount of clothes on hangers—most of her clothes were T-shirts and jeans lying in drawers—then eyed the shoes Jessica had neatly placed on the closet floor. "Women wear high heels when they dress up."

"They often do," Jessica said. Should she go with the pants or the skirt? Pants.

"Can I wear a pair of your high heels?"

Jessica whipped around. "What? It must be a long walk to the other side of town. Have you ever worn high heels?"

"No, but I want to give it a try," Sophie pleaded. "I can picture myself stepping into a lawyer's office wearing a beautiful dress and high heels. I know that's how the lawyer will be dressed."

From wearing sneakers, even to church, to high heels? And walking a long distance? This had 'bad idea' written all over it. Jessica tried to throw her off. "Sophie, I don't know if we wear the same size shoe."

Sophie glanced from her feet to Jessica's. "I think we're pretty much the same size. How about if I take my normal shoes in a tote bag?"

"Well . . ." Jessica paused. "That seems to make sense. Then you can change if you need to." Jessica pulled a pair of black high heels out of the closet and set them on the floor by Sophie's bed. "Even if these do fit, I think you're going to regret this. But they'll go with almost anything, and the heel is low enough that these are probably the easiest I have for you to walk in."

Sophie startled her by taking a beautiful teal dress out of the closet and slipping it on. "This is my best dress. My mother said

I would need it someday." She shrugged. "Might as well wear it now."

When she reached for the shoes, Jessica stepped between her and them. "You know, it took me a while to learn how to walk in high heels. And I was on flat ground in the city."

Sophie grinned and reached around her for the shoes. Trying them on, she exclaimed, "They fit. We wear the same shoe size."

Jessica didn't think Sophie would be as happy about that later. Turning, she checked out her own appearance in the mirror. The black pants and white blouse came off as professional but not over-the-top. Then she thought about her choice of shoes. Sneakers would work for the walk. She'd put heels on when she got to the lawyer's office.

She picked up her purse, slipped her cell phone out of its pocket, and set it on the dresser. Good reception seemed to be limited to times when she really didn't need a phone. Then she picked the phone back up. With everything that was going on, it might come in handy.

Sophie put the papers into a surprisingly cute denim tote bag. When they got to the door, she turned back, tottering a little on the heels.

Jessica hoped she'd come back wearing sneakers, but she just returned holding up their feather.

"We'd better drop this off on the way," Sophie said. She tucked the feather into the bag and they started off, Sophie walking slowly but steadily.

Jessica kept an eye on her, keeping to the edge of the paved road for the smoothest path to town. By the outskirts of Pine Hill, Sophie was walking tenderly, putting more pressure on her left foot. A block from the sheriff's office, she began wincing when she put down her right foot.

Jessica gently pushed Sophie in the direction of her favorite bench. "Sit here and I'll run the feather in to the sheriff."

When Sophie quietly sat as she'd asked, Jessica knew she wasn't herself.

Jessica took the feather out of Sophie's bag, then into the sheriff's office. She found the sheriff seated at her desk and held out the feather to her.

Tucking it into an envelope, Sheriff Valeska asked, "Where's Sophie?"

"She's learning to walk in high heels, so she's resting on a bench outside."

The sheriff's eyebrows shot upward. "Sophie? Is she okay?"

"I hope so," Jessica answered, turning to leave. Almost out the door, she turned back. "I know she'll ask later if we can see the feather if we want to."

The sheriff wrote something on the envelope before she answered. "I agree that she will ask. Tell her I'll consider it and that I'm starting to realize there's more to this mystery than I'd thought."

Jessica walked back to Sophie. She knew her cousin would love hearing that. But right now she didn't think it would register with the brain of the girl on the bench, staring blankly straight ahead.

11 LEGAL MATTERS

Jessica and Sophie continued on, Sophie now giving a little hop each time she took a step. By the time they arrived at the two-story building the lawyer's office was in—thankfully, on time—Sophie was almost dragging one foot and then the other. But she hadn't complained. Actually, she hadn't said a word in about twenty minutes. She just had a stupid grin on her face.

Jessica sat down in the lobby and slipped off her sneakers, trading them for high-heeled, tan strappy sandals she'd brought in a pink tote bag. Then she got up and they followed the sign with an arrow that led them down the hall to the lawyer's office, and Jessica told the secretary why they were there. Sophie kept that stupid grin the whole time.

While they sat on a sofa and waited for the lawyer to finish with her previous appointment, Jessica studied Sophie, who was definitely breathing but not moving otherwise. Could painful feet hurt you in other ways? "Sophie?"

Sophie turned toward her.

"You okay?"

"I think so," she said softly.

The phone on the secretary's desk rang. After speaking on it, she quickly ushered the girls through a door to her right and into an office.

A woman wearing an elegant red business suit with black high heels stood beside a desk. Sophie nudged Jessica with her elbow. Her expression said, *I was right. Lawyers dress in beautiful clothes.*

Sophie dug the papers out of her tote bag and handed them to the lawyer. "Do you have any idea what these mean?"

"Please sit down, ladies."

As the girls sat in the padded leather chairs in front of the desk, Mrs. Samuels walked around the desk and sat down. Reading the papers one by one, she nodded her head. At one point her brow wrinkled. She entered something into her computer, then went back and forth repeatedly, comparing that to one of the pieces of paper. When she'd read through all of them, she said, "There's only enough here to know that this is a real estate contract."

"A what?" Jessica asked.

"Someone wants to buy property. What I have here appears to be a standard agreement to do that."

Jessica saw Sophie's face fall.

"There's nothing strange here?" Sophie asked.

Mrs. Samuels flipped back to one of the pages. "There is one 'strange' thing, as you put it. There is what's called a legal address on one piece of paper. That's the series of numbers and letters. Every house, business, or vacant piece of land has a different one. I've been your parents' lawyer, Sophie, for so many years that it seemed familiar, so I checked and it's for the building Great Finds is in, your mother's shop."

Sophie wrinkled her brow. "Do you mean someone wants to buy Mom's shop?"

Mrs. Samuels said, "It would seem so. Has she mentioned anything about this?"

"No. Not a word."

Mrs. Samuels stood and handed the papers back to Sophie. "That's about it, ladies. I hope I've helped."

"Thank you very much for speaking with us." Sophie stood, wincing as she put weight on her feet and immediately grabbed hold of the desk.

The lawyer rushed around it and steadied Sophie before Jessica even had a chance to stand. "Are you all right?"

Sophie, her face bright red, said, "New shoes."

"Ah." Mrs. Samuels nodded and looked down. "Very pretty."

Sophie turned and walked very carefully through the doorway as the lawyer and Jessica watched. She vanished out of sight, but Jessica knew it would take her a long time to reach the chairs in the lobby.

Mrs. Samuels said, "You should get her to take those shoes off and put her feet up."

Jessica liked the woman. "I know. She wouldn't listen before." Jessica leaned to the right and could see that the secretary had stepped away from her desk, so maybe Mrs. Samuels had a few minutes. "Can I ask you what some of these words mean?"

The lawyer seemed surprised. "Sure."

Jessica asked about a few of them and listened carefully as Mrs. Samuels explained the meanings.

"You have an amazing command of language for someone so young. Have you thought about being a lawyer?"

"Sometimes. I'm not sure what I want to be." Jessica heard the door to the office open and close. "Thank you."

She passed the secretary as she left and found Sophie sitting in a chair in the lobby, with her sneakers on her feet and the high heels on the floor. She stood when Jessica neared.

"Oh boy, when you are right, Cousin, you are right." Sophie grabbed the high heels and stuffed them in her bag. "Whew, my feet still hurt. But not like with those instruments of torture. How can you wear them?"

Jessica laughed. "First, I'm used to them. Second, as I

mentioned when you weren't paying attention, this is a long walk in heels. I wore sneakers."

"I heard you. But I figured *I* could do it. I thought that if I could run up Cutoff Trail, I could walk across town in high heels."

"It isn't the same."

"Tell me about it."

"Let's go home. I'm curious what your mom will say tonight about the real estate deal."

Sophie walked slowly out the door, limping each time her right foot touched the ground, and saying, "Ouch" each time her left one did.

"I think it's going to take a while to get home," Jessica muttered to herself as she followed Sophie out the door.

When they got to the corner of the block, Jessica checked her watch. Ten minutes just to get there.

A car pulled around the corner and the driver, who turned out to be Mrs. Samuels, rolled down the window. "Can I give you ladies a ride?"

Jessica pulled out her phone. "Three bars." She gave a thumbs-up and handed it to Sophie. "Call your parents first."

Dialing, Sophie said quietly, "They'll be fine with it." A minute later she hung up. "Let's go."

As Sophie slid into the backseat, Jessica gratefully opened the car door and climbed into the front seat. If they'd had to walk home, tonight's dinner would have been about ten o'clock— tomorrow morning.

———

Aunt April served burgers and fries. When her aunt went into the kitchen to get dessert, Jessica waited for something exciting, like strawberry shortcake, but she returned with the not-so-exciting bowl of fruit.

Sophie nudged her and whispered, "Go get the papers."

Jessica was about to ask why she couldn't do it herself when Sophie raised her feet and wiggled them.

After running to get the papers, Jessica handed them to Sophie, then grabbed the peach she'd had her eyes on.

"Mom, are you selling your shop?" Sophie asked.

Mrs. Sandoval paused, with her apple half-peeled. "A man offered to buy my building and my inventory today. Where did *you* get the idea?"

"Remember the papers the thief dropped in the alley?"

"I know your overactive imagination believes there's a thief." Mrs. Sandoval smiled at the girls, then continued peeling.

"You'll believe in the mystery when you read this." Sophie handed her mom the pieces of paper.

Jessica added, "Mrs. Samuels says these papers, or at least some of them, are part of a contract to buy the Great Finds building."

Mrs. Sandoval flipped through them. "It's hard to tell that from what's written here. I'll take Sara Samuels' word for it, though. To answer your question, I have no plans to sell Great Finds." As she set the papers down, she said, "I have a question for you. Did you give away the whipped cream?"

"Huh?" Sophie stared at her mother.

"I noticed the other day that all of the whipped cream was gone, so I wondered if you'd given it to the neighbors. Jessica said we had enough for us *and* them."

"Uh, no." Sophie looked over at Jessica with a giveaway, panicked expression.

They'd forgotten to buy whipped cream to replace what they'd used. Uncle Lucas had warned them.

"We did use quite a bit that night. Um, did I tell you I wore high heels today?"

Sophie'd handled that diversion well. Thinking about her in high heels would be enough to throw anyone off, and it did.

Mrs. Sandoval dropped a slice of apple, then sat with her

mouth open for a minute. She said, "I guess you tried on a pair of Jessica's to see what they were like."

"Sophie walked to the lawyer's office in them." Jessica giggled. "'Walked' might be exaggerating. She hopped and dragged herself to the lawyer's office."

Sophie glared at her.

Mrs. Sandoval exclaimed, "Oh, Sophie, your feet must be hurting."

Sophie moved a foot and winced. "Let's just say that it will be a while before I try high heels again. Maybe you can check out my feet after dinner?"

"Of course." Mrs. Sandoval put her hand on Sophie's shoulder. "There does seem to be something mysterious going on in Pine Hill. Be careful. Don't take any chances. Both of you."

"We won't, Aunt April." Jessica thought about the feather they'd given to the sheriff, and the papers. No matter how hard it was to believe, they'd landed right in the middle of a real mystery.

12 A MYSTERIOUS WOMAN

Ring.

Sophie blinked awake, then started to roll over.

Ring.

"It's the phone," Jessica said into her pillow.

"Dad'll get it." Sophie stretched and yawned.

On the fourth ring Sophie leaped to her feet and ran for the phone in the living room. "Dad must not be in his office," she called behind her.

"Okay, Mom," Sophie said into the phone, moments later. Then after a pause, "Yes, we'll be there soon."

She hung up and came back to the bedroom. "When the phone rang, I hoped it was someone with a clue." She laughed. "Of course, who would call with a clue? Anyway, Mom wants us to come to her shop and deliver something."

"In case you forgot to be afraid of me in the morning, I think I'm waking up nicer. Maybe it's all the exercise."

Sophie raised an eyebrow. "I *had* forgotten that I shouldn't talk to you."

Jessica sat up. "I *am* better."

Laughing, Sophie said, "I'm still afraid to talk to you, in case grumpy Jessica returns."

"I think I'll have a good morning. Beach later?"

"Absolutely."

They showered and ate, then dressed with bathing suits under their clothes. Sophie put her shoes on when they were ready to leave, and winced. "Ouch." She went to the medicine cabinet, got two bandages, and covered her two blisters, one on each foot. Then she put her shoes on again. Letting out a big sigh, she said, "So much better."

Leaving, Sophie went in the direction of the shortcut through the woods.

Jessica stopped. "With the guy in the brown suit *and* the guy asking about feathers out there, I'd like to stay by the road."

Sophie didn't want to say so, but Jessica was right. She turned back toward the road. "It'll take longer. There's a gravel path beside it so we don't have to walk where the cars go."

They walked side by side for a while. Then Sophie thought she heard something behind them, so stopped.

Jessica, now a few feet ahead of her, looked back. "Hey. What's the idea?"

"Shh." Sophie held her finger to her lips.

A crunching sound came from somewhere behind them. After a few seconds, it stopped. Jessica walked back to her.

"I think someone's following us," Sophie whispered.

Jessica rolled her eyes, then in a normal voice said, "A criminal followed the detective in that old movie we watched."

Sophie glared at her, then whispered, "I can prove this. Walk."

When they'd taken four steps, the crunching started again. They stopped and it stopped a few seconds later. Sophie and Jessica looked at each other.

Sophie whispered. "You know, this road has so many curves in it that we wouldn't see someone who's close to us."

"Let's do it again."

Sophie hoped she would *only* hear birds singing. They were too far from her house to cut through the woods and run back.

As soon as they started walking, the crunching began. When they stopped, the crunching stopped. Stuff like this only happened in books and movies.

Jessica whispered, "I'll call the sheriff." She pulled her cell phone out of her purse. "No reception." As she put the phone away, the crunching started again.

"Run!" Sophie yelled.

Racing toward town, Sophie felt her heart pounding. She wouldn't admit it to anyone, but having someone follow them had scared her. Sophie whipped around the corner of the first street in Pine Hill, her cousin right on her tail.

Jessica called out, "Stop. No one's behind us."

Sophie pushed her heels into the sidewalk. Jessica swerved to miss her and stopped.

Panting, they sat on the curb. Sophie looked up to realize she was directly across the street from the Down Shoppe. "Strange that a mysterious pursuer would chase us right back to the Down Shoppe."

Jessica leaped to her feet. "I've got it!"

Sophie jumped. "Ooh, you startled me. What?"

"The French woman, and I use that phrase loosely, shook her head to say no."

"And?"

"The French shrug." Jessica raised her shoulders to demonstrate. "They don't shake their heads to say no, like Americans do. Something's fishy at the feather place."

Sophie grinned. "Good work. Let's take another peek."

This time, when they peered through the windows, there wasn't even a person in the room.

Sophie tilted her head to the side. "I know a little about business because Mom and Dad both own their own businesses and they talk about them. I think people should be working here to turn this into a real store if they want to open in a few weeks."

"That makes sense."

Jessica sat down on the curb again, and Sophie paced back

and forth between the corner and the front of the Down Shoppe. She stopped and stared at the building.

"We'd better get to your mom's shop."

"Yeah. The sooner we get there, the sooner we're at the beach."

They walked a couple of blocks to Great Finds. "You haven't seen the inside. Be prepared for a lot of really old stuff."

Her mom was arranging items on a shelf toward the back. Sophie walked her cousin around the shop.

"You're right," Jessica whispered. "I've never seen so many old things in one place. Furniture, plates, vases, even a case with jewelry. Some of it's kind of pretty."

"She does like them."

The bell at the front of the store rang, and Sophie ushered Jessica into the back room. "Mom wants it to be peaceful in the store. Unless I'm in the middle of a project, she likes me to be in the back when customers come in because she says I can be 'a disruptive influence.'"

"You sure have been in my life. I never would have gone hunting for a mystery." Jessica sat on the one stool, so Sophie leaned against the wall.

"You know, I thought my brother was going to have the exciting summer, going out with Uncle Bill on his fishing charter boat."

Sophie heard the door's bell ring again.

"You can come out now, girls."

As soon as they entered the room, her mother said, "Over here, Soph. Arms out."

Mrs. Sandoval set a huge box in her arms. Sophie could barely see around the side of the thing.

"Sorry, Soph. I hadn't realized how big it would seem in your arms."

Sophie pulled away when, out of the corner of her eye, she saw her reach for it. "I can carry it. But, Jessica, you're going to have to help guide me."

Mrs. Sandoval said, "Okay, if you can do it, take it to the high school. The mayor's wife called this morning and asked if I could give something for a charity raffle today."

Sophie said, "Don't people normally ask earlier?"

"Always. She told me that the owners of a fishing supply store had promised her something a while back, I think she said a fishing pole, but they're out of town."

Jessica took hold of Sophie's arm and steered her out the door. With her head to the right side of the box, she had a narrow area of vision.

Outside, a man in a brown suit stopped, staring in Great Finds' direction. Was he the same man they'd seen before? A woman wearing a flowered dress and a hat with matching flowers walked in his direction, then seemed to hesitate when she saw him. Had he just shaken his head at her? The woman speeded up, passed him, turned left at the corner, and disappeared out of sight. Then the man glanced around and went around the same corner.

"Jessica, I just saw the strangest thing. Get me to the school and I'll tell you about it." Sophie gave directions from behind the box, then let her cousin lead her.

Sophie's arms were very tired when Jessica said, "I'm happy to report that we've actually arrived at a high school."

After handing the box to the mayor's wife, Sophie shook out her arms. "Whew. I'm glad I didn't have to carry that any longer." She rubbed her upper arms. "Let me tell you what I saw."

Jessica listened, then asked, "So you think they knew each other?"

"It seemed like they did." Sophie shrugged. "Maybe."

On the way to the beach, they went up the street with the Down Shoppe. Sophie thought about the last time they'd looked inside and wondered if maybe Jessica was right, and there wasn't a connection with their mystery.

"Hey." Jessica pointed to the building. "The Down Shoppe has something in their window."

13 FEATHER FINDERS

Sophie and Jessica stood in front of the Down Shoppe and stared at the window.

"Sophie," Jessica squeaked, "there are feathers and fluffy white things in this store window."

"It's like what was in the briefcase."

They looked at each other, then back at their surprising find in the store window.

"Get down." Sophie pushed Jessica's head down, and they crouched under the window. "I thought I saw movement in the back of the shop. This might be important. We'd better tell the sheriff."

"Agreed. Let's get to her as fast as we can."

They squatted and hopped for a few feet until they were away from the window, then stood and took off running.

"Sheriff Valeska," Sophie called out as they burst into the sheriff's office.

A deputy sheriff jumped. "She isn't here, Sophie."

"Where can we find her?" Sophie asked, panting.

"She's working. Can I leave her a message?" He picked a sheet of paper up off his desk and walked over to a file cabinet against the wall.

"Tell her we found the feathers."

The deputy turned toward them. "The feathers from the briefcase? Where?"

Jessica said, "They're in the window display of the new Down Shoppe on Olympic Street."

He chuckled. "They're supposed to have feathers in their window display."

Sophie didn't think he understood at all what this meant. And she didn't particularly like being laughed at. "But they're the same kind."

"I know you want to help. I'll leave her the message." The deputy opened a drawer in the file cabinet and dropped the paper in a folder.

Sophie couldn't think of anything else that would convince him. Trudging over to the door, with a deflated Jessica close behind, she pulled it open and ran headfirst into Sheriff Valeska.

The three of them jumped back, the sheriff's hat flying off her head. As Sheriff Valeska reached for it and pushed it back on, she asked. "Do you need something?"

"We have to show you what we found. Please come." Sophie tugged on her arm.

The sheriff cocked her head to the side, then shrugged and followed along.

"We found an important clue. Just around the corner." As they crossed the street, Sophie asked, "Have you learned more about the toy from the accident?"

"There are an adult's fingerprints on the toy, but we don't have a match for them."

"So you have more clues but no answers," Jessica said. "Will you be able to figure out whose fingerprints they are?"

"We sent both them and those from the briefcase to the FBI and hope to have a match soon. I also want you girls to bring in those papers tomorrow so I can make a copy. I'll keep the originals and have someone go over them for clues, even though I don't think it's going to lead anywhere."

When they stopped in front of the Down Shoppe, Sophie swept her hand toward the window like a game show host. "See what we found?"

The sheriff frowned. "I see an empty window display."

Sophie whirled around to the window. "We saw a pile of feathers mixed with white fluffy things, just like those in the briefcase, right here."

"Are you sure they were the same?"

"Exactly," Jessica said.

All traces of their amazing clue had disappeared, and blue fabric was in its place. Pointing at the shop window, Sophie said, "Get a search warrant. Those feathers are in there."

"Sophie, I can't get a search warrant without evidence of a crime."

Sophie put her hands on her face. "But we saw them. They weren't there this morning. Then they were there a few minutes ago, and now they're gone again."

"I believe you, but as far as I know, you're the only ones who noticed them. The feathers have to be in the window display for me to even have a chance of getting a search warrant."

"They must be criminals." Sophie pressed her face to the window. "How else can you explain the feathers being there, then disappearing?"

"They decided to change the display because every time they opened the door, the air coming inside blew white things around the room," Jessica suggested.

"Hey, I thought you were on my side."

"I am. But it is possible."

"Yeah. But it isn't likely. Sheriff, can we at least knock and ask about the feathers?"

"Yes, we can. But they don't have to answer." Sheriff Valeska knocked on the glass door.

Sophie was sure she saw a shadow move in the back of the shop for just a second, but then nothing stirred.

"I'll have one of my deputies drive by here every once in a while."

"Thanks."

Sophie wasn't happy as she trudged away. Jessica tugged on her arm. "There isn't anything else we can do about this now, right?"

"I don't think so."

"Then we've done enough crime-solving. Ready for sun, sand, and water lapping on the shore?"

Sophie perked up. "The beach!"

Jessica pumped air with her fist.

———

"This is gorgeous." Jessica stretched out on her beach towel and stared at the sky through her sunglasses. "A soft, sandy beach, blue sky, and water. What more could I ask for?"

Sophie rubbed on sunscreen. "You've been to a beach before."

"Not one I could walk to anytime I wanted for a whole summer. This is great."

"I think I know something that could make it even better for you."

Jessica closed her eyes and sighed. "What?"

"Tony."

"Where?" Jessica shot straight up and looked around.

"Try to be a little more subtle. He's over there." Sophie nodded to her right.

Jessica lowered her sunglasses to see more clearly. "He's cute. But I don't know anything about him. I might not even like him if we talk about more than sandwiches."

Sophie laughed. "He's a nice guy."

Just as Sophie spoke, Tony started walking their way. Jessica ran her fingers through her hair. "How do I look?" she whispered.

"Superb," Sophie whispered back.

"Hi, Soph." Tony nudged Sophie to the side and sat beside her on her towel.

"And you remember my cousin."

"Jessica," he said.

Jessica's heart pounded at the thought that he'd remembered *her* name. "Thank you for remembering."

He gave Sophie a crooked smile. "In a town this small, you know everyone's name."

"Oh." Jessica was disappointed. She'd thought he knew her name because he was interested in her. It was a good thing that she had these sunglasses to hide behind.

"I'd better get back to work." Tony stood and brushed sand off his pants.

"Mom will probably have us in Great Finds soon. We'll come over for lunch then."

"Great." He turned toward Jessica. "Do you like ice cream?"

Jessica nodded.

"I'll give each of you a sundae next time." He walked away but looked back when he was almost to the street. The girls waved at him before he turned toward the deli and disappeared out of sight.

"Wow," Sophie exclaimed.

"Wow what?"

"He asked you if you like ice cream, and then he said he'd give us some."

"So? What's your point, Cousin?"

"He's never given me anything free. And I've known him most of my life."

Jessica grinned. "Do you think Aunt April will ask us to help in her shop soon?"

"Maybe we'll volunteer."

"Excellent! I guess he doesn't mind braces." Jessica lay back on her beach towel. When she thought about Tony and the sundaes, she started grinning. She was still grinning when they packed their towels away and started for home.

———

After dinner, they sat on the couch, Jessica with the newspaper and Sophie with a magazine. Aunt April and Uncle Lucas had taken cups of coffee out onto the front porch after dinner to enjoy the evening, her uncle said.

Jessica said, "You know, Sophie, we could go to the newspaper office and read whatever they've written about the Down Shoppe. It's a new business, so there must be something."

"Mr. Avinson, the owner of the *Pine Hill Press*, is a nice man, so I'll bet he will find us exactly what we need."

Sophie asked her parents if she could call the newspaper owner to see if he would help them. They agreed, and Sophie quickly had him on the line. A few seconds later, she hung up the phone.

"Are we on for tomorrow?"

"No. He's going to be out of town for a couple of days, so we can't meet him until Friday."

"Too bad." Maybe the mystery would leave them alone until then. A summer filled with mysteries wasn't what Jessica had expected when she came to Pine Hill, but Tony was making things better and better.

———

The next day, Aunt April quickly agreed to their helping at Great Finds. The upside was that Jessica might get to see Tony. The downside was that "helping" meant dusting. She swept a feather duster over things on low shelves, on high shelves, and around the edges of furniture.

At one point, she and Sophie worked near each other. Jessica brushed the duster over small antiques on a shelf and glanced around. "Sophie, there's a lot of empty space on these shelves. Doesn't your mom want to have more to sell?"

"Summer's always busy so there'll be more and more empty space. Mom takes trips in the winter to buy things for the next summer. This year, she's going to Paris." Sophie sighed deeply. "She went a couple of years ago and met up with your mom there."

"You should try talking her into taking you this time." London was a short trip away from there, so they could have a day or two together in Paris while her aunt shopped.

"Don't think I haven't tried. She said that I need to get better grades in my native language before she'll take me to a country where they speak another language."

Jessica laughed, then paused. Sophie didn't know just how good she was at English or French. Or most other subjects. With them living so far apart, she probably wouldn't want her for a tutor anyway. Her secret could stay safely locked away—and she could stay guilt-free for not offering.

Jessica hoped for a trip to the deli for lunch, but Aunt April ordered in Greek food. Sophie shrugged when her mom placed the order on the phone. The gyro, good though it was, did not take the place of talking to Tony.

Jessica stopped working to check out a shelf full of blue-and-white plates, and to give her dusting arm a chance to rest. As she reached for the feather duster again, Sheriff Valeska walked into Great Finds and said, "April, can I speak with you alone?"

"Sure. Why don't you girls go outside and get a little fresh air?"

Sophie nudged Jessica. "See, I told you, Cousin. We're really big on fresh air here."

Both girls laughed as they went out the door. Jessica stopped to see the posters of exotic places in the window of the travel agency next door. Sophie grabbed her by the arm and pulled her back in front of Great Finds.

"Look," she said to Jessica.

"What?"

"They're talking." Sophie pointed at her mother and the sheriff.

"They're supposed to be talking. This mountain air is shrinking your brain."

"Yeah, but Mom seems concerned. Sheriff Valeska is using the phone. Now Mom's waving us in."

Back inside, Sophie's mom said, "Girls, Sheriff Valeska came to me first to make sure Lucas and I wouldn't mind what was about to happen. I said we would cooperate."

Jessica said, "Cooperate with what?"

Just then, a man in a perfectly fitting gray suit with a crisp white shirt and navy tie walked into the shop. Jessica stared at him. He seemed familiar.

"It's him," she called out and ran over to the sheriff.

"Who?" Sophie asked, staring at the man in front of her. "It *is* him."

14 A GOOD GUY

Sophie stepped forward. The sheriff may be here, but criminals wouldn't hide behind the law when she was around. "Who are you, really?"

"What's going on, girls?" Sheriff Valeska asked.

"I think I should explain," the man said to them. "Girls, I'm Agent Dallas from the FBI. I had a description of the two girls who had found the briefcase, so I knew who you were when I saw you at the resort. I decided to find out what you knew and warn you to be careful." He looked up at the adults. "They misunderstood and ran away. I hurried after them to explain, but they disappeared."

"We knew you were chasing us, but we also thought the man in the brown suit was after us," Jessica said.

"What man in a brown suit?" he asked.

"The one we've seen over and over again since we found the briefcase."

Agent Dallas pulled a notebook out of his pocket. "Describe him in as much detail as possible. Try not to forget any details no matter how small."

As Jessica did as he'd asked, Sophie studied the FBI agent, trying to learn about his character from his clothes and, more important, the way he moved. Mystery movies and books often said that the way a person stood and gestured showed how he really felt. Nice suit, pretty tie. He stood straight and still like a soldier. When Sophie looked at his feet, she found the shiniest shoes she'd ever seen. She could probably see herself in them.

Jessica stopped talking, so Agent Dallas turned to Sophie. "Anything you would like to add?" He held his pen over his pad.

"Not right now." Turning to Sheriff Valeska, she asked, "Did he show you his ID?"

"Sophie!" her mother exclaimed.

The agent pulled his identification out of his suit pocket and handed it to her. "That is an excellent question."

The ID showed a photo of the man, one that made him appear slightly more dangerous. His perfectly arranged features seemed tougher. Maybe the FBI wanted their agents to look tough in photos. In person, his eyes were a little bluer and his hair a darker shade of brown.

He started to put it away but Jessica stopped him. "Can I see it?"

"Certainly." He handed it to her.

Jessica held up the ID, glancing from it to Agent Dallas. "It sure looks like you."

"It does seem to be official," Sophie said as Jessica handed it back to him. "We'll trust you, since Sheriff Valeska is vouching for you."

"Sophie!" her mother admonished her again.

"The identification is genuine." The agent slipped it back into his coat. "Can you tell me more now?"

In her mind's eye, Sophie could see the man running away from them with the briefcase. "Well . . . he's tough looking. His hair is dark brown or black and kind of wild. And he always wears a brown suit. It's like he doesn't have any other clothes."

"But his suit isn't as nice as yours," Jessica added. "And his shoes were cheap. I know fashion."

"Thank you. Now that we have that out of the way, I need to ask you more questions."

Mrs. Sandoval said, "If this is going to take a while, we could go somewhere where we can sit down. Maybe the deli?"

Agent Dallas said, "I prefer this location. I'd like to keep this situation quiet for now."

"What is 'this situation'? I need to know so that I can protect my daughter and niece."

"We aren't sure. But strange things are happening in Pine Hill."

"You can say that again," Jessica said.

Sheriff Valeska stepped over to the two stools that usually stayed beside the cash register, sat on one, and took a small note-book and pen out of her pocket. Sophie knew they'd told her everything before. Maybe she wanted to be exacting in front of the FBI agent.

Agent Dallas spoke. "Girls, from the beginning, tell me about finding the briefcase."

Sophie told him everything that had happened. When she forgot something, Jessica added it.

"Don't forget about us being followed," Jessica said.

"Followed!" Mrs. Sandoval practically shouted. "You never said anything about that."

"We were never sure. We just had that crawly feeling you get when someone is watching you," Sophie said.

"And a branch broke when we were in the forest." Jessica shuddered.

Sophie said, "And on the trail, we heard crunching on the gravel behind us."

Mrs. Sandoval groaned and sat on the stool next to the sheriff.

"Go on," Agent Dallas said. "Describe what happened at the resort. I ran after you to tell you not to worry, but you had vanished."

Sophie jumped in. "We thought we'd seen the man in the

brown suit there earlier—" She looked up at the agent. "We forgot to mention that. Anyway, we didn't know who you were, and you chased us through the resort."

"How did you get away?" he asked.

"There's a hidden tunnel behind the waterfall."

"Well, that is about it." He closed his notebook. "I'm still not sure if the papers you found are anything other than trash, but I would like a copy of them."

Sheriff Valeska stood. "I asked the girls to bring them in today so I could copy them."

"Here." Sophie pulled the papers out of her pocket. Her mother offered the use of her copier, so the sheriff took them and went into the back room.

Agent Dallas put his notebook in his coat pocket. "You've been a great help, girls. Either I or my partner, Agent Able, who is arriving in town tomorrow, will be in touch with you if we have any more questions. I'll leave my card in case you think of something you want to add." He handed it to Sophie. Then as soon as the sheriff returned with the copies, he took the originals and gave the girls and the sheriff copies before leaving.

"Wow," Sophie said.

"Wow is right, Soph." Mrs. Sandoval checked her watch. "It certainly was an action-filled day. We need to close and get home. Your father is going to be getting hungry. I've got some hot dogs in the fridge, so we'll have a quick dinner. Will one of you girls go across the street to the deli and get two pounds of potato salad?" She pulled some money out of her wallet.

"Great." Jessica grinned, put out her hand for the money, and after taking it, hurried out the door.

"Why don't we run over to Bananas and get dessert?" Sophie asked hopefully.

Laughing, Mrs. Sandoval took out more cash, then paused as she was about to hand it to Sophie. "Nothing coated with sugar. But maybe I should call first and tell her what I want."

"Trust me, Mom."

"Don't let me down. You'd better hurry if you want to catch up with your cousin." She handed Sophie the money.

When Sophie walked into the deli, Tony was setting the container of potato salad on the counter. She waited by the door.

"Thanks, Tony." Jessica picked up the container and smiled the whole way to the door.

"Mom wants us to get dessert at Bananas and hurry back." Sophie walked as fast as she could, and Jessica stayed beside her.

"Yum," Jessica said when they went into the bakery.

Mrs. Bowman was on the phone when they walked in. "A down comforter?" she said into the phone.

Sophie and Jessica stopped in their tracks and turned to each other.

The older woman glanced up at them. "I have to go," she said. "Yes, I'll talk to you later."

"Down?" Jessica whispered.

The woman hung up the phone, then asked in what Sophie thought was a nervous voice, "Are you here for a sweet treat?"

Sophie gulped. Were they looking at a thief? She shuffled her feet. "Sorry to interrupt, Mrs. Bowman." Waving Jessica over, she said, "Help me choose something."

Jessica had a panicky expression on her face. Sophie worried she'd freeze up again, but when she looked in the glass bakery cases, the distraction of it helped. She sounded normal when she said, "There's so much to choose from."

"Remember, Mom said 'low sugar.'"

Mrs. Bowman reached into one of the cases and pulled out a cheesecake. "This one isn't too high on the sugar."

Sophie leaned forward to see it better.

"Chocolate swirl banana cheesecake."

Jessica said, "Yum. My mouth is watering."

Sophie agreed, and the older woman packed it up for them.

When they were outside again, Jessica asked, "Do you think she's involved with the criminals?"

Sophie shrugged. "I just don't know. We'd better keep an eye on her."

They were almost back to Great Finds when Sophie said, "The sheriff and FBI agent don't seem sure that the papers we found are important. We've already used them to find clues. I wonder why they can't see that they're valuable?"

"They don't appear important at first. We've done enough work with them to know they are."

"Too true," Sophie said.

On the way home, in the car, Mrs. Sandoval had a bag with some paperwork beside her on the seat, so the two girls sat in the back. Jessica put her hand on the yellow box sitting between them. "That looked so good."

"I know I should have asked you girls earlier, but what's in there?"

"Cheesecake." Sophie held up her hand to stop any protests. "Mrs. Bowman said it was low in sugar. She said it wasn't low in calories, but our family wasn't dieting."

They all laughed.

———

When Jessica took a bite of her dessert, she said. "This is the best cheesecake. Ever."

Sophie nodded in agreement. "I know. It's strange how all these banana things taste good. And you don't really notice there's banana in most of them."

"What is it with the owner and bananas?"

"No one knows." Mrs. Sandoval added cream to a cup of coffee. "The whole town just figures that she loves them."

"Are you sure you don't want some, Mom?"

She sat down, hesitated for a few seconds, then put a thin slice of the cheesecake on a plate and took a bite. "You're right. This is delicious." She took another bite, then said, "I called the sheriff when you were at the deli and bakery. She said that things seem quiet and safe, so if you promise to stay around people and not wander off without telling me"—she gave Sophie a firm glance—"I think you should take a day off from the mystery and go to the beach again tomorrow."

"Good idea." Sophie gave a thumbs-up to Jessica.

"Yesss! Beach, here we come."

———

Sophie glanced around at the woods lining the road as they walked to the lake. "You know, Jessica, after all that's happened, I wonder if anyone *is* watching us."

"Good question," Jessica agreed as she scanned the area. "There isn't a car or a person in sight. It's pretty deserted here right now. Let's move faster until we get to people." Jessica started running, so Sophie ran after her, pouring on the speed to pass her a minute later. This time it wasn't quite as easy to get ahead of her cousin.

At Main Street, Sophie stopped, then bent over with her hands on her legs. Panting, she said, "I'll be glad when the FBI and the sheriff arrest the bad guys."

"No kidding." Jessica panted beside her.

"You check really carefully this way," Sophie pointed in the direction of Great Finds, "and I'll check back where we came from. See anything?"

"Nothing suspicious this way."

"Nothing suspicious this way, either." Sophie bent over and got into a racing start position. "Let's go to the beach."

Five minutes later, they'd arrived, peeled off their outer clothes, and were lying on their towels on the beach. The sun felt warm on Sophie's face. "I had to work a little to pass you today."

"Uh-huh. Better watch out."

A cool shadow fell across Sophie, so she opened one eye to look at the cause of it. Agent Dallas towered over them, wearing a suit and dress shoes on the beach. If he'd trailed them here, he must need something from them.

15 SEARCH AND FIND

Sophie nudged Jessica.

"Huh?" She blinked and looked up. "Oh. It's you."

Agent Dallas smiled. Sophie hadn't been sure that FBI agents were allowed to smile. They never did in movies.

He knelt down. "Can you girls take me to the place you found the briefcase? I've got a team that needs to go through the woods there."

Jessica shrugged. "We've already searched."

"These are professionals. They might find something you missed."

Sophie and Jessica got up, repacked their bags, and slipped their clothes on. "At least I've got the right shoes for it." Jessica pointed at her feet.

Sophie giggled. "Better than the first time."

"Whew. Much better."

The agent watched them curiously. "Follow me to my car."

"Car? It's just a short walk to the trail," Sophie said.

"Even if that's the case, I wouldn't want to leave my car here."

"Leave it at my house. We can walk from there."

At Sophie's house, Agent Dallas took off his suit coat and tie, traded his shoes for hiking boots, and carefully locked all the car doors, pulling on a door handle to check it after he'd closed the door. Obviously from the city. Not many cars were stolen in this small town.

More than one person had told Sophie that Cutoff Trail was difficult for visitors who weren't fit. She looked the agent over. He wasn't overweight and seemed reasonably healthy. He should be fine.

He took off at a fast pace. He wasn't as fit as he appeared to be, though, because ten minutes later he was breathing hard. "Is it much farther?" he asked between breaths.

"It's at the top of the hill and around the bend." Sophie wondered about him. Even Jessica had done better than this— and in flimsy sandals. To be fair, though, Agent Dallas was moving quickly, and Jessica had taken her time that first day.

When they'd walked for a few minutes more, Sophie could hear people talking.

The agent said, "The team must have been able to follow the map Sheriff Valeska gave them." He seemed relieved.

Sophie grinned. She wasn't sure if he was happier to find everyone here or happier to be able to stop walking uphill.

He straightened his shoulders and got his in-charge, FBI look back. "Show us exactly where you found the briefcase."

Jessica walked over and tapped her foot on the spot. "Here."

"We won't need anything more from you girls. Would you like one of my agents to escort you home?"

Jessica and Sophie glanced at each other.

"I want to watch," Sophie said.

"Me too," Jessica agreed.

"Then stay out of the way."

The FBI team made a circle from the briefcase's location out. A dozen people searched behind every bush and under every rock. Some of them moved out of view down the path.

"They *are* searching more carefully than we did," Jessica said.

"That's because they're getting paid to do it."

Jessica giggled.

Just then, an agent walked up to Agent Dallas. Sophie could barely hear her low voice telling him they'd found something. She watched as Agent Dallas followed the woman down the path, around the corner, and out of sight.

"I'd love to see their clue."

"Why don't we casually walk down the path?" Jessica started walking slowly, whistling as she went and looking around.

All the agents stopped what they were doing to watch her.

Sophie laughed so hard that she couldn't move. "Jessica, wait," she choked out when she could and hurried to catch up with her. "Instead of whistling, maybe you should scream at the top of your lungs."

"Huh?"

"You made so much noise that everyone stopped working so they could see what you were doing."

When Jessica paused and saw all the agents watching her, her face turned bright red. "How embarrassing. They do that in the movies and everyone ignores them. Shows you how real movies are."

Sophie spotted the agent by the nail-polish rock. "Hey, look!" Sophie pointed to her. "She and Agent Dallas have knelt next to the rock we turned over."

The girls walked up to the agents and overheard the woman say, "Nail polish wouldn't normally be here, and it being hidden by flipping the rock could make this important."

Sophie and Jessica giggled.

"Can I help you girls?" Agent Dallas asked with an annoyed tone.

Sophie said, "Actually, I think I can help you."

"How would you do that? We have an important clue here that you girls overlooked. I told you professionals could find things you had missed."

Sophie resisted the urge to roll her eyes. Jessica reached out her hand and held it next to the polish on the rock.

The agent looked from Jessica's nails to the rock and back again.

"Did you do this on purpose?" Agent Dallas gave them a look that Sophie figured had made grown men cringe in fear.

"No. I dropped the bottle of polish. We turned the rock over because we didn't want to leave a mess."

The other agent set the rock back down and glared at them. She definitely wasn't happy that her evidence was really just part of a bungled manicure.

Jessica nudged Sophie and gestured uphill with her thumb. Sophie headed up the hill after her. Agent Dallas might ask them to leave if they stayed there any longer.

From the top they watched the proceedings. Sophie cocked her head to the side. "You know, I forgot to search over the side of the hill."

"That isn't a hill. It's a cliff. It goes straight down." Jessica rubbed her arms like a chill had gone through her.

"Actually, it just looks like that from here. There are lots of ledges. You can climb down from ledge to ledge."

"Really?" Jessica approached the edge but stopped a few feet from it.

Sophie walked over to it, lay down, and scooted on her stomach to peer over the edge. Still facing down, she waved Jessica over. "Look!"

Jessica lay down next to Sophie and slowly scooted toward the edge. "It's a suitcase!"

"Do you think Agent Dallas is going to like it if two girls find him a clue?"

"Not a bit."

"Maybe we should make the guy look good."

Jessica slowly grinned. "What did you have in mind?"

"Let's talk about the hill over by him. Maybe he will overhear us and do something about it."

"It's worth a try."

They found him near the nail-polish rock. People still combed the woods for clues. A few feet from him, she and Jessica paused and turned toward each other. Sophie winked.

"You know Jessica, something might be over the side of the hill," Sophie said loudly.

"But that's a cliff, Sophie. Anything that fell over would be in the lake at the bottom."

"No, it only seems like a cliff to strangers to Pine Hill. You can climb down it fairly easily."

Agent Dallas froze. They had his attention now.

The girls walked back near the edge and sat on a boulder to see what happened.

Jessica could hear Agent Dallas shout at one of his team members. "Hey, Morgan, go check over the side of the hill." He pointed in their direction.

"The hill?" The man turned where his boss pointed. "You mean the cliff? Maybe we should bring a boat around the lake to inspect the base of it."

"Just do me a favor and check over the hill."

The man shrugged. "Sure."

He and Agent Dallas walked to the top of the hill then slowly edged forward to peer over.

"Look!" Morgan pointed down the cliff.

Jessica smiled at Sophie. "Your word exactly."

"I'm a genius with language."

Jessica laughed.

Morgan scooted backward over the cliff and came back with a large, blue suitcase.

Sophie kept her eyes on the suitcase until Morgan carried it out of sight. "I'll bet there are a lot of clues in a suitcase that size. I wonder if they'll let us see what's inside."

The girls moved close enough to the agents to hear that it would be opened back at the lab.

Agent Dallas motioned them over. "Thank you."

"For what?" Sophie looked at him innocently.

"You know. I appreciate your help." He walked away.

"Our work is done here," Sophie said. She'd helped the FBI. If only she could tell someone about everything that had happened.

———

Back at the house, Jessica knew something different was up when Sophie went into the kitchen, opened the fridge, and pulled out chicken and vegetables.

"I would ask if you're making a snack, but it would be a strange snack."

"I haven't made dinner in a while, and it might make Mom and Dad happy if I do. They seemed a bit overwhelmed by the idea of us working with an FBI agent."

"Working with the FBI is a bit of an exaggeration. He asked us questions. Will your parents be happy eating something you cook?"

"I can cook. Mom taught me how when I was little." After grabbing a large pan, Sophie next moved everything to a cutting board. "How does a chicken stir-fry and fruit salad sound?"

"Great. Can I help?"

"Sure. Get out a big bowl for the fruit salad. Then cut up whatever fruit is ripe, making enough for the four of us."

Jessica carefully cut up a couple of peaches, a plum, and some cherries.

Sophie put rice on to cook, then cut up the chicken and veggies. "I saw blueberries in the fridge. Throw some of those in there. And pour a little orange juice over it so the fruit doesn't turn brown."

A few minutes later, Jessica stood back and admired her work. "I did it. I made a fruit salad. Anything else?"

"It's good as is. You could add some honey and cinnamon to yogurt and make a sauce. Then it's more of a dessert."

Jessica grinned. "I'm on it." She got out the three ingredients, combined them, and tasted as she went. "This is great. I'll make this when I get home." She didn't think her mom would be too happy if she made a whole dinner because of the possible scary results, but Sophie's parents were happy and appeared relaxed when Sophie told them about their day.

Uncle Lucas leaned back in his chair and listened as Sophie described how she'd found the suitcase. Shaking his head in amazement, he spooned some fruit into a bowl. "If the FBI want you to go back there with them, I'll take time off work and tag along."

"Is business okay, Dad? To be able to take time off in the middle of the day?"

"It's fine. I did meet a man the other day who asked me about buying my business."

Jessica said, "Just like Aunt April."

"Not quite. Your aunt and I own the building Great Finds is in, and if she sold the business, she would also sell her inventory —all of the antiques in the store. Her business is worth a lot to anyone. My business is different. It's based on my brains, and my office is a room in our house, so without me, it isn't worth much. The offer doesn't make sense."

"That's another strange thing that I'll have to think about." Sophie slowly put a bite of fruit into her mouth.

Her dad rolled his eyes. "Our little crime fighter. Right, April?"

Her mother sighed. "Yes."

After dinner Jessica sat down in an old, comfy chair, and Sophie settled onto the couch while her mom and dad cleaned up in the kitchen—their thank-you for dinner. Sophie almost immediately sprang to her feet and began pacing back and forth across the room.

"Sophie, stop!" Jessica closed her eyes and tried to ignore her. That proved to be impossible when Sophie kept going. "Not one more lap across the room! Please."

"I want to *do* something. I need to get out into the fresh air. Maybe go camping or something like that. I know Mom and Dad *won't* let me do that right now." Sophie perked up. "Hey, maybe we could sit outside tonight. Talk about the mystery. That might be the closest I come to camping under the stars until this is solved."

Jessica didn't want to sit outside, but Sophie seemed so sad about not being able to go camping, something Jessica wanted to do even less, that she agreed. "Okay." How bad could it be?

"Great. I'll make some snacks."

An hour later Jessica brushed a couple of mosquitoes off her arm, two of what seemed like thousands that were trying to eat her alive. "Pass me the popcorn." When Sophie did, she tossed some into her mouth. "I wish mosquitoes ate this instead of me."

"Sitting out here in the dark makes me think about the guy who dropped his briefcase in the night and ran. Why would someone do that?"

Something swooped above Jessica, diving close to her head. She dropped forward onto her knees, popcorn flying into the air. "What was that?"

Sophie stood next to her and chewed on her lip. "Don't worry. It wouldn't hurt you."

Jessica glared at her. "I know you aren't telling me something. What was it? It didn't seem to be a bird. Besides, it's dark and I don't think birds fly at night. I remember you told me bats and owls flew at night. An owl?"

Sophie scuffed the ground with the toe of her shoe. "A bat."

"Did you say a *bat*?"

"Uh, yeah."

"I'm out of here." Jessica ran for the back door. "The bat can have my popcorn."

Sophie chased after her cousin. "Bats don't hurt you."

Jessica stood inside the open back door. "Are you sure?"

"Uh-huh. I'm pretty sure they don't eat popcorn either."

Jessica paused to think about it. "I'm sorry, but I think I've had enough of the outdoors for tonight." When she started to walk away, she stopped. "I also think that bat answers loud and clear why anyone would get scared in the woods at night and abandon their luggage."

When Sophie came into the bedroom an hour later, she told Jessica about the possum with its babies she'd seen. But even cute possums couldn't make up for bats.

16 CLUES IN THE NEWS

On the way to the newspaper office, Jessica and Sophie decided they had no choice but to tell Mr. Avinson about the two pieces of newspaper they'd found. After explaining, they showed them to him.

"Hmm. It can't be." He held the piece of an article close to the light, carefully examining it.

"What can't be?" Sophie asked, moving closer to the light.

"The style of type—that's the way the letters look—is the same. The page's layout is the same." Mr. Avinson turned to them. "I believe these are corners of articles from the *Pine Hill Press*. I have a computer list of all the articles going back fifty years. We can search it for some of the words we see here." He sat at his computer and started typing. "The word 'Down' is at the edge of one of the pieces of newspaper, with the rest of the sentence torn away, and it's capitalized," he said as he typed.

"What?" Sophie exclaimed.

Both girls crowded closer to read the computer screen.

"Why didn't we notice that?"

"Only one subject matches it: Down Shoppe."

Sophie and Jessica stared at each other, then Sophie said, "It's a new business over on Olympic Street, but it hasn't opened yet."

"Hmm. Three articles." Mr. Avinson's forehead furrowed. "I know we wrote something about it, but that's too many articles for a business that hasn't opened." He paged through the list. "I can read summaries of the articles here. Yes. This explains why. There was a Down Shoppe seven years ago, and two of the articles are about the earlier business."

He put his elbow on the table and rested his chin on his fist. "That was before I bought the newspaper, so I don't remember those articles. I do remember the fishing store that was there last year, but I guess they closed permanently. Let's print a list of these dates and get the papers for you." He hit Print and picked up the pages that slid out of his printer.

Taking them, he walked over to shelves lining the wall that were stacked high with newspapers and pulled three out, one by one. "Come on over and sit down." He set the newspapers on a table and added his printout to the pile. "This sheet shows which article is on which page. I have to finish an article for the newspaper, so I'll let you ladies work on this." He walked back to his desk and sat in front of a computer.

Jessica went through the list. "I can read the old articles, Sophie, and you can read the new one. How's that?"

"As long as my one article is twice as interesting as yours, that's okay." Sophie laughed.

Jessica handed the newer paper to Sophie and picked up the printout. "Your article is on page 2." Jessica found her articles on the list and turned to them. As soon as she saw the first one, she felt like jumping up and down and shouting. Excited, she studied the photo that went with it and read the entire article. Then she reached for the second newspaper, hoping to find something just as good.

When she finished hers, she saw that Sophie had finished too. "Look at this!" Jessica held up the first newspaper she'd read. "This article matches the corner of the one we found."

She held the actual newspaper next to their corner of newspaper.

"Score!"

"There's more—the new Down Shoppe looks just like the old one in the photo."

Mr. Avinson walked over to the girls and bent over them to see the photo. Shaking his head, he said, "This certainly is odd. I haven't been on Olympic Street in a couple of weeks, so I haven't seen the new Down Shoppe sign. Maybe we made a mistake and used an old photo for the new story."

"Uh-uh." Sophie shook her head. "We walked by there a few days ago, and it's exactly like this photo. Maybe the same people started both businesses."

"It doesn't seem likely," Jessica commented. "My second article mentioned that the earlier business never opened because the owners suddenly decided to move to Italy."

Sophie leaned back in her chair. "Mine didn't say much about the new shop. Maybe the reporter didn't find many facts."

Mr. Avinson said, "That's an interesting observation. I remember her saying that she had to ask around to try and find information for the article because she couldn't get ahold of the owners."

"Why did you publish the article, then?" Jessica asked.

He chuckled. "Sophie, I think you can tell her."

Sophie smiled back. "Because anything new in town is news. Right?"

"Right."

Sophie snapped her fingers. "My article said that the new owners hadn't been to Pine Hill until a month ago. How can the two businesses look the same?"

Mr. Avinson furrowed his brow. "Everything about this is unusual. I believe we should explain the situation to Sheriff Valeska."

"Agreed," Jessica and Sophie said in unison.

"Are you sure you've only been together for a week or two?"

They nodded excitedly.

———

"We have a clue," Sophie called out and waved the newspapers in the air as they entered the sheriff's office.

Sheriff Valeska put her head on her desk. "No more!"

"This is a fascinating development," Mr. Avinson said.

The sheriff lifted her head. "I didn't see you behind the girls, Frank. Is there really a clue?"

The three told her what they'd found. As they stood there, the phone rang.

The sheriff answered, listened a moment, then said, "Yes, April. I'll make a note of it." She hung up.

"Did my mom call to check on us?"

"No. A woman offered to buy Great Finds."

"That's strange. First Mom, then Dad, now Mom again. Jessica, let's run by Great Finds and ask her about it." Sophie said good-bye to Mr. Avinson and the sheriff, then ran over to her mom's shop.

Once there, Sophie grilled her mother. "Can you describe her?"

"She'd be hard to forget with a bright flowered dress and matching hat. It was a bit much for downtown Pine Hill."

"She sounds like someone we've seen before." Sophie then told her mother about what they'd learned at the newspaper.

"You girls stay out of trouble."

"Of course," Sophie answered.

"I hope trouble stays away from us," Jessica added quietly.

Sophie led Jessica to the back of the shop. When they sat down, Sophie on the floor, Jessica on the stool, Sophie said, "We need to know a lot more about down. I know that Mom and Dad have a down comforter on their bed."

"So?"

"So, maybe we can carefully open it and see if what's inside is the same as what we found in the briefcase."

"Oh, Sophie! If your parents found out—"

"I know. But we have to solve this mystery."

There must be a way to go about it that wouldn't get them in what Jessica knew would be big trouble.

"Well?" Sophie asked.

A solution came to mind. "It might help if we knew more about what was going on in town when the other Down Shoppe was here. Maybe we could look through more newspapers."

"Let's call Mr. Avinson." Sophie ran to the phone, and soon received an answer that had her smiling. "He says we can go back there right now. If it's okay with Mom, he's going to leave the key with us so he can go to a meeting and we can lock up when we're done."

Her mother agreed. "It's fine with me as long as you're back here by about four o'clock. I'm thinking of closing early today."

The girls hurried to the deli—Tony wasn't there—and picked up some sandwiches and chips to go before heading over to the newspaper.

When they arrived, Mr. Avinson said, "I certainly enjoyed our research earlier."

Sophie said, "We did too. Thank you for letting us come back."

He took them back to the same table. "In case you girls didn't notice where I was getting the newspapers for our research, this area is for the year when the other Down Shoppe existed, and"—he stepped a few feet to his right—"here are the recent issues. If you're comfortable working alone on your project, I'm going to my meeting."

"No problem," Sophie said.

As he gathered up his things to take, including a briefcase, Jessica asked, "How do you become a newspaper reporter?" Images of working in exotic places, writing about important stories, excited her.

"Most people study journalism in college. I did. Is newswriting something you're interested in?

Jessica glanced over at the stacks of newspapers. "Maybe. I know I enjoy writing, but I've never written a newspaper article."

"If you'd like to write one, I'll read it. If I like it, I'll publish it in the paper."

"Thank you. I'll keep my eyes open for exciting ideas. You know—"

Sophie interrupted her. "Give it time, Jessica. You can bounce ideas off me."

Yikes. She'd almost spilled the story. And to a newspaperman.

"Here's a key." Mr. Avinson set it on his desk. "It fits both the back and front doors, but the front door lock can be a little fussy, so I'll lock it now. Go out the back door and drop the key through the front mail slot." He locked the front lock from the inside, jiggling the knob a bit as he did so.

When he went toward the back door, Jessica called out, "Thank you again, Mr. Avinson."

"Yes, thanks." Sophie added.

He waved as he pulled the door closed.

As soon as it closed completely, Sophie said, "Jessica, you were going to tell him about our mystery. He knows some of what's happened, but not most of it."

"Sorry. All of the recent activity on the mystery is so exciting that it immediately came to mind."

"Maybe you can write the story about our mystery after we solve it."

"I've been thinking about doing that." Jessica spotted the bag from the deli and realized she was hungry. "But let's eat before we work." As she unwrapped her sandwich, she asked, "How far back before the articles do you think we should read?"

Sophie tore open her bag of chips. "I've been thinking about that. How about a month before, and for the older ones, a month after?"

"Sounds good to me."

After eating, they washed their hands and got to work.

"I'll get the earlier ones." Jessica sorted through the newspapers and pulled four of them off the shelf. "I'm quite happy the *Pine Hill Press* only comes out once a week."

Sophie walked over to the later newspapers and pulled off a stack. Both girls set their papers down and read in silence for a while. When Jessica reached for the second to last newspaper, she said, "I'm almost through the time when the other shop was there."

Sophie kept reading and muttered, "Uh-huh." Then she stretched and asked, "Have you found anything interesting?"

Jessica flipped the page. "Not until now. Sophie . . ."

Sophie sat up. "What'd you find?"

"On the other side of the article about the first Down Shoppe, the one we found in the alley, there's an article about all of the money residents make off visitors each summer. The idea of a lot of money might bring in criminals. Pine Hill was called the 'richest little city in the state.'"

"I remember learning about that in school." Sophie rested her elbows on the table. "Other newspapers printed the articles. After that, people flooded into town trying to buy up land for the boom they expected to happen. But I don't think it ever did. Does it say that?"

"No. At the end of the article, it says to see the next issue for the conclusion." Jessica picked up the last newspaper. "It was front-page news in the next newspaper. The town went wild with people wanting to make a fortune off visitors to the city."

Sophie laughed. "I doubt that's an article we need. We'd better keep reading."

The phone rang a couple of times, but they didn't think they should pick it up.

When Jessica finished the little reading she had left, she

rubbed her eyes. "No more newspapers, please. I don't even want to see one for a while."

Sophie closed her eyes and rolled her shoulders. Looking up, she said, "We haven't found anything that seems important. But maybe we've missed something."

Jessica felt the same way. "If we have, maybe we'll know later. There might be a piece of the puzzle we won't know is important until we have the rest of the pieces fitted together."

Sophie gathered the newspapers together. Then she checked the time. "Jessica, it's after four. We're late, and I don't think Mom will be happy."

"Understatement of the century." Jessica returned the papers to the shelf in the order they'd found them. "I want to make sure we leave things as we found them."

"Me too. It was really nice of Mr. Avinson to let us stay here without him."

Sophie turned off the lights, and Jessica went out the door first. While Sophie locked it, Jessica stood behind her in the alley. Something moved to her right.

Jessica gulped, slowly turned to the right and saw . . . a stack of empty boxes waiting for trash pickup. She let out a deep breath. "I'm getting jumpy."

"Why do you say that?"

"I thought I saw something move, but when I turned that way, all I saw was garbage."

Sophie looked around the shadowy alley and shivered. "Maybe the flap on a box moved in the breeze. Let's get back on Main Street."

They dropped the key through the mail slot, then hurried to Great Finds.

Once there, Sophie opened the door and put on a big smile. "Hi, Mom."

Her mother pushed some paperwork to the side, an angry expression on her face. "Why are you late?"

"Well—"

She held up her hand to stop her. "I was worried about you. I called the newspaper office and no one answered."

"We didn't think we should answer the phone there."

Her mother glared at her, picked up her purse, and ushered them out of the building.

As they walked to her car, Jessica couldn't think of anything to say. The normally short drive seemed to take forever. When Aunt April pulled up in front of their house, Jessica hurried out the car door and rushed inside.

When she and Sophie got to the bedroom, Sophie quickly closed the door. "Whew, I haven't seen Mom that mad since I forgot to clean the house and the mayor came for dinner."

Jessica giggled. "You must have gotten in a lot of trouble."

"That's the truth." Sophie flopped down on her bed. "The good news is that she cools off pretty quickly. Unless she gets Dad involved."

A knock sounded at the door.

"Yes?" Sophie called out.

"It's Dad."

"Uh-oh." Sophie fell backward on her bed. "Come in."

He started talking the second he opened the door. "Sophie Eileen, your mother was worried about you today."

She sat back up. "I know, Dad. We were safe. When we did see we were a little late, we still had to straighten up."

Jessica heard her uncle Lucas sigh. Then he turned to leave. "I'll explain the situation to your mother," he told Sophie. "She'll understand that you were trying to follow the rules."

Sophie turned to Jessica when he closed the door. "Whew. That was better than I expected."

Aunt April didn't seem angry when they sat down to dinner, and by the time they finished, she was smiling. But she didn't bring out any dessert. Not even fruit.

After dinner, Sophie pulled out a pad of paper and a pen, along with the papers they'd found. "Let's list all of our possible clues to see if anything helps."

Jessica could certainly get behind the idea of bringing organization to their efforts. "Why don't we make two columns, one with things we know are clues and the other with things that might be clues."

Sophie nodded. "I like that."

When it came to the newspapers they'd searched through today, Jessica argued against Sophie's take on them. "I don't think we can put the newspapers we read in the clue column. We don't know if they really helped."

"Sure, they did. We know there was an earlier Down Shoppe."

"But we don't know if that means anything."

Sophie argued. "It has to. The new Down Shoppe is a clue."

"Agreed."

"Then the old one has to be, because they look the same. They must be connected."

Jessica sighed. "You win. All those years of reading and watching mysteries did teach you something."

They looked through the legal pages and the newspaper bits one more time, but nothing new stood out.

When Jessica went to bed that night, she picked up one of Sophie's mysteries to read. Maybe she would get some ideas from it.

17 BAD GUY ALERT

After breakfast, Sophie got a surprise when Jessica said, "Let's go by the Down Shoppe. Just to see if anything's different."

"I like that. You're starting to think like a detective. Let's case the joint."

"I think that's what criminals say before they check out a place they want to rob."

No other awesome detective sayings came to mind. "Let's go see what's what."

Not far from the Down Shoppe, Sophie noticed a man following them. "Jessica, is that the guy in the brown suit, or am I seeing things?"

Jessica looked in the same direction. "I don't know. He's so far away that I can't even tell what he's wearing. It could be a man in a suit, but he might be wearing jeans and a jacket. It could be anyone, including Uncle Lucas."

"Let's walk faster and see if he follows us."

"Two things: What if that man, whoever he is, already planned to walk this direction? And even if he is the man in the brown suit, he's far enough away that he probably doesn't know who he's following."

They walked a little faster, then a little faster than that.

Sophie looked over her shoulder. "He's wearing navy pants and a tan jacket, and he's going faster than we are. He's gaining on us. Run to the sheriff's office!"

The girls ran the three blocks and plunged through the door.

"Girls, what's wrong?" Sheriff Valeska hurried over to them.

"Man," Jessica panted, "chasing us."

The sheriff pushed open the door and surveyed the area. "I don't see anyone."

Sophie checked. "He's gone. But you've got to believe us."

"I do." Sheriff Valeska pointed to the chairs. "Sit, ladies, and rest. We received the results on the fingerprints in the briefcase a few minutes ago. Now I see why the FBI was so interested. They must have suspected something like this."

"Like what?" Jessica bent forward in the chair, still panting.

"The fingerprints belong to a serious bad guy. You must stay in public and together. And if you see anything suspicious, call immediately." Sheriff Valeska sat behind her desk. "Do you understand, girls?"

Jessica took a big breath. "I sure do."

The sheriff leaned toward Sophie. "Listen carefully to me. Do not wait. Do not investigate. Call."

"We understand," Sophie said. The excitement of having a real mystery with a real criminal slipped away from her.

"It's best this way, Sophie."

"I know, but it isn't as exciting. For a little while, it was like living in a detective book or movie."

The sheriff grabbed her hat and headed for the door. "I'd planned to call your mom today to tell her about the fingerprints. Since you're here, I'll walk you over there. Would you like to listen in?"

"Yes. Thanks." Sophie felt like smiling again.

A few minutes later, Sheriff Valeska explained to her mother, "We've received the fingerprint report. The man whose fingerprints were in the briefcase is a known criminal. He's someone the FBI has been after for several years."

Mrs. Sandoval gasped.

"I know you've been watching the girls carefully, but I want you to fully understand what's going on. We don't want them vulnerable to strange men, like earlier today."

"Earlier?"

"That's right. You couldn't know yet. A man chased them into town. Keep them in public and together." The sheriff walked over to the door.

"I'll keep them here during the day."

Sophie's summer crumbled to the ground. "Oh, Mom."

"You're safe here, Soph," Mrs. Sandoval said.

The sheriff agreed. "Yes, this should all be over in a few days," she said as she left.

"Jessica, I've got a good news, bad news scenario," Mrs. Sandoval said.

"You're going to call my mom and dad, aren't you?"

"I don't want them to worry, but I can't keep something like this from them. I'll call tonight."

"Great. I haven't talked to them for a few days." Jessica didn't seem worried about the call.

The bell at the front door rang as Agent Dallas came into Great Finds. He started speaking as the door closed behind him. "Sheriff Valeska told me what happened this morning. Are you girls all right?"

"They're fine," Mrs. Sandoval said. "Will you solve this soon?"

The agent grimaced. "We get one clue that leads nowhere. Then we get another one . . ."

Sophie said, "That's exactly what happened to us. We wrote down everything we knew about the case last night and studied the papers. But we didn't notice anything new. What clue are you working on now?"

"That's right," he said slowly. "We're working on the original papers in our lab. But you still have copies. I'll come by tonight to get them. You aren't safe as long as you have any evidence that might be associated with this case."

Jessica asked, "If the bad guy *thinks* we have them, aren't we in danger even if we don't?"

"I admire your logic, but I don't want you to have anything associated with this crime. I think you'll be safest without them."

Mrs. Sandoval said, "Let's hope the criminals are paying as much attention as you think they are."

When Agent Dallas turned to leave, Sophie said, "Wait. What was in the suitcase?"

He stopped, not moving for a few seconds, then faced them. "Mostly clothing."

"Men's or women's?" Sophie asked.

"I shouldn't tell you anything. But it was both. And that's all I'm saying. Now, I have to be going." The bell signaled his departure.

When her mother went to the back of the store, Sophie said, "That suitcase was a great clue."

"It was filled with clothes, Sophie. How is that a great clue?"

Sophie felt like the mystery was starting to come together. "It shows that there's a man and a woman in this."

"You're absolutely right. Maybe it's the man who just chased us and the pretend French woman."

All of the people they'd seen doing odd things flashed through Sophie's mind, but Jessica's theory was as good as any. "Might be."

After dinner they called Jessica's parents. Sophie could tell from Jessica's answers that her mother was worried.

"No, Mom, everything's fine. I'm safe. The FBI is taking care of us."

Sophie winced when her aunt Stephanie, Jessica's mother, shrieked so loudly she could hear it. Jessica jumped and moved the phone a few inches from her ear. She heard a few more loud things Aunt Stephanie said. Her cousin nodded and said, "Yes, Mom" over and over. Then she held out the phone to her aunt April. "Mom said, 'Put my sister on.'"

After taking the phone, she said, "Yes, Sis. They're fine." Then she listened for a while, not saying anything, before passing the phone back to Jessica.

When Jessica hung up, Mrs. Sandoval said, "Your mother was concerned."

"Tell me about it. She didn't know about the FBI until I told her, and it totally upset her that the situation required major law enforcement, not just the sheriff. Big mistake."

"But it *was* right to tell her."

Later that night, the girls watched one of Sophie's favorite mysteries from her library of movies. As the end credits rolled by, Jessica said, "You know, I'm surprised that Agent Dallas never came to get the papers."

"As much as I didn't want to give them to him, I find it strange too."

18 CATCHING CLUES

"Let's give the FBI a call."

"They aren't going to care about a call from someone our age."

"Let's try." Jessica dialed the phone number on Agent Dallas' card and asked for him, explaining that they had a clue for him.

A minute later, Jessica hung up and sighed. "The woman told me he wasn't available and took a message. She didn't seem to think this was important."

"Told you so."

"They must get a lot of calls from people telling them they have clues, so I doubt that it's because I'm twelve. She can't see through the phone."

"And you don't sound like a little kid."

"Thank you. I tried to sound older."

The whole situation puzzled Jessica. Why hadn't an FBI agent done what he'd said? "Maybe we'll get a call from Agent Dallas tomorrow. He could just be busy with the case."

During church the next morning, Sophie thought about the rest of the day. Staring straight ahead, she said out of the corner of her mouth, "How about a hike?"

Jessica wrinkled her nose. "I don't think so."

"Okay," Sophie said slowly. "Then how about walking down by the lake like last Sunday? It should be fun on a sunny summer Sunday. Ooh, I like how that sounds. Sunny summer Sunday."

"Shh." Her mother put her finger over her mouth and glared at them in a way that made Sophie cringe. Her mom had thankfully refocused on the minister's lesson when a minute or two later Jessica nudged her and gave a thumbs-up.

The whole family ate lunch in a small Mexican restaurant. Then Sophie's parents dropped them off at the lake with directions to stay together and around people. They'd be back to pick them up in a couple of hours.

Sophie hoped they'd be less protective after a while. A man had chased them, but he hadn't caught them. Walking toward the water she said, "Let's go over by the boats."

"Are they far?"

"Nope. Just over to the right."

As they got close to the docks, Jessica said, "There are boats tied up in all colors and sizes. The lake's bigger than I realized."

A big, burly man on a large boat came into view. Sophie said, "Hey, Captain Jack."

"Hello, lassie."

Jessica turned to Sophie. "From Scotland?"

"Yes. He's a friend of Dad's. But how do you know those things?"

"Scotland's attached to England, the country I live in."

Just one more thing that she and Jessica didn't have in common.

As they stepped to the side of the boat, Sophie said to the captain, "I'm surprised to see you at the dock this time of day."

"I'm not booked today and was getting ready to go fishing by myself. You know, I haven't taken you fishing in quite a while." He rubbed his bearded chin. "Would you like a short trip?"

Sophie explained to Jessica, "Captain Jack owns a charter boat. People pay him to take them fishing."

"My uncle Bill does that too," Jessica said, then asked, "Will your parents allow us to go? I can call." She pulled her cell phone out of her purse. "No, I can't."

Captain Jack smiled. "No one's phone works here, so we use the pay phone onshore. Lassie, why don't ye call and ask?"

Sophie raced up to the phone and came back in two minutes. "We can go."

As Captain Jack prepared to leave and the girls waited on the back of the boat, Sophie told Jessica, "Mom was thrilled. She said we'd be safe on the water, where no one could get to us."

Jessica glanced over at the shore. "When you put it like that, being on the boat does sound better than being on land."

Once they were on the lake, Captain Jack slowed the boat to a crawl, reached for two fishing poles, and handed one of them to Sophie. Then he walked over to Jessica.

"I'm not fishing." Jessica crossed her arms in defiance.

Captain Jack stopped in front of her with a pole. "Don't you like fish, lassie?"

"I love fish. On a plate. But I'm not putting a hook through a wiggling worm to catch one."

Captain Jack roared with laughter. "Lassie, I don't want you to miss the fun of fishing." He reached into a cabinet and pulled out a bag of marshmallows. "Would this suit you?"

Jessica eyed him suspiciously. "Are you teasing me?"

"No. The fish love them." He tore open the bag and put one of the marshmallows in his mouth. "Matter of fact, 'tis true that I like them too."

Jessica smiled. "Cousin, let's each catch a big fish."

"Deal," Sophie said and baited her hook with a marshmallow. Jessica copied what she did.

As Captain Jack motored them slowly across the smooth lake, with their lines pulling in the water, Sophie looked around them and up to the sky. Several large birds flew high in the direction of the boat. She shaded her eyes with her hand to watch them.

Captain Jack looked up. "Those ducks are beauties.Have ye become a bird-watcher?"

"No. But we are trying to find the bird that matches a feather we found."

The birds dipped down toward the water, then up over the boat. A couple of feathers fell off of them as they passed overhead.

Excited, Sophie asked, "Can we catch a feather, Captain Jack?"

"There's a breeze today, so I'm not sure where they'll drop. I'll try to maneuver the deck under them, but you lassies need to grab a fishnet each and be ready to scoop them up." Sophie reached for the net beside her, and Jessica rested her pole against the side of the boat so she could grab another.

The captain cut the motor and, staring upward, carefully turned the wheel. At the last minute, the breeze shifted sending one feather into the lake and out of sight. When the other feather fluttered above the water for a second, Jessica scooped it up in her net.

Sophie plucked it out of the net. "Jessica, take a look at this feather. I think it's exactly like ours! And there's some of the fluffy white stuff with it."

"That's a bit of the down from the duck," Captain Jack said.

Sophie blinked, startled. "Down comes with duck feathers?" How had they missed this fact?

"Aye, Lassie. And geese. I'm surprised someone who enjoys the outdoors as much as you doesn't know about our winged friends."

"Me too. I'll be learning more." She pulled on the bit of fluff and muttered, "So down comes *with* duck feathers."

They fished for a while longer but didn't catch anything.

Jessica handed her pole to Captain Jack when they reached the shore. "I'm not sure if I should be sorry I didn't catch anything or glad I didn't have to touch a slimy fish."

He chuckled. "I'll make sure you catch a fish this summer. You and Sophie can come out with me another time."

"Thank you. I think." Jessica smiled at him. "A bat attacked me and I survived, so I guess catching a fish is next. This is a summer of adventure. Thank you for helping us catch the feather."

Sophie held the feather up in the light as they walked back down the pier. "I can't wait to take this over to Sheriff Valeska tomorrow so we can compare it to our old feather."

"Are you sure she isn't there on Sunday? Maybe we should try."

"The office isn't really open. There's just a deputy on call for emergencies."

Sophie called her parents from the phone she'd used earlier, and her dad drove over to pick them up.

Back at home, Jessica stretched out on her bed and put her hands behind her head. "We've had quite a day."

Sophie grinned, "We couldn't ask for more than a piece of the puzzle falling from the sky."

———

They were in their robes after their morning showers and sitting on their beds talking when someone knocked on the bedroom door. Sophie called, "Come in," and her dad stepped inside.

"Girls, I'm heading out early for a meeting, so I can drop you off at Great Finds. I think you're safe as long as you're together, but you may as well take advantage of the ride."

Sophie answered, "Sounds good to me, and I don't think Jessica will argue."

"Not a chance I'll say no." Knowing they were inside a car, so no one would follow or chase them as they walked to town, was all good.

When her uncle had closed the bedroom door, Jessica headed for the closet. "It's great that you have a dad like that."

"I like your dad too. I haven't seen him in a long time, but I remember he's nice."

"I love my dad. But he's gone a lot, and I don't really know what he does at work. Your dad is here all the time."

"My dad's here all day. But I don't understand accounting. Your dad is gone for months at a time. Are you missing him again?"

Jessica wondered what her mom and dad were doing right now. "I miss my whole family."

"Even Frog Boy?"

Jessica's brother was going out on a boat every day, so he may not have even noticed that she wasn't there. But she still thought about him. "Yes, I even miss him."

On the way to town, Sophie asked her dad to drop them off at the sheriff's office instead of Great Finds.

"Sheriff Valeska," Sophie called out as she opened the door and hurried inside.

"Yes, Sophie." The sheriff sighed.

"We found a feather. Can we hold it next to the one from the briefcase?"

The sheriff hesitated, then said, "Why not?" She disappeared into the back, then returned a few minutes later with the feather in a labeled plastic bag.

The girls held theirs next to it and smiled.

"It's a match," Sheriff Valeska said in amazement.

"It's from a duck. Captain Jack knows which kind."

"Thanks. The waterfowl biologist is on vacation, so the feather hasn't been identified."

Huh. The sheriff had to call Fish and Game too.

———

At Great Finds Jessica set her purse down on a back shelf and picked up the duster—her job. Again. Glass shelves seemed to attract dust.

"Girls, I usually put out a Be Right Back sign in the window when I need to run an errand, but since you're here . . ." Her aunt's words trailed off and she stared at them.

"Mom, we can handle things for a few minutes."

"Okay, Soph. If a customer wants to buy something, you know what to do. If they have a question you can't answer, get their phone number, and I can call them as soon as I get back."

"Sure." Sophie smiled sweetly.

"I'll only be gone about forty-five minutes," Mrs. Sandoval said as she walked out the door, glancing back once as the door closed.

Sophie turned to Jessica. "It isn't like I'd sell something for a dollar instead of a hundred dollars." She shrugged.

"No. You seem to understand about the pricing. And it isn't as though you could find a mystery here in the next half hour."

Sophie grinned. "Actually, there is a mystery."

"Oh no!" Could Sophie find a new mystery in this short of a time?

Sophie motioned for Jessica to follow her to the back room. "Don't worry. I can't get into trouble with this. It's just that the floor seems hollow right here." She stomped her foot on the wood floor. "Mr. Braden, the owner of the boat store, used to play professional football and is a big guy. When he visits Mom, he won't step here because he says he's afraid he'll fall through."

Jessica walked over, stomped there, then stomped in a few other places. "You're right. It doesn't sound like the rest of the floor." She leaned against the shelves and watched as Sophie stomped again.

"Huh. It sounds stranger than usual. Kind of hollow. Maybe there's a secret passage under here."

"Sophie." Jessica rolled her eyes. "Next you'll tell me there's a secret passage to somewhere like Narnia. It's probably just an old floor that's getting worn-out."

Sophie jumped high up in the air, landing with both feet on the spot.

"No! What if it cracks?" Jessica cried out.

A crunching, creaking sound came from beneath Sophie's feet, and Jessica watched her cousin disappear through the floor.

"Aaaahhhhh!" Sophie screamed.

19 UNDERGROUND ESCAPE

"Sophie? You okay?" Jessica called out. "Sophie?"

"Just a second," said a faint voice Jessica barely recognized. She started to run toward the phone to call for an ambulance.

"I'm okay."

She stopped.

"That would have been much easier with stairs," the quiet voice said. "Please get the flashlight so I can see what's down here."

"Where is it?"

"Under the cash register," Sophie said more loudly, sounding more like herself already.

Jessica ran over to the counter, found a yellow plastic flashlight, and ran back. She pushed the button on the outside and stood a few feet from the hole, shining the light through it as well as she could from there.

"Can you bring it closer?" Sophie shouted.

Jessica lay down and scooted closer to the hole. "Does that help?"

Sophie shouted back, "Yes. I can see that I'm lying on a big fabric thing that's soft. But I still can't see what's around me. Can you point the light straight through the hole for a few seconds?"

"I'll try," Jessica shouted back. She edged a few inches closer and held her hand over the hole, pointing the light straight down.

"That's perfect."

Jessica felt one of the boards under her crack. Everything moved in slow motion as she slid through the hole. The floor of Great Finds moved by; then she was surrounded by darkness. *Whap!* She hit bottom.

"You okay?"

Jessica wheezed in air. Her chest hurt, but she could breathe. That had to be the scariest thing ever. Wiggling each leg and arm, Jessica declared, "Everything seems to work."

Sophie scooted next to her. "I found the flashlight." She clicked the button.

Jessica squeezed her eyes shut. "But there's a bright light in my eyes."

"Oh, sorry." Sophie moved the light to the side. "Fortunately, the flashlight landed on the other side of me, not on my head. At least we're both okay." She shined the light through the hole in the floor. "It's a long way up."

Jessica stared up at the hole filled with light from the shop. She could feel Sophie moving around like she was going to get up. "I think we should stay right here until someone comes to help us. We seem safe here."

"This *is* soft."

"But it's kind of smelly. You know, it's strange how nice this feels under us. Like a pile of mattresses. What's it look like in the light?"

Sophie shined the light all around the thing they'd landed on.

Jessica sat up. "If it didn't sound so strange, I'd say this was a pile of comforters." She pressed against it with her hand. "It's almost as fluffy as a stack of down comforters."

"Hey!" Sophie cried out.

Jessica jumped. "What? What?"

"Maybe this is filled with down. Someone from the Down Shoppe could have put it here."

Jessica put her hand on her racing heart. "You scared me. Don't *do* that. Besides, the Down Shoppe is almost a block away. How could they get it here? And who would be stupid enough to hide evidence under your mom's shop? I'll bet everyone knows you're working on the mystery."

"They might be smart criminals, not stupid. Until now, there was no door into the basement, so this was very safe. It might help solve the mystery."

Jessica groaned. "The smelly thing we were lucky enough to land on to prevent broken bones can't be a clue." She looked completely around them. Something looked back. "Sophie." She gestured behind them with her thumb.

"What's so important? I'm solving the mystery."

"A rat."

"Where?" Sophie asked nervously.

"There." Jessica pointed. Creepy just got creepier.

"If you're pointing, I can't see you." Sophie shined the light in Jessica's direction, then to where she pointed.

"There are *two* sets of eyes. Maybe we *should* try to get out of here."

"Mom said she'd be back in forty-five minutes. I fell through the floor right after she left, so we've probably got a half hour left before she'll be here to help us."

"Let's get up and walk around, shining the light on the walls as we go. Maybe there's another way out of here. A ladder or something."

"Deal."

Jessica watched her cousin rise, then slowly got up off the comforter herself. "I'm relieved that everything works while I'm standing, too."

Sophie lifted each arm and moved it around. "Me too. Let's go."

Standing in the middle of the room, they turned around

slowly, the light revealing stone walls with a door on the left and the right sides.

Sophie actually seemed to hesitate. "Should we try one of them and see what's on the other side?"

"I'm surprised you'd stop to ask."

"You're right. We seem safe here, and who knows what's through that door. We should probably stay here." Sophie shined the light up to the ceiling and around the room one more time.

Jessica took a deep breath of the stale basement air, then regretted it. Coughing, she said, "There are rats here. Isn't the travel agency next to Great Finds on one side and the fur shop on the other?" *Calm, try to stay calm.*

"Oh, that's good. We know what's above it, so it should be safe just like here."

"Yep. I'll be brave." Jessica hurried to the door that led to the fur shop's basement and tried the doorknob. "It's locked."

Sophie followed her and tried it. "This won't budge. Let's try the other one."

With Sophie behind her, Jessica ran across the room, keeping an eye on the rat corner. Twisting that knob, she said, "It moved a little."

"Let me try." Sophie handed her the flashlight and grabbed the doorknob with both hands, twisting hard. After a few seconds, it gave way and the door opened with a spooky, creaking sound.

Jessica gulped. Then she nervously shined the light through the doorway. "It's like here. Empty." The light played off the wall on the other side of the room.

"Another door. You want to keep going or wait for my mom?"

Jessica glanced around. It seemed like almost anyplace would be better than where she was. "I'd like to get out of here."

"Me too." Sophie put her arm through Jessica's. "Let's go together."

Something skittered away into the corner of the Great Finds

basement. "Yuck. Let's hurry." She returned the flashlight to Sophie. "If something small and furry bumps me, I might drop this and run."

The second door opened easily, and the girls soon found themselves in another empty basement, this time with a red door on the opposite side.

Sophie said, "There's a men's clothing store above here. Let's keep going."

Sophie stopped in front of the third door. "You know, I can't figure out where that door leads." Sophie shined the light on the door. "The men's clothing store is on a corner, so the street should be above whatever's through here."

"Do we go back or keep going?" Jessica didn't really want to do either. She just wanted to be back at ground level. "I hear the sound of tiny feet scurrying behind me." She rushed over, reached for the doorknob, and opened it.

Sophie shined the light inside.

"It's a tunnel," Jessica exclaimed. "The walls are made from blocks of stone and curved to make the tunnel round."

"I'd think this was really great almost any other time."

While Sophie shined the light around the walls, something bumped into Jessica's leg. "Let's get out of here." When Sophie stepped into the tunnel, Jessica followed close behind. "I don't know if we're breaking any laws, but you've got the light, so I'm with you."

At the end of the tunnel, shadows lined the walls. Sophie said, "I see some stuff piled in the corner, but I don't know which direction the tunnel took us in, so I'm not sure whose shop it would be near."

Jessica didn't care overly much about what it might be. She took a few more steps into the tunnel, but the light stayed back with Sophie. Her cousin shined the light into the corner, where Jessica could barely make out the shadows of some long, stick-like things.

Sophie said, "I would normally want to see what they were, but I just want to keep going and get out of here."

At the end of the tunnel, they faced yet another door. "There's only one way to find out what's in there." Jessica gulped, then turned the knob, while Sophie shined the light on it. "It's locked."

"No! It's got to open." Tucking the flashlight under her arm, Sophie pulled on the door. It creaked a little. "I think it's just old and rusty." She handed the flashlight to Jessica, then braced her feet on the ground and pulled. The door slowly creaked open and a feather blew out.

"Uh, Sophie," Jessica whispered as she looked up a well-lit stairway, "the Down Shoppe might be through this door."

"Uh-oh." Sophie peered through the doorway, then stepped back. "I think this is a way out, and all that light is sunlight coming through windows upstairs." The floor above them creaked. Sophie whispered, "Someone's up there."

Jessica whispered back, "Let's go up the stairs very quietly and see if we can sneak out. I'd rather be outside than in here."

"Me too. There's a wall next to the stairs, so I *think* we'll be safe."

"Who goes first?" Jessica felt her legs start to shake as she thought about who and what might be upstairs.

"I will."

Jessica watched Sophie gently step on each stair. Almost at the top, Sophie stopped and seemed to relax a bit, then waved Jessica on.

Just a few steps up, when Jessica could almost see out the windows, a woman spoke.

"George, I tell you, this isn't working."

Sophie backed against the wall. Jessica froze, with her right foot on one step and her left foot in midair.

20 JESSICA'S SECRET

When Jessica opened her mouth to speak, Sophie shook her head and held her finger over her lips. Sophie was right. They probably would hear even a whisper this close.

"Eva, it *will* work. Give it time."

There were two people in the room, not just one on the phone talking to someone. The man's voice sounded so close that Jessica felt like she could reach out and touch him if the wall weren't between them.

When the woman spoke again, she sounded as if she'd moved closer. "We've run out of time. We'd be fine if you hadn't taken the down."

"They didn't know what they had," the man snarled.

The woman laughed shrilly. "But you made them wonder about it when you took it."

"I wouldn't have lost it in the first place if you hadn't told me to stay at that motel. When it was full, I took that terrible path through the forest in the middle of the night and tripped over a root."

"Then you almost finished it for us when you dumped the feathers in the window display."

"But Eva, that's *why* we wanted them in the first place."

"Not anymore. Those kids were making people suspicious."

A loud thump was followed by the words, "I'm getting some fresh air."

He'd see them if he looked back as he opened the door. Jessica slinked down the stairs. At the bottom, she carefully slipped through the door and took off running. Sophie was right behind her. Two minutes later they were back where they started, staring up at the hole Sophie'd made in the floor. The light from the flashlight suddenly dimmed and flickered.

"Oh, no. The batteries are low. What—" Jessica stopped talking when the bell from the shop door rang. She could hear footsteps on the floor above them.

"I hope it's Mom. We're here!" Sophie called.

"Where?" her mom called back.

"Go into the storeroom," Sophie yelled.

The footsteps stopped nearby. "Soph? Did you fall through that hole?"

The flashlight went dark. Jessica thumped it a couple of times, but it wouldn't come back on.

"Mom, help! Get us out of here."

"And hurry," Jessica whispered. "There's a rat convention going on here."

Sophie turned toward the rat area and saw four sets of eyes. "Yuck."

"Are you girls okay, or do you need a doctor?"

"We're fine, Mom. We landed on something soft."

Footsteps moved overhead. Then Jessica could hear bits and pieces of a conversation. The footsteps quickly came back toward them, and then Mrs. Sandoval peered through the hole at them.

Sophie shouted, "Be careful, Mom. Don't get too close."

Mrs. Sandoval stepped out of sight. "The sheriff is on her way."

"Good." Jessica sighed.

A few minutes later, she heard footsteps and voices, then a

bright light shined through the hole, and someone lowered a rope with a loop in it to them.

Sheriff Valeska said, "One of you, slip the loop over your head and under your arms. Let me know when you're ready."

The rope landed on Jessica's lap, so she slipped it on. "Ready." The rope harness became taut, and her feet dangled off the ground as someone lifted her up. Back in the storeroom, she discovered both the sheriff and one of her deputies. "I am *so* happy to see you."

Jessica quickly crawled away from the hole, then stood and pulled off the rope. It vanished down the hole. Then they pulled Sophie up in it.

With the two of them sitting off to the side, Sheriff Valeska studied the area around the hole. "I can't figure out what happened to the floor. The rest of it appears quite solid."

Jessica pointed at the hole. "It seemed hollow where it broke."

Mrs. Sandoval said, "Sophie and I both knew there was something odd about the floor there. Bill Braden wouldn't stand in that spot because it seemed weak."

"Makes sense. What did you do, Sophie?" Sheriff Valeska asked suspiciously, turning toward her.

All eyes looked her way. "Why is everyone staring at me?" Sophie fidgeted nervously.

They continued to stare at her. Mrs. Sandoval tapped her foot on the floor.

Sophie, staring first at the floor, then at the ceiling, said, "Okay. So I wanted to know why the floor felt hollow."

Sheriff Valeska turned to Jessica. "So she jumped on it?"

"Weeellllll, . . ." Jessica hedged.

"You mean you did this on purpose?" Mrs. Sandoval reeled backward.

"Weeellllll, . . ." Sophie stared at the floor.

"Sophie Eileen, you are going to be punished. You won't

know what's going on around town for a while because you'll be at home gardening and cooking and cleaning."

Sophie didn't argue. "Can you shine a light through the hole again?"

Mrs. Sandoval said, "Forget it, Sophie. It's time to go home."

"*Please?*"

Sheriff Valeska flipped on a floodlight she'd positioned over the hole. "It looks like a pile of down comforters." The sheriff sounded surprised.

Sophie turned to Jessica. "Trust me. We know they're soft."

"They can't be, but they look clean from here," Sheriff Valeska added. She turned toward her deputy, "Bruce, get Oscar McBride to unlock the door to his basement and go down his stairs to recover whatever they landed on."

"Through the fur shop?" Mrs. Sandoval asked. "Don't you mean through this hole?"

"No. Most of the basements are connected through the town. A hundred years ago, everyone knew that, but not many people know today." Sheriff Valeska gathered her rope and light. "Oscar McBride has stairs and locks his basement door. He says that he doesn't want just anyone going through his basement, and that makes sense since he has a lot of expensive fur coats in his store."

"Uh, Sheriff," Jessica called out just as the sheriff was pulling open the door, "we went through the basements and into the Down Shoppe."

The sheriff turned back toward them. "Trespassing, huh?"

"More like sitting in a dark basement with rats and really wanting to leave."

"I'll have Bruce check and make sure that all the doors are closed. I'm sure the other store owners will forgive you."

Jessica sighed. "Thanks, Sheriff."

The sheriff put her hand back on the door.

"But there is one more thing," Sophie said.

Sheriff Valeska paused. "What would that be, Sophie?"

"We heard the people in the Down Shoppe talking about stealing the briefcase from the police station."

"Think carefully. What were their exact words?"

Sophie repeated what they'd said.

"You heard the man say that he took the down and that he shouldn't have. We need something more concrete than that. While it might be criminal, it might not."

The sheriff left quickly, probably so no one could ask her any more questions.

"Okay, girls," Mrs. Sandoval said, "go home and take showers. What you landed on may have been soft but"—she sniffed at the air—"you stink."

Sophie laughed. "I'm so relieved that we're safe at street level that I'm going home without another word."

"And when you finish cleaning up . . ."

"Yes?" Sophie asked.

"Stay there."

Sophie sighed. "Will do. And," she added excitedly, "we can think about the evidence at home."

Jessica rolled her eyes. "She's unstoppable. Let's go to your house, Miss Stinky."

"Me? What about you?" Sophie sniffed the air as they went out the door.

Walking down the sidewalk, Jessica went through everything that had happened from the moment she fell through the hole to the rescue. "You know, Soph—"

"Hey, I think that's the first time you called me Soph."

"Oh, sorry. You know, Sophie—"

"I like being called Soph."

"Okay. I save a whole syllable." Jessica grinned.

"What were you going to say?"

"Oh yes. Those down comforters were soft, but not as soft as the one I have at home. It felt like they'd put harder feathers—"

"Yes!" Sophie exclaimed. "Not like the feathers we found in the briefcase."

"Exactly. If I was going to make a down comforter, and I'd never been around feathers—only seen a picture of them—I might think any feathers would work."

"You're right. They might have made the comforters with the wrong feathers, and when they didn't turn out soft and fluffy, they had to get rid of them." Sophie snapped her fingers. "That cinches it. The Down Shoppe is a phony."

"*If* they made the comforters. I wonder why the people from the Down Shoppe would drag them all the way over here. Maybe they're from the business that was in this location before your mom owned it. Maybe they sold comforters and just stored them there."

"It was a bookstore. And remember that they were clean, not rat-messed up, so they're newer. I just know the comforters are a clue." Sophie paced across the room. "We have to get Mom to let us out of the house tomorrow so we can see what Deputy Bruce pulled out of the basement."

Jessica wrinkled her nose. "I hope he puts some of the feathers in a plastic bag. That thing we were lying on smelled terrible."

———

After dinner, Jessica started in the direction of their room. "Tonight's a good night to read. It's quiet and calm. How's that sound to you?"

"I'm reading a great spy thriller," Sophie said as she followed her.

Jessica shuddered as they entered the bedroom. "How can you read that stuff when real bad guys are chasing us?"

"The book isn't real, and I know that. That man who chased us the other day was real. This takes my mind off him."

"It makes sense in a strange way."

Sophie threw her pillow at Jessica.

"Hey, you'll mess my hair." Jessica patted her hair with her hands, then threw the pillow back at her.

Sophie giggled. "I'm so glad you don't care about your hair and makeup as much as you did when you got here."

"Me too. I can even be smart here."

Jessica clamped her hand over her mouth.

"What?" Sophie giggled. "You aren't any smarter than I am." Then she paused and stared at Jessica. "But you do use very large words sometimes."

"Forget I said anything." Jessica sat down on her bed and pretended to read. Maybe Sophie would just pick up her book.

Sophie sat on the edge of her bed. "Are you really a brainy type?"

No chance Sophie would ignore what she'd said. Jessica cringed as she answered, "Yes."

"I should have suspected as much. Sometimes you seemed smart. I remember when you first read the papers. You seemed to know what you were reading. Did you?"

Jessica looked down. "A lot of it."

"Why do you hide being smart?"

As tears filled her eyes, Jessica tried to blink them away. "Please, please don't tell anyone, Sophie. People think that you're supposed to wear ugly clothes and sit alone in the corner when you're smart. No one will like me anymore."

"Dry those eyes, Cousin. No one here will treat you any differently." Sophie went back to her bed and threw her pillow again, ducking when Jessica threw it right back at her. "Although I may call you during the school year and have you help me with my homework."

Jessica smiled. "As you would say, 'Deal.' I felt like I was living a lie. At least I can be myself here." Jessica got into her pajamas, under the covers, and happily started reading for real this time.

21 THE WRONG FEATHERS

Sophie pushed aside the curtain on the front window of the house, letting in the light of a bright, sunny day. This would be a great day to be hiking, but with Jessica she would have suggested the beach. They were trapped in the house instead.

"Mom, can we—"

"No, Sophie."

"But, Mom, we can't stay here all day every day."

Her mother stopped polishing a silver teapot. Glancing up at the big grandfather clock in the corner, she said. "The carpenter should be finished with the floor by now, so we can go to Great Finds."

"We get to leave the house?"

"Jessica's not being punished, so I could let her leave anytime, but I want the two of you together at all times."

"Yippee!" Sophie hollered.

"Hang on. You have to stay with me in Great Finds. Or your father or I, or another adult we've approved, has to be with you." She held up her hand when Sophie started to speak. "Don't bother to argue. With criminals running around, your father and I agreed this was what we needed to do. Besides, you're grounded right now."

Sophie and Jessica went into the bedroom, and Jessica changed into what she called "more suitable clothes" to wear to Great Finds. Sophie stayed as she was—jeans and a T-shirt. As they were leaving, Sophie grabbed the papers out of her box.

Jessica rolled her eyes. "What do you want with those? We've looked and looked at them. The FBI doesn't even care about them because Agent Dallas didn't pick them up."

"Maybe we can find time to look again. I figure if we solve this crime, then the FBI and the sheriff will take away the bad guys. I love a mystery, but being watched and staying inside all the time is too much."

"This is one time when I like the way your mind works." Jessica grinned. "Aunt April's shop is okay, but . . ."

Mrs. Sandoval called from the kitchen, "Girls, since you're going to be at Great Finds every day, I'm going to pay you."

"Excellent!" Sophie exclaimed.

"Being there just got better."

They met Mrs. Sandoval in the living room. "Don't get too excited. It won't be a lot, but it will buy you some new things for school this fall."

As they drove to the antique shop, Jessica excitedly said, "New clothes, Sophie."

Clothes would be fairly low on Sophie's list of priorities. "What I have is fine."

Jessica put out her foot. "Maybe shoes?"

Sophie shrugged. "Nothing for school—but new hiking boots would be good."

"We're definitely different."

Sophie grinned. "You got that right, Cousin."

The carpenter was packing up his tools when they arrived.

"Thanks for the quick work, Joe."

"Happy to be of service, April. The place your daughter crashed through was a basement access that had been covered up years ago. I repaired the damage and added a hinged door." He put his hammer in the toolbox.

"Funny thing is . . ." His voice trailed off as he spoke and stared at the floor, shaking his head. Then he focused on Mrs. Sandoval again. "The underside of the floor looked altered in an odd way. It sounds impossible, but it seemed that somebody cut it. And recently. That's why Sophie was able to crash through so easily."

"So it wasn't completely my fault?" A glimmer of hope that her grounding would be lifted flickered into Sophie's mind.

"Don't think you can get off easily, Sophie. You still jumped on it, and that's why it broke."

Glimmer extinguished.

Mrs. Sandoval checked out the new door. "Joe, I don't see how it's possible that someone cut the floor. Maybe it just appeared to have been cut."

He said, "Maybe." But Sophie didn't think he was buying that idea.

"I made a ladder so you could go down there. Will that do? I could come back and make you some stairs."

Mrs. Sandoval peered down the hole into the basement. "Let's try the ladder and see how it works. I need to get Hank the electrician to install a light in there."

"There already is one, from the days when the basement was used."

"A light?" Jessica asked. "We sat in the dark, and a light was waiting to be turned on?"

"You couldn't have reached it, but I made the chain longer so you could now. When you're on the ladder, reach to the right and feel for the pull chain." Joe climbed into the hole. "Oh, and I had the exterminator come, and the rats are all gone. It'll just take me a few minutes in the basement to finish up."

Sophie suddenly had a not-so-happy vision of trips up and down the ladder with merchandise in her arms. Her mom had talked about more storage space for years.

Just then, Mrs. Bowman came into the shop, carrying a yellow box.

Mrs. Sandoval said, "I didn't want you to think I'd completely forgotten about you, girls. I called Bananas and asked Abigail Bowman if she would do us a favor and bring over some of her banana-blueberry muffins for a snack."

Mrs. Bowman set down the box and left. Then the girls each grabbed a muffin.

Sophie said, "Wow. Thanks, Mom."

"Yes, thank you, Aunt April."

After eating, Mrs. Sandoval gave them chores to do.

Almost three hours later, Sophie came over to where Jessica was working on a project. "How's it going?"

Jessica blew her hair off her face and groaned. "This will take forever."

Sophie nodded. "Mom must believe that as long as she's paying us, we can get some bigger projects done for her."

"*We?* This one's all *me* right now. Hurry."

"I'll clean as fast as I can." As she went out front, Sophie said, "Mom, it must be time for lunch."

Mrs. Sandoval checked her watch. "It is. It's one o'clock. You and Jessica only have permission to go to the deli. I can clearly see you walking over there. Get your lunch and bring it back here. But call me before you return so I can watch you."

"The deli's fine." Jessica's grin almost split her face.

A few minutes later, Tony put their lunches in a paper bag. "I hear you made an entrance to the basement under Great Finds."

"Very funny." Sophie unwrapped her straw, put it in her soda, and took a sip.

"How'd you know?" Jessica asked.

Tony looked over at Sophie and smiled.

Jessica answered her own question. "It's that small-town thing again, right? The whole town knows?"

"Probably. Were there a lot of rats?" Tony asked.

Jessica shuddered. "Yes. I was so glad to get out of there."

"And Sophie, I hear your mom won't let you out of her sight." Tony continued grinning.

"But that's because . . ." Jessica started, then stopped and looked at Sophie.

Sophie jumped in. "You're right, Tony. I've spent a lot of time dusting. Need anything dusted? I've become an expert."

Tony laughed. "No thanks. I'm the youngest, so I'm the duster here."

"Can I use your phone? Mom wants me to call when we're coming back."

"Whew. She sure is watching you. Here." Tony handed Sophie the phone, then turned to Jessica. "Maybe you'll get to eat here next time and I can make those sundaes."

Jessica got a silly grin.

As they left the deli, Sophie said, "You almost told. Again."

Jessica frowned. "I'm sorry, but I stopped before I said anything too suspicious."

Back at Great Finds, a plan formed in Sophie's mind as they ate. Their next step would be to see the feathers from the comforters they'd landed on.

"Mom, you must want to visit your friend the sheriff," she said, once they'd resumed working.

"Not right now." Her mom rearranged some yellow flowers in a blue glass vase. Then she placed some teacups with painted flowers on them next to the vase.

Sophie paced the shop. "Maybe Dad has something he needs at the sheriff's office."

"I doubt it."

"Can I—"

Her mother raised her hands. "I give up. The sheriff's office isn't far. You're in the public eye in town. Go. Quickly."

Sophie called, "Jessica, let's go."

Jessica came out of the back room, pushing her hair out of her face. "Huh?"

"Mom's letting us go to the sheriff's office."

"Great." Jessica ran to the bathroom, and came back with her hair neatly combed.

———

Sheriff Valeska picked a clear plastic bag full of feathers up off her desk when Sophie and Jessica walked through the door. "I can guess why you girls are here." Handing it to Sophie, she said, "Once again, you've found the evidence, so I'll let you see it."

Sophie turned the bag from side to side, studying this clue. When she handled evidence, she felt like a real detective. She handed it to her cousin.

Without reaching into the bag, Jessica shifted the feathers around to separate one from another. "When I press against these feathers, they're harder and they aren't anywhere near as fluffy as those in the briefcase."

Sheriff Valeska leaned back in her chair and said, "That's an excellent observation. Since the expert at Fish and Game was on vacation, I sent over a scan of a few of them to a professor of ornithology at the college, and he said they were chicken feathers."

Sophie turned them into the light. "They aren't the right feathers for a down comforter. Only someone who was a phony would make a down comforter out of hard chicken feathers. Every clue points more and more to the Down Shoppe as a criminal hangout." Sophie stared at the floor while she paced back and forth across the room. "The question is, why would someone do this? What does it all mean?"

Jessica stepped in front of her and put one hand on each shoulder. Sophie looked her in the eyes and Jessica said, "You're making assumptions again based on something that might be a coincidence."

"What? Please speak English."

"You're guessing. Oh, and you asked two questions again."

Sophie grinned. "This is a solid clue. Right, Sheriff?"

The sheriff said, "Those comforters aren't there for any

logical reason we know of, so I think they are. You didn't find them in the usual way, but I guess I should thank you anyway."

———

They came back the long way, around the block, instead of taking the more direct, shorter route to Great Finds. Sophie wasn't breaking rules—because they didn't stop—but it gave her a little more time outside.

As they passed Simpson's Shoes, Mr. Simpson was standing in front and said, "I understand you're solving mysteries for the sheriff."

Sophie laughed.

"We have a mystery here at Simpson's Shoes."

22 UNLOCKING A MYSTERY

Jessica's heart dropped to the ground. "*Another* mystery in Pine Hill?"

"Yes, and we're puzzled by it. Why would anyone keep unlocking our doors at night?"

Sophie jumped right on it. "Sounds interesting. Let's ask Mom if we can come over and help."

The two of them ran over to Great Finds where Sophie's mom quickly agreed that Simpson's Shoes would be a safe place.

They hurried back, then followed Mr. Simpson into his shoe store. He asked, "What do you think of the new window display, girls?"

"Very pretty. I like these shoes." Jessica touched her finger to a pair of navy flats.

"Nice choice."

He seemed ready to say more about what Jessica thought was a display filled with beautiful shoes, but Sophie couldn't stand the delay. "Show us what's happened," she said with excitement.

Mr. Simpson said, "I'll give you the chance to solve this mystery. Twice now, we've come in and found the front door and the door to the storeroom unlocked. We had the locks changed the first time, but whoever it was opened them again."

"Is anything missing?"

"Barely anything. A doorstop and one pair of women's shoes. That's another strange part of this."

Jessica asked, "What kind of shoes?"

"High heels. Red leather. Size 8."

"Let's look around, Jessica." Sophie turned toward Mr. Simpson. "If you don't mind."

"Please do. I know the sheriff didn't find any clues, but since you've been helping her, maybe you can find a clue here."

Jessica whispered as they walked away, "He thinks we're a combination of Nancy Drew and the head of the FBI."

Sophie laughed.

Jessica checked out the shoes as she walked through.

"See anything?"

"A lot of shoes I want."

Sophie groaned. "This isn't a shopping trip. We're detectives."

Jessica giggled. "There's always time to shop. There are so many shoes. It's like heaven for a shoe lover."

"Mystery. Think mystery."

"Okay. Okay." After checking under and around everything, Jessica said, "Not a shoelace out of place."

"Very neat. If there had been a clue, the Simpsons probably swept it away by now."

"I wonder what's through there." Jessica pointed at a door in the back of the room.

"Let's find out." Sophie walked over and put her hand on the doorknob.

"Shouldn't we ask Mr. Simpson if it's okay to open it?"

"He said we should look around. This is part of *around*." Sophie opened the door and flipped on a light switch just inside. "Stairs. Maybe they have a basement."

Both girls stared down the stairs for a minute, then at each other.

"Do you think?" Jessica said.

Rushing downstairs, Sophie said, "Maybe there's a door into the tunnels."

"My thought exactly." Jessica followed her.

At the bottom they found a large door.

"Let's see what's in here." Sophie turned the doorknob.

Jessica put out her hand to stop her. "There might be rats waiting to run in here."

"No," Sophie said. "They'll stay where it's dark."

"Yuck." Jessica cringed and cautiously watched the door open. No rats.

"Hey!" Sophie reached through the doorway for something on the floor. "It's a doorstop, probably the missing doorstop. But why would someone take a doorstop from upstairs and use it down here?"

Jessica closed then reopened the door. "It's like the door leading into our garage at home. It closes by itself if you let go."

"Ah, so they had to prop it open to move something in or out of here."

"Exactly."

"But what were they moving?"

"Did you girls find something?" Mr. Simpson asked from the top of the stairs.

"Your doorstop. Do you have a flashlight?"

"I'll get it for you." He hurried away.

Sophie pushed the doorstop under the door. "Why would they use this to come through here when they can easily come and go through their own building? They only took one pair of shoes, so they must not have come here to steal."

"They must have been hiding from someone."

"Could be. Or maybe they just didn't want to be seen near their building but didn't mind being seen outside another one."

"Very good. Could be either." An image of rats' eyes glowing in the dark popped into Jessica's mind. "I hope Mr. Simpson has a large flashlight. I don't want to be the guest of honor at another gathering of rodents."

"You have got a point there." Sophie stood proudly. "I told you Simpson's Shoes was a clue."

"I agree with you. Now."

Mr. Simpson returned with two large flashlights and handed one to each of them. "What are you going to use them for?"

"We're going to check out what's beyond here." Sophie pointed at the now propped-open door.

He shrugged. "It's a basement we rarely use."

"We'd still like to see what's there."

"Must we?" Jessica asked.

Sophie looked at her and Jessica sighed. She knew the answer. "We must."

"Shouldn't we call the sheriff?" Mr. Simpson asked.

"We've been in the basements before," Sophie said as she stepped inside. They found a door on one side of the room, opened it, and shining the light inside, found a rounded tunnel like the one they'd been in before.

"Do you think it's the same one?" Jessica asked.

"Think about it. We aren't under the men's shop, so it can't be."

"Good point. Maybe there are lots of them connecting everything under the streets."

Cars drove by overhead as the girls moved through the tunnel. At the end of the tunnel, another door led them into a basement.

"I remember this red door," Jessica said as they walked into the room. "I think that now we're in the basement of the men's shop." She scraped golden dust off the floor with the toe of her shoe. "We have twice the light this time. Sophie, I think this is sawdust."

Sophie crouched and held her light over the dust. "You're right." Standing, she looked around the room.

"This store only has a hole for access, just like Great Finds, and the sawdust is right under it. I wonder if the owner closed off their basement access too."

Sophie nodded. "This means the carpenter had the right answer about why I fell through the floor. Someone tampered with the access here, so they probably did that under Mom's shop too."

"Exactly."

"Let's keep moving." Sophie pointed across the room. "That red door leads to another tunnel."

"What you mean is that it leads toward the Down Shoppe."

At the end of the tunnel, a familiar door was in front of them. Sophie put her hand on the doorknob. "I wonder if we could sneak inside and take a quick look around."

"Sophie! The sheriff would say that's breaking and entering."

"We'd be walking through a door that's probably still unlocked, so not breaking, just entering."

"I don't believe that makes it legal."

Behind them a door opened and closed. Then footsteps echoed through the tunnel, coming closer and closer by the second.

Jessica's heart pounded as she and Sophie crawled behind some of the stuff piled in the tunnel and turned off their flashlights. She shivered as the footsteps grew louder and louder, then stopped right in front of them.

"Sophie. Jessica."

Jessica let out a huge sigh of relief.

"We're here, Sheriff." Sophie stepped into the bright light of the sheriff's flashlight, and Jessica followed behind her.

"What are you two up to? Sophie?"

"We're on the trail of a clue."

"What clue? Mr. Simpson told me you found his doorstop."

"Yes. No. I mean, the doorstop was outside their basement door. Someone must have used it to prop it open. We wanted to see if the tunnel in his basement connected to the one that leads to the Down Shoppe." Sophie pointed at the door. "It does."

The sheriff sighed. "Even if the Down Shoppe people were guilty of something, you couldn't accuse them without evidence. And you shouldn't be here."

"Why not? You can hear cars driving overhead, so we're under the street. We're not on private property."

"Let's go, girls."

Sophie said, "What about all this fishing gear that's just laying here?"

"Huh?" the sheriff and Jessica asked.

"Remember the tall, skinny things in the shadows, Jessica?"

"Yes. But—"

"Those were fishing poles. I saw them when I ducked in here. There are also tackle boxes and a lot of other fishing things, like what we used on Captain Jack's boat."

All three shined their flashlights into the area.

Jessica stepped closer. "When we were here before, there were more of the tall, skinny things that I now know are fishing poles. I think they've gotten rid of a bunch of them."

"Yes, ladies. This is strange, but it doesn't prove guilt. It just makes me wonder why all this valuable property is here. It could be sold for a tidy sum of money." The sheriff shined her flashlight back the way they'd come. "Time to go."

"Look here," Jessica called. She ran over and picked up something from the floor.

"It's just an empty shoe box," the sheriff said.

"Not just any empty shoe box. Mr. Simpson said that whoever unlocked their doors stole a pair of red, size 8 high heels." She shined her flashlight on the end of the box. "There's a picture of red high heels, and it says size 8."

The sheriff took the box and tucked it under her arm. "This *is* an important clue. I'd assumed the Down Shoppe owners had rented their space from the building's owners. That happens all the time in business, but none of this makes sense." She looked at the door to the Down Shoppe. "I would love to go inside, but I'd lose my job. Let's go back, girls. I hope we find something soon that is big enough to talk a judge into issuing a search warrant."

Sophie and Jessica followed the sheriff back to Simpson's Shoes. When they arrived, Mr. Simpson was waiting in the basement.

"Did you discover something?" he asked.

Sophie looked up at the sheriff.

"We have suspicions, but nothing confirmed," the sheriff said.

"I think you'll know more soon, Mr. Simpson," Sophie added.

———

Back at the antique shop, while Jessica dusted and Sophie cleaned, Sophie told her mother what they'd seen. Before long, it was time to go home. When they were heading out the door, Sophie grabbed the box of leftover muffins.

As Mrs. Sandoval locked the door, she said, "I'm surprised Sam and Charlotte sold the business."

"Huh?" Sophie turned toward her mother.

"The building the Down Shoppe is in was a fishing shop last year. Remember, Sophie? Hook, Line & Sinker?"

"That's right. I only went there once, when we bought Dad a new fishing pole for his birthday."

Mrs. Sandoval chewed on her lip. "The business owners, Sam and Charlotte Cross, actually owned the building their shop was in. They weren't just renting it. When they closed for the winter, they told me that they would reopen in the spring for the fishing season. You could see all of their fishing gear through the window so I assumed they'd come back when they could."

"Do *you* know where they're living? The sheriff didn't mention that she did. Otherwise I think she would have called them," Jessica said.

Mrs. Sandoval stabbed at the air with her finger. "Yes, I do." She turned back into the store, walked over to the phone, flipped through a small notebook sitting next to it, then dialed. "Charlotte?" she said, seconds later. "This is April Sandoval in Pine Hill . . . Yes, thank you. We were surprised you'd sold or rented your store and wanted to check on you . . . What? . . . Someone *is* in there, with a sign out front saying, 'The Down

Shoppe.'" She gave the phone number for the sheriff, then said good-bye.

Turning back to the girls, she said, "It's supposed to be their shop and closed until they can return. They had to attend to a family emergency and weren't able to come back in the spring."

"Wow! So Sheriff Valeska can go in." Sophie jumped up and down. "Yes, yes, yes!"

"But Sam and Charlotte want to drive here first so they can see what's going on."

Jessica could feel the mystery ramping up. "Sophie, if we can figure out why the doors on Simpson's Shoes are being unlocked, we'll have this solved." Solve the mystery, have a simple summer vacation. Not that anything about her stay in Pine Hill had been simple, but she could hope.

Sophie leaned against the counter. "I think I know about the doors."

"Are you sure?" Jessica asked.

Mrs. Sandoval paused. "Okay, what's the reason?"

"The phony Down Shoppe people needed to get rid of the fishing shop products, and they didn't want to take them out through their door. People might think it was strange that all the fishing stuff was still there if Hook, Line & Sinker didn't plan to reopen."

Jessica got excited now. "So they're going through the basements and out Simpson's Shoes in the middle of the night."

"Yes."

"That does sound plausible, Soph," Mrs. Sandoval agreed. "But why do they need a phony Down Shoppe? Anyway, the Crosses said they'd be here tomorrow. I'll call Mandy Valeska and let her know." She picked up the phone again.

While her mom was busy, Sophie spoke softly to Jessica, "We should call Agent Dallas."

"We did the other day, and he hasn't called us back."

"True. Something must have happened to him. We have to rescue him."

"Seriously? *If* something has happened, the FBI must know that. You think that the entire FBI hasn't been able to help him, but we can?"

"Yep."

Jessica rolled her eyes. "What do you propose?"

"I'm working on it."

Mrs. Sandoval hung up the phone and said, "By the way, Jessica, Frank Avinson told me you were going to write an article for the *Pine Hill Press*. Remember all of the details about this. It will make an exciting story."

Jessica happily sank into a comfortable, old chair. "That's a superb suggestion. In fact, it's magnificent."

"Superb? Magnificent?" Sophie laughed.

"What happened to the way you usually speak?" Mrs. Sandoval asked.

"Our little Jessica has been hiding something from us. She's very, very smart."

"I've suspected that for a while." Mrs. Sandoval reached down and hugged Jessica. "I'm glad you trust us enough to be yourself."

Jessica felt even more relieved than when Sophie had found out. "Thank you, Aunt April. I felt like I was lying and didn't want to do it anymore."

Her aunt smiled. "Now you can help Sophie with her homework."

Sophie laughed. "I already told her that."

"You girls get your things and we'll go home."

As they rode home, both girls in the backseat, Sophie said, "The owners are coming here tomorrow, so we'll get new clues from inside the building and we might even solve the whole mystery."

Jessica answered, "I can't wait. When the mystery is solved, we can go to the beach, shop, and eat for the rest of the summer."

"And go for hikes," Sophie added.

"I'll have to think about that."

Just before 5 a.m., Sophie's parents got ready to meet the Crosses. The sheriff told them she, four FBI agents, and two deputies would also meet them at the Down Shoppe. Unfortunately, when they were finishing breakfast, Mr. Sandoval said, "Stay here."

"Dad! How can you say that? We're the ones who found out about the Down Shoppe. We need to be there."

"Stay here." He grabbed his coat off the hook and put it on.

"Mom?" Sophie watched her mother put her coat on.

Mrs. Sandoval shook her head, and they left.

Sophie slumped down on the sofa. "This is so frustrating. Here we solve everything, then they leave us at home." She stood and circled the room. This was not how she'd pictured the end of the mystery. "Let's go upstairs. Maybe flashing lights from the sheriff's vehicles in town will show through the trees and we'll know that they're at the Down Shoppe."

The two girls stood at the windows that faced town.

Sophie couldn't see anything beyond the trees. "Nothing."

"No."

"Did you hear that?" Sophie asked.

Jessica stared at her. "What? Can you hear sirens?"

Sophie held her finger in front of her mouth. "Shh."

Downstairs, a creaking sound was followed by a thud.

24 TALKING TO TONY

Sophie motioned for Jessica to follow her across the hall, through another bedroom, and to a window.

Jessica whispered, "Do you think your parents are back already?"

"Uh-uh." Sophie pointed down the driveway to a black car partly hidden by trees. "I think all the sounds are coming from the front of the house. Let's sneak down the back stairs to the kitchen and go outside."

Her cousin went pale. "But Sophie, if they come into the kitchen, they'll see us."

Sophie nodded. "That's better than staying upstairs and not being able to get out if they come here. Be ready to run. As we walk, put your foot where I just put mine. I know where the floors creak in this old house."

Sophie could feel Jessica right behind her as she went down the hall, then crept down the stairs. Slowly, ever so slowly, she opened the door to the kitchen. Empty. Running across the room, they both reached for the doorknob on the back door, but Sophie got her hands on it first and jerked the door open. Out the door, she ran for the closest trees, with Jessica so close on her heels that she thought she might trip her. Sophie kept running until they'd circled the house. Then they crouched behind a large tree.

Jessica spoke in a low voice. "Maybe we can identify whoever comes out the door."

"My thoughts exactly."

A while later, Sophie guessed about ten minutes, the "French" woman from the Down Shoppe stepped out the front door of the house. And she was eating what looked like a left-over banana-blueberry muffin. "Maybe we should try to stop her."

The woman looked around, threw the muffin to the side, and ran to her car. Before they had a chance to do anything, she was backing out onto the road.

"Oops. I think she heard me."

"I think she did. I wonder why she came here." Jessica stood.

"Breakfast?"

Jessica giggled nervously.

When they stepped through the front door, they found a mess. Drawers and shelves were empty, with everything from them littering the floor.

Jessica picked up a sofa cushion and put it back where it belonged. "Amazing. She even pulled the cushions off the sofa."

"Criminals always do. At least she didn't slit them."

"Should we clean the room before your mom and dad come home?"

"I don't want to disturb the crime scene. But this is a mess, and Mom really hates messes. Normally I'd leave it for the sher-iff, but this woman must have left plenty of fingerprints on everything else in the house, including the plastic bag Mom put the muffins in." Sophie reached for a pile of papers.

"Hey, let's take photos."

Sophie rolled her eyes. "Why didn't I think of that?" She ran to her room and came back with her camera.

Walking around the torn-apart sections of the house, she

snapped dozens of photos. Done with that, Sophie said, "Now, we clean."

When her parents walked in the front door later, the house was almost back to normal.

"What's going on?" Mrs. Sandoval asked as soon as she saw Sophie with the vacuum.

"A woman broke in and took the place apart."

Mr. Sandoval stepped forward. "I'm going to make sure there's no one else here." He checked every room downstairs, then went upstairs.

"We saw her drive off, Dad." Sophie put the vacuum in the hall closet.

Mrs. Sandoval hugged Sophie, pulling Jessica into the hug. "Are you girls okay?"

Jessica said, "Yes. We ran out the kitchen door."

"I'm glad you're safe. Is anything missing?" Mrs. Sandoval looked around the room.

Sophie shrugged. "I don't think so. She wasn't carrying anything when she left."

"Except a muffin." Jessica giggled.

Mrs. Sandoval cringed. "She got into them after she got dirty searching the house? I'll be sure to get rid of the rest."

"We thought the police could use the plastic bag for her fingerprints."

Mrs. Sandoval nodded agreement. "We'll be careful not to touch it. Now let's call the sheriff."

Sophie suddenly remembered where her parents had gone. "Hey, what did the sheriff and FBI find in the Down Shoppe?"

"Other than more fingerprints, not much," Mrs. Sandoval answered.

Jessica jumped in. "I'm sure they'll match these. We think this is the same woman we saw in the Down Shoppe and around town."

Mrs. Sandoval sat down on the sofa. "The Down Shoppe was totally empty. Except for a few feathers. Sheriff Valeska said they were the same kind of large feathers that were in the comforters you landed on. It tied the comforters in with the people in there."

Sophie and Jessica sat next to her as Mr. Sandoval came down the stairs, shaking his head. "The upstairs rooms are fine. It's just the downstairs that she messed up."

Sophie already knew that, but her dad seemed to need to check it out himself. She asked, "What did Agent Dallas have to say when you saw him?"

"He didn't come."

"Did other FBI agents come?"

"His partner, Agent Able, and two other agents."

"Hmm. I wonder. . ." Sophie tapped her fingers on the arm of the sofa.

"You wonder what?" Jessica asked.

"I wonder where Agent Dallas is."

"Probably wherever the criminals are. Doing his job," Mrs. Sandoval answered.

"It seems strange that he wasn't there." Sophie couldn't understand why they'd take the agent off the case who knew the most about it.

Mrs. Sandoval stood. "Unless we decide to leave a sign at Great Finds that says, Out Catching Criminals, I think we'd better go to work."

Sophie laughed. "I like the sign idea."

"Can we get sandwiches from the deli today?" Jessica asked as they stood.

Mr. Sandoval asked, "Aren't you girls getting tired of sandwiches from the deli?"

"I am," Sophie said. "Last time, I had soup."

Mrs. Sandoval laughed. "They also have salads, Soph."

"Sandwiches are fine with me." Jessica grinned all the way to the deli when they were told they could go later.

They'd almost finished their lunches when Tony came over and asked what kind of sundaes they'd like. When he brought

Jessica's hot fudge sundae and Sophie's pineapple sundae, he said, "You're our only customers right now, so I can talk for a minute. How's summer going?"

Jessica took a bite of her sundae, "Great! We're hot on the trail of some criminals."

Sophie dropped her spoon. "Jessica!"

"She's kidding, right?" Tony asked Sophie.

Jessica stuck her spoon in her sundae and swirled it through the hot fudge.

Sophie sighed. "What now, O wise one?"

Tony sat down, his eyes sparkling. "This sounds a lot more exciting than life in a deli. Tell me what's going on."

Jessica took a bite of her sundae, then looked at Tony. "We aren't supposed to tell about the FBI part—"

"Jessica! Eat and stop talking."

"The FBI? Here in Pine Hill?" Tony leaned forward in his chair.

Sophie took another bite of her sundae. What could they do now? "He knows enough that maybe we should tell him what's going on. Another point of view might be good."

Jessica nodded excitedly. "I've wanted to tell someone for the longest time. You're trustworthy, aren't you, Tony?"

"If you mean, will I tell this to anyone else? Nope."

"Okay. It all started with a briefcase we found on Cutoff Trail." Sophie told the story, with Jessica putting in pieces now and then.

When they'd finished, Tony sat back in his chair. "Wow! Your summer hasn't been dull."

"I think it only seemed really dangerous when a man sat down at our table in the resort. But he turned out to be an FBI agent."

"You skipped that part." Tony leaned forward again.

"Oh," Jessica went on, "he just wanted to know what we knew, but we didn't find out he was an FBI agent until later. We ran and hid in the tunnel behind the waterfall."

"Do you girls need help with your crime?"

Sophie and Jessica looked at each other. Jessica pleaded with her eyes for Tony to help them.

"Why don't you come over tonight," Sophie said.

Tony rubbed his hands together. "See you about seven."

Back at Great Finds, Jessica hummed as she cleaned.

"What's going on with your happy cousin?" her mother asked Sophie.

"Tony's coming over tonight to hear all about the bad guys."

Her mother placed the antique quilt she was holding on a shelf and turned around. "Sophie, you know you weren't supposed to tell."

"I know, but Jessica spilled it, and then it was too late."

"Do you think Tony can keep the secret?"

Sophie nodded. "I think so."

25 OPERATION DALLAS

After the girls had gone through all their clues that night and told him about calling Agent Dallas, Tony asked, "Have you heard from him?"

"No. And we haven't seen him either."

"Strange," he muttered. Shrugging, he said, "It could be good news."

Jessica wondered if inviting Tony to help had been a big mistake. What he'd just said hadn't made any sense at all.

"Maybe he's so busy he doesn't have time to call," he added.

Now he made sense. "But for your idea to work, we have to assume he's been sent somewhere else. I'd think either they'd tell us that when we called or he'd call to explain."

"Or maybe he can't call," Sophie said.

"What?" Tony turned to Sophie.

"In the movies the bad guy takes the good guy hostage."

Tony laughed. "Too many movies." He twirled his finger next to his ear.

"Her idea may not be as crazy as it sounds," Jessica said. "I didn't think these things really happened when I arrived here. But after helping the FBI, I'm starting to think anything's possible."

Tony sighed. "I see your point. Let's call Agent Dallas again and see if he answers."

"It isn't as exciting as a rescue, but it does sound like the right thing to do," Sophie agreed.

A few minutes later Jessica hung up the phone. "This time they said he's late calling in for his messages. They took another message from me. If he isn't checking his messages . . ."

Sophie chewed on her lip. "Where would bad guys put an FBI agent?"

"Where would bad guys put themselves?" Jessica raised her hands and shrugged. "We haven't figured that much out."

"Is there a basement under the Down Shoppe?" Tony asked.

Sophie said, "When we walked through all the basements from Mom's antique shop to the Down Shoppe on our attempted escape, we opened a door that led to stairs going to the front door of the Down Shoppe. We weren't in a basement under the store, more like beside the building." She paused. "I don't think there could be a basement."

Tony got a cute, intense look. "If there are basements under your mom's side of the street and under our deli, too—"

"And under Simpson's Shoes," Jessica added.

"All the buildings were built about the same time—"

"So there should be one under the Down Shoppe, and maybe someone is hiding an FBI agent in it," Jessica said excitedly. "Good thinking, Tony!"

"We need to call Sheriff Valeska to learn more about this morning's search."

Sophie dialed and talked to her.

"So the FBI went over the building with a fine-tooth comb and didn't find a basement? . . . Thank you." Sophie sighed and hung up. She stood and walked across the room, then turned, walked back, and sat back down. A few seconds later, she got up and walked across the room again.

"Knock it off," Jessica said.

Sophie perched on the arm of the sofa. "I think we should go look anyway."

Jessica shrugged. "But Sheriff Valeska said—"

"I know what she said, but it would be really weird if every building we know of had a basement except that one."

"You're right, but how do we get in?" Tony asked.

"The owners went home but left the key with Mom and Dad, so it's easy to get inside."

"That's right," Jessica exclaimed.

Sophie said, "Now the only problem will be getting permission for 'Operation Dallas.'"

"Great name. It sounds official," Jessica agreed.

"I'll bet your parents will want the FBI to rescue their own man," Tony said.

"We called the FBI and got nowhere. We called the sheriff, and she says the law enforcement people searched and there is no basement. We have to do this ourselves."

Tony touched Jessica's hand for a second, and her breath caught in her chest. *Breathe*, she told herself.

"Now I see how you got in the middle of this thing." Tony shook his head.

"You in or out?" Sophie asked.

"I'm in," Tony said.

Jessica tried to concentrate on the conversation.

"We know the owners and they know us. Mom's at a meeting, so let's ask Dad about going in. Then we can call the owners and get permission if he thinks we need to."

Jessica thought it went well when they asked her uncle. There was just one catch. He was driving them over there, checking the place out first, then standing guard in the car. Tony called his parents about going, and they thought it was fine as long as Lucas Sandoval was going, too. Then Mr. Sandoval called the owners and got their permission to enter.

When they pulled up to it, Mr. Sandoval went inside, and the three of them sat in the car waiting, flashlights in hand. He turned on the lights inside the building and motioned them over.

As Sophie was stepping out of the car, she said. "Let's hurry. I just saw something move out there."

Tony shrugged. "Does it matter? I doubt anyone would follow us."

Jessica and Sophie looked at each other, and Sophie said, "I guess we forgot to tell him part of the story."

Tony looked over his shoulder. "You mean someone has been following you?"

"Uh-huh. Once he chased us all the way to the sheriff's office."

"Now I wonder if I should be glad I'm involved in this."

Sophie paused. "You can go home if you're chicken."

"No one's called me that since I was six. And he got a black eye for it. I'm going."

Sophie called to her dad, "We're going to walk around the building and see if there are any signs of a basement."

"I'm coming," he called back. He followed them as they studied the front, then walked around the corner of the block to the alley that went behind the building.

"There aren't any basement windows like on our building," Tony said.

"My mom's building doesn't have windows there. Let's go inside and try to find an entrance to a basement."

When they went around to the front again, Mr. Sandoval walked toward his car, saying, "I don't think you'll find a thing, but I'll be out here, just in case." He got inside, turned on the dome light and picked up a book.

Inside, the trio began their search in a back room that held a desk and phone.

"Our basement entrance is a flap in the floor. How do you get into your basement?" Sophie asked Tony.

"We use ours all the time for storage, so we have a regular door and stairs."

Sophie said, "Let's look for anything that seems strange. And remember, the FBI didn't notice it, so it won't be obvious."

Inside, Sophie stepped into the first empty room. Jessica and Tony continued down the hall. The three of them went from room to room, checking around and under furniture.

Soon Jessica could hear someone scuffling around in the room next to her. Then she heard Sophie say, "This is weird."

"What is?" Jessica came into the room with Sophie.

Sophie pointed at the wall. "This area is sun bleached and about the same size as the bookcase on the facing wall."

"That is weird. Hey, Tony," Jessica called.

He walked into the room. "Did you find something?"

"Sophie did. Someone must have moved this bookcase." Jessica pointed to the wall and told him about it. "You know, it's possible that they just needed it on another wall."

Tony said, "Let's see if anything's behind it."

The three of them pushed it to the side.

"A door!" Jessica exclaimed.

"Let's see what's behind this."

When Sophie reached for the doorknob, Jessica put her hand out to stop her. "Hey, maybe we should get your dad."

Sophie paused and looked like she was thinking about it. "Let's see if it's worth getting him. It might just be a closet." The door creaked as Sophie pulled it open. She said in a low voice, "There are stairs." Turning on her flashlight, she reached inside. "Let's see if there's a light switch."

When it flipped on, they could see that the stairs led to a dark basement.

"See anything down there?" Sophie whispered.

"Now who's chicken?" Tony laughed.

"I'm not chicken. I'm"—she paused—"cautious."

"That's a first." Jessica giggled.

Sophie glared at her, then grinned. "I think Dad might be angry if we don't get him right now."

Jessica said, "I think you are exactly right."

Sophie ran out of the room and came back with him.

His eyes opened wide when he saw the door and the stairs beyond. "You mean to tell me that you actually found something the FBI missed? Maybe we should call them."

"Dad, they haven't called us back, and we think Agent Dallas is missing and in there." Sophie pointed. "We have to rescue him."

He rolled his eyes. "Fine. Let's see if there's anything mysterious downstairs."

Sophie stepped through the doorway before anyone could stop her. Mr. Sandoval followed, then Tony and Jessica. Sophie stumbled slightly on the bottom step. "Watch that last step. It's taller than the others."

Mr. Sandoval and Tony came down the stairs fine, but Jessica took the last step flying, hit the concrete on her knees, and slid across the floor.

"Are you all right?" Tony raced to her side.

Her knees stung but her face felt hotter. She thought, *Just completely humiliated*, but said, "I'm okay." She felt stupid but liked it when Tony helped her to her feet.

He said, "This is a small and neat, empty basement. There isn't a single piece of junk and only a little bit of dust and a few cobwebs."

Sophie banged her hand on her fist. "This is frustrating. I thought we'd found a clue."

"But, Sophie," Jessica asked, "if there was nothing to hide, why was the bookcase moved?"

Tony walked around the room. "Look here. It's cobweb-free in this corner." He gestured to the rest of the basement. "*Only* in this corner."

"And there's a storage area with shelves there. It's kind of a bookcase, and a bookcase hid a door upstairs," Jessica added.

"Jessica, I doubt anyone would use the same ploy twice," Mr. Sandoval said.

"I'd be cleverer," Sophie agreed.

Tony put his head against the wall and tried to peer behind the bookcase. "I can't see anything." He and Mr. Sandoval pushed it to the side.

"Another door," Sophie whispered.

26 DARING RESCUE

"Calling the sheriff might take too long. I think we should go in there and rescue Agent Dallas." Sophie crossed her arms and stood firmly in her place. They needed to do this.

"My dear cousin, we don't know if he's there. He might be having dinner at the resort right now. This place might be filled with bad guys. Or rats."

"I'm not afraid." Tony glared at Sophie. "I wouldn't want to find criminals or rats, but I think we should see what's in there."

Mr. Sandoval sighed. "I can't believe I'm agreeing with your reasoning, but let's go in." He shook his head. "What will your mother say, Sophie?"

As Tony slowly opened the door, Sophie crouched low and peered through the gap. She first saw a single lightbulb dangling from the ceiling in the middle of the room, giving off a small amount of light. Then, as the door swung wider, she could see a man sitting on the floor, tied, blindfolded, and gagged. A strange sound came from inside the room.

Sophie stood. "I was right. There's Agent Dallas."

"No, it's Mr. Merkle, the shoe salesman who came into the deli," Tony whispered beside her.

The other three looked at him.

Sophie smiled and nodded. "I get it. Being a shoe salesman was his cover story."

"Must be. Who goes first?" Tony gestured toward the room.

"I will." Sophie started through the door.

"Soph," Mr. Sandoval whispered, but she didn't stop.

When Sophie stepped into the room, she could see a woman sleeping on a cot in the corner, wrapped in a fur coat and wearing red high-heeled shoes. The strange sound she'd heard earlier was her snoring in a way that sounded like a chainsaw cutting through metal. Sophie turned back and whispered, "Get her," then pointed toward the woman.

She heard Jessica say, "Who?" Then, "Oh."

As Sophie crouched next to Agent Dallas, she saw her dad move to stand over the woman, ready to pin her down if she woke up. Jessica had pulled off her belt and was wrapping it around the woman's hands. When she tightened it, the woman awoke and kicked out at them until Tony sat on her legs.

"That will keep her still," he said.

Sophie untied Agent Dallas, then removed his gag. "Are you all right?" she asked as she started on the blindfold.

When the blindfold was removed, he blinked and rubbed his eyes. "I am now."

Mr. Sandoval helped Agent Dallas to his feet.

"Let's get her over to the sheriff's office," Agent Dallas ordered and took a step toward the bound woman. Then he weakly slumped against Mr. Sandoval. "I'm weaker than I thought." Tony supported him from the other side as they made their way out of the basement.

Sophie and Jessica pulled the woman to her feet. She didn't fight them, so she must have sensed they had her outnumbered.

As they pushed her along behind the men, the woman said, "You nosy girls. Our plan was going well until you stuck your noses in this."

Maybe she'd spill the whole story if she thought they already knew about the crime. Sophie said, "That day at the Down Shoppe, we didn't believe you were French."

The woman glared at them. "I remembered just enough French from high school to throw you off."

"So it *was* her," Sophie said.

"Who's he?" The woman gestured with her head toward Tony.

"Never mind. How did you think you would get away with such a scheme?" Sophie asked.

Jessica looked puzzled. "What are—"

"Jessica, she knows we've figured it all out. We were smarter than they were."

"Ha! You kids don't know anything."

Sophie went through the clues one by one in her mind. Feathers, newspaper clippings, real estate contract . . . yes. "You tried to buy Mom and Dad's businesses to get us off your trail."

"They wouldn't sell, so I tried to scare you today so you'd leave town for a while—but you weren't home."

"You planned everything so you would have access to all the stores in Pine Hill," Jessica added.

Sophie stared at her cousin in amazement. Could she be onto something?

The woman turned to Jessica. "You do know! We were going to rob this town."

Sophie felt like a lightbulb had switched on. "You planned to steal and use the tunnels and connected basements to get everything out."

The woman sneered. "If you hadn't come along, we'd have cleaned this town out tomorrow night."

Jessica smiled at Sophie. Then they pulled the woman up the stairs, out the door, and down the street to the sheriff's office.

Sophie pushed open the door to the office. Sheriff Valeska slumped in her chair and sighed. "What now, girls? I'm almost ready to leave for the night."

When Sophie pulled the woman in behind her, the sheriff's

mouth dropped open. And when a grimy and weak Agent Dallas followed, supported by Mr. Sandoval and Tony, she seemed frozen in her chair. Agent Dallas stumbled, almost pulling all three men to the ground. Sheriff Valeska jumped to her feet and pulled a chair over to the agent. "Here. Sit down."

"Please lock this woman up," he said in a shaky voice as he sat. "She and her husband surprised me one night in the dark, knocked me out, and kidnapped me."

Sheriff Valeska took the woman away. When she returned, she said, "That looked like the fur coat that the owner of Elegance Furs reported missing and assumed shoplifted. Her red shoes must be the ones stolen from Simpson's." She sat down and said, "Tell me what happened."

"These four just rescued me from the Down Shoppe's basement."

Sophie thought about telling him that it was really Hook, Line & Sinker but didn't think he'd care right now.

"There was a basement? The FBI didn't find one."

Agent Dallas sighed and leaned back in his chair. "I heard many footsteps over my head earlier, and thought I was about to be rescued. Then it got quiet." He sniffed the air. "That coffee sure smells good."

"I'll get it for you. I'm used to getting coffee." Tony walked over to the coffee maker.

The agent looked confused at Tony's statement. Sophie explained, "His family owns Donadio's Deli."

Agent Dallas smiled weakly. "I knew he seemed familiar. You guys make the best turkey on wheat that I've ever had."

Tony grinned. "My mother thanks you. Cream or sugar?" he asked.

"Two sugars." Agent Dallas ran his hand through his hair.

"How did you end up in that basement?" Sheriff Valeska asked.

"I sent my partner to follow Jessica and Sophie. Then I circled through the woods toward town. That's the last I remember until

I woke in what felt like a basement, with my hands and feet tied, tape over my mouth, and a blindfold." The agent sighed in a way that almost sounded like a groan. "I have no idea how long I was there."

"It's Wednesday."

Agent Dallas leaned forward in his chair and rested his elbows on his thighs. "Four days. It seemed longer than that." Then he sat straight in his chair. "I need to call Agent Able."

Sheriff Valeska handed him the phone just as Tony gave him his cup of coffee. He looked at both and seemed too tired to figure out what to do, so Tony took the cup from him and set it on the desk.

"Thanks. I'm a little confused." He dialed the phone and hung up a few seconds later. "No answer. Have any of you seen Agent Able?"

Jessica shrugged. "We don't know what he looks like."

"He's tall and thin, brown hair, mustache, often wore dark pants and a tan jacket."

The girls looked at each other.

"He's the man who chased us."

"Chased you?" Agent Dallas took a sip of his coffee and closed his eyes. "I missed this." After another sip, he said, "Yes, it's coming back to me. I remember you said someone chased you."

Jessica said, "We assumed a bad guy chased us, but we felt fairly confident that the man wore a tan jacket and navy pants. It must have been Agent Able."

"I told him to follow you. He's very efficient, so if he thought you were in danger, he might have given chase when you ran." Agent Dallas rubbed his eyes. "Have you seen him since then?"

The girls looked at each other again, and Sophie answered, "No. But we don't really know what he looks like up close."

He turned toward Tony. "Able loved your family's chicken salad on rye. Has anyone ordered one lately?"

"I remember an order that we delivered to the resort this afternoon."

Agent Dallas sighed with obvious relief. "We were staying there. Maybe he's out searching for me and will be back later."

One thing still didn't make sense to Sophie. "We left messages for you, but no one returned them."

He looked at her oddly. "No one?"

Sophie answered. "No one."

"Strange." He nodded his head, obviously considering what they'd said as he took a long sip of his coffee.

"Can I give you a ride back to the resort?" Sheriff Valeska asked.

Agent Dallas nodded. "Yes. But I'm filthy. I'd love a ride to the *back door* of the resort."

Jessica giggled and held her nose.

He raised his eyebrows at her, then smiled. "I'd be offended if I had enough energy."

Mr. Sandoval stood and offered, "I'll get our car and bring it around here so we can give Agent Dallas a ride. You've got enough to do here, Mandy."

While they waited, Sophie asked, "What about the woman we brought in?" She pointed toward the back of the sheriff's office.

Agent Dallas and Sheriff Valeska looked surprised, as though they'd forgotten about her. The sheriff said, "We can hold her on the kidnapping charge. Tomorrow we'll sort everything else out."

"We'll be here first thing," Sophie said.

The sheriff said, "Stay home. We can handle it, girls."

Sophie raised one eyebrow. "I guess you don't want to know what she told us." Her dad had pulled his car in front of the building, so she started to walk out the door.

"Okay, be here about eight," Sheriff Valeska called after her.

"Hey, what about me?" Tony asked. A second later he said,

"Never mind. My sister's gone tomorrow, so I have to be at the deli. But please let me know what happens."

They dropped off Agent Dallas, then Tony, and finally pulled into Sophie's driveway. Her father turned off the lights and opened his car door. "We're a lot later getting home than I'd expected. I hope your mother wasn't too concerned about us, Sophie. At least we know that Agent Dallas is back on the job."

As they started up the steps, Mrs. Sandoval stood in the doorway, waving her jacket. "Where have you been for so long? I've been out looking for you."

"Sorry," Mr. Sandoval said. "We rescued Agent Dallas." He hung his coat in the closet.

"You're kidding." She sat on the sofa.

"Nope. The kids were right about him. Girls, go get clean clothes on, and let's have some popcorn."

"Yes!" Sophie pulled her fist through the air. They ran into the bedroom, changed their clothes, and were back in minutes. A bowlful of popcorn already sat on the coffee table.

The girls told Mrs. Sandoval all about what had happened. As she listened, she popped the popcorn in her mouth, handful after handful, like she was at an exciting movie.

"Wow. Until this 'George' is caught, I'm keeping you girls with me at Great Finds."

"Can't do." Sophie grabbed a handful of the popcorn. "Tomorrow morning we have to go to the sheriff's office. They're going to interrogate the woman and said we could watch since we tricked her into telling the truth about the crime."

27 SWEET SOLUTION

Mr. Sandoval dropped the girls off at 8 a.m. at the sheriff's office, then drove to a meeting with a client. Sophie noticed that Agent Dallas looked well rested. They sure trained FBI agents to recover quickly.

He greeted them when they walked in. "Nice to see you girls. Now that I've had a couple of meals and can think clearly, I have to thank you again. What you did still amazes me."

"You're welcome." Jessica blushed at the praise.

"And Agent Able is safe. He spent a lot of his time following you and searching for clues to my location. I found him in his room last night, eating the leftover half of his sandwich from the deli."

Sophie and Jessica laughed and sat down.

"Able chased you because he thought you were in trouble when you ran. He didn't know you'd only run because you'd seen him behind you." He sighed.

"Why didn't he call us back when we left messages?" Sophie asked.

Agent Dallas grimaced. "I'm embarrassed to say this after everything you've done, but he recognized your names and didn't think kids could help."

Sophie almost got mad, but then she remembered how much they *had* helped, and Agent Dallas did seem grateful.

"Let's see what my kidnapper has to say for herself." He nodded at Sheriff Valeska, and she went to the back for the prisoner.

When they returned, Jessica stared at the woman. "We didn't just see you at the Down Shoppe. You stood out wearing flowers on a dress and hat."

"After ugly prison clothes, I liked wearing things with flowers on them. I got to wear anything I wanted, including furs." The woman glared at them.

Agent Dallas leaned back comfortably in his chair. "Now you'll get what the law wants—a new prison sentence."

Sheriff Valeska turned to the girls. "Tell us what she said to you last night."

The woman jumped in. "Those girls have been trouble from the first day they knocked on the door to the Down Shoppe. We tried to buy the building the mother's business is in and even offered to buy the father's business to get them to leave town." She slowly grinned in a way that made Sophie shudder. "That antique shop is also right next to a fur store and on an alley where we could park a large truck."

Jessica explained. "They planned to use the tunnels to steal from every business in town."

"Tunnels? Steal?" Agent Dallas leaned forward, intent on her words.

"Sophie and I, uh, *found* connected basements and tunnels under Pine Hill. They planned to break into the businesses through the tunnels. We heard them talking. Her name's Eva."

Eva glared at them. "A man we met in prison told us about the basements and tunnels under Pine Hill. His grandfather helped build them. He also had old newspapers that said the town was loaded with money from tourists." She put her hands on her hips and chuckled. "Even before we got out of jail, we had a great idea. We could use stairs for access, and when there weren't any, we would cut away pieces in the floor above so that it would only take a few minutes to break through into the shops. Jewelry, furs, money, antiques. We would have gotten away with it all."

Sophie sat on the edge of the sheriff's desk. "So it wasn't all my fault that I fell through the floor. You made it break more easily."

Eva nodded. "We'd already taken care of the entrance under your mother's shop. You girls caused more problems for us after you fell through the floor and found that we'd stuck those stupid comforters of George's there. After he bungled them, we thought they might still turn out to be useful as a soft place to land if we were in the antique shop and needed a quick escape." She sneered and pointed at the girls. "They got the briefcase full of down, full of what was supposed to go into the window to make us look legit. When George went back the next day, the idiot couldn't find either of them."

"George who?"

"I shouldn't have told you anything." Eva crossed her arms and glared at them. "I'm not saying another word until I get a lawyer."

Sophie tried another question. "Did you think you could steal things as you went?"

Eva chuckled. "This coat and shoes were my prizes. George can unlock anything. Not another word " This time she stayed silent.

Sheriff Valeska signaled for a deputy to take her back to her cell.

Agent Dallas stood. "I guess that's it. They'd planned a big heist. I wonder what gave them all their crazy ideas."

"One of the pieces of newspaper we found had an article about the old Down Shoppe on one side and that article on the other about the amount of money visitors spend here each summer."

All of the clues were coming together. "Maybe when they

came to town and Hook, Line & Sinker was closed, they decided to take it over and re-create the business they'd read about over and over again in those clippings—the Down Shoppe. That's why George had the down."

Jessica said, "They probably figured no one would remember it from before or try to find out what happened to the owners of the store that was supposed to be there." She smiled at Sophie. "They shouldn't have done that. Not in a small town."

Sophie said, "Exactly. Can you imagine if they'd cleaned out every shop in Pine Hill?" She rested her chin in her hands as she thought. "Whew, they must have planned to have a huge truck ready that night."

Agent Dallas shook his head. "You girls solved the whole thing. But until we find 'George,' stay out in the open."

"We know." Jessica sighed, obviously frustrated.

"We never get to be part of the action," Sophie muttered when the door to the sheriff's office closed behind her.

Jessica stopped in her tracks. "Are you kidding?"

Sophie laughed. "We did rescue an FBI agent."

"When no one else could find him. And captured a criminal."

While they walked up the street toward Great Finds, Jessica pointed at a man across the street. "That's . . . that's . . ."

Sophie studied him. "That's the man in the brown suit. George."

Jessica nodded and gulped.

"Let's turn around and tell the sheriff."

"Good idea. Hurry." Jessica pushed Sophie along the sidewalk. "Oh, no."

Sophie glanced around. "What?"

"He's coming this way. I think he's seen us. Run!"

Sophie and Jessica ran down the street.

"I've got an idea." Sophie panted between words. "Go ahead of me to Bananas and get two banana cream pies from Mrs. Bowman. I sure hope she has some."

She slowed down to give Jessica time to get there ahead of

her. When Sophie ran into the bakery, Jessica set a pie in her hand. The man pushed through the door a second later. Sophie hit him in the face with her pie. Then Jessica splatted hers on top of that. He clawed at his face to pull off the creamy mess.

"Push him down," Sophie shouted and shoved at his back.

Mrs. Bowman shrieked when the man hit the floor.

Jessica sat on him. "We need to tie him up." She looked around frantically for something to use. "Hurry."

Sophie tried to pin down his arms. "Use your belt again."

Jessica looked down and nodded. She unfastened it and wrapped it around the man's wrists. He started bucking and fighting, kicking with his feet so hard that bits of pie flew off him and splattered onto them. "Tie his feet," Jessica shouted when he almost kicked her off.

When Sophie sat on his feet, Mrs. Bowman ran over with a roll of string.

"You tie his ankles," Jessica ordered.

The older woman looked timidly at the man's feet, then stepped forward and wrapped the string around them.

Sophie glanced over at the phone on the wall. "Now we'd better call the sheriff."

Just then Sheriff Valeska and a deputy rushed through the door.

Sophie looked up at them, confused.

Mrs. Bowman answered the silent question. "I called the sheriff, Sophie, after you hit him with the pies. I didn't know what was going on."

"Thank you. Sheriff, we think this is George." Sophie and Jessica stood.

"How do you kids know my name?" the startled man sputtered.

"Because we freed the FBI agent last night and captured Eva."

The sheriff and her deputy pulled the man to his feet and

directed him through the open door. He muttered, "I hate bananas."

"Well—" Mrs. Bowman exclaimed. "How rude."

Going out the door, Sophie said to Jessica, "There isn't anything worse to her than someone who hates bananas."

"It's a good thing she had banana cream pies today. We owe her for them."

Sophie started laughing. "I just thought of something. I think you can say that we creamed him."

ONE MORE PUZZLE

One question is left unanswered in the book. Mrs. Bowman, the owner of the bakery, is seen in front of the Down Shoppe and she's overheard talking about down. Jessica and Sophie are suspicious of her. Is she involved in *The Feather Chase*? After you've read the book, solve the last piece of the mystery. Go to shannonlbrown.com/more to find a puzzle that will give you the answer. (All links are for 18 and over.)

WHAT'S NEXT?

For more fun, this Mystery Writing PDF kit is FREE.

Find it at shannonlbrown.com/writeamystery. (*Ages 18 and older only please on this and all links in this ebook. Includes a teacher's guide.*)

THE TREASURE KEY

THE CRIME-SOLVING COUSINS MYSTERIES

1 KEY TO A MYSTERY

Jessica Ballow yawned and slouched into her chair. "We need *something* to do." Pine Hill had become every bit as boring as she'd imagined when her parents first told her she was going to spend the summer in this small town in the mountains. On top of that, she had to stay with her cousin Sophie, whom she hadn't seen since they were little. They got along well . . . now.

Sophie Sandoval fell backward onto the sofa. "Agreed. Maybe we should go into town."

"Why not? At least we won't just be sitting in your living room. We found our first mystery, *The Feather Chase*, right after I got here, so I barely had time to be bored." Jessica yawned. "Now I am."

"I doubt we'll find another mystery, even though I love mysteries—"

Jessica groaned. "I know. The next couple of months might be b-o-r-i-n-g." An endless summer of small-town life stretched in front of her.

"Pine Hill isn't boring."

A picture of lying on a sandy beach on Pine Lake with the sun overhead popped into Jessica's mind. "You're right. Let's get our swimsuits on."

This time Sophie slouched, her ponytail of brown hair smashing against the back of the sofa. "Again? We went to the beach yesterday. Wouldn't you like to go hiking on Cutoff Trail?"

The image in Jessica's mind switched to one of a trail climbing through a pine tree–lined path. With bugs. And wild animals. "*Like* isn't the word I'd use." When she paused, boredom began to sink in again. "I might not survive to my thirteenth birthday if I'm this bored. Let's do it."

Sophie instantly stood. "Really?"

"Pine Hill was way more exciting than home for a while. It's Tuesday, so most of a long week of nothing is in front of me. I'm ready to do something." Sometimes Jessica wished she could be with her parents, but they were on the other side of the world because of her father's job, and both she and her brother were spending the summer with relatives.

As Sophie ran into the room they were sharing, she said, "I think we'll both make it from twelve to thirteen, even if we are bored." She ran right back out with her backpack. "Let's go."

Jessica giggled as she followed Sophie to the door. "You aren't taking any chances that I'll change my mind, are you?"

"When the girl who loves shopping and is used to living in big-city London, England, says she'll go on a hike, we're on our way out the door." She glanced at Jessica's feet and stopped. "Sneakers."

"I forgot." Jessica raced into their bedroom. After slipping off her pretty pink sandals, she put on her boring-but-useful white sneakers and hurried back. Standing at a mirror beside the front door, she checked her makeup and tucked her blonde hair behind her ears, saying, "Sophie, maybe we'll find another mystery on Cutoff Trail."

Sophie got a faraway look in her brown eyes and sighed. "Oh, that would be *amazing*." She opened the front door and stepped out.

With one foot in midair, she froze.

Jessica peered over her shoulder. "Is something wrong?"

Sophie stepped to the side and pointed down. Right in front of her sat a perfectly gift-wrapped package. The wrapping paper had tiny pine trees on a white background and was encircled with a forest green ribbon and bow.

"Is today a holiday I don't know about?"

"I don't think it's even Mom and Dad's anniversary or anything like that." Sophie picked up the box and shook it. "I can't feel anything moving around inside it." Stepping back into the house, she held the box close to her ear and shook it again. "I wonder if we should open it."

"What if it's supposed to be a surprise for your mom or dad?"

"I don't think someone would leave a package for one of them and not put their name on it."

Jessica said, "That made sense for a second. Then I thought, why would someone *ever* leave a package with no name on it? What if it's for you? Or even for me?"

"All good points." Sophie shifted from one foot to the other. "I'd like to see inside. But I really don't want to get in trouble."

Jessica reached for it. "I'll open it so it won't be your fault. I'm going home at the end of the summer, but you have to live here all the time."

Sophie grinned and handed her the box. "I like the way you think, Cousin."

Jessica carefully removed the wrapping paper and set it on the nearby dining room table. When she opened the lid, an old-looking, yellowed envelope with the word *Desk* handwritten on it lay inside. "Whoa."

"What is it?"

Jessica stared at the envelope. Had someone set a mystery on Sophie's doorstep? The odds were totally against finding another mystery so soon. Maybe even impossible. Laughing, Jessica stepped back from the box. "Hey, you set me up. You knew I was bored and you did this to cheer me up! Making the envelope appear old was a master touch."

Sophie leaned over and tried to see into the box. "Uh-uh. It wasn't me. Did you say there's an old envelope in there?"

"Yes." Jessica picked up the envelope. "And there's something inside." She rubbed the envelope between her fingers. "I think it's a key." A sense of excitement ran through her. "Could we have found another mystery?"

"On the doorstep? I agree with your first thought: someone's playing a joke on us." Sophie reached for the envelope. "Let's open it up." She pulled on the end to tear it.

"Wait! We may already be in trouble for opening the present—"

Sophie dropped the envelope as if it were on fire. "And get in much bigger trouble if we open this too." She stared at it. "I'll open it carefully, just in case it is a clue for a real mystery. Or mom or dad think it's important." She went into her mom's office, which was just off the living room. "Being careful doesn't mean I won't get in trouble, but maybe it will help."

When she returned with something that looked like a knife with fancy decorations, Jessica said, "You're kind of off the hook for opening the package, so maybe I should—"

"Good idea." Sophie handed the letter opener to Jessica. She carefully inserted it in the end of the envelope and made a clean cut before tilting it and dumping out a key that hit the table with a clunk.

They both stared at it.

Sophie said, "I want to get excited about all of this. But I keep feeling like I should look over my shoulder for someone who's making a video of us opening their package. I don't know if it's a pretend mystery, or if another real mystery has landed at our feet."

"Cousin, you're the mystery expert. If you don't know, we're in trouble."

Sophie stood straighter. "You're right. I've read so many mystery books and watched so many mystery movies that I am an expert." She picked up the box. "Let's start with crime-solving basics and examine the clues."

Jessica smoothed out the wrapping paper. "Basic Christmas paper. Except that I'd put a red bow on it to make it more Christmassy. Anything interesting with the box?"

Sophie turned it from side to side, then set it back down. "No." She snapped her fingers. "I wonder . . ." Quickly grabbing the paper, she flipped it over. Frowning, she said, "Blank."

Jessica grinned. "Did you think there'd be a message written on the back?"

Sophie sheepishly nodded. "It could happen."

"Maybe it's in invisible ink."

"Maybe," Sophie slowly said.

Jessica could tell Sophie was intrigued by the idea for a second. Then she set it down.

"Nah. I think it's just wrapping paper. We could take it by the sheriff's office. We haven't visited Sheriff Valeska in a couple of weeks."

"Yes. She told you to come back"—Jessica changed her voice to sound like the sheriff—"if and when you found another mystery."

"It was fun working with her last time. I hope we get to do it again."

"Speaking of solving mysteries"—Jessica leaned over the table—"this paper seems familiar."

"I don't remember seeing it before, but it looks like a thousand other Christmas wrapping papers."

"That's it!" Jessica picked up the gift wrap. "Remember all that time I spent cleaning out the back room of your mother's antique shop, Great Finds?"

"Sure. While you cleaned out the back room, I dusted and did other stuff."

"I think this was old wrapping paper your mom had there. I remember her saying that she thought the pine trees would be right for a store in Pine Hill, but everyone said it looked like Christmas paper so she stopped using it."

"You mean Mom might have set us up?" Sophie glared at the box. "I wonder if she thought this would be funny."

Jessica shook her head. "I've been here long enough to know that doesn't sound like my Aunt April. She doesn't seem like the sneaky type."

"I've been so sad since we solved the last mystery that she might be trying to help." Sophie walked through the living room and peered down the hall. "The door to Dad's office is closed, so we'd better not bother him. I think Mom said something about him being extra busy right now with his accounting business."

She dropped the key back in the envelope and handed it to Jessica. "Here. I don't need my backpack just to go to town, and this will get less rumpled in your purse than it will in my back pocket." She headed for the door. "Let's go talk to Mom." Sophie stopped halfway down the steps. "Are you okay with taking the shortcut through the woods, or should we walk along the road?"

"Shortcut. The sheriff arrested the bad guys that chased us when we were trying to solve our last mystery, so we're safe walking through the woods again."

As they walked down the path, Jessica stepped on a branch, and it made a loud cracking sound. She wiped her brow with her hand. "Whew. I'm so glad I don't need to worry about hearing someone else making that sound when we're supposed to be alone in the woods."

"I know. Part of me is happy that life is quiet again."

At the edge of Pine Hill, Sophie yelled, "Race you!" and took off.

Jessica ran after her. When she could see Main Street, Sophie was leaning against the brick front of Simpson's Shoes.

"You're getting slow, Jessica. A twelve-year-old should have more energy."

Jessica leaned over, panting. "It's only been a couple of weeks since I had to be fast on my feet. We need to do something so I don't get out of shape."

"Since we aren't going hiking today, Cutoff Trail tomorrow?" Sophie looked so excited that Jessica didn't have the heart to tell her no.

"Sure. We'll find out what's going on with the box and envelope today. Tomorrow we go hiking."

They walked the short distance to Great Finds. When they pushed the glass door to the shop open, a bell rang and a voice called from the back room, "Welcome to Great Finds. I'll be right with you."

Jessica pulled the envelope out of her purse and tipped the key into Sophie's hand.

Sophie peered around the shop, probably checking to be sure they were alone. When Mrs. Sandoval stepped into the shop itself, Sophie held up the key. "Mom, was this a joke?"

Mrs. Sandoval walked toward them, smiling. "I'm glad you figured out the wrapping-paper clue. I hoped you would."

"You played a joke on us? Mom!"

"There is a real mystery." She pointed to the front of the shop.

Sophie raised one eyebrow. "It's a big piece of furniture. There aren't any drawers on the front, and something curved is over the top of it, but I kind of think it's a desk. Right?"

"A special desk, a cylinder desk. A curved piece of wood rolls over the top. The owner could leave their work on the desktop, roll the top down to hide it and lock up when they finished for the day."

"It's still just a desk."

The three walked together to where the desk sat. Jessica smoothed her hand over the curved cover. "The whole desk is beautiful." She leaned to see the side. "I love the flower design on it." Old furniture, dishes, lamps, even jewelry, filled Great Finds. But this desk seemed as though it had been around longer than most of the things her aunt had for sale. "Is it old?" she asked.

"Oh, yes. It was made in the 1700s." Mrs. Sandoval stared at the desk in a way Jessica could only describe as lovingly. She sighed and said, "It's exquisite."

"Let's see if the key fits." Sophie tried to insert it in the lock on the front of the cylinder. "The key is too big."

"I know." Mrs. Sandoval reached over to the cashier stand and picked up another key. "When it arrived, this key was in that keyhole. The envelope with your key was tucked into a cubbyhole, a storage space inside the desk." She smiled widely. "I did seal the envelope, though, to add an air of mystery."

Sophie flipped the key in her hand, and Jessica grabbed it in midair, saying, "Maybe it's to another desk."

"I don't know what desk that would be. This is the only desk the man was known to have owned, at least in his later years." Mrs. Sandoval walked over and flipped the sign on the door to Closed. "I have to go to a meeting, so I'm going to close for a while."

Sophie stood proudly. "We could watch the shop for you, Mom."

Jessica pictured the problems that could come up. Sometimes Sophie had a way of finding trouble.

Mrs. Sandoval raised one eyebrow.

"Okay, so maybe I wasn't good at doing that once. But I can!"

Mrs. Sandoval shook her head. "I'm not ready to try that again. I rarely close during the day, but this meeting is important." She stepped out the door, and the girls followed her outside.

As she was locking the door, she said, "The desk belonged to Harold Laurence."

Sophie shrugged. "Never heard of him."

"Yes, you have. You just don't remember the name. He owned that big old house on the hill overlooking Pine Lake. He died a few years ago at 102 years old."

Jessica furrowed her brow. "If he died years ago, how did you get his desk now?"

"That's an interesting story, Jessica. Mr. Laurence said in his will that it had to stay in Pine Hill. I knew it was sitting in that big empty house all these years, so I asked about it."

Sophie said, "But you have customers from lots of places. One might buy it and take it away from here."

"No. I worked with the estate's lawyers, and whoever buys it has to agree to keep it in Pine Hill. It's a beauty with a story attached to it, so I thought it would be good to have it in my shop, even if it didn't sell right away because of its high price."

As the three walked away from the shop front, she added, "The rumor of a lost treasure makes anything from Mr. Laurence more interesting."

2 HIDDEN CLUES

They hadn't made it five steps before Sophie spun around and started to head back toward the door to Great Finds. Before she could get out of reach, her mother grabbed her sleeve. "Sophie, where are you going?"

"I need to see the desk again. You didn't tell us about a treasure." Sophie peered over her shoulder at her mother, who hadn't moved an inch back toward her business.

"Soph, the key didn't fit anything on the desk. I thought I'd spice up your day, but I don't have time for this."

"Please, Mom. I have to see if there's something hidden in the desk. You said the envelope was inside a cubbyhole. Maybe one of the cubbyholes has a lock and we missed it, or something else inside the desk does." Sophie pleaded with her eyes. "Maybe there's a *treasure* inside."

Mrs. Sandoval slumped. Looking at her watch, she said, "Twenty minutes. The meeting's across town, and I was going to walk, but I'll drive instead." Putting the key in the front door lock, she added, "You'll have to come back later if you aren't successful in that amount of time."

Sophie ran over to the desk, lay down on the floor, and

scooted under the front part of the desk where the chair would go.

Jessica's green eyes stared down at her. "Uh, Sophie, what are you doing?"

Sophie lifted her head up. "In detective shows there's often something taped underneath furniture. There aren't any drawers, but I thought maybe . . ." There was silence for a moment as Sophie rooted around under the desk.

Jessica asked, "Find anything?"

Sophie scooted back out. "Nope. Jessica, check the outside of the desk, and I'll see if there's anything else in the cubbyholes and the rest of the inside."

Mrs. Sandoval tapped her watch. "You have seventeen minutes."

Jessica crouched in front of the desk. "What are we looking for?"

"Anything that doesn't seem right."

A moment later, the girls heard, "Sixteen minutes."

"I can't work like this, Mom!"

Mrs. Sandoval started for the back room. "I'm going into the back to pack up something I need to ship later."

"Good idea, Mom."

When Mrs. Sandoval stepped into the back room, Sophie whispered, "I think I can focus on this now that she isn't telling me the time every minute."

Jessica stared at the desk. "It doesn't seem right to me that the desk doesn't have drawers."

Sophie leaned back to see the front. "True. There's a big space on the left side where drawers would usually be."

Jessica rubbed her hand over the front of the desk. Then she leaned in and looked underneath in the place where the chair would fit and ran her hand over the sides there. When Jessica continued to the left and to the underside of the area too low to the floor to slide under, she jumped in surprise. "Sophie, there's a bump here."

Sophie crouched beside her. "It's old. Is it just a broken piece?"

"This is odd," Jessica said. "I wonder . . ." She pushed on the spot, and the front of the left side of the desk popped out.

"Oh no! Mom is not going to be happy. I hope it can be fixed." Sophie leaned down and checked under the piece, moving it slightly up and down. As she lifted it, a large drawer became visible. "It's a door." When she'd raised the door all the way, she gently pushed it out of the way into what appeared to be a slot made for it.

The two of them silently stared at the hidden compartment for a few seconds before Sophie said, "Wow."

Jessica said, "Wow is right, Sophie."

Sophie pointed. "There's a keyhole."

Jessica pulled the key from the envelope out of her purse and handed it to Sophie.

"I'd better be very careful. Mom said this was old and valuable."

Jessica leaned over Sophie as she tried the key.

"Doesn't fit. Let's try the small one that fit the top."

Sophie felt her heart speed up as the key slid into the lock. "This is it!" She turned it to the right, and the whole drawer popped forward, pushing her to the floor. As she scrambled to her feet, Jessica peered inside.

Standing up, Sophie asked, "What's inside? Is there a treasure map?"

Jessica answered. "Not a thing."

"Nothing? A key opens a hidden drawer and there isn't anything in that drawer?"

"I don't have any answers, Soph. Maybe Mr. Laurence liked the desk, but didn't keep anything in it."

Sophie squatted in front of the drawer. "I'm not giving up yet. Let's check for something taped to the top."

Jessica shrugged. "Why not?"

Sophie felt around inside the drawer area. "The top is clear. Maybe we should pull the drawer out and check behind it."

"That sounds like something you should ask your mom."

"Probably. Mom!"

Mrs. Sandoval hurried over. "Is something wrong?"

"No, Mom." Sophie pointed at the desk.

Kneeling in front of it, Mrs. Sandoval said, "This is exciting."

"Mom, can we pull the drawer out to see if something's hidden behind it?"

"I don't see why not," her mom answered, "provided that we aren't damaging it in any way. But let me do it." She bent over and gently pulled the drawer forward. "It stopped."

Sophie leaned closer. "It won't come out? Are you sure? All of the drawers in our furniture at home come out."

Mrs. Sandoval turned, her eyes suspicious. "How do you know that?"

Sophie felt her cheeks turn pink. "I checked to make sure nothing was hidden behind them. It was in the book I was reading."

Mrs. Sandoval chuckled. "I will say that you're right, Sophie. Drawers can usually be removed."

Sophie crouched beside her. "Jessica found a button for the cover. Maybe there's another one that makes the drawer removable." She felt around inside the drawer. "Hey, here in the back there's a piece that seems loose."

"Careful. If the wood is cracked or broken, don't make it worse."

"It has smooth edges, so it doesn't feel like a broken piece." Sophie stood and moved to the left of the desk, bending over to reach inside. "This time, I'm not going to stand in front when I push it. Let's see what happens."

When she pushed on the wood, the drawer jumped forward and swung to the left, shoving her backward. She landed on the floor—again.

Jessica laughed. "You may be onto something. I know by watching you what I shouldn't do."

"Ha-ha."

Sophie crawled around the corner and looked into the open space. "There are hidden drawers behind the hidden drawer! Three of them!" She reached for the top drawer handle. "Maybe there's treasure inside."

Jessica said, "A tiny treasure. Two of those drawers aren't more than an inch deep."

"Diamonds are tiny," Sophie said.

Sophie pulled the three drawers open one by one. "Nothing . . . Nothing."

When she opened the third drawer, the largest one, she froze.

"Is there something in it?" Jessica asked as she and Sophie's mom leaned in closer.

"It's a piece of paper. Maybe it has a treasure map on it." Sophie reached into the third drawer and pulled it out, then said, "It's just a photo of a house with 'Hilltop' written on it." She handed it to her mom.

Mrs. Sandoval scrunched up her face as she studied the picture. "That's the Laurence house. Both the house and grounds have changed a lot since this was taken, and not for the better." She pointed at the faded photo. "This building has the same tower on each corner. It's definitely his house."

Jessica peered into the drawer. "Anything else in there?" She reached into the drawer. "Empty."

Mrs. Sandoval stood. "I have to run now. Please come back this afternoon and dust for me. Right now, why don't you get some lunch at Donadio's Deli?" She reached into her purse, checking her watch at the same time. Handing Sophie some money, she added, "I'll be back in an hour. Two at the most." Then she turned and headed for the door.

Jessica put the key back in the envelope and slid it into her purse.

Waving the girls over, Mrs. Sandoval opened the door. "I can just make my meeting." She hurried them outside, locked up, and rushed down the sidewalk to her car, parked nearby on the street.

As she unlocked her car door, she looked back at them and said, "Maybe go see Nezzy." Before they could answer, she climbed into the car, started it, and drove away, waving as she passed them.

Sophie and Jessica stared at each other. "Did you understand what Mom said?"

"I heard the words but don't understand. What's a *Nezzy*? There's a Loch Ness monster in a lake in Scotland, and they call it Nessie. We went to the lake for a weekend once, but didn't see the monster. I doubt she meant that. Anyway, it's mystery break time! Maybe we can go shopping after lunch."

Sophie swallowed hard. If they had to decide between doing something outdoors, like hiking or fishing, or shopping, Sophie would always pick the outdoors. She said, "Let's go with food first. I definitely can't think about shopping when I'm hungry."

Jessica laughed. "I can always think about shopping. Maybe your mother will take us sometime."

Sophie hoped her face didn't give away how much she *didn't* want that to happen anytime soon. "Let's go to lunch at the deli. Tony's mother is usually there. Maybe she'll know what 'Nezzy' means."

"I'm always happy to eat at the deli. They make good food."

"They do. But you might also like to see Tony there today."

Jessica stared at the ground. "He's a friend of yours, too."

"Yes. But he's never given me a hot fudge sundae, and he did give you one."

"You're right." When Jessica looked up, Sophie grinned.

3 WHAT'S A NEZZY?

A smiling, older man brushed by the girls as they stepped through the door into Donadio's Deli. Sophie knew she'd seen him before but couldn't remember who he was.

She and Jessica walked up to the counter. Jessica got a silly grin on her face as Tony, the owner's dark-haired son, took their order. Once they'd ordered their sandwiches, they went to find a table.

As they sat and waited for their food, Sophie tapped her fingers on the table. She still couldn't remember who that man was, and it was starting to bug her. When Tony brought their lunches, she asked him.

"He's Mr. Jenkins, and he must be the nicest man in town. He took good care of Mr. Laurence as his butler when he was alive, and lives in the house now as the caretaker. He comes here almost every day and talks about what a great man Mr. Laurence was. He says he does that to keep his memory alive."

"I think Mom and Dad had him over for dinner once when I was young. Mom said something about a 'Nezzy' today. Would you ask your mom if she knows what a Nezzy is?"

Tony laughed as he leaned against the table. "I can answer

that. Nezzy isn't a what. It's a who." He clearly liked knowing something she didn't.

"Okay. *Who* is Nezzy?"

"Nezzy Grant. You know Mrs. Grant."

"Oh. Sure, I do." Sophie smacked her forehead with her hand. Turning to Jessica, she said, "Nezzy is old lady Grant, and she must be a hundred years old."

Tony stood. "She's ninety-nine. I know because she loves our chicken salad sandwiches, and that's what she wanted for her ninety-ninth birthday lunch."

Sophie popped a chip in her mouth as Tony headed back to the counter. "We don't have time to visit Nezzy and go to Hilltop today before we need to go back to Great Finds to help Mom."

Jessica took a sip of her lemonade. "I've never been to Hilltop, and it was Mr. Laurence's house. I say we go there."

Lowering her voice and glancing around to make sure no one could hear her, Sophie said, "Maybe holding up the photo and looking at the house at the same time will show us something important." She ate another chip, then bit into her sandwich.

"Kind of like the game where you have to see what's different between the two pictures." Jessica spread some extra mustard on her turkey sandwich.

"Yes."

"I've always liked that game."

Just then Jessica's phone made a frog's *ribbit-ribbit* sound, and Sophie knew a message had come in from Jessica's brother.

Her cousin pulled out her phone. "I guess Donadio's Deli is one of the few places in Pine Hill where cell phone reception is good. I just wish my phone worked at your house."

"Cell phones and Pine Hill definitely aren't good together. The mountains block the signal most of the time, but at least the mountains are pretty."

Jessica turned her phone so Sophie could see it. "Frog Boy sent a photo of himself with a giant fish he caught off Uncle Bill's fishing boat."

"Are you sure your brother doesn't mind being called Frog Boy?"

"He didn't mind when he was really little," Jessica answered, then frowned. "I might have to start calling him Jake now that he's almost ten."

After tucking her phone away, she asked, "Do you know where Hilltop is?"

"Everyone in Pine Hill knows that house," Sophie said. "I just didn't recognize it in the photo. Mom took me there a couple of years ago for a party the city had for people who helped out with Hilltop. I remember that it's kind of creepy, even driving in."

"We need to ask the owners if we can see it."

"The city owns it, so I guess it would be like going to a park. I don't think we can go inside without asking Mom or Dad. There might be an awesome clue to the treasure on the outside though."

"Right," Jessica said. "It's been sitting outside the house, and no one else noticed it. Not in close to a hundred years."

"It could happen."

"Sure." Jessica took another bite of her sandwich. After she'd swallowed, she said, "We don't know if there really is a treasure. Your mom said there was a 'rumor' of lost treasure. That means it may or may not be true."

Sophie shoved the last bite—maybe two bites—of her sandwich into her mouth. When she'd swallowed, with the help of her drink, she stood. "Some people believe it. I plan to be one of those." Sophie could picture the looks on everyone's faces when she found the treasure. She took a step toward the door. "Are you coming?"

Jessica ate the last bite of her sandwich, then said, "Let's go."

"Another mystery." Sophie waved her on.

Jessica groaned but joined her. "Here we go again."

"Admit it. You're a little less bored now. You're happier."

"I am happier." She paused. "As long as there aren't any bad guys, especially any bad guys *chasing us*."

4 MYSTERIOUS MANSION

Going out of the deli, Jessica followed Sophie as she turned right and headed up the street. Sophie pointed beyond Pine Lake and said, "Hilltop's over there. I think Mr. Laurence's house used to have a great view of the lake, but trees and bushes grew up in front of it. Now you can barely see it even when you're in a boat."

Once they'd walked past the lake and beyond the downtown area, Sophie turned left onto a narrow, gravel driveway filled with potholes and overhung by trees. Even though it was a sunny day, it was cooler and felt like dusk with all the shadows under the trees.

"Spooky," Jessica said.

"I told you it had a haunted-house thing going on. And you haven't even seen the house yet."

Breathing hard, Jessica stopped. "I also see why it's called Hilltop. We're definitely going uphill."

"I know," Sophie answered, also stopping. "Mr. Laurence must have seen everything around here from his windows, sitting above the town, the lake, everything—when you could still see through the trees and brush, that is."

They continued up the sloping drive and soon came around a

curve, where a massive house sat in front of them. Jessica pulled out the photo and held it up. "It's no wonder your mother didn't recognize the house in the photo at first. It was a beautiful mansion, and now it looks like it might fall down any minute!"

"It has some holes in the roof—"

"Big holes in the roof."

"But the city says it's safe." Sophie walked over to the side of the house and pushed on it. "See, the walls are still standing."

"This is brick, so people here must have liked bricks for a long time. I'm still surprised at all of the brick buildings in this town." Jessica stared at a hole in the corner of the roof that over-hung them. "Why is a mansion like this in such bad shape? The owner must have been rich to have built this."

"I don't think he had much money when he got old."

Jessica started to step forward, then paused. "Didn't Tony say Mr. Jenkins was the butler? Poor people don't have butlers."

"True. I don't know the story, but Mom will. Anyway, Mr. Laurence didn't have kids, so he left the house to the city in his will. I don't know why it's such a mess."

"I think it would be very expensive to repair. It isn't just the holes in the roof. They must have let in a lot of rain—and other things—over the years." Jessica pointed at the roof. "There's a bird's nest at the edge of that hole. Maybe the city doesn't have enough money sitting around to fix everything."

Sophie surveyed the area. "You're probably right. It would cost thousands of dollars to fix all of this."

"Thousands and thousands."

"Let's walk around the house and look for clues."

"I ask again: what would give us a clue to a treasure's hiding place? If there is a treasure."

Sophie started to speak, but Jessica held up her hand to stop. "We don't even know if the photo was an actual clue to the treasure."

"Of course it's a clue. Remember that the last time I told you we'd found a mystery, we really had."

"That's true," Jessica said. "But that doesn't mean you're right again. Maybe Mr. Laurence was just sentimental. He likes holding on to things with memories, so he kept an old photo."

"Jessica, the man had a treasure, and we found the photo hidden in a secret area of his desk."

"People believe that he had a treasure. He might have just liked this photo and wanted to keep it safe."

"Stop being so negative. Clues are often in unexpected places."

"At least we have something to do." Jessica waved Sophie forward.

Sophie had that *I'm on the trail of a mystery* look. "I just know we'll find something exciting."

As they continued around the house, Jessica said, "It must have been pretty here." She pointed to their left. "I think there used to be a flower garden with a rock wall, like we have in England. Now there's just a pile of rocks."

As they neared the corner of the house, Jessica pointed to the edge of the roof. "There's another giant hole." She took steps backward until she could see more of the roof.

Sophie pointed at the hole. "A squirrel darted inside it." Laughing, she started to turn toward Jessica.

Jessica watched what happened next as if in slow motion. Someone raced around the corner of the house, swinging his hands around in the air, and slammed sideways into Sophie. As she started to fall, Jessica raced toward her and prayed she'd get to her before she hit the rocks.

A man and woman followed the blur around the corner, and the man grabbed Sophie's arm, stopping her fall.

"Are you okay, Sophie?" Jessica asked when she got to her side.

Sophie leaned against the house. When she reached up, her hand was shaking. "I thought I was going to land face-first in those rocks."

Jessica turned and saw a girl a few years older than them

standing beside the man and woman now. The woman asked Sophie, "Are you injured?"

"No. I'm fine." Sophie straightened and turned toward the man. It didn't take her long to recover. "Thank you for catching me."

The man spoke. "We're the Coopers. These are our kids, Madeline and Cody."

"Cody?" Jessica hadn't noticed a boy about their age. Then she realized he'd been the blur.

Sophie glared at Cody. "You ran into me."

His face turned bright red. "I had hornets circling around me. I was trying to get away from them. I'm sorry you almost got hurt."

Sophie rolled her eyes and muttered, "City boy," just loud enough for Jessica to hear. She then thanked the boy's parents and moved quickly around the corner of the house, with Jessica right behind her.

"It's too bad he's a jerk," Sophie said. "He's cute."

Jessica stopped in her tracks. "What did you say?"

"Huh? I said he's a jerk."

"No. After that."

Sophie blushed. "Well, he is cute."

"Yes, he is. But I didn't think you'd notice. You hadn't paid any attention to Tony."

Sophie laughed. "Tony and I played together when we were babies. He's like a brother. Ick."

"Well, I think Cody *tried* to be nice and apologize to you."

Sophie looked around and tapped her foot. "He did, didn't he?"

Jessica nodded.

Whirling around in the other direction, Sophie said, "I could have been a little bit nicer to him."

"A little bit?"

Sophie's face turned a darker shade of red. "Maybe a lot. But it hurt when he slammed into me." Pointing to the house, she said, "Let's get to work. Pull out the photo of Hilltop and hold it up."

Jessica did, and they both glanced from the photo to the house and back again. "One difference is that the photo is of a house with a whole roof, and this one only has part of a roof."

Sophie shrugged. "My first idea might not work. The house is in worse shape than I remembered. We'd better do some actual detective work. Walk around the house and see if anything stands out. See if there are any clues."

Sophie turned one direction, and Jessica the other, studying the house as they went. When they finally met on the other side, Jessica asked, "Did you see anything helpful?"

"Uh, no." She stared up at the house. "I keep hoping something will stand out."

"I don't see any clues."

Sophie frowned. "Me neither."

Jessica would rather get a milkshake at the resort or do something else fun instead of working on the maybe-mystery, but Sophie looked so sad that she said, "Tomorrow morning we can go meet Nezzy Grant. Maybe she can give you—or rather, us—some help."

Sophie perked up. "Great idea. We go to the next place for clues."

5   NO TIME TO LOSE

Two hours had passed by the time Sophie and Jessica hurried back into Great Finds. Mrs. Sandoval was helping a customer, so the two girls quietly stepped to the other side of the shop to wait.

Sophie watched as Jessica spun slowly in a circle. "Uh, Sophie, what's different about this picture?"

"Huh. Are you saying—" Sophie immediately looked at the place where the desk had sat earlier. She walked through the shop and came back to Jessica. "It's gone! Mom must have sold it."

Sophie paced back and forth by the front windows, impatiently watching her mother taking her time with her customer. Finally, she said quietly to Jessica, "Maybe the person who bought it will let us check it out if we need to."

Jessica stared at Sophie.

"Well, they might," Sophie said hopefully.

It seemed to take forever for her mom to finish helping the customer and ring up the purchase. As soon as the woman opened the door to leave, Sophie and Jessica hurried toward the cash register. When they were halfway across the room, Sophie blurted out, "Mom, who bought the desk?"

Mrs. Sandoval smiled. "Someone close to you. Don't worry."

When Sophie started to speak, Mrs. Sandoval said, "Just a minute. I have to write this down before I forget it." She made a note on a pad, then looked up. "Sorry for keeping you in suspense. Ever since we discovered the hidden drawers, I've thought about that desk. I finally decided that I didn't want to let it go. At least not yet. So I had it taken to our house, and it's in my office." She pointed across the room. "There's my old desk."

A couple entered the shop just then, and she went over to help them.

Sophie leaned against the counter, feeling dazed. "It's at our house," she whispered.

"Even I was a little nervous," Jessica said. "I don't want to lose the one place where we've found a clue—if it is a clue, which we aren't sure about." She shook her head as though she needed to clear it. "I didn't want it to be gone forever—just in case."

The customers left after browsing, and Mrs. Sandoval came back and dropped into a chair. "Other than the fun with the desk, my morning didn't turn out as I'd hoped."

"What happened?" Sophie asked.

"We need to protect treasures from the past. I tried to explain that, but I lost the battle. The city council voted to tear down Hilltop. It will be taken to the ground in a month."

Jessica gulped. "That fast?" The clock was ticking on solving this mystery.

"It costs them every month to keep it. I had hoped that the town would find the money to restore the house and turn it into a convention center or art center, something that could be used by a lot of people. Instead, the land, all thirty acres of it, will be a park." She stood. "I guess that will have to be okay."

Sophie and Jessica followed her to the back room, where she retrieved a couple of dust rags. She started to hand them to the girls, then snatched them back before they could take them. "Let's do this another day," she said, as she laid the rags down where she'd found them, before heading back onto the sales floor.

Sophie watched her mother walk to the front of her shop and stare out the window. "I've never seen Mom like this. I sure hope we can find the treasure in time to save the house."

"Me too! It could be a beautiful house again."

———

Walking home, Sophie said, "Remind me when we get home to put the key in my secret hiding place."

"That is so cool! How many people find a hidden metal box under a loose floorboard in their closet?"

"We have to remember to put everything we find for the mystery into the box."

"If everything fits."

"Last time our clues were pretty small."

The phone was ringing when they stepped in the door, but it stopped ringing before Sophie could answer it.

"Is that you, Sophie and Jessica?" Lucas Sandoval called.

They both answered, "Yes."

"Jessica, your mom and dad are on the phone. You can use the phone in my office."

Jessica ran out of the room, wearing a huge smile. When she came back a short time later, she was grinning from ear to ear.

"Mom says it's very expensive to call from where they are, but she knows cell phones and texting aren't reliable here." Jessica sat down. "It feels so good to talk to them. I'm used to having Mom around all the time, so this summer has been strange."

"Do you think both your mom and dad will come back to London this fall?" asked Sophie.

Jessica gave a dreamy sigh. "That would be so nice. Sometimes I wish Dad had a normal job that didn't take him all over the world."

———

After dinner, the girls were sitting on the couch when Sophie said, "We went to see Hilltop today, Mom."

Mrs. Sandoval set down the newspaper she'd been reading. "Find any treasure?"

Mr. Sandoval groaned. "Don't tell me you girls are searching for the Laurence treasure now."

"Sure, Uncle Lucas. Do you want to see the photo we found in Mr. Laurence's desk today?"

"Why not?"

Sophie ran to her room to get the photo from its hiding place. When she returned, she gave it to her father.

Once he'd checked it out, he handed the photo back to Sophie. "You found an old photo in an old desk. That isn't surprising."

"It's a clue," Sophie said with confidence. "Now we need to see if there are more clues inside Hilltop."

Mrs. Sandoval said, "I don't want you inside the house without one of us. Mr. Jenkins lives there. It's his home, even if it does belong to the city."

"Can you or Dad come with us tomorrow?" Sophie asked.

"I wish I could, Soph, but I was closed quite a while today and can't do that again tomorrow. And I know your dad's been working on a special project that needs to be completed as soon as possible. Just stay outside the house."

Sophie sighed. "Okay." As she picked up the remote so she could put on a mystery movie, she muttered, "We have to find a way to get inside."

6 ANY BODY HERE?

Sophie eyed Jessica warily from her bed the next morning, watching her cousin stretch and yawn.

"Don't worry," Jessica said. "I didn't wake up grumpy like I do sometimes."

Sophie raised one eyebrow, but didn't say a word.

"It could be more than *sometimes*."

Sophie nodded slowly, but still didn't say anything.

"When I wake up excited about the day ahead, it pushes all of my grumpiness away."

Jessica threw back the covers and got out of bed.

Sophie stared at her. "You *seem* okay."

"I think I'll get in the shower first thing, just to make sure. That always wakes me up completely. I wouldn't want to promise what I can't deliver."

Sophie slipped into her robe and tied the belt. "I'll have a breakfast surprise for you when you get up."

As Sophie cooked, a plan started and grew in her mind. She *thought* she could talk Jessica into it.

When Jessica walked into the kitchen, she sniffed appreciatively. "Yum. I wondered what you'd make since I've only seen you cook dinner, and a stir-fry sounds rather unpleasant at 9:00 a.m."

"French toast." Sophie set a plate with two slices of French toast and some strawberries on the table, then sprinkled powdered sugar on top.

Jessica sat down and took a bite. "This is sooo good."

Sophie sat next to her. "I can show you how to make it. You could surprise your mom and brother."

Jessica put another bite into her mouth. "Dad would love this when he gets to come home from his job."

———

Sophie took a shower after breakfast. She thought that by the time she'd dried her hair and dressed, Jessica would be done with her hair and makeup and they could leave. She was wrong.

Sophie perched on the end of her bed and watched her cousin put on blush and lip gloss, things she'd only recently learned the names for. If someone had a question about how to put up a tent, she could help. Jessica didn't have a clue. She was girly all the time.

A glimmer from Jessica's teeth caught Sophie's eye. "Do braces hurt?" she asked.

Jessica stopped with an earring halfway to her ear and stared in the mirror. "Sometimes. But generally not. I'll be super glad when they're removed next year."

"I don't usually notice they're there."

After putting in the earring, Jessica said, "That's what Mom tells me." She inserted the other earring and added, almost in a whisper, "I wish she was here," reminding Sophie of how good it was to always have both her mom and dad with her.

Standing tall, Jessica turned her head from side to side in the mirror, Sophie figured to make sure she'd done a good job. Nodding once, she turned to face Sophie. "I'm ready to go."

Halfway through the living room on their way out of the

house, the phone rang, and Sophie answered. Right after she'd said, "Hello," their plans for the morning were thrown out the window. Her heart sank as her mom talked.

"But we want to visit Nezzy today."

Her mother told her that they could visit Nezzy later, to remember that the old woman was eccentric and to be respectful —but first, they had a job to do.

After hanging up, Sophie sat down on the couch. "That was Mom."

"I could tell. We have a new project at her shop, don't we?"

"No." She gestured around the room. "Vacuuming, dusting, picking up."

Jessica plopped down next to Sophie. "Maybe it won't take too long."

"I think we can get out of here in about an hour. Let's make some cheese sandwiches for lunch and take them with us. We can head over to Nezzy's this afternoon, then get a ride home with Mom."

"Sounds good. Well, I shouldn't say that cleaning *sounds* good."

"Never." Sophie stood and held out her hand to help Jessica up. "Let's get this done. Then we can have our lunches at a picnic table in a park before we go see Nezzy. I know the perfect place."

"Have I been there before?"

"No. It's Dogwood Park, on the other side of town. I have an idea, and this will be good. By the way, Miss Smarty Pants, what's 'eccentric'?"

"Unusual. Maybe a little odd."

"That's how Mom described Nezzy. I can handle odd."

"I'm used to odd, being around you all the time." Jessica grinned and ducked.

"*Funny.*" Sophie tapped her cousin on the shoulder with her fist.

———

They ate at a wooden picnic table in a park that had tall pine trees. It might be a pretty place to sit and admire—if Sophie hadn't fidgeted like she was nervous about something. When they'd finished their lunches, Jessica picked up their trash and said, "You're acting like something's wrong. What's going on?"

"Since we haven't been able to get inside Hilltop, there's only one other place tied to Mr. Laurence that I know of where we haven't checked for clues."

Jessica furrowed her brow. "Where?"

"You aren't going to like it." Sophie winced. "*I* don't really like it."

"You're making me nervous. Just say it."

"It's a place where we won't see many people."

Jessica glared. "Another hike?"

"The cemetery."

Jessica looked heavenward. "Uh-uh. No way. I'm not going there." She stared at Sophie for a minute before speaking again. "I guess I should calm down enough to ask—why?"

"In the book I'm reading—"

"Oh, now I see. They found a clue inscribed on a tombstone?"

"On the cemetery's entrance sign. We've seen stranger things than that."

Jessica nodded once. "You're right about that. Okay."

Sophie took a step backward. "You'll go?"

"Other than being irrationally afraid—terrified, actually— that something creepy, like a body moaning in a grave, will happen there, I can't find any *good* reasons to say no."

"I think we're safe. It's just a few blocks from here."

"Now it all makes sense, Sophie. We passed two other parks on the way here, not to mention the picnic area by the beach."

"I thought that already being near the cemetery when I mentioned it would mean I could talk you into it more easily, and we would have a short walk to get there once you said yes."

"You mean *I* wouldn't have time to back out."

Sophie just grinned.

Neither girl said anything as they walked the five or six blocks to the cemetery at the edge of town. When they could see it ahead, Jessica glanced around. They were in a lonely area. "It's certainly away from the center of town."

"I have a feeling no one wants a cemetery near their house."

Jessica giggled nervously as they walked under the sign that said "Pine Hill Cemetery" and stepped onto the path that wove through the grounds. "We shouldn't see much activity here."

"Let's hope not. When I asked Mom this morning where Mr. Laurence is buried, she told me the area it was in and said most of the town came to his funeral here."

Walking from tombstone to tombstone, Jessica said, "Nope . . . Nope . . . Here it is!"

Sophie said, "Harold Laurence. His birth and death dates."

Jessica shuddered. "There's something creepy about being here. It's *very* quiet." A skittering sound to the left made her swing that direction. "A squirrel." She let out a big breath.

Sophie had her hands up to ward off an attack. Jessica coughed to hide her giggle. Her cousin was scared too, and that made Jessica feel much better.

Sophie said, "Let's hurry." She crouched beside the tomb stone. "Even up close, there isn't anything on the front other than the words I read."

Jessica walked to the back. "Nothing here. It's blank." She leaned over the top of the tombstone. "And it's just dirt on top of the grave itself."

Sophie twisted to the side. "You're right. But other graves have grass on top, or there's a stone with words carved in it set in the ground." She rubbed her hand over the grave. "It's loose dirt. I guess rain must have washed dirt over the grave."

Digging her fingers in deeper, she found something hard.

"Jessica! There's a flat stone under all this, and I can feel something carved into it."

Jessica hurried around and helped wipe the dirt away.

Both girls sat back on their heels.

Jessica read, "'Wisdom is the key to knowledge.'" She brushed off the edges to make sure there wasn't anything else hidden. "Sophie, this dirt was really fluffy. Rain would make muddy water. Wouldn't it dry hard?"

Sophie nodded. "You're right. That means . . ." She scanned the area. Lowering her voice, she said, "That means someone put dirt here so no one would see these words. They must have thought they were a clue to the treasure."

"People who live here would know what it said."

"Maybe. Maybe not. I doubt most of the people I know in Pine Hill could tell you what's on any of these graves, not unless it was someone close to them."

"You're right." Jessica was surprised to see Sophie glance around nervously before she spoke again.

"Someone came before us, but not long before us, because it rained a couple of days ago, and they poured fresh dirt all over this."

"They planned it ahead of time because they had a shovel or a bag of dirt."

"That also means we could be making someone nervous, someone who's looking for the treasure and is slightly ahead of us. They're trying to hide clues."

As Jessica stood, movement caught her eye. Something big and black moved behind a stone building. She grabbed Sophie's sleeve and tugged her away from the headstone. "Let's go."

"Huh? I'm not done." Sophie stood.

"Yes. You are. I just saw *someone* hide. Someone wearing black." She pointed to her left.

Sophie looked that way. "It's probably a crow."

"A six-foot-tall crow?"

Sophie stepped back from the stone. "You sure?"

"I know what I saw."

They broke into a run.

Sophie led them to the edge of the city, then slowed down when they were out of breath and well away from the cemetery.

Jessica took in a big gulp of air. She said, "I've been thinking . . . Maybe I saw a plastic tarp or something like that." She played it over and over in her mind. It had looked like a person, but maybe she was wrong. "I don't want to have bad guys following us again."

Sophie shook her head. "Me neither. Let's go see Nezzy now. There are lots of houses around her, so we *shouldn't* see anything suspicious."

The two girls moved more slowly than usual, neither one saying anything. In her heart Jessica felt sure she'd seen someone and that someone had hidden. If so, their mystery had just changed, and not in a good way. Sophie led Jessica up one street, down another, over a path between two large houses, finally stopping in front of a house that sat on a small hill above them.

Jessica looked up. "Wow."

"It's something, isn't it?"

Nezzy Grant's house had wild, crazy things in the design. It was brick, of course; almost everything in Pine Hill—except Sophie's big, white, antique house—was brick. A bright orange flag flew from a turret, purple drapes hung at the sides of a porch that curved around the front of the house, and wooden trim painted blue and yellow added a dizzying element. Jessica knew she wouldn't wear an outfit made up of those colors.

"I remember being here once when Mom needed to bring something to Mrs. Grant. We stayed outside, but the door stood wide open. Wait until you see inside."

Jessica kept staring at the house. "I'm curious, for sure. Look. There's a large stained glass window that adds even more colors." Turning to Sophie, she said, "I wonder if we should have called first. Even with all of the, uh, unusual details, this is a really fancy place. Another mansion." Jessica pulled out her lip gloss and ran it over her lips, then slipped her fingers through her hair.

"Mrs. Grant came to my church before she got so old, and her housekeeper, Amanda Easton, still does. I'm sure it's fine."

They climbed the steep stairs—brick, as Jessica pointed out— and knocked on the front door.

A woman opened the door. "Well, hello, Sophie. What can I help you with? Are you two selling something?"

"No, ma'am. We wondered if we could speak to Mrs. Grant."

"I'll see." She gestured them inside, then disappeared through a doorway off a long hall.

Standing in the entryway, Jessica couldn't focus on any one thing, there was so much to see. She whispered, "This is a crazy mix. There's a stuffed bird." She pointed toward the ceiling. Turning around to the wall, she said, "And here's a collection of lace."

Sophie whispered, "Maybe this is what Mom meant by eccentric."

As Jessica opened her mouth to speak, Miss Easton entered the room. "She'll see you now." She gestured for them to follow and led them down a long hall and into a large living room with fancy furniture that had lace doilies lying over the back, a totem pole in one corner, a suit of armor in another. Jessica said, "This is eccentric."

"Thank you," an old lady's voice came from the corner of the room.

Jessica gulped. "I'm sorry, Mrs. Grant."

The old woman cackled the way Jessica always imagined the witch in "Hansel and Gretel" would right before she got ready to eat the children. "Why ever would I be offended? Please sit down and tell me the reason for your visit."

Sophie and Jessica walked over to her and sat down in red leather chairs.

Sophie said, "My mother thought you could tell us about Mr. Laurence and Hilltop."

Mrs. Grant narrowed her eyes. "April Sandoval sent you, huh?" She leaned back in her chair and rubbed her chin, studying them. "Learned about the treasure, did you?"

Sophie spoke up. "Yes, ma'am."

The woman slapped her knee. "Nezzy."

Both girls jumped.

"Excuse me, ma'am?" Jessica edged back in her chair, away from Mrs. Grant, and tried to keep a happy expression on her face.

"'Ma'am' and 'Mrs. Grant' make me feel old. My name is Esmeralda, or Nezzy. I don't like that newfangled 'Ms.' thing."

Jessica replied, "Yes, ma'am. I mean Nezzy." The girls looked at each other. It wasn't polite, but it was what she wanted.

Sophie asked, "Did you know old man—I mean, Mr. Laurence?"

Nezzy guffawed. *"Old man Laurence!"*

Sophie nodded slowly. "Yes, ma'a—Nezzy."

Nezzy cackled again. "Get comfortable. I know everything you'd want to about Harold Laurence. Except the location of the treasure."

Sophie, her brown eyes sparkling, moved to a chair closer to Nezzy. "There is a treasure?"

The old woman got a faraway look in her eyes. "I'm not positive, but I believe there is. The story begins when my family moved to Pine Hill right after I'd turned sixteen. The first day we came to town, I was about to step into the general store when the most handsome man I'd ever seen walked across the street. I was so caught up with watching him that I tripped and fell. He hurried over and helped me up. I really thought I'd marry him, but life can bring unexpected surprises. Mr. Grant moved to Pine Hill the next year and swept me off my feet."

"Was there anything about Mr. Laurence that was unusual?"

Nezzy guffawed again. "Almost everything about that man

was unusual. Harold built the mansion about the time he got married, and you know that cost a pretty penny. He started spending money like it was water."

Sophie's eyes grew round and big. "Did he rob banks?"

"Naw. The man I knew wouldn't do anything like that. In the beginning some folks thought that."

"Then where did he get the money?"

Nezzy raised her hands. "I asked him, but he wouldn't say. I always did enjoy talking to that man. Still enjoy going through my memory books."

Jessica tried to pull her back on track. "So people think there's a treasure just because of all the money he had?"

Sophie sat back in her seat and crossed her arms. "That doesn't seem like much of a clue."

"No. There's more to it than that. Many years ago, a man everyone trusted, Doc Jones, said he'd taken a shortcut through the woods in the middle of the night and saw Harold there— with a big bag of gold. There was a bright, full moon that night, and he said it reflected off the open bag and lit it up for him to see clearly."

The girls were silent for a minute.

Sophie said, "Wow. How did Mr. Laurence explain the gold that night when Doc Jones stopped and asked him about it?"

"That's the problem. Doc was hurrying to help someone who was very sick, so he couldn't stop. Harold always said Doc Jones had been mistaken in the dark, that it wasn't him."

"And what about the place where the doctor saw the gold? Could the treasure be hidden there?"

Nezzy shook her head. "Seemed like the whole town went out to look for it. Harold owned that land and more, but he didn't stop anyone from looking."

Jessica glanced out the window. She could see the sun dropping low in the sky. "Sophie, we'd better hurry to Great Finds, or we'll miss the time we told your mother we'd get there."

Sophie turned to the window, then jumped to her feet. "Nezzy, we've really enjoyed our visit."

"Me too, ladies. Please come back. Oh, there is one other thing. Harold's desk was the one piece of furniture that he kept near him as he moved from room to room in that rotting house. When he was nearing the end, he told me, 'The beauty of the desk isn't just skin-deep. It goes deeper than anyone imagines.'" She shook her head. "I've never been sure what that meant." Shrugging, she added, "But it might be a clue to the treasure."

———

On the way to Great Finds, they passed a building with a poster in the front window and Sophie stopped in her tracks. "Jessica, a carnival's coming to Pine Hill! We haven't had a carnival here since I was a little kid."

"We have a giant Ferris wheel in London called the London Eye, and we go to that every once in a while. Even so, I'd like to go to a carnival. Do you think it will cost a lot?"

"I have a feeling it would take our whole allowance. And we might need money for things to solve the mystery. Look!" She pointed at the poster. "It's going to be on the grounds of Hilltop to raise money to save the mansion."

"Sophie, I wonder if we should go, just so we can keep our eyes on the house."

"I know what you mean, but they won't let us in for free." Sophie laughed and grabbed Jessica's arm. "We'd better hurry."

When they arrived at Great Finds, Mrs. Sandoval waited just inside the door for them. "I'm ready to close, so I'm glad you're here." She paused with her hand on her purse. "I just remembered that we have company for dinner tonight. I've been so busy today that I forgot. It's a good thing I made lasagna ahead yesterday." She reached into her purse, pulled out some money, and handed it to Sophie. "Girls, please run over to Bananas and get dessert for me."

Going out the door, Sophie asked, "Who's coming over?"

"Huh?" Her mom looked up from the key ring in her hand. "Oh, a couple of people who also want to save Hilltop." She smiled. "After dinner—and dessert—you can stay with us if you want, or you can go out on the porch or to your room so you won't be bored."

Once outside, Sophie said, "I'm for going where we aren't bored."

Jessica laughed. "Me too."

As they stepped into the bakery, Sophie saw Jessica pause and take a deep breath. In a low voice, her cousin said, "It smells so good in here. Kind of makes you forget that everything Mrs. Bowman bakes has banana in it."

"I know. It's weird, but everything is delicious. And she did try chocolate chip cookies without bananas," Sophie added.

Mrs. Bowman finished up with her customer, then walked over to them. "What do you need today, ladies?"

"Mom sent us over for dessert. We're having company tonight."

"My Triple Berry Cobbler came out especially good today." She pointed at a crumb-topped pan of dessert with a bright berry color around the edges.

Sophie looked over at Jessica, and her cousin's expression seemed to say: *Bananas and berries?!*

Jessica said, "The berry part sounds good. Um, does it have bananas?

Smiling broadly, Mrs. Bowman said. "I tried making it without bananas, but it just didn't taste right. It's wonderful now."

Sophie knew it sounded strange, but it would probably be delicious. "Sounds good to me."

Jessica seemed a little less certain.

The older woman pulled the foil pan of cobbler out of the glass case and reached for one of her yellow boxes. "Is anyone I know coming to dinner?"

"Mom said she'd invited a couple of people." Just then, an idea popped into Sophie's head. Mrs. Bowman probably knew everyone in town. "Does Mr. Jenkins come in here?"

"Oh my, yes. He's such a nice man. He's been wonderful to my sister. So kind." Mrs. Bowman tucked the pan into the box and started folding the sides in.

"Why is he wonderful?" Sophie asked.

"Emma Jean retired from teaching a few years ago, so she had extra time in her day. She offered to clean the old Laurence mansion for free to help out the city. Every Thursday and Saturday she spends a couple of hours there cleaning the safe areas, the ones that are in decent shape. Mr. Jenkins kindly said she didn't need to clean the area he sleeps in, and that saves her a lot of time. She says he always has a smile for her and insists that she not bother with his rooms." Mrs. Bowman set the box on the counter.

Sophie paid her. "He does sound nice."

As she walked to the cash register, Mrs. Bowman said, "He asked about you two the other day when he bought some muffins. Banana chocolate chip."

"Really?" Jessica asked.

"Yes, they're my personal favorite muffin. I love the chocolate scattered through them."

Jessica blinked.

Sophie knew that wasn't what she'd meant.

Jessica said, "I'm sure they're delicious. What did Mr. Jenkins want to know?"

"He'd heard about the mystery you solved and wondered if I knew more about what had happened. I guess he asked because everyone knows I helped you."

Sophie put her hand over her mouth to hide her grin. "Helped" probably wasn't the right word. Mrs. Bowman never learned that she'd been one of their suspects in the last mystery.

As the older woman handed Sophie her change, another customer walked in the door.

"What did you tell him?" Sophie asked quickly.

"I told him you were great detectives. I thought that would make him happy, but it didn't seem to."

As they left the bakery, Jessica said, "Everyone seems to love Mr. Jenkins. That was odd that he asked about us though."

Sophie thought about it. "It is, but we haven't heard anyone say anything bad about him." She shifted the box in her arms. "I doubt there's anything suspicious about him."

8 NOISES IN THE NIGHT

A *clunk* woke Jessica.

Clunk again. Had someone broken into the house?

Another sound came from the wall on the other side of the bedroom, this one more like tapping. Tapping, tapping. Heart racing, Jessica turned toward Sophie's bed. She gulped. Sophie wasn't there. Knowing Sophie, she'd woken up and gone to check out the source of the noise that Jessica thought came through the wall from Aunt April's office.

Jessica reached for her phone. The off-and-on reception in Pine Hill might make it iffy for calling people, but it still told the time: 2 *a.m.* She silently slipped out of bed and crept out the door, which had been left partway open by Sophie, or whoever had snuck into the house.

When the tapping stopped, Jessica froze. After a minute, she continued toward her aunt's office, which she was confident was the source of the noise. She found the door shut, so she gently turned the knob and pushed it open an inch. Someone sat on the floor next to the desk, almost out of sight from where Jessica stood. The person turned, and she saw who it was. "Sophie!"

Her cousin jumped about six inches in the air. "Ooh, you scared me!"

"*I* scared *you*? I was scared stiff when I woke up and heard strange sounds. Then you were gone . . ."

Sophie hurried over and pushed the door shut, turning the knob as gently to close it as Jessica had to open it. "I couldn't sleep. I kept thinking about the key. It has to fit something in the desk. Help me?"

Jessica rolled her eyes. "Sure. Why not? I can't think of a thing I'd rather be doing in the middle of the night. Other than maybe sleeping. But if I help you, we might both be able to go back to sleep. You have one hour."

"Deal."

Jessica crouched beside the desk, with Sophie kneeling beside her. "You know, there probably isn't anything else hidden in this desk. I suspect Mr. Laurence was just old and meant to put a different key in the envelope."

"Think about what he told Nezzy about the desk. All we found was a photo. That doesn't seem worth mentioning to her."

"It's definitely not the treasure people have talked about for close to a hundred years."

Sophie's eyes got big. "Sooo, you agree there may be something else hidden in the desk."

Jessica shrugged. "Maybe. Now that I'm up, let's look for it. What now, O wise one?"

Sophie stood. "Let's start with what we know." She pointed at the side with the hidden drawer.

Jessica reached inside and pushed first the button to open the large drawer and then the button inside it to cause it to swing to the side.

"We stopped examining the desk when we found the hidden drawers. What if they were just the easiest hidden places to find?"

"It seemed like there should be drawers. I think that makes them something people would look for."

"*Very true.*" Sophie studied the desk.

Jessica crouched at the side of the desk and ran her hand underneath the bottom edge. "I'll pick up where I left off."

"Me too." Sophie rolled the top back and leaned over the front of the desk.

They worked without speaking for a while. Then Jessica said, "We should have gone to the library and searched on the computer for 'desks with hidden compartments.' We might have gotten some ideas about where to look and saved some time."

"I wonder . . . No, I don't think Dad would be happy if we went into his office in the middle of the night."

A man's voice said, "He wouldn't be happy if you woke him up either."

Mr. Sandoval stood in the doorway with a metal fireplace poker in his right hand and a flashlight in his left.

Jessica leaned against the wall, hand on her heart.

"You scared us, Dad!" Sophie said.

He glared at them. "How do you think I felt when I heard tapping in the night?"

"Um, maybe this wasn't my best idea?"

"Now you're thinking right." He pointed at the desk. "What's going on?"

Sophie said, "We—"

Jessica cleared her throat.

"Okay. I decided to see if there were more hidden compartments in the desk."

"Uh-huh. And?"

"Nothing so far. Would you like to help?"

Mr. Sandoval seemed to fight a battle with himself, first looking annoyed and then interested. He finally grinned and set down the fireplace poker. "I wouldn't miss it. Let's try to keep it down so we don't wake up your mom. No more tapping, okay?"

Both girls nodded.

Inside, across the back of the desk there were three rows of small storage places: two rows of open boxes big enough to hold a letter or two—cubbyholes, her aunt had called them—and under those, a row of tiny drawers that could hold a handful of paper clips each. Between each drawer there was a round piece of metal for decoration. Sophie peered first into the cubbyholes. "Hold your flashlight here, Dad." She pointed at the spot.

Jessica stopped what she was doing to watch. "Find something?"

"Maybe." Sophie groaned when her dad shined the light into the box. "Dirt. It's just dirt on the back of a cubbyhole."

Jessica giggled. "It's probably antique dirt."

"Maybe Mom would like it." Sophie grinned.

Mr. Sandoval chuckled. "She might. You know, we could be on an impossible mission. Consider all of the people who have looked for the treasure for more than a hundred years."

"And not found it," Jessica added.

Sophie pulled out a tiny drawer and peered into the hole it left. "None of them were friends with Mr. Laurence."

"I think *every* one of his friends would have looked for the treasure," Mr. Sandoval said.

"You may be right. There's something about the word 'treasure' that gets people excited. But Nezzy had special information. He told her the desk was important."

Sophie bent over the side of the desk. "Whoa!"

"What?" Jessica crowded next to her.

"When I looked at the hole from the side, I noticed that the metal decoration between these two drawers looks like a button, not just a pretty decoration."

"And?" Jessica stood.

"Let's see." Jessica stood on one side of her and Mr. Sandoval on the other, both leaning in as Sophie pushed the piece of metal. The tiny drawer swung sideways to reveal a hidden cubbyhole behind it.

Jessica leaned over the side of the desk. "Wow!"

Sophie reached her hand into the hole. "*Nothing*. I was *so* sure . . . I'm starting to wonder about the treasure myself."

"Let me check. There must be more." Jessica nudged Sophie

to the side and put her hand inside the hole. "Hey, the bottom is loose!" She pushed on it, flipping the end of the board up so she could lift it out. When her uncle shone the light inside, she craned her neck to peer into it. "Empty! This is so frustrating. I really thought we'd found something."

Mr. Sandoval said, "Let me see." Jessica stepped aside and he handed the flashlight to Sophie. "What about the little drawer at the back of the hole?"

The girls leaned in. He reached inside and slid out a tiny drawer.

Sophie groaned. "Nothing! There should be a law that secret compartments must have something great inside." She lifted it from her dad's hand and turned it upside down. "There isn't anything underneath either."

"Maybe . . ." Sophie reached inside and flipped up a board under the new drawer. "There are layers upon layers of hidden places in this desk." Bouncing with excitement, Sophie reached her hand inside. "I feel like we're close to a big discovery." Then she sighed and pulled her hand out. "Nothing."

Jessica stepped back and studied the desk. "You know, Sophie, if this drawer on the left side of the desk has all of this, the drawer in the same place on the right might too."

Sophie smacked her head. "Obvious. My detective brain cells must be asleep."

"Perfectly reasonable since it's the middle of the night," Jessica muttered.

Mr. Sandoval chuckled. "If there isn't anything here, we'll need to go back to bed and try another time. During daylight hours."

Sophie focused intently on the desk. She pushed the center of the medallion between the two drawers on the right, watched as the drawer swung out, this time designed with a glass jar in the center. Sophie said, "I've seen something like this before. Mom told me it would have had ink in the jar before modern pens, from when people wrote with pens they dipped into ink."

Jessica reached inside the open compartment and flipped up the bottom board. Then she reached inside to open the little drawer. "It's stuck."

Mr. Sandoval shone the light into the slot so she could see better. "Should I get a tool to help open it?"

When Sophie peered inside, her jaw dropped. "This drawer has a keyhole." She reached into her robe pocket and pulled out a key. "I brought it just in case." She fit her hand inside the hole. "You couldn't have a large hand and do this. Everyone ready?" She looked up at her dad and Jessica. After a few seconds, she whispered, "It fits."

Sophie slid the drawer out and they peered into the tiny, empty space.

Mr. Sandoval groaned. "I thought you'd found something. Well, we'd better all head back to bed. Morning will come quickly."

"Just a sec, Dad. We should see if there's a space under the drawer, like on the other side. This one was locked, so maybe it's more important."

Jessica reached in and flipped out the board. "Yep." She reached her hand into the hole and hit something cold and metallic. She ran her fingers over it, feeling the outline of the object. "Not again!"

Mr. Sandoval asked, "Jessica, are you okay?"

She wrapped her fingers around the object, slid her hand out, and held up a large key.

Instead of looking frustrated, Sophie's eyes gleamed with excitement.

Jessica raised both hands in exasperation. "Now we have to find something else with a keyhole."

Mr. Sandoval said, "Since this is a larger key, my guess is that your treasure hunt just took a turn away from the desk."

Jessica dangled the key by the end. "You're right, Uncle Lucas. This is a different kind of key. And it's kind of pretty, like keys were a long time ago."

Sophie lifted it from Jessica's hand. "Maybe this time when we find the place the key fits, we'll also find the treasure."

Sophie fought a yawn as she watched Jessica dry and style her blonde hair, then put on makeup. It was so much work *every single day*. After wondering for just a second if she should give it a try, she quickly shifted her mind to their mystery and went through their clues. Everything came back to Hilltop. An idea popped into her mind. She'd be extra helpful at Great Finds. Then she'd ask her mother to help them get into Hilltop.

They walked into town and to her mother's shop.

When Sophie found her mother with no customers, she put her plan into play. "Do you need us to do anything, Mom?" Sophie made herself smile broadly.

Mrs. Sandoval picked up her mug of coffee and peered over the rim as she took a sip. "You must want a favor."

"Wellll . . ."

So much for sneaking up on her mother with the idea.

"I'll take you up on your offer later. Right now, I have good news for you. Your father talked to Mr. Jenkins about letting you see Hilltop."

Sophie froze. There could be a clue in the house. Would they find the treasure today? "And?"

"He said you could come over today."

Sophie felt a real smile spread over her face. "Are you or Dad coming with us?"

"Neither. Emma Jean Walker is going to be cleaning there today. Your father and I have known her for years."

"That's great!"

"Try not to pester Mr. Jenkins with your questions. Also, remember that Hilltop may belong to the city, but it's his home right now. Think of it like a museum. Don't touch anything."

"Mom! How can I investigate if I can't touch *anything*?"

Her mom paused. "I'll revise that. Touch, but be very careful not to break."

Sophie nodded. "Deal."

"When are we scheduled to go?" Jessica asked.

"I'll run you over right now. I want to make sure Emma Jean is there."

Jessica left the room to brush her hair.

As Sophie watched her cousin leave, she felt less girly than she thought she should. Leaning close to her mother, she said, "Mom, would it be okay if I wore makeup?"

Her mother reared back. "What?"

Sophie watched her but didn't say anything else.

"I want you to wait to wear makeup."

"But Jessica—"

"That's between her and her parents." Mrs. Sandoval rearranged teacups on a shelf. "I'm willing to let you wear a very light pink lip gloss, but that's all."

"Thanks, Mom." Sophie reached up and hugged her.

———

As Mrs. Sandoval drove, Jessica pictured the Laurence house. "There are some very large holes in the roof, and I suspect some large rodents have decided to call it home."

Sophie laughed. "Just be ready to run if any rats come out to meet us."

Mrs. Sandoval gazed up at the sky. "The forecast said we could get some severe thunderstorms today. Be careful when you're out."

"We will, Mom."

When they turned onto Hilltop's driveway, the car dipped into a big rut and bounced. Jessica grabbed the door handle and held on. "The road seemed bad when we were walking." Her voice vibrated on the rough spots. "But it's a bumpy mess in a car."

When they arrived at the front of the house, Jessica gladly got out. "Whew! I'm happy we're walking home."

"Me too!" Sophie stepped out and shut the door.

As her aunt climbed out of the car, she studied the sky. "The clouds are getting darker. Sophie, I want you to promise me that you two won't go outside if there is thunder or lightning."

"Sure, Mom. Why so serious?"

"There are a lot of trees here, and they're a magnet for lightning. Stay here until the storm passes. Jessica?"

"Yes, Aunt April."

Jessica was happy when Miss Walker greeted them at the front door since they couldn't go in if she wasn't there. They stood inside the entry as her aunt waved and climbed back into her car. Miss Walker waited beside them while Mrs. Sandoval drove away. Then she said, "Girls, I'll be working in the house, but never far away if you need me."

When she reached over to dust a table beside her—she must not like dust to be anywhere—Sophie leaned over and whispered to Jessica, "I have the weirdest sense that maybe we should have asked Mom to stay."

Thunder, lightning, and a house even Jessica had to admit was more than a little creepy didn't make her excited to see that car go down the driveway either. Even she had to wonder if it was right to be here. Jessica pulled out the photo of the house. It still amazed her that this used to be a fabulous place.

At that moment Mr. Jenkins stepped into the entryway with a big smile on his face.

Jessica tucked the photo back into her purse. "Aunt April said we could see the inside of the house. Is that possible?"

"I'm happy to show around someone who's interested in this old place." Turning toward Miss Walker, Mr. Jenkins said, "Emma Jean, go ahead and start in the kitchen. I'm going to give these two a tour."

Miss Walker bent over and reached into a bag that had paper towels and cleaning supplies sticking out of it, rifled through it, and stood back up. She said, "I stopped for supplies this morning but just realized I missed one thing. Mr. Jenkins, please let me know when Sophie and Jessica leave. I'll need to run to the store." She added, "These are smart girls, so don't leave out anything interesting." She went through the door.

He said, "Girls, I want to warn you: the house is in terrible condition. Old Mr. Laurence let it run down around him. He just kept moving his bed and desk to an area that was livable and dry. Then he moved again when that one deteriorated."

Jessica turned in a circle. A dusty crystal chandelier hung from the two-story ceiling over a staircase that split at a landing in the middle, curving elegantly to the right and left. Floors in the entry were what looked to be gray and white marble, Jessica guessed, but they were too grimy to tell. This must have been a beautiful house when it was new and when it was clean.

"I thought Miss Walker cleaned the house."

Mr. Jenkins frowned. "The city told her to only clean the areas I actually use. They said they didn't want to take advantage of her kindness by having her clean a building they may tear down." He ushered them on. "I'll show you where the old man lived."

They followed him past a closed door and down a hallway with vacant spaces on the walls from pictures, the dust and discolored paint around them leaving ghosts of what once hung there. A room with a large desk and dark wood-covered walls lined with bookshelves, all in good condition, sat to the left.

"My office," he said, pointing as they kept walking.

Jessica asked, "What happened to the paintings that used to hang on the walls?"

"Mr. Laurence had to sell them," Jenkins said glumly. "He sold most things of value in this old house to pay bills."

They entered a bedroom, or at least a room that had a bed in it.

"This was the family's informal dining room before the old man moved in here."

"Why here?" Sophie asked.

"His bedroom had always been on the second floor, but the condition of the upstairs got worse and worse. The roof leaked and some windows wouldn't close right. Mr. Laurence also had more and more trouble climbing the stairs. He decided to move to a part of the house that was in good shape and on the ground floor."

Sophie asked, "Where do you live?"

"I live in the basement," he said. "There are old servants' quarters next to a shop of sorts where things were made and repaired. It's warm and mostly dry."

The girls checked out Harold Laurence's room. There wasn't much furniture, just a twin bed, a small dresser, and what must have been a comfy chair, but now had a rip across the seat and stuffing coming out of one arm. Wallpaper with green and pink flowers had peeled off about half the walls. A cleared area in the corner looked like the only space large enough for the desk at Sophie's house.

Seeming to read her mind, Mr. Jenkins said, "The desk Sophie's mother has in her shop was there." He pointed to the spot Jessica had noticed.

Neither girl corrected him about the location of the desk. Jessica figured it would probably go back to the shop eventually anyway.

"I can answer any questions you have. Let's go to the front parlor." He led them back down the hall and opened the door they'd walked by before. The parlor was filled with dining room furniture.

"I helped him sell whatever he didn't use. The parlor's furniture was the most valuable, and he didn't leave his room in the last years, so he didn't need it. Once it was gone, I moved the dining room furniture from his bedroom space in here so visitors would have somewhere to sit other than the kitchen table."

The phone rang just as everyone had taken seats at the dining room table on worn, faded green velvet seats that matched the wallpaper in Harold Laurence's last bedroom. Mr. Jenkins stood, saying, "If you'll excuse me, I've been expecting a business call and will take it in the office." He hurried down the hall they'd just come down and Jessica heard a door close behind him.

As soon as he'd left the room, Sophie said in a low voice, "I want to check out Harold Laurence's room when Mr. Jenkins isn't there so he doesn't wonder what's going on. Maybe he left a clue there."

Jessica bit her lip. "I'd like to see too, but someone should stay here." She waved her arm at the room.

"Agreed." Sophie stood and started to walk away.

"Hurry!" Jessica said in a hushed voice. "He might be back in a few seconds." She watched Sophie disappear down the hall.

Jessica arose from her seat and nervously wandered around the room, stopping at the fireplace to pick up each figurine on the mantel to check it out—for what, she didn't know. They must not have been valuable anyway since they were still here. Another empty rectangle over the fireplace told her a picture had been sold. Knowing Mr. Jenkins would be coming back soon, she sat back down, but then stood again and pulled out her phone. *Photos of the inside of the house might be important later.*

She raced around the room, snapping pictures, then stepped out into the entrance and hurried down the hall, pausing every few seconds to take a shot. Knowing she'd been taking a chance on how long Mr. Jenkins would be gone, Jessica raced back to the dining room and stood next to her chair. Tapping her fingers on the table nervously, she wondered where Sophie was. Peering around the corner of the doorway, she saw Sophie stopped in front of the office door.

Jessica waved her over, but Sophie didn't seem to see her. Her cousin leaned against the office door, her eyes getting bigger as she did so. Then Sophie hurried over to a chair, slid into it, and pointed at Jessica's chair. Jessica sat only seconds before a smiling Mr. Jenkins walked into the room.

"Sorry, ladies. Just a small problem with my dear old mother's car."

"No problem, Mr. Jenkins." Sophie stood. "I think we've learned enough today, don't you, Jessica?"

Jessica reared backward. They'd had a tour but hadn't asked any questions. And they certainly hadn't told him about the hidden compartment in the desk.

Sophie continued smiling. "Thank you for your time. We can see ourselves to the door." And without another word, she turned and left the parlor, Jessica on her heels, and closed the door to that room behind her.

Jessica followed her to the front door. She whispered, "What's going on?"

Sophie put her finger to her lips. "Shh."

"Sophie, what's going on?"

"I don't know. But I can tell you that Jim Jenkins isn't who he's pretending to be."

As she opened the big, old door, thunder crashed overhead.

10 HIDE-AND-SEEK

Jessica had known something wasn't right when Sophie glanced back toward the closed parlor door with a spooked expression on her face. Sophie hurried out the front door, and Jessica stayed on her heels. Another, louder clap of thunder sounded, followed quickly by lightning streaking across the sky.

They whirled back around and into the house. Sophie pulled Jessica away from the entrance to the parlor and whispered, "As I walked by Mr. Jenkins' office, I heard him speaking in an angry way. I thought, *That's weird, because he seems like such a nice man.*

"When I leaned against the door, I heard him say, 'Yeah, Lester, I hear you, but get off my back. I'm good for it.' Lester must have talked then, because it was quiet. Then Mr. Jenkins said, 'The old man was loaded. I'll get my share.'"

Jessica whispered back, "Wow! Now I see why you wanted to leave."

"But we can't. I promised Mom we'd stay inside if a storm struck."

"Miss Walker is working here. Maybe we should go find her."

"Good idea!"

Just then, a little gray car drove by the window.

"Uh-oh. Mr. Jenkins must have told her we'd left."

Lightning lit up the sky again. "It's getting worse out there. I know I have to keep my promise to Mom." Sophie's breathing quickened. "I also know we shouldn't stay right here."

Jessica pointed through the doorway of the room in front of them. "Maybe we can stay *here*. It's filthy, so he probably doesn't even come into this room. Then when the storm's gone, we'll quietly leave."

Sophie glanced over her shoulder. "Maybe he won't know we were here."

"Exactly."

When they entered the room, Jessica discovered that it had a cracked window, and it looked like an animal had built a nest in the corner. "I don't think this room is on any tours."

Sophie looked around. "Me neither. Even Miss Walker has abandoned it. I'm going to go through the door on the other side of the room. Maybe it's a better place to be." Sophie slowly opened the door. "It's a butler's pantry, and the kitchen's next to it."

"A what?"

"A small room between the kitchen and dining room. I've seen them in other old houses Mom's taken me to. I guess that in the old days it was a place where a butler worked on things he was about to take into the dining room."

When they went through into the kitchen, Jessica felt a lot safer. Speaking in a normal voice, she said, "This is clean and seems like a nice, safe place to wait. I doubt Mr. Jenkins comes here very often."

Sophie pulled the old-fashioned ruffled curtains shut, closed the door that opened to the hallway, and both girls sat at the small, round kitchen table.

Jessica nervously rubbed her hands together. "Do you think Mr. Jenkins is dangerous?"

Sophie pursed her lips. "I don't know. He seems so nice. Everyone thinks he's nice."

"I assumed he was just as nice as everyone thought, even Tony. Then you overheard his conversation. Are you sure you heard the words clearly?"

"Yes. And I don't think 'Lester' is someone I'd like to meet."

A shadow passed by the curtain. "I'm glad Miss Walker is back."

"Me too!"

A knock on the door made them both jump. Jessica whispered, "*Not* Miss Walker. She has a key." A louder knock made Jessica jump again.

"That's going to bring Mr. Jenkins here in a hurry!" Sophie dropped to her knees. "We need somewhere to hide. There are two doors we haven't opened. You try that one"—Sophie pointed—"and I'll try the other. Stay low."

They crab-walked across the room, and Jessica pulled a door open. "Pantry. We could hide in the corner."

Sophie tried hers. "Stairs to the basement. Let's go." She was halfway down the stairs before Jessica could even decide what to do.

Jessica had stepped through the basement door and almost pulled it closed when Mr. Jenkins came into the kitchen and opened the door to the outside.

"Lester! What a pleasant surprise." Jessica could tell by his voice that the visit was less than pleasant.

When the men walked out of the room, Jessica pulled the door closed the rest of the way and went down the stairs. "Sophie," she whispered. "Sophie!" she said a little louder.

"Over here." Sophie stepped out of the shadows in the corner of the room. "I wanted to see if we had a way out of here, so I checked out every room, including Mr. Jenkins'." She glanced back to those shadows. "Tell me what you think about what I found."

"Sophie, we shouldn't invade his privacy. It's his room."

"The whole house belongs to the city, and this is important. Follow me."

Sophie led her through the shadows, opened a door, and they stepped into a fully furnished room. Sophie closed the door as Jessica turned in a circle, checking it all out. Paintings hung on the walls, and what appeared to be other treasures sat on shelves.

Jessica said, "Why would these things be here? Mr. Jenkins said he'd helped Mr. Laurence sell everything of value."

"That what I thought! He kept these and hid them in his room."

Jessica examined several of the paintings. "Sophie, I think at least some of these are worth a lot. They remind me of things I've seen in museums."

Sophie opened the door and peered out. "Let's get out of here. We don't know when he might come downstairs."

Jessica had just closed the door behind her when the one at the top of the stairs opened. The girls ducked into the shadowy corner. Jessica hid as far in the corner as she could fit. She bit her lip so she wouldn't yell out loud when she leaned against a rough brick, and stayed there as still as she could.

"Lester, I tell you I've got the money covered. I can lay my hands on a lot of cash in a hurry."

Lester almost growled when he said, "Then do it! I want my money now. Turn on another light, Jenkins. It's dark in here."

Sophie grabbed Jessica's arm. They'd be discovered if he turned on a bright light!

"That tiny light hanging from the ceiling is the only one that's electric, and the old gaslights don't work anymore. Old man Laurence never spent money in this part of the house." He sounded very pleased with himself when he added, "I wired my room and connected it to the electric box so it's well-lit and warm."

The door to his room opened, and he flipped on the light.

"This stuff must be worth a bundle. Sell it and give me my money."

"I've been holding on to all of this, the best of what the old man had, until I know it's safe to sell. Most of these artists are so well-known that someone might notice the sale, and I'd end up behind bars."

Lester chuckled. "Wouldn't be the first time."

"I'm never going back. I play it safe now. I'll pay you when I find the treasure."

"Right. You're going to find what no one else has. I know better men than you that tried."

"None of them were inside the house. I have access to every clue the old man left."

"What if someone else finds it first?"

"Everyone else seems to have given up. Except a couple of girls." He started to close the door. "And if they get in my way—"

The door cut off the rest of his words.

Jessica rose on shaky legs. She pointed to the stairs and moved as softly—but as quickly—as she could up them and out the door, with Sophie on her heels. When she opened the kitchen door, she saw Miss Walker drive around the corner and park. Jessica almost waved to her, then realized she might accidentally say something to Mr. Jenkins that would give away the fact that they hadn't left earlier, and that could be very bad for them.

After pulling the door closed, Jessica tugged Sophie into the hall and both girls raced toward the front door. Sophie passed her in the hall and opened the door. The weather had been so bad that no visitors were out there, so they closed the door behind them and ran unnoticed down the drive.

When they were out of sight of the house, Jessica stopped, leaning forward and panting. "The storm seems to have passed." She pointed up to patches of blue sky peeking out between the clouds.

"Jessica, we've got bigger problems than thunder and lightning."

11 HIDDEN TRAIL

Sophie thought trouble had followed them when she heard gravel crunching. Jessica had reached down to retie her shoes so she didn't seem to notice. Sophie waved her arms to get her attention, then put her fingers over her own lips to tell Jessica to be quiet when she opened her mouth to speak.

Gravel crunched again. She grabbed Jessica's arm, pulled her into the woods, and pushed her behind a boulder. Someone laughed and Sophie started to relax. When a little kid squealed, she knew it was a family and gave a big sigh of relief. Definitely not bad guys.

Both girls stood.

Sophie really looked around them for the first time. "Jessica, there's an old trail here. I wonder where it goes."

"What trail? I just see bushes and trees."

"Here." Sophie pointed at the ground. "It's a little overgrown."

Jessica slowly shook her head from side to side. "A little? I missed it completely."

Sophie pushed a branch aside. "Let's check it out. This must have been a path in the olden days. Maybe there's a clue at the end of it."

"And maybe there are only snakes and other creepy things."

Sophie grabbed the back of Jessica's shirt when she started down the trail, and held her still. "Just don't touch anything I didn't touch."

Jessica looked at her in confusion, so she added, "Poison ivy. This might be a trail that was used more in the past, but it's rarely used by humans these days. I think it's a game trail now."

"A what?"

"A trail deer and other animals use. See how it used to be a lot wider?" She pointed at the edge of the trail. "There are scruffy weeds and grass now but no trees have grown in."

"I wonder if it was used more when Mr. Laurence was younger."

"He might have walked here often if it was a special place."

"And he might have buried treasure in a special place."

"Uh-huh."

After they'd walked about five minutes on a trail that turned and wove through the trees, Jessica said, "This makes Cutoff Trail look good. At least the bushes and bugs weren't crowded around me."

They stopped at a fork in the trail. "Which way, Sophie?"

Sophie pointed to the right as if she knew the way, but she wasn't sure. She didn't want to admit it, but taking this path might not have been her best idea. Every step took them farther away from the road into an unknown she might have trouble backing her way out of. They passed two trees that had grown twisted together. "This is unusual, so we can remember it, if we get lost."

"Are we going to get lost?"

"No one knows they're going to get lost, or they wouldn't do it."

Jessica glared at her.

Sophie pushed aside a tree's branches and a flock of birds exploded into the air.

Jessica clutched her hand to her chest. "That's it. If we don't find civilization in the next two minutes, we're turning around."

Sophie gulped. She wasn't sure she could get them back to the road. She pushed through the trees and stepped into a clearing, or at least what had been a clearing in the past. Grass stood about a foot tall and would be much taller later in the summer.

Jessica stepped beside her. "I'm sorry I doubted you."

"I was actually getting a little, um, concerned, myself."

Jessica rubbed her arms nervously. "I'm glad I wasn't alone on that."

Shifting bushes caught Sophie's eye. She whispered, "I see something moving. Over there." She pointed toward a clump of trees.

A deer stepped out from the trees, saw the two of them, and flicked its tail in the air before running off through the woods.

Jessica's voice shook when she said, "I need peace and calm. Two mysteries so close together have made me edgy." She looked down just then and stared at her arm.

"Is something wrong?"

Jessica moved her arm so Sophie could see it. A key about the size of a candy bar was imprinted on it.

Sophie reached out and touched the red mark. "How did you get this?"

Jessica shook her head. "I don't know. Wait! I do know. I was pressed against a rough brick when we hid in the basement. The brick must have had the key design on it."

Sophie shook her head in amazement. "Jessica, this may be a clue."

Jessica rubbed her arm. "It's already starting to fade away. How do we get back into the basement to search?"

"Let's figure that out when we're done here." Sophie motioned around them. "We're near Hilltop right now, maybe even on Hilltop's land, so let's examine everything here very carefully." Sophie started around the clearing. "And be careful of plants with three leaves together. It's probably poison ivy."

They both explored. Jessica stopped for quite a while at a tall, skinny bush, so Sophie walked over to see what she'd found.

Jessica pointed. "I thought this was a big bush at first, but it was funny-shaped. Look closely." Stone peeked out between the green leaves.

Sophie squatted down to see the bottom of it. "It's an old fireplace and chimney!" She tugged at the vines.

Turning in a circle, Sophie said, "I'm guessing this was a cabin that burned down. Look: there are stones that make the edge of it, and there are some scattered on the ground." She stopped and stepped inside the remains of the old cabin. "Maybe we should check under each of the stones."

"That would be so much work." Jessica glared at them. "But I just remembered what Lenny and Mr. Jenkins said about us. If we find the treasure, maybe they'll move away. On second thought, I'd be happy to check those stones."

Sophie turned away from her cousin, who now crouched on the ground and pushed stones back one by one. Starting on the chimney, Sophie checked each of the stones.

A half hour later, Jessica stood and groaned. "My legs are aching. I don't know if this is helping, Sophie. Anything over there?"

Sophie stepped to the side of the chimney. "I've pushed on about half of the stones here, hoping one is loose and hiding something."

Jessica moved over to the chimney. "Walking feels so good." She bent to her right side and stretched one leg, then the other. "Did you check inside the chimney to see if there was anything odd?"

Sophie moved around in front of it. "I think the only thing that would be odd is if I stuck my head up a chimney."

"Still . . ."

Sophie sat down and scooted backward into the fireplace. "You know, this is so big that I can almost stand up." As she tried to do that, a storm of dirt, leaves, and soot poured down and out.

Coughing, Jessica ran about ten feet away. When the dust settled, she asked quietly, "Sophie, are you okay?"

Sophie crab-walked out of the fireplace, covered in debris, but with her shirt pulled up over her face. "I felt it starting, so I made sure I'd be able to breathe. I feel okay."

Jessica came over to her and pulled an eggshell off her head. "I think a bird must have made a nest in the chimney." Jessica cleared her throat to hide the laughter that tried to bubble up.

Sophie saw the shell and started giggling. Standing, she stretched. "I don't think we'll find any clues in this chimney. Let's see if there's anything else in the clearing." Sophie reached down and picked up a couple of skinny tree branches from the ground. "Lift branches up with this. Oh, and, be careful of anything that moves."

"Because . . ."

"There could be snakes."

Jessica froze with one foot in the air. "Now you tell me?"

"Well, they like to lie in the sun, and the sun's coming out."

"Just call me Wilderness Woman." She took a stick from Sophie and walked around the clearing.

Sophie could hardly believe her eyes. "Why aren't you running away?"

Jessica kept working. "I hate to admit it, but I want to know if there's something here that will help us solve the mystery and find the treasure."

Sophie laughed. "I've got you hooked." She leaned over and poked around in the weeds with her stick.

"I know I want to find the treasure, if there is a treasure, before Mr. Jenkins does."

Sophie said, "Ouch!" and rubbed her knees. "My legs hit . . . I don't know what." She used her stick to pull aside bushes and weeds. Stones like those in the fireplace were stacked on top of each other and formed a circle with a hole in the center.

"It's a well. I saw one at an old house in England."

"Let's clear the area to look for anything that's unusual about the well." Sophie held a bush up on her stick. "This is strange. These bushes seem to be dead, like someone piled them here."

They both reached in and swiped at everything with their sticks. When they'd cleared it all away, they walked around the circular well.

Sophie leaned over the well's opening. "It's deep."

"Be careful, Cousin!" Jessica held on to the back of her shirt.

"I'm okay." Sophie picked up a small rock from the ground and dropped it in. A splash came seconds later. "It sounds deep."

Jessica knelt at the side of the well. "I thought it would be made of rough stones, but it's kind of pretty. The stones are smooth. Here's one with a key on it. Mr. Laurence did love keys."

"What if it's a clue, Jessica?"

"It's a rock in the side of a well. I don't plan to go down in the well to see if something's hidden there."

Sophie thought about the wet, dark hole she'd tossed the rock into. "I don't think I do either." Dropping her stick, she said, "We should head back now, before Mom has a chance to worry."

"Definitely. I think we've panicked and worried enough for all of Pine Hill today."

"You got that right." Sophie studied the area around them. She didn't want to add to Jessica's worry, but she wasn't sure where they were.

Jessica watched her. "Uh-oh. You don't know how to get us out of here."

Sophie made herself smile. "Sure, I do. We can go back the way we came. But I'm not loving the idea of getting that close to the mansion again today."

"Me neither."

Sophie circled the clearing and found another trail, maybe the same trail, as it kept going into Pine Hill. "There's a path heading this way, and I think that's the way to town." She pointed. "The good news is that if I guessed wrong, we'll probably find the lake and know to go the other way."

"That is good news. Well, your woods skills are better than mine, since those are nonexistent, so you lead and I'll follow."

Sophie chose a trail and they went down it for a while. Then she went to the left at a fork in the trail and they followed it for a few minutes. Feeling as if she'd led them deeper into the woods instead of closer to town, she stopped, a panicky feeling working its way up her body.

"You're lost, right?" Jessica asked.

"Maybe just a little bit." Sophie held her thumb and forefinger close together.

"If we had a hill to climb, maybe we could see around us."

Sophie snapped her fingers. "Of course, I should have thought of finding a high point. I'll climb a tree." Staring up into the trees around them, she chose one with a heavy branch low to the ground. Moving over to the base of it, she climbed onto it and worked her way up the tree. Just over the height of Jessica's head, she could see beyond them to the lake.

Sophie pointed. "It's like I said. I can see the lake, so I know we go that way"—she pointed to her right—"to get to town."

"I'm very glad to hear those words. I've had enough excitement for one day."

12 SHARING SUSPICIONS

Fifteen minutes later, the girls could see the town. Sophie was more relieved than she'd expected to be. There were people here. "I may normally like being in nature, but I'm happy to see buildings right now."

"I am too. I've been thinking as we walked. We should tell Sheriff Valeska what happened at Hilltop."

Sophie sighed. "You're right. Part of me doesn't want to because she'll probably say she can't do anything about it and that we may have misunderstood his words."

"Part of *me* agrees with you, Sophie. The other part thinks we'd better tell her so she knows Mr. Jenkins may not be as nice as everyone says."

"Right."

They went down Main Street, then stood across the street from the sheriff's office for a minute. "I say we go in, Jessica. You with me?"

Jessica nodded once. "I'm with you."

Sophie said, "I don't think there's any point in telling her about the desk. We don't know if it matters."

"Agreed. We stick to what just happened."

When they stepped inside, they were greeted by the new

secretary, Clare Morton, who hadn't looked happy to see them the few times they'd stopped by since she'd taken the job.

Sheriff Valeska called out from her desk. "Can I help you ladies?"

Sophie and Jessica looked at each other, then went over and sat down in the chairs in front of her desk.

Sophie spoke first. "Sheriff, we just found something out, and it's going to be hard to believe."

The sheriff leaned back in her chair. "That wouldn't be the first time with you, Sophie. Go on."

Sophie began with going to Hilltop and told her what she heard.

Then Jessica picked up the story with going downstairs. "Mr. Jenkins scared us when he said he'd do something to two girls who were also looking for the treasure if they got in his way."

Sheriff Valeska looked startled. "I agree that the situation sounds odd. Who have you talked to about your treasure hunt?"

"Sheriff, we didn't tell anyone that wasn't trustworthy," Sophie said. "You didn't tell anyone I don't know about, right, Jessica?"

"No. We only talked to your parents and Nezzy about it. I don't think any of them would tell another person what we'd said."

The sheriff nodded. "While that all makes sense, how could he have known? Did you make a mistake today and give him that impression?"

"Uh-uh. We said we were interested in seeing the old house. And we were interested in it."

Someone coughed and they all turned that direction. Clare Morton said, "Sheriff, I might be the one who said something."

"You!" Sheriff Valeska tapped her fingers on her desk. "Tell me what happened."

"April Sandoval stopped by the other day and mentioned that the girls were searching for the lost Laurence treasure."

Both girls both swung back toward Sheriff Valeska.

"We hadn't talked for a while, and she stopped by to visit. I see that expression on your face, Sophie. Your mother did not come here to tell your secrets. Continue, Clare."

"I passed that nice Mr. Jenkins on the street, and since the treasure ties into Hilltop, I mentioned that two girls were looking for it."

"I see." The sheriff did not look happy. "Why did you do that?"

"He seems so harmless and is always polite and nice. And I thought it was funny." She smiled at them. "I'm sorry, but they're just kids."

"Clare, everything that is said in this office, *everything*, is confidential. You aren't to tell a single person outside of here anything you've overheard. You're new in town, so you don't know that earlier this summer, these two girls foiled a criminal plan and helped us arrest the culprits."

"Really?" She looked from Sophie to Jessica with an expression of disbelief.

The sheriff added, "It would matter to someone that these two were also looking for the treasure."

"Yes, ma'am."

"We'll talk again later, Clare." Turning to Sophie and Jessica, she said, "Here we are again, with me telling you to be careful. I'll check into Jim Jenkins' background and see if something turns up."

———

Walking away from the sheriff's office, Jessica said, "It's just sinking in that Mr. Jenkins definitely knows that we are searching for the treasure—"

"And that he did mean *us* when he talked about *two girls*."

Jessica shuddered.

"Even I thought this would be a fun little mystery."

"I know. Something to make summer vacation more interesting. We were bored, but . . ." They arrived at Sophie's favorite bench on the sidewalk, the one she always went to when she needed to think.

"The main question is: does this change anything?" Sophie sat down. "Other than us having to keep our eyes open for anything unusual."

Jessica stood beside the bench. "Remember when I said I saw someone wearing black at the cemetery?"

"The crow!" She turned to Jessica. "I'm sorry I doubted you."

"I only caught a flash of black and thought, *Who would care about us checking out a grave?*"

"So you think he's been following us." Sophie started to twist in her seat, then faced forward. "You're standing, so it won't be as obvious. Casually look around us."

Jessica shaded her eyes and checked first down the street, then around in a circle until she could see up the street. "I don't see anything odd. He could be inside a building, watching us, though, and we wouldn't know it."

Sophie stared at the building across the street. "You're right, of course. We need to move into danger mode. We can't assume at any time that we aren't being watched. Well, other than when we're inside a building ourselves. Away from the windows."

"Soph, I wonder if we should tell your parents about what happened today. I can keep it a secret from my parents, since they aren't here and would only worry."

Sophie chewed on her lip. "If we tell my parents, they'll worry too. Remember how they were with the last mystery? Everything turned out fine, but both my parents and yours were a mess."

Jessica said, "Images from that mystery just flashed through my mind. Your parents called my parents. Wow, did they worry. As much as I want to tell them, I guess we should wait until Sheriff Valeska learns for sure who Mr. Jenkins is."

"Yes. Let's wait until we know more."

13 VIEW FROM ABOVE

When Jessica and Sophie entered Great Finds, Mrs. Sandoval held up two small pieces of paper. "Look what I got! The mayor heard about a carnival that was passing through this area and talked them into coming to Pine Hill for a weekend between locations to do a fund-raiser to save Hilltop. I agreed to donate some of my sales from this weekend to help save the mansion, so the carnival owner gave me and others doing the same thing free passes for the whole family."

She waved the tickets in the air, then frowned and held them close to her chest. "No, you wouldn't like to go to a carnival and go on the rides as many times as you wanted, would you?"

Sophie grabbed at the tickets, but Mrs. Sandoval moved faster and hid them behind her back. "It sounds like fun, Mom."

"Your father and I could meet you at the carnival when I've closed for the day. And we can eat dinner there."

Sophie put her hand on her chest. "Eat fair food? For dinner? Mom, are you okay?"

Mrs. Sandoval laughed. "Just this once. Don't expect us to do this kind of thing very often. And only one dessert."

"I can live with that. How 'bout you, Jessica?"

"Absolutely. I'd like a break from this mystery."

When she heard Sophie gulp, she realized her mistake. What if her aunt asked if they'd learned anything new? She wouldn't lie, and she knew Sophie wouldn't either, but she wasn't sure what her aunt would do if they told her.

Mrs. Sandoval turned and started toward the back of the shop. "I have to put prices on some things that just arrived. You girls can head over to the carnival right now. We'll meet you there about six."

————

Jessica could hear carnival music as she and Sophie turned down the road to Hilltop. When she could see the mansion, she could also see people swarming over Hilltop's grounds like the hornets around Cody a couple of days ago. There were lines at every ride and all of the food booths.

They gave their tickets at the gate, then wandered around a bit. Sophie stopped in front of the cotton candy booth. "Do you have any money with you?"

"My allowance. I'm not going to buy *that* though." Jessica pointed at the fluffy sweet. She didn't eat sugar straight out of the package, so she didn't see how that could be any good.

"Come on. It's pure sugar. Either pink or blue."

"Maybe I've lived in other countries too long, but that doesn't sound good to me, so unless they come up with a chocolate variety, I don't want to try it."

"Are you saying you've never eaten cotton candy?"

"Uh-huh."

"I need to talk Mom into it. *Everyone* needs to try cotton candy."

They continued on, and Jessica stopped at the deep-fried candy bars.

Sophie held up her hands. "Seriously? After what you said about the dessert I wanted?"

"You're right. But it does sound fun."

"We must both be getting hungry. I hope Mom and Dad get here soon."

After going on three different rides, Jessica felt as if she would forever be spinning and turning from side to side. Holding on to her head, she said, "I need a break from rides."

Sophie slowly turned in a circle. "It's still too early for Mom and Dad. What do you want to do?" She stopped. "Hey, there's Mr. Donadio, Tony's dad. Maybe Tony's here."

Jessica looked that direction. "Where?"

Sophie pointed at a man wearing navy blue pants and a light blue polo shirt.

Jessica felt her face flush as she scanned the area. "Do you see Tony?"

"No. Mr. Donadio is alone right now and seems to be in a hurry."

Jessica looked straight ahead and up. "Let's go on the Ferris wheel."

Sophie grimaced. "After all of the fast-moving rides we've been on, why would you want to go on an old-fashioned Ferris wheel?"

"Ferris wheels are quiet. And they don't move much."

"Exactly."

"I've been flipped from side to side, spun in a circle, and sped downhill screaming enough today. Quiet wins."

"I'd rather flip, spin, or speed again, but I'll go with you."

"And we can't talk about the mystery."

"But—"

"I need a break, Soph. Just peace and quiet."

"Okay. You got it."

The girls showed their tickets, climbed into the seat, and were latched into place.

When the Ferris wheel began its slow circle, Jessica leaned back and felt the stress of the mystery become less and less as they climbed higher and higher. "This is what I needed. And I've never seen Pine Hill from more than a second-story building."

"I think we'll have a good view of the lake from the top." Sophie leaned over the side. "Staring down at all of these people makes me realize that I should never search for clues on the grounds of Hilltop. Too many people have gone back and forth across here over the years. I'm glad we get to have fun here today, but I'm certain we won't find anything to do with the mystery tonight."

When they'd almost reached the top, Jessica pointed to the ground on her side of the Ferris wheel. "There's Mr. Donadio again." She paused for a few seconds. "Oh, no! He's talking to Mr. Jenkins."

"This is a small town, and they know each other, so they must just be *talking*."

"No. Mr. Donadio handed something to Mr. Jenkins, and he handed something back to him. Now they're shaking hands."

Sophie twisted and turned in her seat, obviously hating it that she couldn't see what was happening. When she leaned forward, Jessica grabbed her arm. "Hey, you'll fall out. They're both gone now anyway."

Sophie blew out a breath. "I missed the whole thing!"

Their seat rolled over the top of the wheel and started down the other side.

"Now that I can see below us, there isn't anyone special except my second grade teacher. Miss Becker was nice."

The ride made a few more rotations; then they found themselves stopped at the bottom again, and the attendant was lifting the protective rail so they could get out. As they stepped off the ride, Jessica searched the crowd for Mr. Donadio.

Sophie blew out a deep breath. "I *still* don't see either Mr. Donadio or Mr. Jenkins."

"Sophie, what should we do about what I saw?"

"I don't know, Cousin. It's probably easily explained. I don't want to think Mr. Donadio could be a criminal too."

"Me neither." Jessica scraped her toe on the ground. Suddenly looking up, she said, "What if Mr. Donadio doesn't know about Mr. Jenkins and ends up in danger because we didn't tell him?"

Sophie grimaced. "I hadn't thought of that. I figured he was an adult and could take care of himself. But no one else in this town knows what we know about Mr. Jenkins. They *all* think he's a great guy."

"Soph, we need to find out more. We need to talk to Tony."

"If I didn't know you were a nice person, I'd think you were trying to find a way to bring Tony into another mystery."

"He did help last time."

Sophie sighed. "Yes, he did. I wanted the two of us to solve this one together."

"Maybe next time."

Sophie grinned. "I love that you're into mysteries now."

Jessica held up her hand. "Don't get too happy. I don't think there will be another mystery in this small town in the near future."

"You said that last time."

"I know. I thought we were safe searching for treasure that hundreds of people had searched for."

Sophie checked her watch. "It's almost dinnertime. We're going to have to wait until tomorrow to see Tony. I don't think we should talk to him about it on the phone."

"Definitely not."

"Let's see if Tony's at the deli in the morning and talk to him outside, where no one can eavesdrop."

"It's a plan." Jessica pointed. "I see your dad now. I'm going to push this out of my mind and have fun tonight."

"Me too. Fair food for dinner? I want to enjoy every bite, because I'll probably be ready to graduate from high school before Mom says we can do that again."

"That's the truth. She loves to eat healthy."

They hurried up to Mr. Sandoval.

"Sophie, your mother has a surprise," he said. "Come on, both of you."

As they turned to follow him, Jessica could hear loud voices from the other side of the carnival, growing louder with every step they took. When they could see the source of the shouting, they found a woman on a seat overhanging a water-filled dunk tank. People threw balls at a target on the side of the tank, hoping to hit it and drop her into the water.

As they neared it, Sophie shook her head. "I wouldn't want to be that woman."

"Your mother surprised me when she agreed to hop up there."

Sophie pointed. "That's Mom?"

Mr. Sandoval nodded.

Jessica giggled. "At least she didn't ask you to do it."

They watched for a few minutes. Then Mr. Sandoval got a sneaky smile on his face that reminded Jessica of his daughter. He left for a few minutes and returned with a basketful of balls.

"Do you girls want to give it a shot?"

Sophie spun around and stared at her dad. Then she got that same smile. "Yes, I do." She picked up three of the balls and stood in line.

Jessica pictured her aunt falling in the water because of a ball she'd thrown. "I think I'm going to pass on this."

Mr. Sandoval said, "Go ahead, Jessica. April won't be angry. She did it to support Hilltop."

"If you're sure . . ."

He nodded.

"Okay." Balls in hand, Jessica waited behind Sophie. "I doubt I'll hit anything."

Sophie turned toward Jessica, her dark brown eyes sparkling. "I was on the softball team when I was little. I'll hit it."

When her turn came up, Sophie stepped forward and her mother cried out, "Oh, no!"

Sophie took aim and threw the ball. A bang signaled the ball hitting the target, and a splash told the rest of the story. Jessica handed the balls back to her uncle. "I think one person in the family knocking her down is enough."

He gave the balls to some people watching off to the side. "You may be right. Let's get something to eat."

14 GUILTY DAD

When Jessica and Sophie found a list of chores posted on the refrigerator the next morning, Sophie groaned. "At least there isn't any housecleaning involved. We don't have any clues to chase this morning, and the deli won't open until 11:00 a.m, so helping Mom is no biggie."

She read through the list again. "This is Dad's handwriting, so Mom must have called him. She wants us to bring paper towels from home to her shop and to mail some things at the post office. We can do all of that this morning."

Sophie carried the three-pack of paper towels under one arm. When they were about a block from Great Finds, Sheriff Valeska drove by in a sheriff's car. She pulled over to the curb, and as they were passing by, rolled down the window. "Are you girls being careful?"

"As careful as we can be when we're not sure what we're being careful of."

The sheriff blinked, then nodded. "It's surprising to me, but I actually understood what you meant." She motioned them closer.

Sophie leaned in the car window and asked in a low voice, "Any news on Mr. Jenkins?"

"Nothing."

Sophie stood so quickly she bonked her head on the window frame. She rubbed the spot and winced. "How is that possible?"

"When I say 'nothing,' I mean absolutely nothing. It's as though he didn't exist until he started working for Harold Laurence."

Jessica leaned next to her, "What does that mean?"

Sophie pointed to her chest. "I know. He isn't who he says he is, right?"

"Most likely. I don't know any more yet. I hope to soon. In the meantime—"

Sophie interrupted. "Be careful."

"Yes. We don't know who he really is. He might be a nice man who just changed his name because he didn't like it. But he might also have a criminal reason for his name change."

As they watched Sheriff Valeska drive off, Sophie said, "Let's hurry up so we can get to the deli."

"I hope your mom doesn't ask us to work and make it so we can't get to the deli."

"I agree. We *need* to talk to Tony, but I don't want to tell her—or anyone else—about what we saw until we know more. It wouldn't be right for people to think badly about Mr. Donadio if he's innocent."

Mrs. Sandoval was busy with a customer when they got back to the shop. They put the supplies away in the back, picked up the mail where she said she'd put it, along with the cash needed to pay for the postage, and hurried back out. Sophie gave a little wave to her mother as she opened the door to leave.

Mrs. Sandoval called out, "Come back here this afternoon. I have a couple of projects for the two of you to work on."

"We weren't fast enough," Sophie said to Jessica as the door closed behind them.

"You could never be fast enough to get out of work with your mom."

Sophie shrugged. "True."

Once they'd reached the post office, they waited in line, mailed Mrs. Sandoval's things, then hurried over to Donadio's Deli. Every time Jessica pictured them talking to Tony, it didn't go well. "Sophie, it might stand out less to everyone else if we eat lunch and try to talk to Tony quietly there."

"You're probably right. It's a good thing we *did* save our allowance."

Tony placed the Open sign in the window as they arrived. Eating earlier than normal, they had the deli to themselves. As the glass door closed behind them, Sophie whispered, "Remember: the fact that we're searching for the treasure and all of the clues we've found are secrets. We're only here to ask in a sneaky way about Tony's dad so we can take him off the list of suspects. Since everyone thinks Mr. Jenkins is super nice, we'd better only tell Tony about him if we absolutely have to."

Jessica could keep a secret with the best of them. "Yes. We'll be subtle. I won't tell any secrets." Scenes of their last mystery flashed through her mind. Jessica had spilled the secret to Tony then. Heat climbed up her neck, which she knew made her face red. "I really *can* keep a secret."

"I hope so."

"I know I didn't keep the secret last time, but I will this time."

As they ordered their food from Tony, Jessica felt melty inside.

Tony smirked as he set their food on the table minutes later. "Hot on the trail of any criminals?" He walked over to the counter and picked up a spray bottle and rag, then sprayed the table beside them and started wiping it off.

Jessica leaned forward. "T-r-e-a-s-u-r-e," she said slowly.

Sophie stared at her cousin. "Jessica!"

"I opened my big mouth again, didn't I?" The secret spiller had struck again.

Tony stopped what he was doing and eyed them suspiciously. "Actual treasure?"

Sophie said, "Sort of." She wavered her hand. "Yes, but no."

"Yes, you found treasure or yes, you're searching for treasure?"

Jessica excitedly added, "We're hunting treasure." She did a happy dance in her seat. "I love how those words sound. Jessica Ballow, treasure hunter."

Tony threw down the rag and sat in a chair at their table. "With pretty much anyone else, I'd say, no way, you won't actually find treasure. But you guys have a track record."

Sophie said, "The 'yes, but no' is that it's the Laurence treasure."

He pushed back his chair. "Not only have I looked for it, but my parents, grandparents, and great-grandparents all looked for that treasure. They didn't find anything, and as far as I know, no one ever has."

Jessica said, "Yes, but we know things no one else in town knows."

Sophie poked her cousin's arm. "Jessica!"

Jessica sheepishly said, "I'm sorry."

Tony leaned forward. "What?"

Jessica stared at Sophie. Then Sophie said, "Okay. Tony helped us last time."

"Give." He motioned forward with his hand.

Sophie glanced over at the door when it chimed, announcing a group of four people entering the restaurant. "I think we should talk to you outside, Tony."

The girls got up and went outside. Tony joined them a few minutes later.

Jessica took a deep breath to calm her nerves and asked him, "How well do you know Mr. Jenkins?"

"How well?" Tony shrugged. "He's a customer. He lives in Pine Hill."

Sophie scanned the street, probably to make sure no one could overhear her, but leaned closer to Tony anyway. "Mr.

Jenkins hasn't been to your house for dinner? Your dad doesn't play golf or bowl with him or anything like that?"

Tony scrunched up his face. "No. Why are you asking me that? Hey, you aren't investigating my dad, are you?" His face quickly turned stormy.

Jessica touched his arm. "We don't want to. It's just that we saw your dad at the carnival last night." She didn't add that she'd seen him with a criminal.

"So what? Most of the town was there." He crossed his arms over his chest and glared at them.

This wasn't going well.

"Sophie, let's just tell him."

"Tell me what?" he said.

"We saw your dad with Mr. Jenkins, and it looked like they were doing business together." When Tony seemed confused, Jessica added, "Mr. Jenkins is not who you think he is."

Tony raised his hands. "This is about Mr. Jenkins? He's a nice guy. What are you talking about?" He stepped toward the door of the deli. "I need to get back to work."

"We overheard Mr. Jenkins talking to another man. There's no question that they're both criminals, and Mr. Jenkins is conning the town."

"That's ridiculous. He took good care of Mr. Laurence and everything in the house."

"Tony, he has many of the house's treasures in his room in the basement, treasures that everyone believes were sold to help Mr. Laurence."

He leaned against the window. "He couldn't. I know for a fact that Mrs. Bowman's sister cleans Hilltop. She would have seen that and told her sister, and you know Mrs. Bowman can't keep a secret."

"Mr. Jenkins does her a favor by not having her clean his room."

"Wow. It's hard to believe." He suddenly stood up straight and his eyes narrowed. "But you asked about my father."

Jessica explained what she'd seen.

Someone else walked past them and into the deli. "I have to get back to work," Tony repeated. "When I see my dad, I'll tell him you saw him at the carnival and see if he explains why." He opened the door to the deli. "And if I can, I'll come over tonight, and you can tell me what other clues you have."

As the door closed behind him, Jessica blew out her breath. "I wasn't sure about that for a minute."

"Me neither. I didn't think enough about this to realize we were accusing Mr. Donadio of being a criminal. That was stupid."

"Yes, it was. We might have lost a friend for our carelessness. I hope Tony has good news for us tonight."

Just then, Nezzy's housekeeper, Amanda Easton, walked by the deli. She carried a bag with the town's craft store's name written across it in bold red letters. When she noticed them, she stopped. "I'm glad to see you girls. Walk with me while I go to the candy store. Nezzy loves their cherry-filled chocolates."

She raced down the sidewalk, and they hurried to catch up with her.

Sophie said, "It must be fun to work for Nezzy."

"Oh, my, yes. She's delightful, but a little demanding." Miss Easton smiled to soften the comment. "I just bought her a new book for her memories. This will be her second one this year, her B. She asked me to invite you over to go through her many memory books, if you'd like to."

Jessica pictured being bored for hours reading through an old lady's memories.

Sophie gave a polite, but not-quite-real smile. "Please thank her for the offer."

Jessica said, "I've never heard of memory books. That must be something you do around here."

Miss Easton stopped. Laughing, she said, "Of course you'd say no to something with that name. They're scrapbooks filled with things from Nezzy's life. Mr. Laurence was her friend, so many of the memories have to do with him."

Sophie felt her heart race. They'd figured the newspaper wouldn't have much to help them, but they might finally get some answers from the scrapbooks. "Can we come over tomorrow afternoon?"

Miss Easton smiled at them. "Certainly. I'll expect you at two." She waved as she hurried away, turning the corner onto Dogwood where Sophie knew the candy store sat.

"Jessica, we'd better get over to Great Finds. Let's hope that the work we have to do is something we don't mind."

"I just hope I don't have to dust. I've learned that there's a lot to dust in a shop filled with antiques."

When they got to Great Finds, they discovered that they were to unpack some new items. Mrs. Sandoval directed Jessica to one cluster of boxes, and Sophie to another. Each item was to be carefully unwrapped. Then Mrs. Sandoval would price the item and set it in its proper place for sale.

Jessica peeled bubble wrap from around a large, green-and-yellow vase. "I love doing this. It's a little like Christmas."

Mrs. Sandoval said, "I feel that way too, even though I saw everything when I bought it. We have one more box to do, and then we can all go home to dinner."

After dinner, Sophie offered to do the dishes and said Jessica would help. When they were alone in the kitchen, Sophie explained, "I did this for a reason. I thought we could talk about what we'll do if Tony's dad turns out to be one of the gang." Sophie rinsed dishes and handed them to Jessica to load into the dishwasher.

"Now that I've had time to think about it, I doubt that's what we'll discover. Mr. Donadio isn't someone who just came to town. He's lived here a long time."

"As long as I remember."

"Let's assume he's okay." Jessica tucked a pot into the corner of the bottom rack. "I hope that's all the dishes, because this is almost full."

"That's it." Sophie added, "The more I think about asking Tony about his dad, the more I realize that we might have started something ugly. Let's wait on the front porch so we can talk to Tony alone when he gets here."

Jessica blew out a big breath. "Good idea. If there is a problem, maybe we can talk to him quietly before we have to tell anyone else."

"Like the sheriff."

"Yes, like the sheriff. I still have the photo and keys in my purse. I'll get it so we can show them to Tony."

They sat on the porch, Jessica on a rocker and Sophie on the porch swing. A car pulled into the driveway at about seven o'clock. Tony stepped out of the car, closed the door, and waved as his dad backed out and drove away. Then he walked toward the girls, carrying a bulging bag that he held up when he got closer.

"Ice cream and toppings. We can make sundaes."

"Chocolate?" Jessica asked.

"Of course. I wouldn't forget the hot fudge sauce for you. Or the strawberry sauce for Sophie. And I have whipped cream and nuts."

Sophie and Jessica looked at each other. Did this mean everything was okay? Which one of them should ask? Jessica pointed at Sophie.

"Is everything all right at home, Tony?"

"Very subtle. I did what I said and told my dad that you'd seen him at the carnival. He got upset."

Sophie stood up. "I'm sorry, Tony."

"No, not because he was guilty of something." He motioned for her to sit back down. "Because he was handing Mr. Jenkins a bill for a dinner the deli catered at Hilltop for Mr. Jenkins and some of his friends."

Jessica beat her to asking, "Why would that upset him?"

"He'd mailed the bill to Mr. Jenkins six months ago and again two months ago, but it hadn't been paid. Mr. Jenkins said it never arrived, so Dad told him he'd personally bring it to him at Hilltop. Except when he got there—"

"There was a carnival." Sophie did sit down now, feeling more relieved than she thought she would at learning that Mr. Donadio wasn't guilty.

"Dad had to track him down at the carnival. You saw him handing Mr. Jenkins the bill and Mr. Jenkins handing Dad a check for the amount." He lifted up the bag again. "Are you ready for dessert?"

"Always," Jessica held open the door for him and he carried it through to the kitchen.

Inside, Sophie explained to her parents that Tony had brought dessert. Her mother didn't want a sundae, but her dad asked for one with hot fudge. Sophie made his, brought it to him, and fixed her own after Tony and Jessica.

The three of them took their sundaes onto the front porch— Sophie returning to the porch swing, Jessica and Tony each taking a rocking chair. All three dove into their frosty desserts.

When they were about halfway done, Tony asked, "Do you have any actual clues to the treasure?"

Jessica held up her purse and stared at Sophie, who nodded once. Jessica pulled out the photo and two keys. She started the story of how they'd found each, with Sophie jumping in to add things Jessica'd missed.

Tony took the photo of the house from Jessica, turning it over to check the blank back. "It just says 'Hilltop.' He handed it back. "I know the story of the gold in the moonlight. I don't see anything that seems like a clue. Who knows what that second key fits?"

Sophie hated to admit it, but Tony was right. How would these help them find treasure?

"These things must be clues," Jessica said, laying the keys and photo on the arm of her rocking chair. "Two of them were hidden in secret compartments in Harold Laurence's desk."

"That makes them more interesting, but I still only see a photo and two keys, one that's already been used for its purpose. The photo says, 'Hilltop.' That isn't very helpful."

Tony stared into his ice cream. "Nezzy Grant told you the desk was important?"

Jessica dipped her spoon into the fudge sauce. "Uh-huh. I know it looks like an old photo and keys, but who would hide unimportant things that well?"

Sophie held her spoon in the air. "Especially the second key, the larger one. That took a while to find."

Tony reached over and picked up that key, turning it over in his hand. "I admit this *key* could *unlock* the secret of the lost treasure . . ." His voice trailed off and he grinned, obviously waiting for comments.

Jessica groaned. "I can't believe you said that."

Sophie snickered. "I can't believe I didn't say it."

Laughing, Tony added, "When you consider the number of doors and other things with keyholes in Pine Hill, this could take a long time."

Jessica scraped the last bite of hot fudge from her bowl. "We could never try them all."

Sophie set down her empty bowl and reached for the photo. "Wouldn't Mr. Laurence want someone to find the treasure? Otherwise, why leave the key in the desk?"

Continuing, Sophie said, "I just thought of something: what if Mr. Laurence wasn't the man in the woods that the doctor saw that night? It was dark, and the doctor was in a hurry."

Jessica tapped her fingers on her cheek. "I see how you're thinking. Or what if it was him, but it wasn't really a bag of gold? Maybe it was a bag of nails to build his house, or something else that could shine in the moonlight."

Sophie added. "Or a stranger who was about the same size as Mr. Laurence and had his hair cut similarly who did have gold, but he put it on a wagon and drove away with it that night?"

Jessica said, "Oh my, Soph, that is good."

Tony added, "Or we may be missing something. Go over everything one more time. I have to work tomorrow, my family is doing something that night, and Sunday we're taking inventory at the deli. I can't help either day."

Jessica said, "Did we tell you that Mr. Jenkins asked about us at Bananas?"

Tony stopped with his spoon halfway to his mouth. "Let me get this straight. You just told me that Mr. Jenkins knows you're looking for the treasure because Clare at the sheriff's office goofed?"

Sophie said, "Right. But he hasn't bothered us."

"He asked about you two at Bananas. He told Lester about two girls. And you're certain that Mr. Jenkins isn't a nice man."

A clatter sounded when Sophie and Jessica both dropped their spoons.

Jessica reached to pick hers up from the porch floor. "I don't like hearing all of those things combined."

"Sophie and Jessica, you'd better be careful and keep looking over your shoulders."

Tony's dad pulled into the driveway a short time later, and they watched him drive away with Tony. Even with what their friend had said, Jessica knew the treasure was out there and they would be the ones to find it. She also knew they had to be very careful.

15 CLEANING FOR CLUES

Sophie wasn't sure she'd fall sleep with all of the clues running through her head, but she'd dropped right off. Probably because she was so tired.

Stretching in bed the next morning, Sophie could see Jessica moving around like she was awake. "Let's grab something for breakfast in town this morning and get right on the mystery. We didn't come up with anything new last night."

Neither she nor Jessica had mentioned the key mark on her arm to Tony the night before. She felt a little guilty about that, but she wanted to see if the two of them found anything first. Besides, he had to work and wouldn't be happy about not being in on the search.

Jessica grabbed her robe, but didn't say a word as she headed for the bathroom. She must realize she woke up grouchy. Mornings hadn't always gone well before they'd come up with the system of having her head straight for the shower without conversation.

When the door closed and the shower turned on, Sophie said, "Whew! I'm glad we figured this out." She picked up a book to read as she waited for Jessica.

"Much better," Jessica said a short time later when she

stepped out of the bathroom, rubbing her hair with a towel. "I thought anything I tried to say this morning would come out grumpy."

"It amazes me that someone as smart as you can't work around that." Sophie climbed out of bed, headed into the bathroom for her shower and came back afterward feeling ready to take on the day. She found her cousin putting on makeup.

Jessica set her mascara down on the dresser. "I didn't fall asleep for a while last night. I think chocolate is a good idea this morning."

"Chocolate for breakfast? Where? And can I get something without chocolate there?"

"A chocolate chocolate-chip muffin from Bananas would work."

An image of one of Mrs. Bowman's awesome banana-blueberry muffins popped into her mind. "Deal."

"Let me get my sneakers and jeans on."

When Jessica was ready, she searched for Sophie and found her dressed and on the front porch. The cousins walked down the porch steps, but then Sophie paused. "Shortcut through the woods or beside the road?"

Jessica stepped beside her. "I never thought I'd have to pick one over the other because of bad guys again." She looked to her right toward the woods, then down the driveway to the road. "Road. I think we'd better be careful."

"Yes. We haven't seen anyone dangerous yet—"

"Hold it. Mr. Jenkins and Lenny were creepy and sounded dangerous to me."

"I guess I was trying to see them as fellow treasure hunters."

"Who just happened to sound scary when they talked about us?"

"I see your point. The road wins."

As they walked beside the road, Jessica said, "We need to check out the inside of Hilltop. *Really* check it out. And we have to see if the brick with the key on it is part of the mystery."

"I know. The mansion has to be the answer to everything. We didn't have a chance to search for clues inside the house." Sophie snapped her fingers. "I remember that Miss Walker works at the mansion on Thursday and—"

"Saturday," Jessica said. "I'm fairly certain Mrs. Bowman said that. Since she was at the mansion two days ago . . ."

Sophie pumped air with her fist. "Yes! She must be there today. Maybe we can look around inside when Mr. Jenkins is at lunch."

"He could come back any second. And how would we explain being there again? I lay in bed last night trying to come up with a way around Mr. Jenkins. I don't want to try to search again when he's there. And he isn't only there sometimes. He lives in the mansion, so he's almost always there."

They walked without speaking. Jessica was trying to come up with a plan and figured Sophie was too.

After a bit, Sophie said, "Maybe we'll get a break in the case and Mr. Jenkins will go to the city for the day. Or fishing. Or something else."

"Those things only help a little, because Miss Walker will probably tell him we were there when he arrives home later today, and it will stand out if we were the only unexpected visitors."

The girls opened the door to Bananas—and froze. The man they'd been talking about stood at the front counter, handing Mrs. Bowman cash. With his usual smile on his face, he said to her, "I'm sure these muffins will be delicious as always."

Mrs. Bowman blushed. "You'll have some homemade muffins for your drive and the first couple days of your vacation. Make sure you eat a good breakfast the rest of the week."

"Nothing will be as wonderful as what you make." He picked up a yellow box and turned to leave. When he spotted them, he said, "I hope you girls didn't get drenched in the storm two days ago."

Thinking quickly of something honest to say, Jessica politely answered, "No, sir. We ran down the road when we left."

Mrs. Bowman put her hand on her cheek and sighed when he went out the door. "What a nice man."

Jessica could tell that Sophie was having to grit her teeth to not tell her the opposite. "Is he going on vacation to a beach or somewhere beautiful like that?" Jessica watched him climb into a car parked at the curb and drive off. This could be their chance.

"He never says. Mr. Jenkins is here almost every day when he's in town, but he's gone about a week most months. He always brightens my morning when he comes in."

Sophie and Jessica quickly bought a muffin each, Jessica's filled with chocolate and Sophie's fruity, ordering them to go instead of choosing to sit at one of the small tables Mrs. Bowman had recently added.

Outside, Jessica said, "I'm so glad we heard that."

"Mr. Jenkins will be gone from Hilltop for days." Sophie stood in front of Bananas with the bag of muffins clutched in her hand.

"Soph, are we going to eat our muffins?"

Sophie held out the bag as if she were in a trance.

"Hello? Sophie?"

"Huh?" She blinked at Jessica. "Oh, sorry. I've been trying to figure out a way for us to get back inside Hilltop, but have it seem natural, not like we're on a treasure hunt. It's city property, so it's legal for us to be there, but I don't think we should ask for another tour."

An idea popped into Jessica's mind. She tugged on Sophie's sleeve and pulled her over to a bench on the sidewalk. "Sit. Eat. I have an idea."

An hour later, they were knocking on Hilltop's kitchen door. When Miss Walker answered, Sophie spoke. "We noticed when we visited before that there was more work here than you had time for. Jessica and I would like to help."

Jessica held up a bucket filled with cleaning supplies, all borrowed from Great Finds. "The room at the front of the house is so pretty that we wanted to make it shiny and clean."

The older woman smiled and ushered them inside. "That's kind of you two. As much as I hate to admit it, I can't do much more than clean the same rooms each week in the two days I give to the city. I have too many other things going on in my life to take on the rest of the house."

Miss Walker walked them into the connected room. "Now that they've voted to tear it down, there probably isn't a point, but I'd like to see it clean one more time. If you girls need me, I'll be upstairs. I'm working on a project in one of the bedrooms."

The girls pulled out their cleaning supplies as Miss Walker left. When she disappeared up the stairs, Sophie said, "I wish your idea hadn't included us cleaning."

"I hope it's worth it."

Sophie pulled on rubber gloves, opened a trash bag, and started filling it with garbage. "Let's clean as quickly as we can so we'll have time to check things out. I want to make sure we have lots of detective time while we're here."

Jessica glanced around the room and started for the door. "There's icky stuff in piles on this side of the room's floor." She left the room, returning minutes later with a broom. While sweeping, she said, "You know, Sophie, Mr. Jenkins has lived here for years. He must have checked everywhere for the treasure."

Sophie set aside the bag of trash and picked up paper towels and window cleaner. She sprayed a window, then wiped it dry. "I know Mr. Jenkins did everything he could think of, but he didn't have the clues from the desk." Sophie stepped back to see her work, nodded approval, and moved on to the next window.

"Uh, Soph?"

"Yes?" Sophie turned around to find Jessica staring at the

floor. "The animal that got inside left these little brown pellets behind, didn't he?"

Sophie laughed. "Yes, he—or she—did. And you definitely want to wear gloves if you get anywhere near those pellets."

"I thought so. It's poop." Jessica put her gloves on and wiped the messy part off the floor, then carefully dropped the paper towel into the trash bag. "Yuck. I can't believe I'm actually doing this. It's even harder for me to believe that I'm doing this so I can help solve a mystery."

When they'd almost finished, Sophie stepped back and looked around. "This must have been a fancy room when it was new."

"I know." Jessica dropped a final paper towel into the bag. "I'll dust and you get the mop."

A half hour later, Sophie said, "Gorgeous. We finished quickly."

"It's pretty now. Let's hurry downstairs and see if that brick is important. After that, we can go through the rest of the house. I hope Miss Walker is too busy to check our progress."

"Me too. She thinks Mr. Jenkins is wonderful and would tell him about our treasure hunting."

They hurried to the kitchen and down the stairs. Sophie pulled out a small flashlight she'd tucked in her back pocket and pointed it at the corner.

Jessica knelt and ran her hand over bricks until she found the rough one. "This is it!"

Sophie knelt beside her and pushed on the sides of the brick. "I think this is loose. I need something to pry it out with."

Jessica stood and ran around the room. "I finally found a screwdriver on a workbench in the corner." She moved beside Sophie and put the blade of the screwdriver into the area beside the brick, working it loose. When it was about to fall, Sophie caught it.

Jessica said, "Nice save. That might have made a crash that would be heard throughout the house." Sophie shone the light into the hole left by the brick, and Jessica tried to see inside. "There's a white thing in here." Jessica reached into the hole and brought out a wooden box that wasn't much larger than the photo they'd found.

Sophie shone the light on it. "This box has a key painted on it."

"Mr. Laurence sure liked keys." Jessica lifted the lid and Sophie leaned over to see. "A piece of paper is inside. It's yellowed, so he must have put it here a very long time ago."

"37B is written on it. Nothing more. What could that mean?" Sophie picked up the brick and slid it back in place. "We'd better get out of here. I don't want Miss Walker to tell Mr. Jenkins we were down here. He'd wonder why."

Back upstairs, they returned to the room Mr. Jenkins had left them in while he was in his office. Sophie said, "We can spend more time on the box when we leave here. Let's search the mansion while we have the chance."

Jessica wandered through the parlor, now dining room. "What are we looking for? Do you have any idea? Or is this another of those 'we'll know it when we see it' times?"

"To answer your questions: I don't know. I don't. And yes."

Jessica laughed.

They went from room to room. "Whatever we're looking for wouldn't be obvious. It has to be a place that wouldn't have occurred to Mr. Jenkins."

Sophie paused at the stairway and gazed up.

Jessica said, "I don't think we can explain why we're upstairs. Unless you want to clean more."

Sophie shook her head. "Considering the holes in the roof, I have a feeling that the upstairs is much worse than the main floor."

Jessica brushed her hands on her pants. "I've had enough of this place. Dirt and things I never, ever wanted to get close to are all around me. And on me. I don't think there are any clues here." She sat on the bottom step, feeling discouraged.

"I'm surprised, but I agree with you."

"Really?" Jessica brightened up. "I thought you'd tell me we had to keep at it, that we'd find the clue if we tried harder."

Sophie sat beside her. "I'm starting to think you're right about what you said earlier. If there was a clue in here, if the treasure was in the mansion, Mr. Jenkins would have found it earlier. He didn't find the brick, probably because it was in a dark corner of the basement, but I bet he's been through every inch of the rest of the house." She stood. "Let's go home."

"Oh, thank you! We said we'd go to Nezzy's this afternoon, and I want to get that done so I can take a shower to wash all of this grime off me." Jessica stood.

They shouted a good-bye to Miss Walker and grabbed their bucket of cleaning supplies.

Walking toward the door, Jessica said, "Sophie, something just occurred to me. I've thought of finding the treasure as another mystery, something we need to solve."

"It is. What's your point?"

"This may be a mystery, but it's also a lot of money—if what the story says is true. What are we going to do with all that money if we find it?"

Sophie brushed off the front of her shirt with her hand. "If it's in Hilltop or anywhere on the property, the treasure belongs to the city."

"True. What if it isn't?" What if it's somewhere that no one owns, and we can keep it?"

"I see pictures of things I could buy flashing in front of me." Sophie grabbed for the doorknob, holding on tight. "Whew. Thinking about this makes me light-headed."

"Me too. We'd be rich."

Sophie chuckled. "What am I thinking? It wouldn't matter, because our parents would decide what we do with it. They'd be happy if we paid for college."

"Maybe we could do something great with it, perhaps help people."

"I hope we get the chance to figure it out."

Jessica said, "We'd better hurry. We need to get to Nezzy's by two."

"I keep thinking, where else could the treasure be hidden, Jessica? It must be here."

"I wonder if the clue we just found is sending us to a new place. But what's a 37B?"

Sophie patted the pocket of her backpack, which held the box. "Let's make a list of everything that could have a 37B."

"I think that will be a short list. If we decide it might be at Hilltop, we can come back next week—if Mr. Jenkins hasn't returned."

"We need to walk faster to get to Nezzy's on time. Let's think about the next step in solving our mystery on the way."

Jessica held up her hand to hide a smile. Sophie could sound so mysterious. Then she stopped smiling. Last time they'd gotten involved in a mystery, it had gotten more than a little dangerous. Maybe she shouldn't be smiling too much.

16 THE MEMORY ROOM

Climbing the steep stairs to Nezzy's house, Jessica said, "We can spend an hour or less here and still have time to do some other sleuthing today. I don't see how it could take very long to flip through a few old scrapbooks."

When they rang the bell, Miss Easton opened the door and ushered them inside. "Nezzy is resting. I'm to take you to her memory room."

Sophie and Jessica followed the older woman. The house-keeper led them down a hall and stopped at double doors. She reached for handles on the doors and pushed the doors to the side into pockets in the wall. An antique-looking orange-and-gold sofa straight ahead caught Jessica's attention when she stepped into the room. Her Aunt April would probably like it. It wasn't until Sophie gasped that she turned her gaze upward.

Sophie's voice shook a little when she said, "They're filled with books." She cleared her throat. "The shelves are filled with what must be hundreds of scrapbooks."

"Three hundred and thirty, to be exact," Miss Easton said. "There will be three hundred and thirty-one when Nezzy finishes the book she's working on now."

Jessica gulped. They'd be here longer than an hour. A lot

longer than that if they needed to go through every one of these books.

Sophie said, "Nezzy knew Mr. Laurence most of her life, so he could be in almost all of them."

"Quite true. Each is labeled by year." Miss Easton pointed at the spine of the newest book. "I'll leave you girls with your project. If you need anything, pull that cord and I'll come." She pointed at a heavy gold cord hanging next to the sofa.

When she'd left, Jessica asked, "Which 165 books do you want to do?" She giggled.

Sophie stared up at the shelves. "This is a *giant* job. Maybe we should start at the beginning." She crossed the room. Running her finger along the edge of the shelf, she said, "Nezzy's a great record keeper. They're not only labeled by year, but she also has an A, B, C, etc., for the order of them in the year." She pulled four of the scrapbooks off the shelf and handed two to Jessica, who carried hers to a round table in the middle of the room. Sophie sat down on the sofa with her two.

Jessica carefully opened the old book and gently turned the pages. It was filled with photos and other pieces of memories, like a dried flower or a ticket from an event, each held in the book by the little black corners they were tucked into. A strip of paper with a description typed on it was glued under each item.

When she reached the end of the first book, Jessica pushed it aside and opened the next one. "You know, Sophie, this really is searching for a needle in a haystack, as our grandfather likes to say."

"I know. I'm trying to stay positive. We're not only searching through hundreds of books, but we don't have even a small idea of what we're looking for. We're just hoping there's a great clue somewhere in all of this." Sophie waved her hand toward the full bookshelves.

Jessica watched Sophie finish one book and open her second.

"Jessica, hold it. What if—" She stood and went over to the bookshelves, following them along the wall again.

"Soph, what are you doing?"

"37B."

Jessica whispered, "Just like in the box." As she stood, her chair fell backward, but she caught it just before it crashed to the wood floor. Righting the chair, she said, "Bring it over here" and pushed her two books to the side.

Sophie did and set it down. Then she flipped through the pages one by one. About halfway through, one page landed harder than the others. "This page seems different."

Jessica leaned in closer. "Different how?" She lifted it up. "Sophie—"

"What?"

"It's thicker at the top."

Sophie flipped the page back and forth. "You're right."

"The typed words under it say, 'Harold and I in front of the new stained glass windows he bought for the church.' This must be a clue he wanted someone to find."

"I agree."

Sophie laid the book flat in front of her and slipped one corner out of the black piece that held it.

"Careful."

When she'd taken it out of the second black corner, Sophie lifted the photo up and tilted the photo album. A tiny envelope fell out.

Jessica picked it up. "Someone wrote, 'My dear Nezzy Grant' on this. I think it's the same handwriting as the envelope with the key."

Sophie stared over her shoulder at the closed door. "I, um, wonder, um, if we should open it."

"Sophie!"

"Okay. You're right. Let's find out if Mrs. Grant can see us now." She pulled the cord, and it wasn't long before Miss Easton opened the door to the room.

When they told her what they'd found and showed her the envelope, she smiled widely. "Let me take this upstairs. I think

Nezzy will want to see you." She left with the memory book and envelope.

While they waited, they flipped through the rest of the book.

Jessica said, "Other than learning about things that happened in 1937, I don't see anything else that seems to be a clue."

"Me neither."

Miss Easton returned and gestured them over. "Nezzy's very excited. Follow me."

Nezzy's over-the-top decorating style continued at the top of the stairs. What must have been family portraits going back hundreds of years, all in big gold or silver-colored frames, lined the purple-painted hallway.

Jessica said, "I feel like I'm in a castle in England. They often have many old pictures like this. Of course, not with a purple wall."

Miss Easton said, "These aren't Nezzy's relatives. She visited a castle and wanted her home to be like the castle."

Sophie and Jessica grinned at each other, and Jessica wondered whose relatives these were.

When they entered Nezzy's room, they found her propped up in bed. The walls of the room were covered with framed pictures of what must be her actual family and friends, since they were mostly black-and-white photos. From the way people were dressed in them, some must have been taken about the same time as the photo in the 37B book.

"Sit, girls, sit." The old lady pointed at two chairs Miss Easton must have brought over, since they were beside the bed. "It seems my dear friend left me one last note." She held up the envelope and the piece of paper that had been folded up inside it. "The message is actually for you two."

"Us?" Sophie pointed at herself, then Jessica.

Nezzy nodded. "He left other clues, and someone had to be clever enough to figure out those clues and come here. I didn't mention this before, but Herbert loved mysteries whether it was a book or a movie."

"Me too!" Sophie said.

Jessica added, "She does *love* a mystery. That's how we end up in the middle of these things."

Sophie leaned forward. "Is there a clue in the letter?"

"No."

"No! Are you sure?"

Nezzy cackled. "I'm sure. The treasure's story is in this letter. There is a treasure."

Sophie leaned back and fanned her face with her hand. "Wow. A real treasure. I hoped . . ."

"You girls are the first to get this close. Herbert wrote:

"My dear Nezzy,

If you are reading this, you or someone else has most likely found the photo in the desk and the hidden box."

Nezzy looked up at them.

Sophie answered. "Yes. We just found the box."

She nodded and continued:

"Those clues have brought them to you. Tell them to study the photo and the caption. It will lead them to the treasure. I also want the story of the gold to be out in the open now.

"When my father was young, he rode on horseback with a group of four friends in the Wild West. One day, one of them pointed at a wagon train in the distance and commented that it was probably coming from a mine. Another one said they should rob it and be set for life. All agreed to the plan, except my father. He tried to talk them out of it and rode along, hoping to find a way to stop them. But he didn't and they robbed the train, which did have gold from a mine, but in a crazy twist, the gold was under the control of other robbers.

"Those men shouted that they'd hauled that gold a long way and it was theirs. They had a shootout. My father jumped onto the wagon and drove it off so the shooting would stop. The men with my father all trusted him, so when they caught up with him, they asked him to take it to a town, put it in boxes, and ship it home. He did box it up, but

shipped it another direction, hoping to be able to return it to the mine later. He never could figure out which mine it had come from.

"My father moved here, took a new name, and hid the gold. I melted it down and hid it."

Sophie stood. "What a story!"

"Yes. Herbert was a good man. He has one more sentence about the treasure: *'I made sure the gold belongs to Pine Hill.'"*

Jessica stared at Sophie. "That must mean that it's on land that belongs to the city of Pine Hill."

Nezzy said, "Yes. He left his land and home to the city. He added for me: *'And my dear Nezzy, I made my money investing in oil. I never told you that because you love a mystery almost as much as I do.'"* She gave a big grin. "Another mystery solved."

She stared at the open memory book lying beside her in the bed. "Isn't he handsome in this picture? Harold was a perfectionist and meticulous when he was younger. Everything had to be just so."

The girls looked at each other and Jessica shrugged. This didn't sound like useful information, but they'd be nice to her. "Yes, ma'am. You mean how he dressed?"

"Everything. When he paid for the church to be built, the builder didn't put the right stained glass window in the right window hole in the church. He had them remove all five of them and install them again as he requested. And I remember way back, before his early cabin burned down, that he rebuilt the old well there. He said it wasn't in good shape. I said, 'Who cares? You don't live there anymore.' He just nodded and did it anyway."

Sophie said, "We found what was left of a cabin in the woods. I wondered if it belonged to him."

"His father had a larger house, not the mansion, but a good-sized place in the same location as Hilltop. Harold wanted to make it on his own, so he built his cabin when he was young. He moved into the new mansion he built later—Hilltop—and it wasn't too many years before a lightning bolt hit the cabin, burned it down, and that was that."

Nezzy suddenly seemed tired, and Miss Easton stepped forward.

Jessica stood. "Thank you for seeing us."

Nezzy flapped a hand in reply.

The girls walked out of her room, down the long hallway with fake relatives, down the stairs, and out the front door without saying a word. When they reached the sidewalk in front of Nezzy's house, Sophie leaned against the iron fence.

"I can't believe it," she whispered.

"You were right, Sophie. There is a treasure."

"Shhh." Sophie glanced around. "If everyone knew what we just learned . . ."

"There'd be a stampede of treasure hunters."

"Yes. We have to keep it quiet." She held her lips together and turned them like a key. "Locked."

Jessica did the same. "Locked. Now what?"

"Today is"—she looked up as she thought about it—"Saturday! Tomorrow is Sunday. We go to the church and figure out what's in the stained glass windows. There *must* be a clue there."

17 SEARCH THE CHURCH

Sophie sat on the end of the bed as Jessica picked up the blow dryer and stood in front of the mirror. Her cousin went through the clothes she had hanging in Sophie's closet, slipped into a light blue dress, and put on some shoes with a small heel.

Sophie rubbed her hands on her own jeans. She'd chosen her newest pair today, so they weren't faded, but maybe she should dress nicer for church. Fingering her usual ponytail, Sophie wondered if she should care more.

She walked over to her closet. There weren't many of her clothes hanging in it. You didn't need to hang jeans and T-shirts. At least she didn't. "I'd like to wear a prettier shirt to church. Could I borrow one from you?"

Jessica stopped with her brush in her hand. "I like brighter colors than you do. And girly things."

"I wore my one dress not long ago."

"You can wear anything of mine. Go through my side of the closet." Sophie turned and saw Jessica in front of the mirror, putting on makeup. Should she try her new lip gloss?

Sophie flipped through Jessica's clothes. She could pick one of Jessica's tops and not have to wear a dress to dress up. Sorting through the tops one by one, she pushed each hanger to the side as she considered it. Everything there was a bright color, had pretty girly things like ribbons, or both.

A shirt at the end caught her eye. It was a simple pullover, not that different from her usual T-shirts in that way, but it looked fancier. The one problem was that it was—she swallowed hard—bright pink.

After removing it from the hanger, Sophie pulled off the basic brown tee she'd put on earlier and slipped the new top on over her head. Standing beside Jessica, she checked out her reflection in the mirror.

Jessica stopped putting on makeup and watched Sophie in the mirror. "Cute."

Sophie felt that a flashing neon sign would be less noticeable. "Are you sure?"

"Oh, definitely. You're cute in it."

"Okaaay."

By the time she'd found her pair of nice shoes in the closet, the black ballet slippers her mom had bought her since Jessica had come, Sophie had decided she *might* like to look like a girl . . . sometimes. She'd gone far enough though. No lip gloss.

When Sophie stepped out of her room, her dad shouted, "Pink?"

She felt her cheeks turn the same color as the shirt. "I thought I'd look nice."

"You do. It isn't that I don't think you're beautiful in it. I think you're beautiful no matter what you wear."

Sophie hugged him. "Thanks. I'd like to get to church a few minutes early."

He rubbed his ears. "The shock from seeing you dressed up must have damaged my hearing. Did you just ask to be somewhere early?"

"Daaad."

He stared at her. "Why?"

Sophie gave what she hoped was a sweet smile. "Do I need a reason?"

He raised his eyebrows.

"Okay. We're looking for a clue."

"I have to admit that I didn't see that coming. Why would there be a clue in the church?"

"Because Mr. Laurence paid to have the church built. Maybe he made sure the builder added something that's a clue."

"That's a long shot." Smiling, he added, "I'm happy to leave early though."

As they drove, Mrs. Sandoval twisted to see the girls from the front seat and asked, "How have the cousin detectives been doing? Anything new?"

Sophie sat up straighter. "We're doing fine."

Mrs. Sandoval looked first at her, then at Jessica, with a puzzled expression.

Sophie slouched in her seat. "We're kind of stuck. But today we're going to check out the church." She explained why.

Her dad asked, "What did Sheriff Valeska have to say about the things you found hidden in the desk?"

Sophie stared out the window. "Um, nothing."

Her dad pulled the car over to the side of the road and turned to the backseat. "Does that mean you haven't talked to the sheriff about this?"

"Yes." She turned toward him. "What would I say? 'We found hidden compartments with stuff, and we don't know if it's important'? She'd just shake her head." Sophie didn't add that she wanted to keep the hidden compartments a secret.

He stared at her for a few seconds. Then he started up the car and pulled back onto the road.

Sophie waited for a couple of minutes, then couldn't take the silence anymore. "Are you driving to the sheriff's office?"

"They're closed on Sunday."

Sophie wasn't sure if that meant she was off the hook. Or if he planned to call the sheriff at home.

Mr. Sandoval added, "I've thought about it and you're right: she probably will shake her head."

Sophie breathed a sigh of relief.

"Even so, I'd like for you to talk to her in the next couple of days and tell her what you found. It won't be you stopping by to tell her something that doesn't matter. It will be because I sent you."

Sophie nodded. "That's true. And she already knows about Mr. Jenkins."

He pulled to the side of the road again. "What about Mr. Jenkins?"

Sophie swallowed. "Um, that he isn't who he says he is."

Mr. Sandoval slowly asked, "Who is he? And I hope it's good news."

"It isn't. We overheard him." She went through the story with Jessica adding in pieces she forgot. "But we told the sheriff about that."

He let out a deep breath and started driving again. "Why didn't either you or Mandy Valeska tell us?"

"It hasn't seemed dangerous. He pretends to be nice. Maybe she didn't tell because she didn't find anything out about him."

They pulled into the parking lot beside the church.

As they climbed out of the car, Mrs. Sandoval stared up at one of the stained glass windows. "What do you girls expect to find?"

Jessica answered, "Something, anything, that appears to be a clue."

She looked down at them. "That's rather vague."

"That's the detective business, Mom."

They went up the front steps, through the doors, the small entry, and into the church. Five stained glass windows, two on each side and one at the front, rose above them, seeming to dare them to find a clue in them or somewhere else in the church. The sun pushed its way through the clouds at that moment and lit up the rainbow colors of glass.

"Wow!" Jessica said. "I never noticed how different stained

glass looked inside than out. I guess I never paid attention. It's gorgeous when the sun shines through."

They were so early that only a few other people were there, and they sat talking to each other.

Jessica leaned close to Sophie. "What should we do, just walk around and stare at each window for a while?"

Sophie said in a low voice, "Yes. But try not to attract attention to yourself."

Jessica leaned closer to Sophie. "I'm not sure that's possible, Soph. Twelve-year-olds don't usually spend much time fascinated by stained glass windows."

"Just do your best."

"I'll look at the two on the other side."

Sophie studied the first window she came to on her side. Many bright colors of glass surrounded a dove. As she stepped in front of the other window on that side of the church, this time one with the image of a man, she noticed Jessica go from a stained glass window on the opposite side to the steps that led up to the raised area at the front of the church.

When Jessica turned toward Sophie, she gestured for her to go up the stairs. Jessica looked around, probably to see if anyone was watching, and shook her head slightly from side to side. Giving one last glance at the window, Sophie went over to Jessica.

"Find anything?"

"Not that I can tell. There are lots of pieces of glass, making gorgeous pictures."

"Let's go see the one at the front of the church." She stepped forward and Jessica put her hand on her arm to stop her.

"Sophie, the church isn't empty anymore. There are *a lot* of people here."

Sophie glanced over her shoulder. Jessica was right. The pews were filling up quickly. She stared longingly at the front of the church. "I really want to see this one. It's huge and has Jesus with a man kneeling at His feet, plus lots of decorative things around them. We could find a clue in any one of those things."

"Your parents are motioning us over. We have to go sit down."

As they hurried to their seats, they saw Mrs. Bowman across the aisle, and both Sophie and Jessica leaned over to say hello.

"Hello, girls." She smiled broadly. "It was so nice to have both of you and that nice Mr. Jenkins in my bakery at the same time."

"Yes, ma'am." Sophie saw the minister going up the stairs to the pulpit.

"And he even called late yesterday to say he was relaxing on the beach and needed to order a cake for next week. So nice," Mrs. Bowman added. "Maybe your mom will send you over to buy a dessert for the family this week."

Sophie patted her shoulder and hurried to sit down. It was frustrating to be so close and not be able to see if they had a new clue. Or not. She had to keep pulling herself back to the minister's sermon.

When the service ended, her parents sat waiting for everyone else to leave. People gave them odd stares when they just sat there.

When only a handful remained, Mr. Sandoval said in a low voice, "Go to work, girls. See if there are any clues in the large window."

Mrs. Sandoval gently pushed his side. "I think you're curious too, Lucas. Why don't you walk up there with them?"

"I think I will." He winked, then followed them up the stairs. "Anything interesting, girls?"

Sophie examined the window in silence. She turned to Jessica. "Do you notice anything, Cuz?"

"I know detectives are supposed to make note of anything unusual, but I haven't studied stained glass before, so it all looks unusual to me."

"Yes. Pretty but still stained glass. Jessica, take photos with your phone. We can go over them carefully later."

Mr. Sandoval said, "You can download them to my computer so you can see them on a larger screen."

Sophie's brow furrowed. "Mom said you were working on a big project and we shouldn't bother you. Are you done?"

"I did a lot on it and am now trying to keep my work to daytime hours. I like spending the evening with your mom and you girls."

Jessica snapped photos of the glass, then stood back to get photos of the room.

Mr. Sandoval said, "Maybe the sun will come through the window and an arrow will shine onto the wall, pointing toward the treasure."

Both Sophie and Jessica giggled.

As they started to walk out the front doors, Sophie said, "Take some photos of the entry too. And outside around the church. Let's go over everything again later."

18 AFTER HIM!

On the church steps Sophie whispered to Jessica, "I'm not sure what to do next. I wonder if Nezzy could help us more."

"I guess. Maybe." Jessica raised her hands in the air in obvious frustration. "Actually, I don't know."

"Mom, is it okay with you if we visit Nezzy? Then meet you at Great Finds?"

Her mother pulled out a key. When she started to hand it to Sophie, she paused. "Soph—"

"Moooom. You can trust me."

After hesitating for a moment, her mother dropped the key in Sophie's hand. "Let's all have lunch first. Then you can be on your way."

They went to a Greek restaurant they'd gone to before, and everyone had enjoyed. Tony and his family sat at a nearby table.

"I never thought about it, but I guess even people who own restaurants go out to eat." Jessica dipped her bread in hummus.

Mr. Sandoval stabbed a bite of his meal with his fork. "I would think they enjoy it when someone else cooks and cleans up for them."

"Just like I do when you cook dinner, Sophie," Mrs. Sandoval added.

Jessica leaned over to Sophie. "Maybe Tony could come with us today."

Sophie glanced over to his table. "He said something about doing inventory, but his whole family is there—both brothers and his sister—so maybe he isn't needed." She gave Jessica a not-too-serious glare. "Since you've told him about our mystery."

Not wanting to say enough that anyone who overheard knew about their treasure hunt, Sophie walked over to the Donadio's table and asked if Tony wanted to hang out with them for the afternoon. She gave a single wink and hoped he'd realize they wanted him to help with the mystery.

Tony grinned, said he did want to go, and both of his parents agreed.

As they left the restaurant, her parents going one way and the three of them another, Tony told them, "Whew. Thank you for getting me out of doing inventory. I don't like having to go through every single thing upstairs and in the basement and checking it off. It takes hours."

Passing a mostly empty parking lot by a doctor's office, Sophie watched a man slowly climb out of a car parked in a shady corner at the other side of the lot. As he stepped out, he glanced around constantly. When he stood up straight, he looked their way for a second.

"Isn't that Mr. Jenkins?" Sophie turned away from the man to hide her face and pointed his direction.

Jessica squinted. "I think so. He's moving pretty quickly."

Sophie turned back. "He is now. I thought he said he was going out of town for a week."

Tony said, "Maybe he changed his plans. People do that."

"No. Mrs. Bowman told me at church that he'd called her to order a cake for next week and said he was enjoying his vacation. It's odd because he didn't act like he recognized us when he looked our way."

"He was probably thrown off by you in something other than

faded jeans and a white T-shirt. I'm wearing a dress. We both look different. And Tony's dressed up too."

Mr. Jenkins glanced around one last time as he slipped into an alley.

Sophie made a split-second decision. "Let's follow him." She started in that direction.

Jessica called, "Soph, you aren't dressed for pursuit of a suspect."

Sophie noticed her cousin staring at the borrowed shirt, not at the dressier shoes.

"I know, but his being here doesn't make sense." She tugged on Jessica's and Tony's sleeves. "I'm following him. I'll be careful with your shirt, Jessica. You don't have to come if you don't want to."

Jessica rolled her eyes. "Like we'd let you chase a bad guy alone."

"We're coming." Tony added.

When they peered around the side of the building into the alley, Mr. Jenkins was ducking through a doorway toward the end of the alley.

Sophie surveyed the alley and stepped into it. Waving Jessica and Tony over, she said, "This dumpster is the only place to hide."

Jessica stopped in her tracks. Pointing at the dumpster overflowing with trash, she said, "I'm not getting in there."

"Yuck. Me neither. I can smell it from here. Let's hide beside it." She crouched in a place where she could see the door Mr. Jenkins had gone through and hoped he wouldn't leave by another door. Her cousin and Tony crouched beside her.

"Phew!" Jessica put her hand over her nose. "This place stinks. I hope we don't have to wait here very long."

After about fifteen minutes, Sophie stood. Shaking first one leg and then the other, she said, "This didn't go how I'd planned. Sneakers would be better. I'm only going to wait here another five minutes."

At that moment Mr. Jenkins stepped into the alley, glancing around just as carefully as he had before. When he walked their direction, they all jumped behind the dumpster, Sophie grimacing as her sleeve brushed against it.

Mr. Jenkins turned right at the end of the alley and they silently followed him. One block later, he went into another alley. The girls and Tony peered around the corner and saw him exit the alley on the other side, turning left this time.

Tony said, "He's zigzagging through town like he's hiding from someone. I wonder where he's going."

"Wherever it is, we're following him there. Something's up."

"Agreed." Jessica glared at Sophie's sleeve. Sophie followed her gaze to a dirt mark. This chase might cost her a couple of months' allowance if she had to buy Jessica a new shirt.

When they reached the end of the alley, Mr. Jenkins walked quickly away from town and away from the buildings that had hidden them up to that point.

Sophie stopped and raised her hand to block the sun, noticing the color of her sleeve—the hot pink sleeve that was connected to the hot pink shirt.

Jessica pointed at the fading shape of their suspect. "We're losing Mr. Jenkins! Why aren't you following him?"

Sophie gave a frustrated groan. "I can't follow him in a shirt this color. It would be like a bright flag being waved as we walked."

"Can't you crouch low or something?" Tony asked. "There must be some way to hide."

"Even if I crawled, he'd still see a bright blob following him!"

Jessica bounced on her feet. "You're the detective. Think of something, and *fast*. What would a famous detective do?"

Sophie spun on her heels and saw the alley behind them with new eyes. Another dumpster, this one filled with boxes, caught her eye. She ran over and grabbed a large box.

Tony and Jessica stared at her as she tucked the flaps into the box.

Tony asked, "You've had some crazy ideas before, Sophie. What on earth are you doing?"

"Let me find out if this will work. Please watch to see the direction Mr. Jenkins is going."

Jessica turned around, glancing back every minute or so. Sophie lifted the box over her head and lowered it over herself. She grabbed the underside of the box and held on, then tried to run over to Jessica, something that didn't work because the box trapped the top of her legs, and they couldn't move very quickly.

Jessica giggled. "You look like the losing entry at a costume party. We'd better hurry—if you can. Mr. Jenkins went over that hill." Jessica pointed to the left. "If I'm not mistaken, that would be the—"

"Cemetery. My guess is that he's over at Mr. Laurence's grave."

"Hold it. The cemetery? Why would he go there?" Tony asked.

"One of the weird things about our treasure hunt happened there." Sophie told him about the fresh dirt on the grave site.

"And the crow. I don't think we told you about it."

"Right. Jessica is pretty sure she saw someone dressed in black watching us."

Tony frowned. "I thought this was a nice, simple treasure hunt. Nothing like that last mystery."

Sophie started toward the cemetery, saying, "This mystery has been different. But it's anything but simple."

After just five minutes, Sophie's arms began to hurt from holding on to the box. At the entrance to the cemetery, she stopped and leaned against a tree so she could let go of it for a minute. "This *seemed* like a good idea."

"Cousin, it's probably the only thing that would work from what was lying around in an alley. And that no one would care if you used. Unless you wanted to climb into the dumpster to see what it held."

"I would for a clue."

Tony snickered. "I bet you would."

Jessica shuddered. "I'm glad you didn't have to today, for two reasons." She held up one finger. "You'd probably stink, and I'm standing next to you." Holding up another finger, she added, "And because I wouldn't even consider wearing that shirt again if you did."

Sophie pressed her lips together in a frown. "I'm not sure Mom would let me in the house without a shower." Standing upright again, she said, "Let's go."

They went into the cemetery and toward Mr. Laurence's grave.

A minute later, Sophie ducked behind a tall gravestone, folding her knees into the box as she tried to crouch. "Someone's over there." She tilted her head to the left. "Near Mr. Laurence's grave, as I suspected. I wish we had binoculars."

Jessica pulled her phone out of her purse. "I have a binocular app on my phone. I've never tried it." She fiddled with her phone and handed it to her.

Sophie peered around the gravestone, holding up the phone. "It works. I can tell it's him, and I'm pretty sure that looks like Mr. Laurence's grave. But we're too far away even with this to tell what he's doing!"

"Let me try," Tony said.

Sophie handed the phone to Tony, and he slowly raised himself over the gravestone to be even with her. Staring at the phone, he said, "Get down! Mr. Jenkins looked up and over this way." They ducked behind the gravestone again.

Jessica fidgeted nervously. "We'd better leave, Soph. We don't want him to find us here. You move slowly with the box, and without it you stand out like a giant pink flower."

Sophie checked the time on her watch. "We also have to hurry over to Great Finds. Mom and Dad will be there in about twenty minutes, and if we aren't there, they're going to worry."

Jessica swiped her hair off her face and tucked it behind her ears. "And we might be in trouble."

Tony said, "I always try to avoid getting in trouble."

"Me too," Jessica said.

Sophie waddled like a duck, holding on to the bottom of the box, until they were outside the cemetery. Sticking her arms in the air, she said, "Help me out of this thing."

Tony pulled the box over Sophie's head, and she shook out her arms. "I'm glad I don't have to hold on to that anymore. My arms are tired."

Tony held the box in front of himself. "We need to get out of here! Jessica, this is too big for one person to run with. Why don't you take one side of the box, and I'll take the other. We can run back to the alley where Sophie got it."

Tony, Jessica and Sophie rushed back to the dumpster to get rid of the box, then hurried over to Great Finds, arriving just in time to meet Sophie's parents, who had a surprise for them. They offered to take all three of them to a movie and already had Mr. and Mrs. Donadio's permission. Sophie didn't think twice about saying yes when she learned it was a new detective movie.

───────

On the way home from the movie—which they'd all thought was good—they dropped Tony off. Once home, Sophie went straight to her bedroom to talk about their clues again.

Jessica picked up the photo of Hilltop and turned it in the light. "Nothing clue-like on this except maybe the photo itself. Today our clues took us away from Hilltop and to the spooky cemetery. And I thought that old mansion was spooky. By the way, thanks for letting Tony come today."

"There's safety in numbers. I'm glad we had him with us today at the cemetery. Why don't we examine the photos of the church?"

Jessica got her purse and pulled out her phone, flipping to the photos of the large stained glass windows. "These are big windows, and this is a little screen." Jessica opened the first photo and slid her fingers on the screen to make the photo larger.

Sophie leaned closer. "There are a lot of colorful pieces of glass. Make it bigger."

Jessica made the photo larger still.

Rubbing her eyes, Sophie said, "I've learned one thing from looking at these photos."

"What's that?"

"Don't ever try to look at photos of stained glass windows on a phone and expect to see little details."

Jessica set down her phone. "Good point. Your dad said we could use his computer to help with the mystery."

"Let's check with him." Sophie ran off to find her dad, but when she soon returned, her face told the story. "A client had an accounting problem, so Dad is working on it tonight. The good news is that he says he will finish this job tomorrow so we can use his computer tomorrow night."

"Excellent. We can forget about the mystery tonight."

Sophie raised one eyebrow. "You can. I'll probably be working on it while I'm sleeping."

The next morning, after Mrs. Sandoval had left for the antique shop, the girls had breakfast and planned their day. When it was time to get dressed, Jessica put on a sunshine yellow top and shorts. Sophie opened her dresser drawer and pulled out one of her white T-shirts and a pair of jeans. "I'm so happy to be wearing my usual clothes today. It's going to be a long time before I even *think* about wearing a box again."

"Ha! I don't think it was your style."

Sophie slowly added, "I thought it would be nice to dress like a girl, but I'm not sure that bright pink is me either," obviously hoping she wouldn't upset Jessica by saying that.

"Sophie, you look like a girl no matter what you're wearing. I *like* bright colors. You don't have to."

"That's pretty much what I decided."

"So you'll never wear hot pink again."

Sophie thought about it for a minute. "No. I think I learned that I can wear it if I want to, when I think it will be pretty. I don't *need* to wear that to be pretty. And I'll try to never wear the color again when I'm in the middle of a mystery."

Jessica reached out and gave her a high five, then said, "Any great ideas for this morning? We can't use Uncle Lucas' computer, and going through these photos is all I can think to do on the mystery."

"I thought we should go see the outside of Hilltop again. Maybe something on the building will stand out this time."

"We might as well. We will only have pictures of it in a few weeks." Jessica grabbed her purse. "Thinking about Hilltop reminds me of that old cabin. It's close to Mr. Laurence's house, so it's probably on his land, and we're pretty sure it's the cabin Nezzy mentioned. Maybe we should do a better job checking it out."

"Good point. The poison ivy made me a little nervous. I know there are rubber gloves under the sink." Sophie got her backpack and put two pairs of gloves inside. Then she picked up a loaf of bread and got peanut butter out of the cupboard. "Let's take lunches with us. There are some little bags of chips up there"—she pointed to a cupboard—"and some juice boxes in the fridge. Then pick something you want from the fruit bowl. I'd like an apple."

"I would too. They're just hard to bite into with braces. I'm glad your mom bought some softer fruit."

Sophie scribbled a note to her dad. Then they put the lunches they'd made in her backpack and left.

As they walked to town, Jessica said, "I just realized the well might not be on Hilltop's land. We could be trespassing when we're there. And I really don't want to do that."

"I don't think there's a problem. Mom said that the house had thirty acres that went with it, didn't she?"

"But it doesn't have to be in a square. The thirty acres could be behind the house to the lake, out the driveway to the road, or whatever. The cabin's area does fit what Nezzy said though."

When they stopped at Great Finds to check in with Mrs. Sandoval, she didn't want them to work. Jessica noticed that she kept running her fingers through her hair like she had seen her own mother do when she was upset about something. Mrs.

Sandoval listened to their plans, then said, "Just stop here about five and I'll drive you home."

When they were outside the shop, Sophie said, "Mom is usually happy. Or at least not sad."

"The Hilltop situation has gotten her down. If we find the treasure, and there's money to save the mansion, she'll cheer up."

Sophie walked on for a few minutes before she spoke again. "If we don't find something important at the cabin, let's go to the city's land office and see if they have a map of the property. It might give us a clue."

"I realized that I have a bigger, more important question."

"What's that?"

"We wandered through the woods to get out of there. Do you have any idea where the clearing actually is?"

Sophie wavered her hand. "Yes and no. I can get us there again, but the only way I know to get there quickly without a whole lot of wandering in the woods is to go up the drive and down that path we used before."

Jessica checked all around them as they entered Hilltop's driveway.

Glancing around, Sophie said, "I don't want anyone to see us and mention to Mr. Jenkins that we were here. I haven't seen another person so far."

"Those words make me more nervous than happy."

"I know. I almost shivered after I said them."

Feeling the creepiness of the deserted road sink into her, Jessica also scanned the area. "What if Mr. Jenkins is walking down the road or is in the woods and sees us?"

Sophie chewed her lip. "I guess anything's possible, but he doesn't seem like the kind of guy to go for a nature walk. I've never seen him when I'm hiking or heard anything like that about him."

Pausing partway up the drive, Sophie said, "I want to be extra careful now that we think the cabin could be important.

Let's wait a couple of minutes to see if we hear anyone coming down the road."

Sophie kept an eye on her watch. Two minutes later, on the dot, she said, "Okay. Let's move quietly down the side of the road, and jump into the woods if you hear anyone coming."

When they made the turn onto the path at the rock, Jessica looked around. "Still clear."

"I don't feel any of the spooky 'someone's watching you' kind of sensations."

"Me neither."

At the fork in the path, Sophie surprised her when they went left.

"We didn't come this way before."

Sophie said, "I know. We're close to the cabin, so I wondered if anything interesting would be over here."

Five minutes later, Jessica said, "The only interesting thing is that one path can curve around so many times. This is going to take us twice as long."

When they stepped into the clearing, Jessica gave a whoop. "I've never been so happy to be in the middle of nowhere before! At least I know where I am now. I was starting to feel lost." From Sophie's expression, she suspected she'd felt that way too, but it would take torture for Sophie to admit it.

Sophie set her backpack on a large rock. "Maybe we should eat lunch now, before we get started. It's only a little bit early."

"I always seem to be hungry when we're racing around trying to solve a mystery, so that sounds good to me." Jessica reached into the backpack and took out her lunch.

Both girls were quiet as they ate, the chips making the most noise. When Sophie pulled out her apple, she said, "Sometimes I feel like we're close to finding the treasure, and then it feels like we're pushed backward, and I'm further from solving it than I ever was."

"Me too. I guess we need to remember that people have tried to find this treasure for a very long time."

Sophie finished her lunch and stood. Rubbing her hands together, she said, "Maybe today's the day." After pulling the gloves out of her backpack, she handed a pair to Jessica, who put the last bite of her peach in her mouth before taking them. "Even with the gloves, we still need to be careful not to touch poison ivy, then touch our face or hair."

"Got it. Sophie, you, um, spent time examining the chimney last time."

"Yeah. I had to shampoo my hair three times that night to get out the eggshells and bugs. I will be happy to let you finish the chimney, and I'll take the well."

"Maybe we'll notice something one of us missed last time." Jessica moved over to the chimney and pulled back more of the vines. "Everything seems ordinary here."

Sophie walked around the well. "Here too. There are so many weeds and small bushes that they almost seem alive like they're trying to grab at my feet. Whew! One almost tripped me."

Jessica stooped to check out the lower section of the stone chimney, reminding Sophie, "Be careful. You know you can be a bit—"

"Don't say clumsy."

"Danger prone."

"I can live with that. Hey, hey—"

Jessica steadied herself against the chimney as she stood. "Sophie?"

"Help!" a voice that sounded far away cried out.

The stone suddenly shifted, and Jessica almost fell. "Sophie?" Jessica hurried around the chimney. When she saw the bottom of Sophie's shoes, with her toes hooked over the edge of the well to keep her from falling in, she raced to her. "I'm coming!"

"Hurry, Jessica! I'm holding on to a rope that's hanging inside of here. It's probably a very old, rotten rope that's going to break any second."

Jessica grabbed Sophie's ankles and sat down hard, rolling to the side as Sophie slid out of the well and landed on her bottom where Jessica had been.

"Wow. Thank you, Cousin." When Sophie stood, she grabbed for the side of the well. "Whew. I was staring at a long, dark hole and thought for a minute that I was going to find out how deep the water was."

Jessica carefully leaned over and gazed down the well. She tugged the rope toward her. "Soph, check this out."

Sophie brushed off. Then she leaned over the edge, holding onto the side. "That's a fairly new rope."

"That's what I thought, too. Someone must have changed out the rope so they could search inside the well."

"Recently."

Jessica could practically see the wheels in Sophie's mind spinning as she searched for answers.

"That might mean that Mr. Jenkins isn't sticking to just searching Hilltop. Or someone else could be looking too. Half the town has searched for the treasure at one time or another."

"Half? I think it's more like almost every single person in town has searched for the treasure."

Sophie glanced around. "We should probably go soon. Did you find anything interesting?"

"Something is odd." Jessica went back to the chimney. "Come help me."

Sophie followed her, and Jessica pointed at the stone that had moved. "It happened right when you yelled for help."

Sophie said, "Let's pull down all the vines around it. Oh, and you can't be too careful here. Most of this is definitely poison ivy." Sophie started to reach for the stone, then stopped. "You found it. I'm going to let you pull it out. That is, if it comes out."

Jessica worked her right hand into the area that had moved and tugged on the stone. Instead of fighting her, like she thought it would, the stone shifted. "I thought it would be heavier than this, you know, like two of us might have to lift it down, but it's coming out easily."

Enough of the stone now stuck out that Jessica was able to grab it with both hands. She removed a sliver of stone, not a full block. Jessica leaned down and peeked into the hole it had left. "Wow. It only covered the front. Look what it hid."

Sophie peered inside the hole. "It's a big box." Reaching her hand in, she tried to move it. "It doesn't move. I think it's part of the chimney." She rooted around in her backpack and found her flashlight. After switching it on, Sophie pointed the light inside.

"It isn't just a box. It's a box with a *keyhole*."

Jessica peered into the hole. "A big keyhole . . . Are you thinking what I'm thinking?"

"It's like our key."

Jessica peeled off her gloves and pulled the key out of her purse. "You try it. I'm too nervous."

After peeling her gloves off too, Sophie reached into the space and put the key into the hole. "It fits. Now the question is, will it turn and open the box?" Sophie gave it a twist.

"Does it work?"

"Oh yeah. This might be the treasure." Sophie opened the door to the box and pointed the light inside. "It's empty!"

"No, it can't be empty!"

"Maybe Mr. Jenkins got here first."

"He didn't have the key."

"I really don't think that would stop someone like him."

"The box isn't damaged, so I don't think he—or whoever changed the rope—beat us to it."

Sophie reached inside. "It's still empty. There isn't anything that feels like a treasure map or diamonds or jewels." She moved her hand around. "Wait."

"Find a map?" Jessica fought against the sarcasm that tried to seep into her voice. It wasn't Sophie's fault if they discovered that the treasure couldn't be found—that someone had already found it years ago but kept it a secret.

"Not a map, but maybe a diamond." Sophie pulled her hand out of the box as a fist then opened it.

"It's a rock."

Sophie moved it in the light. "It's a white rock with gold-colored rock around it. And it sparkles. It's gold!"

"I doubt that. I think someone found the treasure in that box a long time ago. This is a joke. This whole treasure hunt is beginning to feel like a joke, and that rock is part of it."

"I'm sure it's gold, and it's important to the mystery. Let's hurry home and ask Dad."

"It's just a rock."

"Gold nugget. He may know an expert if he doesn't have the answer."

Jessica and Sophie headed over to Great Finds a little early because Sophie planned to cheer up her mom. Mrs. Sandoval had already perked up a little. This time she smiled when they came in. Checking her watch, Mrs. Sandoval said, "I'm glad you're here early. I want to leave for home soon. I invited a family who's visiting Pine Hill over for dinner. They've stopped at Great Finds a couple of times while they've been here and seem very nice."

"Jessica and I could cook something."

"I think we'll make it easier. Run over to the deli for sides. I thawed some hamburger and won't have time to make anything fancier, but I think everyone will enjoy burgers on the grill. Sundaes will work for dessert, and I have everything for them. Tony left what he'd brought, right? You aren't planning to use the whipped cream on another project?"

"No. It's there." Mrs. Sandoval never had figured out what had happened to the whipped cream that had disappeared a few weeks ago when they'd been working on their last mystery. Mr. Sandoval must have kept their secret.

After running over to the deli for potato salad and coleslaw—buying it from Tony's older sister, since he wasn't there—they all drove home. Sophie and Jessica sliced tomato and onion while Mrs. Sandoval prepared the burgers and Mr. Sandoval put them on the grill. Just as Sophie and Jessica finished setting the table and Mrs. Sandoval was placing a vase with flowers in the center, the doorbell rang. Sophie opened the door and found the family they'd met at Hilltop standing there, with Cody in the rear. "You!"

Her mother wheeled around. "Sophie! Be polite and invite our guests, the Coopers, inside. Cody is also twelve, and Madeline is fifteen."

After the parents came in, Madeline followed, and then Cody stepped through the doorway.

Mr. Cooper chuckled. "It's okay. She and Cody, er, had a rather painful introduction."

Cody smiled, and Sophie looked as though she'd like to wipe that expression off his face. She had seemed almost ready to apologize the day of the accident, but the bruises must have annoyed her.

Cody said, "I was chased by hornets and slammed into Sophie."

Mrs. Sandoval glared at her daughter. "That could happen to anyone. Sophie, be nice."

Jessica didn't like to laugh at Sophie when she was serious about something. But when she saw her cousin smile with gritted teeth before greeting the guests, she almost laughed out loud. "Welcome to our house," Sophie said. "Please come in."

As his parents sat on the couch, Cody stood next to Sophie and Jessica and said, "I really am sorry, Sophie. I stepped into a hornet's nest when we were camping last summer and got stung all over. It's made me kind of . . . nervous around hornets."

"Camping? You like to go camping?"

He nodded. "Sure. We have great camping in my part of Alaska."

"You're from Alaska!" Sophie shrieked.

Her mother popped her head out the kitchen door. "Everything all right here? Sophie?"

"Mom, they're from Alaska!"

"I know, Soph."

She pulled him over to a bench against the wall that her mother had delivered the same time as the desk. "Tell me all about Alaska."

Jessica grinned. Cody's slamming into her was all but forgotten. Learning about camping in Alaska was too good to be missed.

———

After dinner, Sophie said, "We can hang out on the front porch."

Jessica whispered to Sophie. "I guess we'll have to look at the photos of the church later."

She followed Sophie, Cody and Madeline Cooper walked behind her. Jessica hoped the bugs stayed away.

Sophie continued with her questions about the Coopers' home state. "Alaska sounds like so much fun. What do you do there other than camping?"

Madeline shuddered. "I don't like camping. Hiking, yes. Camping, no."

Jessica replied, "I'm with you on camping. I'm trying to like hiking."

"I'm hoping to have her loving the outdoors by the end of the summer."

Madeline asked, "What do you do here for fun?"

Sophie grinned. "We solve mysteries."

Both Cody and Madeline laughed. Cody said, "Is your mystery something difficult, like what to have for breakfast? Have you solved that one?"

Sophie said, "Earlier this summer we helped the sheriff solve a mystery."

Jessica added, "And we're hot on the trail of another mystery right now."

Cody smirked. "Right. Kids solving real mysteries."

"You can't tell anyone about what I'm going to show you. I'm only showing you now because you're visitors and can't beat us to the treasure."

"Treasure!" Cody's eyes widened, and then he laughed. When Sophie and Jessica didn't laugh too, he stared at them. "Actual treasure?"

Sophie said, "Yes."

"Okay, I won't tell."

Sophie turned to his sister.

Madeline said, "Not that I believe this, but sure."

Sophie hurried to get the clues they'd found from her secret hiding place. When she returned a few minutes later, Jessica could see the photo, key, and rock in her hand.

"Exhibit A." Sophie held up the photo. "An old photo we found in a hidden desk drawer."

Jessica snickered.

"Hey. That's how they do it on TV." Sophie held the photo in front of each person, then handed it to Cody. "Pass it to Madeline when you're done."

Sophie reached for the key. "Exhibit B: a key we found in another hidden compartment in the desk. It opened a box behind a stone in the chimney of an old cabin that contained Exhibit C—"

Jessica interrupted. "A rock."

Sophie glared at her. Then she shrugged. "Maybe. But it's a pretty rock."

Cody held out his hand for it. As soon as it landed, he reeled back and stared at the rock. Then he picked it up and checked it from every side before carrying it over to the porch light.

Sophie stepped over to stand beside Cody. "Is something wrong?"

Cody slowly shook his head from side to side. "Where did you get this?"

Sophie cocked her head to the side. "From the box the key opened. Does that matter?"

"Maybe. I think someone hid it for a reason." He blinked and looked a little faint.

"Are you okay? Should we call your parents?" Sophie turned toward the door.

"No." Cody held up his hand. "It's just that this is *gold*."

Jessica laughed. "Sophie gets excited about things and thinks they're important. She thought it was gold too. It must be a plain old rock."

Cody said, "You don't understand. My family goes gold panning and does some dredging—that's mining. I know a gold nugget when I see one."

Jessica's mouth dropped open. Could they be close to finding the treasure?

Sophie was the first to speak. "It *really* is gold?"

Cody nodded.

Sophie's smile started small, then stretched across her face.

Jessica held out her hand, and Cody dropped the gold nugget into it. Rolling it around in her hand, she said, "I thought this was just a white rock with a gold-colored rock around it." She looked up at Cody. "Are you sure?"

"Oh, yes. It's a gold nugget. We can ask my dad, if you want another opinion."

"Wow." Sophie slumped in her chair. "We might actually find the treasure."

"This could be part of it, but this one piece of gold isn't worth a fortune. There'd have to be a lot more for it to be worth much. We could have a nice vacation if we sold this, but not buy a house or pay for college."

Sophie walked across the porch, then turned and walked back. After pausing for a few seconds, she walked the same path two more times before Jessica reached out and grabbed her wrist.

"Sit." Jessica patted the seat next to her.

As she did, Sophie said, "This is amazing. Cody, it's a good thing you visited Pine Hill this summer."

"I just wish we could stay in Pine Hill to help you find the treasure."

———

When their company had left, Sophie and Jessica wandered back into the house. Jessica still felt a little dazed from discovering they'd found a genuine gold nugget.

"Jessica? Hello?"

Jessica turned to Sophie. "Did you say something?"

"Yes. About five times. Do you want to go through our mystery photos on Dad's computer tonight?"

She suddenly felt tired. "Could you see if we can use it tomorrow? I need to think about what just happened."

"I do too. I'll ask Dad."

When she returned a few minutes later, she said, "He has a lunch meeting."

"Okay. We can sleep in and have fun in the morning. I'm excited about taking another look at those photos tomorrow!"

21 STAINED-GLASS SECRETS

Just before noon, Sophie and Jessica stood in the hallway outside Mr. Sandoval's door, waiting. Seeing them there startled him when he came through the door to leave for his meeting.

"I hope you girls find the answers you want. Let me know if you see anything interesting."

"Will do, Dad!" Sophie waved to him as he went around the corner into the living room.

Jessica set her phone on the desk as they sat down in front of the computer. "Soph, do you think we're getting any closer? I know we have our clues, including the gold nugget, but we still don't know where the treasure is."

Sophie shook her head. "I wish I could say, 'Yes, we'll find it any day,' but I don't know. I do think the key Mr. Laurence left in the envelope in his desk—which started this whole mystery—means he hoped someone would search for the treasure. And the second key gave us the gold nugget in the box."

Jessica shook her head as she plugged her phone into the computer and started uploading the pictures. "I don't know. I get excited because I think we've found a great clue. Then it doesn't seem to go anywhere."

"Mr. Laurence pretty much said in that letter to Nezzy that he wanted someone to find the treasure. Are you saying that you want to give up, Jessica?"

"Are you kidding? I'm not sure we'll actually find anything, but sitting around doing nothing was seriously boring."

"I've converted you into being a fan of mysteries, haven't I?" Sophie cocked her head to the side, waiting for the reply.

"I'm not saying I love mysteries like you do, but I am having fun."

"Then let's see if anything in these stained glass windows stands out."

Jessica pulled the first photo up on the computer. "Our adventure continues."

Sophie grinned. "You have a way with words, Cousin."

"Do you think we could go to the beach later? It's a beautiful day, and I miss lying on the sand."

"I'm not sure we'll have time. We haven't even had enough time for me to mention a hike. Or camping."

Jessica clicked on the mouse.

"There's the big window at the front of the church," Sophie said, pointing at the screen. "Even though the rest of it looks like it's really old, the man in it seems modern. I wonder if he's Mr. Laurence. We've only seen small photos of him in Nezzy's book, so it's difficult to know for sure."

"There's probably a valuable portrait of him in Mr. Jenkins' room."

"I wouldn't be surprised. Anything stand out here?"

"No. Let's slowly go through them one by one." Jessica brought up those on the left side of the church first.

Sophie asked, "Do you see anything in here that doesn't seem to belong?"

"Not really. Here are the last two."

At the last window, Sophie stared, then slowly said, "Uh . . . Jessica?"

Jessica leaned closer to the screen. "What? Do you see something?"

"Keys."

Jessica glanced over at Sophie and saw her pointing at an area of the window. "Where?"

"There is a key on every window. They're almost hidden on a couple of the windows."

Jessica flipped through the photos again. "Wow. I have to pay attention on a couple of these because they're hard to find. This key is in with a bunch of flowers. That one's part of a bird's nest."

"What could Mr. Laurence be trying to tell us with keys?" Sophie went from window to window again. "The keys are all pointing toward the back of the church."

Jessica sat back in her chair. "Maybe they just wanted them to be uniform. All of the windows appear to belong together when the keys are pointing the same direction."

"Maybe, but what if Mr. Laurence was trying to tell us something?"

"I don't know, Sophie. Wouldn't the artist be the one who designed the windows?"

Sophie shook her head. "No, remember what Nezzy said? Mr. Laurence gave directions on everything he wanted in the church, including the stained glass windows."

"Sophie, I just thought of something else Nezzy said. She said Mr. Laurence was meticulous—"

"Speak English."

"He focused on details. Remember her story about the stained glass windows in the church? To him, they weren't in the right place."

"If a window wasn't put on the correct side of the church, the key in it wouldn't point to the back." Sophie's eyes got big. "Maybe the key is like an arrow and it's pointing to the treasure."

"Why not? Do you think the treasure is inside the church?"

Sophie pictured the inside of the church and the area near the windows. "I don't think so. I should really say that I *hope* it isn't there, because to say we'd get in big trouble for digging up treasure where the minister speaks is the understatement of the year."

"Maybe outside, behind the church?"

"Do you have the photos you took of the outside? Maybe we can see if anything stands out."

"Like a flashing sign that says, 'Dig here! Dig here!'?"

"Funny."

Jessica searched through the photos on the computer. "This is the back of the church where the keys seem to be pointing. I don't see anything unusual. What's in that direction if you keep going?"

Sophie squeezed her eyes shut. "I'm going to picture it in my mind. The lake's that way"—she pointed to their left. A minute later, she opened her eyes. "Trees, trees, and more trees. I don't think anyone lives there."

"Would it help you if you looked at a map of Pine Hill? Maybe you aren't seeing it all in your mind."

"You're right, Jessica. A good detective shouldn't rely on herself. She should use every tool that's available to her." Sophie went out the office door saying, "There's a map in the living room chest."

Jessica followed her and stood beside her as she opened a drawer on the chest and pulled out the map. Sophie unfolded it and laid it on the top of the chest. "Here's the church. The arrows are pointing this way." She pointed at a green part of the map.

Jessica found Hilltop on the map. "The mansion isn't far from where you're pointing."

Sophie picked up the map and held it close. Setting it down, she said, "I missed it! I'm so sorry."

"It's okay. But what did you miss?"

"Mr. Laurence's cabin and well are right under my finger on the map." She stared at Jessica.

"Wow. The keys in the church windows are pointing at the old cabin."

"Yes. We found the nugget there, so we found the clue he was pointing to even before we found the arrows. I think we're closer to the treasure than anyone else has ever been."

Jessica took a deep breath. "I think you're right. Let's make sure we haven't missed anything in the stained glass." She hurried back to Mr. Sandoval's office.

Again in front of the computer, Jessica flipped through the images.

"Stop." Sophie pointed. "This window shows a well and a woman. The woman looks a little like Nezzy when she was younger."

"Right! Sophie, I only remember seeing one well the whole time we've been on this mystery."

Sophie hopped to her feet. "I've had a couple of nightmares about falling into that well, so believe me, I can picture it clearly. Maybe if we tell all of this to the sheriff, she'll take us seriously and work with us to find the treasure."

"We've seen keys and more keys since the beginning of this case. There was one in the envelope, another one in the desk, one on the brick."

"I feel like we've seen something about a key somewhere else." Sophie tapped her foot as she thought. "Where else did we see one?" She snapped her fingers. "The word *key* was on Mr. Laurence's gravestone. And someone wanted to hide the stone that had that word. Do you think that's important?"

"Until we find the treasure, I'm going to assume everything is important."

"I'm surprised I'm saying this, but let's go back to the cemetery."

22 STAKEOUT TONIGHT?

When the girls neared the cemetery, sunshine made everything bright, but Sophie felt like turning around and heading the other direction. Still, she continued on, moving quickly, checking over her shoulder every minute or two. She couldn't put her finger on why, but she felt something wasn't right.

Sophie said, "At least we know where Mr. Laurence's grave is now. We don't have to spend extra time searching for it."

Jessica answered. "Yes. I know exactly where I'm going in a cemetery. That's more than a little weird."

When they neared the place she was sure it lay, Sophie said, "I guess I'm wrong. That can't be his grave. The grass is dug up all around it."

"No, this is it. See? The name is right." Jessica pointed at the tombstone.

"Jessica, it can't be. It looks like—"

They both jumped back and looked around.

Sophie whispered, "Someone's been digging around here. I'd guess at night, so no one can see them."

Jessica gulped and whispered, "Yes. I'm glad we have a little while before it's nighttime. Let's get out of here!"

As they hurried away, Sophie said, "Wait! We didn't read the words on that stone again, to make sure it did say something about a key." She started to turn back, but Jessica grabbed her arm and pulled her forward.

"We aren't turning back. We can return tomorrow. Maybe with the sheriff."

They ran all the way into town, then stopped, panting and leaning against the front of Kendall's Jewelers.

"Jessica"—Sophie stopped to catch her breath—"someone's probably searching for the treasure around Mr. Laurence's grave. I don't know why, because I don't think it's there."

They stared at each other.

"Mr. Jenkins!" Jessica whispered.

"And Lester. They must be desperate to dig around a grave. I'm pretty sure the word *key* was on the stone, but—"

"He must have learned about the keys somehow. Maybe he heard us talking. I wonder if he's checking everything that has something to do with a key."

"That's stupid. Mr. Laurence couldn't put something there, not in his own grave."

"Maybe they aren't as smart as we thought."

"They're probably just desperate to find the treasure. Hilltop will be torn down soon, and Mr. Jenkins' reason to be in Pine Hill will be gone."

"They might be back tonight."

Jessica gasped. "You're right. Maybe we'd better stop at the sheriff's office."

"Good idea. We'd better hurry so we catch her before she leaves for the day."

Once they could see the sheriff's office, they could also see someone getting into a sheriff's car parked at the curb. "That's her!" Sophie started to run, but the car pulled out and headed down the street.

"So much for that idea! Let's get over to Great Finds before Mom wants to leave for the day too."

When they arrived at the shop, Sophie was surprised to see her dad standing inside.

"A customer arranged with your mother to come in after she usually closes," he said. "I'm driving both of you home." As they stepped out the door, he added, "You barely made it before it started to get dark."

"But we *did* make it." Sophie gave her best smile.

The sun set as they drove. As they pulled into the driveway, an idea came to her. Her dad got out and went inside, but she pulled Jessica aside. "If someone's digging at night, maybe we should be there, watching to see who it is."

"Right. We're going to ask your parents if we, two twelve-year-old girls, can spend the night in a cemetery, waiting for someone who has the guts to dig around a grave."

Sophie couldn't see Jessica clearly in the fading light but knew from her tone of voice that she must have rolled her eyes.

"I see your point." Sophie scrunched up her mouth, thinking, then said, "What if Tony, Cody, and Madeline came along?"

"Oh, so now we have five kids."

"I hate it when you're this right. Let's ask Dad if he will come with us."

When they stepped inside, Sophie asked, "Dad, will Mom be home for dinner?"

He didn't look up from reading a book. "Yes, she expects to be here in about an hour."

Sophie pulled Jessica into the kitchen. When the door closed, she said quietly, "This might be a good night for us to cook dinner. Mom will be happy to have it taken care of, and Dad might be happier about helping us."

"What are you going to cook?"

"Let's check the fridge and see if I can figure out what she was planning to make."

Ten minutes later, they'd started cooking sausage and put spaghetti sauce on to heat.

Jessica stirred the sauce, which was beginning to bubble. "It always amazes me when you are able to make something that tastes good."

"Mom's been teaching me to cook for years." Sophie pulled veggies out of the fridge. "Would you like to fix salads?"

"Just tell me what to do."

"Put lettuce in four bowls. Cut everything into bite-sized pieces. Done."

Jessica peeled and very carefully cut up the veggies. "I've had dried cranberries and pecans in a salad."

"If you find it in the kitchen, go for it."

Sophie took a metal pot out of the cupboard and put water in it for cooking pasta. She had just placed it on the stove when her mom came in the front door and called to them. Sophie answered and her mom stepped into the kitchen. "Making dinner?"

"Yes."

"Thank you, Sophie." She hugged her. "And Jessica." She reached over and hugged her too. "I had a busy, long day, and I'm so happy you're making dinner that I won't ask what you want until after dinner."

As Mrs. Sandoval put her hand on the kitchen door, Sophie said, "It's easy and won't cost anything. Don't worry."

"Music to my ears. I'm going to kick off my shoes and wait for whatever it is you're cooking." She went out the door.

When Sophie and Jessica brought the sauce with sausage, pasta, and salads to the table, Mr. and Mrs. Sandoval were seated there waiting for them.

After topping her pasta and sauce with Parmesan cheese, Sophie took a bite of the meal. "This is good. If I say so myself."

Mrs. Sandoval took a bite and sighed. "I'm glad I taught you to cook. You've made a delicious dinner." When Sophie started to speak, her mother held up her hand. "Wait until we're done."

As Mrs. Sandoval put the last bite in her mouth, Sophie said, "We have a little favor we'd like Dad to do." She took a big breath and smiled sweetly at her father. "We'd like for you to go with us to the cemetery tonight."

Silence. Mr. Sandoval stared at her. "Cemetery? Dare I ask why?"

Sophie explained what they'd found.

"Why were you there today in the first place?"

"Keys. We found keys in the stained glass windows at the church. We've found keys over and over again on this mystery. And the word key is on a stone that sits on Mr. Laurence's grave."

Jessica jumped in and described the keys in the stained glass.

Mrs. Sandoval asked, "And they seem to be like arrows?"

Sophie sat tall in her chair and said confidently, "They are arrows pointing to the woods beside Hilltop."

Jessica cleared her throat. "They appear to be arrows."

"They're arrows. What else would they be?"

"Don't get me wrong, Soph. I think they're arrows too. I'm just not certain."

Her dad jumped in. "No matter what they are and what they're pointing to, I don't believe we should check out a 'key' at the cemetery—"

"Daaad!"

"—without the sheriff or a deputy," he continued. "I'll call and see if someone can come."

"Thanks!"

Mr. Sandoval arose, walked over to the phone, and dialed. When someone answered, the girls listened to his side of the conversation. He hung up a minute later.

"There's a conference the sheriff and most of the deputies are at, over in the county seat. No one can go with us tonight."

Sophie sagged in her chair.

He added, "The deputy on duty said he'd tell the sheriff and ask her to call if she has a chance."

Mrs. Sandoval stood. "Girls, I've had time to relax now because of the dinner you made. I'll do the dishes."

Sophie didn't feel as happy as she should that she didn't have to do the dishes. They *had* to solve the mystery. She got up from her chair and slowly went to her room with Jessica beside her.

"Don't worry, Soph. We'll get to look tomorrow. Let's read. It'll make you happier."

Sophie flopped back on her bed. "We may miss something tonight."

"Relax. There isn't anything we can do about it."

Sophie lay there and didn't even pick up her book.

When the phone rang a few minutes later, Sophie ran to the living room to answer it with Jessica on her heels. She covered the mouthpiece of the phone and whispered, "Sheriff Valeska." A frown turned down the corners of her mouth. "No, it isn't an emergency. But—but—are you sure? . . . Okay." She slowly set the phone on its cradle.

Mr. Sandoval asked, "My guess is that she can't come tonight."

"She's the speaker at a dinner for sheriffs that's about to start, so she said 'nothing short of an emergency' can have her back in Pine Hill tonight."

Her dad picked up the newspaper. "I guess there's nothing else to do about it."

"She said she'd have a deputy drive through the cemetery every hour."

He settled on his chair. "You can stop by the sheriff's office in the next day or two."

Sophie put a hand on her chest. "You don't understand mysteries, Dad. We can't let this clue go cold. She said she'd be in the office in the morning, so we'll stop by then—if it's okay with you."

When they got back to Sophie's room, she did pick up her book this time, but laid it beside her on the bed after a few minutes. "I can't focus on reading," she told Jessica. "I've been going over clues in my mind. I feel like we should have all the clues we need to find the treasure."

"But they aren't connecting in your mind?"

"Exactly!"

"That's how I feel too." Jessica set her book on the night-stand. "I have no idea what's going on in this chapter either."

"We have keys, gold, and a photo. Are the keys on the stained glass important, or did Mr. Laurence just like keys? Does the well in the stained glass matter? We already found the gold nugget at the cabin site." Sophie blew out a long breath in frustration.

The phone rang again, but she didn't get up.

"Soph! Jessica!" Mr. Sandoval called a minute later. He leaned in the doorway to Sophie's room. "The sheriff just phoned to say she'd finished her speech and could come back if it was important. I explained what you'd found and she decided to do a stakeout at the cemetery. We can meet her there in an hour."

"Yay!" Sophie pumped her fist in the air. "Now, let's call Tony and the Coopers."

Mr. Sandoval stood straight. "Why do we need all these people, Soph? Sheriff Valeska agreed to do the stakeout and allow *you and Jessica* to see it—from a distance."

"Due to a slip by my cousin"—Sophie gave Jessica a look —"Tony's been involved in this for a while. I don't think he'd be happy about missing the stakeout. And Cody's the one who told us it was gold. Madeline might like to come too."

When Mr. Sandoval walked away, Jessica whispered, "And Cody's cute."

Sophie grinned and whispered back, "And he's cute."

Once her dad had had enough time to make the phone calls, she stepped over to the door to her room. "How's it going, Dad?"

"The Donadios were easy to reach and gave approval—since Sheriff Valeska's going to be there. The Coopers haven't answered."

Sophie came back and slumped onto her bed. "There are so many pieces to this mystery. And now that we think we're finding answers, we have to get all of the parents to agree."

A few minutes later, her dad stepped into her room. "Let's go, Soph! I finally reached the Coopers. You know how cell phone reception is in town. Madeline didn't want to come, but they're on their way to drop Cody off at the sheriff's office. The sheriff said to drop you two off—Tony's meeting us there—and she'd take you all to the stakeout."

"Yay!" Sophie bounced to her feet. She pulled her flashlight out of her nightstand drawer. "Let's go, Jessica."

"I wish I could be as happy as you are about going to a cemetery at night."

"I won't say we'll have fun, but I think we might see who's doing this. If that person is caught, they might know something about the treasure."

"And you think they'll tell us what they know? Sure. They won't want to get the treasure themselves. They'll be happy to share their information."

"There's no need to be sarcastic." Sophie stopped with her hand on the light switch. "There may be some truth in what you say, but I won't let go of my happy feeling. *This* is the night we've been waiting for."

23   GRAVE DANGER

Sheriff Valeska unpinned her badge, the shiny metal glinting in the moonlight. As she tucked it into her pocket, she said, "Reflective metal and a full moon aren't a good combination. We don't want to alert anyone before they're in our trap." Then she motioned for them to follow her. On the other side of the cemetery, she pointed to a large carved angel. "This is big enough for all four of you to hide behind."

Sophie turned to her. "Sheriff? We'll miss all of the action if we're over here."

"What you'll miss is the danger. Can you see what's happening from here?"

"Yes, but—"

"Could you see the action from your house?"

Ooh. Jessica watched Sophie's quick reaction and bit her lip to hide a grin.

"This is a great spot. Thanks, Sheriff."

Sheriff Valeska gave one curt nod. "I'm glad you agree."

As they crouched behind the headstone, Jessica said, "Soph, seeing the sheriff's badge reflect in the moonlight brought back a part of the case that we pushed aside. There's the original story of the doctor seeing Mr. Laurence in the woods and the moonlight reflecting off of gold."

Sophie brushed the idea away. "No, we decided that couldn't be true. Besides, where would a whole bag of gold be?"

"We should tell Tony and Cody about the windows in the church."

After Jessica told the story, Cody said, "If the well in the window is a clue to lead us to the old well . . ."

Sophie said, "It has a key on a stone, but it's just a stone, and it seems like someone searched down inside the well already. The gravestone has a sentence on it that includes the word *key*, so maybe all of the words on it do mean something more."

"Yes, you're right." Jessica settled down to wait.

Tony said, "Don't you think the arrows in the stained glass are pointing to the treasure?"

"We already checked there." Sophie fought against the sarcastic comment she wanted to make.

"I think we can conclude—" He glanced over at Sophie. "Does that sound like detective language to you?"

She nodded.

"We can conclude that the well has to be where the treasure is. You somehow missed it."

Sophie added, bouncing up and down on the ground, "Everything that had a key on it was important. We'll go check the well again in the morning. And you can come if you want." She softly punched Tony in the arm.

Jessica could see the glint of moonlight off his teeth when he smiled.

All of them settled into the stakeout, finding their positions behind the angel.

———

A short time later, bushes behind them rustled. Sophie checked their group. Everyone was there; Tony and Cody were chuckling about something, and Jessica was focused on the sheriff's hiding place. She nudged Cody and whispered, "Did you hear that?"

"What?" Cody asked.

"Bushes moving," Sophie said.

"You're imagining things." He laughed quietly, then leaned over and said something to Jessica.

Sophie stared over her shoulder. Could she have imagined it? Even if the bushes had moved, it could have been a possum or another harmless nighttime animal. She heard another rustle. The other three were talking in low voices about something. She quietly slipped into the bushes to see what was going on.

———

Jessica stopped talking and focused on the stakeout. The warm summer air hung still and nothing moved, not even a mouse. She turned to Sophie to make a joke about it, but she wasn't there. Jessica looked all the way around them.

When she leaned to the right to check for Sophie on the other side of the angel they hid behind, Tony asked, "What are you doing?"

She whispered, "Sophie's gone!"

Cody heard her too, so both boys checked the area. Cody asked, "Is this something she does, vanish?"

Jessica said, "Absolutely not. I don't understand where she could be." When the bushes rustled, she added. "I'm glad we're getting a breeze, anyway. It's so still, it's eerie."

Cody held his hand in the air. "There is no breeze."

Branches breaking and leaves rustling made them all turn to look.

"Sophie?" Jessica whispered. Then she said her name a little louder.

Tony stood. "This isn't like Sophie."

A crashing sound brought the rest of them to their feet. A muffled voice sounded. Then silence.

Jessica's voice quivered, "Do you think that was Sophie calling for help?"

Cody shook his head. "If it was, I don't think she got to finish what she was trying to say."

A new crashing sound pushed through the woods, moving away from them.

Cody cleared his throat. "My guess is that Sophie was just taken away by someone who was hiding in the woods."

Jessica gasped. She took a step toward the sheriff, but Tony grabbed the back of her jacket.

He said, "Remember, Sheriff Valeska said they would be ready to grab anyone who walked into their trap."

"Then what?"

Cody said, "Let's shout at her."

Jessica said, "Great idea, Cody. On three, shout . . . What do we shout?"

Tony jumped in. "'Criminal!' And point the way the noise went."

Jessica said, "One, two, three!"

When they all shouted, Sheriff Valeska stepped out from where she was hiding and hurried over to them. Scowling, she asked, "What are you doing?"

Jessica said, "Sophie's missing. And we heard footsteps running away."

"Over here!" the sheriff called to her deputies. "Bring all the lights."

Three deputies hurried over with the gear.

"Please tell me what happened, Jessica," the sheriff ordered her.

After she'd finished, Cody added, "I just remembered. She told me she'd heard bushes rustling . . . I'm sorry, but I thought she was imagining things."

The sheriff sent her deputies into the woods to search. Jessica felt like time barely moved as they waited for some sign of Sophie.

A couple of minutes later, a deputy called, "Sheriff, check this out."

Cody, Tony, and Jessica followed the sheriff into the woods.

A shovel lay on the ground, and the powerful lights showed an area where the plants had been flattened. The sheriff crouched and said, "It looks like something, or someone, was pulled for a few feet. Then there are only normal footsteps." She turned to Jessica, Tony, and Cody. "I'll get a deputy to drive you home. We'll find her. Don't worry."

When she turned away, Jessica said, "No, Sheriff. Wait. I know where they're going."

"Where? How do you know?"

"Well, I should say I'm pretty sure I know where they're going. I mean, why would they go anywhere else?"

"Jessica, you're babbling. Take a deep breath."

Jessica obeyed. Then the sheriff said, "Now, slowly tell me what you mean."

"We—that is, Sophie and I—found an old well in the woods, and we believe the treasure is there."

"That's sounds like a good idea, Jessica, but the criminals wouldn't know to go there."

"Actually, they would. We talked about it when we were settling into the stakeout. If they were in the woods, then . . ."

Sheriff Valeska turned to Cody, "Right after that is when Sophie heard the rustling bushes?"

"Yes, ma'am."

"I don't know of a place like you're describing, Jessica. Could you take us there?"

Jessica stared down at the crushed leaves, probably crushed by Sophie struggling to get away from someone. She needed her help. "Yes, I can take you there. The only way I know is down a path leading from Hilltop's driveway."

The sheriff rounded up her team. Once gear was returned to trunks, she ushered Jessica, Cody, and Tony into her vehicle and took off for Hilltop with two more squad cars following close behind.

When they turned in to Hilltop's drive, Jessica said, "Go slowly. I have to find some boulders next to the road."

"There?" The sheriff pointed out the window at the large rocks. When Jessica nodded, she stopped the car. Sighing, she said, "I wish I could tell you to stay in the car, but I need Jessica to show us the way. You may as well all come. But Cody and Tony, please stay to the rear. And Jessica, once we're there, you step to the rear too."

The four of them got out of the car. As they started down the trail with the other officers who had followed them there, the sheriff added, "Everyone, deputies included, walk softly and don't speak. We want to do our best to surprise them."

Jessica recognized the twisted tree and whispered to the sheriff, "We're almost there."

Sheriff Valeska pulled the three of them aside and whispered, "You three kids stay here. I'm leaving a deputy with you." In a voice only slightly louder, she said to the rest of the group, "Lights off, everyone."

A woman who quietly introduced herself as Deputy Story stood beside them as the others continued out of sight.

Jessica waited for sounds of a rescue. She pulled her phone out to check the time and kept checking it every few minutes. Eleven minutes of waiting brought the sheriff back to them.

She spoke in a normal voice. "I'm sorry, Jessica, but they aren't at the well."

"They have to be here. This is the one place they would want to go." She stared up at the sky. "I know! *If* they haven't been here before—and that's a big if—Sophie's taking them on a roundabout trip so we can get here first."

The sheriff pondered that silently. "With anyone else, I'd say that's ridiculous. No one would spend more time with kidnappers than they had to."

"That's how Sophie thinks, though."

"I was about to say that too. Follow me. Let's all hide in the woods and wait for them."

She explained to her deputies what was going on, adding, "Everyone wait for my signal. I'll shine my light in the eyes of the man holding Sophie."

They were soon hidden in a circle around the well, with Tony, Cody, and Jessica together at the rear, the farthest point from the trail. Jessica made sure they hid in grass, not in poison ivy.

24 SETTING A TRAP

Sophie hoped she'd delayed the criminals long enough. She didn't think they'd be very nice if she delayed them any longer. Her heart had raced so much when they'd captured her that she'd thought it would burst through her chest. Then she'd calmed herself down. She knew what she had to do to get rescued and stop the criminals, all at the same time. But she didn't see a way out of this if the sheriff wasn't at the well.

Lester, the man who seemed to be in charge, said in a gruff voice, "This better be it. You took a long way around to get to the trailhead."

"I'm a kid. I'm not used to trying to spot things from a car at night."

"You'd better not be leading us down the wrong path." Lester poked her in the arm and made her yelp, then said, "Hey, keep it quiet, kid."

"You hurt me."

Mr. Jenkins said, "Lester, leave the kid alone. It doesn't matter if she makes noise anyway, because I don't think we're near anything but trees."

They stepped into the clearing and a third man said, "Boss,

we're here." He shined a light around the area. "There's a well over there."

Lester said, "So there is." Pulling Sophie in front of him, Lester tugged her over to the well. "Show me where to find the treasure."

Sophie said, "Let me see it more closely," and crouched in front of the well.

Immediately a bright beam of light flashed on, and Sophie dropped flat to the ground as deputies surged into the clearing, tackling the three criminals. The sheriff herself rushed to help Sophie to her feet. "Are you okay?" she asked.

"I knew, or at least I hoped, you'd come here, and I wanted you to be ready and waiting when we got here."

The sheriff hugged her. "That was smart, Sophie."

"There's something about being captured by bad guys that makes you smarter."

"How did they get you?"

"I guess I didn't start out smart. I heard a noise in the bushes and went to check it out. Three men were hiding in there, listening to us. I thought I could sneak back to the others, but I stepped on a branch, so they knew I was there. When one of the men grabbed hold of me, I tried to call for help, but he covered my mouth. I fought to get away, but they pulled me with them." She took a deep breath. "They had a shovel and had planned to dig more at the grave. But they heard us talking about the well."

Officers had already cuffed two of the men. As the deputy was about to click Mr. Jenkins' handcuffs into place, he shoved the officer to the ground and tore off into the woods.

"Run after him!" Sophie yelled and took off with Tony, Cody, and Jessica right behind her.

"No!" the sheriff yelled. "You kids get back here right—" But before she could finish her sentence, Tony tackled the fleeing man, grabbing his ankles. Cody pinned his arms behind his back.

"Football," Tony said, grinning at Cody.

"Wrestling." Cody grinned back.

When all three men were handcuffed, Sheriff Valeska turned to Sophie. "People have looked for this treasure for a hundred years. How do you know where it is?"

"It has to be here, sheriff. The keys point this way."

"Keys? You're going to have to explain that to me more clearly when we're done here."

The sheriff inspected the well, walking around it and shining the light inside. "I've seen other old wells, Sophie. This one doesn't appear different. A bag of gold is rather large. Where would Laurence have hidden it?"

Sophie knelt in front of the well and the brick with the key on it. "I don't know, Sheriff. I just know it has to be here. Other than being larger than the other stones, the stone with the key on it doesn't look unusual. Of course, it's very grimy and covered with bits of vine." In exasperation, she pushed on it, but the stone was solidly in place like those around it. "They sure built things well in the old days."

The sheriff agreed. "I don't see anything here, Sophie. We'll take these men in for the night, and figure out what to do in the morning."

Sophie kept staring at the stone. The sheriff turned away, then said, "You're going with us."

Sophie knew she didn't have any choice. "Okay."

Sheriff Valeska drove them to her office where they called Mr. Sandoval to pick them up.

While he drove them home, they took turns telling him what had happened. Tony and Cody spoke first, each telling as much of the story as he could before being dropped off, Tony at home and Cody at a campground. They were almost home themselves when Jessica, who was telling the story at that point, got to the part about Sophie.

Mr. Sandoval yelled, "What?! Are you okay, Soph? Tell me the truth."

"Yes. They didn't hurt me, Dad. Well, my wrist feels bruised, but that's all. I'll admit that it was scary, but I'm fine. More or less. Kind of." She paused. "Let's just say that I'm glad we're going home and that those men are locked up."

When they arrived home and her mother heard the story, she hurried Sophie off to a warm bath.

Like that would somehow fix everything.

25 THE FINAL KEY

The next day when Jessica woke up, Sophie wasn't in bed. She pulled on her robe and went into the shower knowing that this morning she needed to wake up fast. She had a feeling that being groggy and grumpy wouldn't be optional.

After showering and drying her hair, Jessica put her robe back on and left the bedroom to hunt down Sophie. She found her in the kitchen, holding a mug.

Sophie looked up and smiled. "Hot chocolate

"In the summer?"

"Mom seems to think that hot baths and hot chocolate are good for you."

Jessica grabbed a couple of slices of bread and popped them in the toaster. "Is she right?"

"She might be. I did feel better after I sat in the hot bathtub last night." Smiling, she added, "I'm not sure about the hot chocolate, but I do know that I like it. It may be the only chocolate that I really like."

"Want some toast?"

Sophie looked down at the mug. "I guess this isn't much of a breakfast. Sure."

Jessica buttered the toasted bread and pulled a jar of peanut butter from the cupboard, handing both to Sophie before she popped two more slices in the toaster for herself.

"I guess the mystery is over, Sophie. We did everything we knew to do. Even the bad guys thought we were right, but the treasure wasn't there."

Sophie dropped her toast on the plate and hugged the mug closely with her hands. "I know. I just feel inside"—she tapped her chest—"that the treasure is at the well. It has to be there. Everything points to it."

Jessica sat at the table, slathered peanut butter onto her toast, then nibbled thoughtfully. "The sheriff's right. Where can it be?"

"I don't know." Sophie set the mug down with a thud. "I'm frustrated. When I picture it in my mind, all I see is a well made up of a bunch of stones."

"Yes. They're all approximately the same size and shape. Except for the stone with the key on it."

Sophie paused with the toast almost to her mouth. "What if that means something? Could you hide something inside a rock? Maybe he carved out the center and poured the gold nuggets inside."

Jessica shook her head. "It wasn't big enough to hold a bag of gold nuggets."

Sophie stood. "Let's go there this morning. I want to see it one last time before I completely give up. I've never given up on a mystery before."

Jessica felt like pointing out that this was only the second mystery they'd worked on, so she'd only solved one. Instead, she told her, "I'll go with you. One last time. Now that I know the only other people seriously looking for the treasure are locked up."

After asking Mr. Sandoval if they could go, they walked silently to town and over to Hilltop's entrance. A few minutes up the road, they turned onto the path to the cabin. Trudging along through the woods, Jessica wondered if this was yet another waste of time.

Sophie first spoke when she saw the well. "It's here. I know the treasure's here."

"Maybe someone found it years ago. If they found it, they might not have wanted to share with family and friends."

"That's true." Sophie studied the ground around the well. "I wonder if we should try digging here?"

"I'm not sure that's a good idea with the big, deep hole of the well so close by. What if it all collapsed?"

"Right."

It wasn't like Sophie to agree with everything Jessica said. Her cousin definitely wasn't herself this morning.

Sophie knelt in front of the key stone again. "That one's so different from the others. It isn't even the same texture."

Jessica crouched beside her. "The other stones have the appearance of being chiseled out of solid rock with a hammer. This one is almost smooth." She ran her hand over the surface. "It's so smooth that it looks modern, like it was made in a mold, not carved by hand."

As Sophie stared at it, her eyes got bigger and bigger. Jessica wondered if she was having an attack of some kind. "Are you okay? Sophie?" She reached out and shook her. "Are you okay?"

A laugh started low, then grew, until Sophie sat back on the ground, holding on to her sides.

Jessica pulled her phone out of her purse, hoping it would pick up a signal. Sophie obviously needed help.

Her cousin reached out and touched her arm. "I'm not going crazy," she choked out. "It's just that it's there." She pointed at the key stone.

Jessica stared first at the stone, then at her cousin. "Okaaay," she said slowly.

Sophie searched the ground around her, picked up a small rock and then another, before choosing one. She got back on her knees in front of the key stone and scraped against it with the rock. "I knew it!" She pointed at the mark she'd made.

Jessica shrugged. "It's still a rock, one with an ugly scrape on it, but still a rock."

"Get closer."

Jessica decided to humor her. The faster they got out of here, the better. Sophie moved to the side so Jessica could get a few inches from the stone. A metal color glimmered out from the scrape. "Sophie, hand me your rock."

Sophie held out her hand and Jessica took the rock and made another scrape, even larger, beside the first one. Jessica gasped. "You found it!"

"When you said it seemed like it was made in a mold, it all came together in my mind. Mr. Laurence melted the gold in the shape of a stone. That's probably what he was doing the night the doctor saw him. Then he painted it the same color the other stones are naturally. The gold has been here at the well all along."

Both Jessica and Sophie stood.

Staring at the rock, now with grooves glinting in the sun, Sophie said, "*We* did it! Let's go tell the sheriff."

———

They raced to town and over to the sheriff's office. When they burst through the door, Sheriff Valeska jumped. "What are you kids doing here? We settled everything last night."

Sophie glanced over at Jessica, then grinned and walked over to the sheriff. "We found it. We found the gold."

A male voice said, "*Sure*, you did. I never found it, but two kids found it today."

The girls both spun to the right and found Mr. Jenkins sitting in a chair wearing handcuffs. Jessica figured they must have been questioning him or something like that.

"Sophie, I'm tired." They turned back to face the sheriff, who rubbed her hands over her face. "We were out fairly late, and I had an early call this morning. There is no treasure."

"Yes, there is. Remember the stone with the key on it?"

The sheriff nodded. "I'll humor you. Yes, I remember the stone. You said the treasure had to be there."

"It is. The stone isn't a stone. It's gold."

The sheriff came to her feet. "Are you sure?"

"I can vouch for her, Sheriff. She scraped it with a sharp rock and I saw gold."

"What?!" Mr. Jenkins yelled. "I searched for the treasure for almost fifteen years, put up with everything this small town had to offer, smiling the whole time, and these kids found it?"

Sophie crossed her arms over her chest. "Yes."

He motioned them over to his chair. "Tell me, did you actually find the bag of gold?"

"He melted it into a block."

"Melted?" He sat back in the chair, head in his hands, muttering softly, "Melted," over and over again as they went back to the sheriff's desk.

The sheriff was hanging up the phone. She asked, "Sophie and Jessica, do you want to be there when we remove the gold block from the well? We have an expert with bricks and stone coming to help."

"Of course," they said at the same time.

When the sheriff laughed, Sophie said, "You already knew the answer."

"Of course I did. I was having fun with you. And I'd ask if someone was pretending to be you if you'd answered no. Let's all go in my car. Notice I *didn't* ask if you wanted to do that. I do have one stop to make."

On the way, Jessica asked, "Do you have any idea how much the gold is worth?"

"We have an estimate based on the size of the stone, as I remembered it from last night, but we won't know for sure until it's weighed."

After a long stop at the site of a car accident, they got to the well. Two deputies were there, along with an expert, who was already at work on the gold block.

Jessica stood to the side and watched him. "I wondered how you would do this."

The expert said, "I've chiseled out the mortar on the edges. We should be able to remove it soon."

Sophie stood on the other side of him. He pointed upward. "We have an old-fashioned block and tackle set up. A pulley system to lift this." He slid a thin wire under the block and used it to pull through another piece that acted like a sling. Then he clipped that onto the rope that hung from the pulley.

His men pulled on it, and the stone rose. Two sheriff's deputies placed the stone in a duffle bag, and each took a handle, carrying it to the sheriff's car with everyone following behind them. One of the deputies got in the passenger seat, and the girls climbed in the backseat.

Jessica said, "I think Mr. Laurence would like to know that the gold was used for something good."

Sheriff Valeska said, "It will be. This was found on Hilltop property, so it belongs to the city. The house will be saved and still be here, Sophie and Jessica, when you're as old as Nezzy Grant."

————

Two days later, when the girls stepped onto the sand at Pine Lake's beach, Jessica felt the stress from the last couple of weeks slide away. "*Yes.*" She sighed. "We finally got to the beach. Now that the bad guys are all locked up."

Sophie put her towel on the sand. "It did turn out well, didn't it?"

"Uh-huh. But I don't want to talk about it. I want to pretend that we never found a criminal in Pine Hill." Jessica placed her towel beside Sophie's and stretched out on it. "Maybe we can avoid mysteries for the whole day."

"After I say this—"

Jessica groaned. "No! Please."

"We found the treasure, saved Hilltop with the huge amount of money the gold was worth, and escaped the bad guys. You wrote an article about the mystery for the newspaper."

"All true and very good. I like writing for the paper, and I'm especially relieved that you escaped from Mr. Jenkins, Lester, and their friend." Jessica put her hands over her ears. "But I need a break from mysteries."

Sophie pulled Jessica's hand away from her right ear and leaned closer. "I just wanted to say that our last mystery turned out well, so maybe our next one will be even better."

ONE MORE MYSTERY

Sophie and Jessica found a rope that looked new inside the well. Who went to the well before them and why were they there? Unscramble each word and put the words together to make a sentence that gives you the answer.

SSMI _____

AKREWL _____

DTENAW _____

OT _____

NFID _____

ETH _____

OLGD _____

_____

Get the answer at shannonlbrown.com/more

THE CHOCOLATE SPY

THE CRIME-SOLVING COUSINS MYSTERIES

1 SOMETHING'S UP

Jessica Ballow put her sunglasses on and lay down on her towel on Pine Lake's sandy beach.

Her cousin, Sophie Sandoval, sat on a beach towel next to her. "So what should we do now?"

Jessica let out a big sigh. "This is pretty good. My heart isn't racing every fifteen minutes now that we've wrapped up our last mystery. My summer in small-town Pine Hill has been much more exciting than I expected, even more exciting than back home in the big city of London, England."

"Even I'm not quite ready to search for a new mystery. But if one found me, I guess I'd be open."

Jessica laughed. "You are *always* ready for a mystery."

Sophie pointed into the distance. "Hey, there's Tony over on Main Street, handing something out to people."

Jessica sat up and slid her sunglasses down her nose. "He's coming this direction. Is my hair okay?" She smoothed her blonde hair, then tucked it behind her ears.

Sophie looked her over. "Great, as usual."

They watched Tony Donadio make his way across the street and toward them on the sand. Tony's parents owned Donadio's Deli, where Jessica and Sophie often ate. He was also more than a little bit cute, went to the same church Sophie and Jessica attended, and was super smart like her.

When he reached the girls, he handed a sheet of paper down to Sophie. Jessica leaned over to peer at it. On it was printed: *Have a sweet summer. Learn how to make chocolates. Classes at Sweet Bites Chocolates now open.*

"Hmm," said Sophie. "Are you interested, Jessica? It's at a chocolate factory not far from here."

Jessica turned toward Sophie. "It doesn't involve a mystery. And it's chocolate? Do you even need to ask?"

Sophie laughed, and Tony grinned.

Tony said, "I knew you'd ordered hot fudge sundaes a couple of times over at the deli, but I didn't realize you had a thing for chocolate."

"Oh yeah. The resort makes those awesome triple chocolate shakes, and there are the sundaes you've made for me at Donadio's Deli. How could I have missed a chocolate factory while I've been visiting here?"

"Not only is it a factory, but my uncle owns it. I'm handing these out for him." Tony held up the stack of papers.

"Your uncle?" Sophie asked. "My class went to see a chocolate factory a couple of years ago, but I thought it was owned by a family named the Wongs."

"My Uncle Sal bought it from them earlier this year. He lived all over the world while he was in the Army and wanted to settle down someplace when he got out."

"Your uncle learned to make candy in the military?" Sophie asked.

Tony laughed. "No. He repaired helicopters in the army. Uncle Sal liked it here when he visited my family, the business was for sale, and he loves chocolate, so he was pretty excited to buy it. The good news is that my family gets samples every once in a while."

Jessica looked at the flyer again. "I wonder if we'll get samples if we take this class."

Tony shrugged. "Probably."

Sophie sighed. "Jessica has been trying to get me to like chocolate. It's *okay*. But I don't want to run toward it every time I see some."

Jessica said, "And I do. For cousins, we're very different."

"That's true!" Tony and Sophie said together.

The three of them laughed.

"Sophie, let's go see your mom and ask if we can take this class."

"I think Mom will be very happy to know where we are while the classes are going on—and that we aren't in the middle of a mystery."

"You two managed to get into the middle of some danger with *The Feather Chase* and *The Treasure Key*," Tony said.

"Not just the two of us, Tony. You were right in the middle of it too. *Three* twelve-year-olds solved the mysteries."

Tony shrugged. "We have had some exciting times this summer. I hope you'll let me know if you find another mystery."

Jessica shuddered. "Whew. I hope that doesn't happen."

Sophie nudged Jessica with her elbow. "You know you had fun. But could we find another mystery this soon? Even I wonder about that."

A loud sound came from over the hills in the direction of Cutoff Trail. Sophie, Jessica, and Tony all turned toward it. A helicopter flew toward heir direction, barely above the many tall pine trees that gave this town its name. Sand blew around them as it passed overhead.

Jessica covered her eyes with her hands, only pulling them away when the sound faded. The aircraft now hovered in the sky on the opposite side of town, then dropped below the trees and buildings.

Sophie stood and brushed herself off. "Wow! A helicopter! I think it landed near the resort."

Jessica combed her hair with her fingers. "What's so unusual about a helicopter? I see lots of them."

"Not in Pine Hill. I only remember seeing a couple. And it turned out later that someone was very sick, and the helicopter had come to take them to the hospital. Oh no! I hope everyone there is okay."

Sophie grabbed her towel and shook it out. Jessica stood and did the same. They both rolled their towels up as they started walking toward the helicopter's landing spot at the top of a nearby hill with Tony at their side.

When they crested the hill and could see the front of the fancy resort hotel, they also saw people they knew crowded around in front of it. Businesses around town must have closed with the sound of the helicopter so their owners and workers could rush to see what had happened.

Tony said, "There's a landing pad on top of the resort. The construction crew came into our deli and bought lunch a few times while they were building it a few months ago. I didn't think anyone would ever use it."

One person was pointing at the roof, so Jessica guessed it was as Tony had suggested: the aircraft had landed on the roof of the resort. Mrs. Bowman, the owner of Bananas Bakery, was among the onlookers, and they all knew her, so they hurried over there.

When they reached her, the older woman glanced briefly at the trio, then returned her gaze to the roof. Before they could even ask what happened, Mrs. Bowman said, "Did you see it? A helicopter just landed up there. Tony's dad went inside to check and make sure someone isn't sick. If they are, we could get Doc Adams to come over here to help. The people working at the resort may not know about him."

Mr. Donadio came out of the resort with a smile on his face and said to the small crowd, "Everything's fine. We can all leave. They had a guest arrive in a helicopter. I guess that can happen now that they have the helipad on the roof, so we don't need to worry every time we hear the flapping sound of a helicopter."

Someone said, "Good!" and others agreed.

"Mrs. Bowman and I should mention that you can have a

wonderful lunch at Donadio's Deli and follow it up with a delicious baked good, such as a muffin or a piece of cheesecake, over at Bananas Bakery."

"Please do," added Mrs. Bowman.

Smiles on faces told Jessica that some of the people in the crowd might do that.

Jessica watched everyone walk away, including Tony, who headed back with his parents to the deli. "Sophie, do you think he minds working in the summer?"

"No. I asked him once. He likes helping out his family, and he still gets to do other things, like when he works with us." Sophie looked in the direction of the deli. "It's downtown, so it's also close to a lot of things."

"I'm not sure I'd be that nice," Jessica said.

Just then, a man came out of the resort and hurried away. He glanced over his shoulder as he went around the corner of the building and toward the center of Pine Hill. The man wore a suit and tie and sunglasses, and he reminded her very much of Agent Dallas, the FBI agent they'd met while working on a mystery.

"Sophie? Did you see that man go around the side of the building?"

Sophie turned back. "What? Where?"

Jessica pointed.

"Did he seem suspicious or mysterious?" Sophie asked with too much excitement in her voice, more than Jessica wanted to hear. She'd had enough of mysteries forever.

Jessica shrugged, trying to act casual so that Sophie wouldn't become too interested and try to follow him. "He was a man in a suit. I know you've said before that there aren't very many of those in town."

"It's probably just another man here to do business."

Jessica didn't say anything, but she wondered about that. Could the helicopter have brought a new mystery to Pine Hill?

2 CAN YOU KEEP A SECRET?

After leaving the resort, Sophie and Jessica hurried over to Great Finds, the antique shop owned by Sophie's mother. When they got there, they pushed open the glass door, and a bell announced their arrival. Sophie called out, "Mom, it's just us."

April Sandoval stepped into the doorway of her back room, drying her hands on a towel. "I was washing up some new teacups and vases."

"We went to see who was in the helicopter."

"Helicopter?" Mrs. Sandoval tossed the towel off to the side. "I guess I didn't hear it over the running water. Who's in trouble?"

"No one," Sophie answered. "It's okay, Mom. I didn't know that the resort had a helipad now, and it was just someone coming to stay there."

"I knew they'd built it, but I didn't think anybody would ever use it."

Jessica smiled. "That's what Tony said."

Sophie handed her mom the class announcement that Tony had given them, and she read it. Looking up at the two of them, she asked, "Do you want to go to this?"

"Sure." Sophie shrugged.

Jessica nodded. "It's chocolate."

"Well, it sounds like a good way for me to know where you are several mornings in the next week." She glanced at the flyer. "I wonder why the classes skip days in between. Anyway, you'll be there bright and early in the morning."

"Morning? I didn't notice the time, Mom." Sophie leaned over to read the paper again.

"You'll need to leave the house before me. If you come to Great Finds after class, you can help me. When you do, I'll treat you to lunch at the deli. Jessica should like that."

Jessica smiled at the thought of seeing Tony at lunchtimes.

"But Mom—"

Mrs. Sandoval gave Sophie a look that told her she wouldn't win this one.

"Okay, Mom. The morning class."

Jessica wasn't too happy about the time either. Morning definitely wasn't her favorite part of the day.

"Unless you don't want to go, Jessica."

"I love chocolate, so I guess I'm willing to get up early."

With Sophie and Jessica looking over her shoulder, Mrs. Sandoval picked up the phone and dialed the number on the paper. "Sophie," she said as she waited for someone to answer her call, "can you take the trash outside to the Dumpster, please? There's some here and more in the back room."

"Sure, Mom," Sophie answered. She picked up the trash can, which was full to the brim, and carried it out the back door. "Be right back," she said to Jessica.

As Jessica heard her aunt tell the person why she'd called, she glanced toward the window and saw Sheriff Valeska walk by the front of the shop. If anyone knew whether or not the FBI was back in town, the sheriff certainly would.

"I'm going to run out and see if the sheriff knows who was in the helicopter, okay?" Her aunt gave a nod of agreement, so Jessica hurried outside. Anywhere else, she might have used her cell phone to ask her question, but with the hills surrounding Pine Hill, you never knew if a cell phone would work or not.

The sheriff had stopped to talk to a man about half a block away. Jessica waited until the man walked off before she moved closer.

When Jessica had met Sheriff Valeska the first time, she'd expected a sheriff to be hard-as-nails, like the sheriffs and police officers she'd seen on TV and in the movies. She'd been surprised to find a woman sheriff, and Sheriff Valeska did a great job. While she might not always appreciate Sophie's tips about possible mysteries, because Sophie often saw mysteries when there weren't any, she'd been very kind when they had found a real one. She'd also let them do some things that Jessica wasn't sure every sheriff would allow kids to do.

When the sheriff started in the opposite direction, Jessica called out, "Sheriff! Sheriff!"

Sheriff Valeska turned back and paused to allow Jessica to catch up with her.

"What can I help you with?"

Jessica glanced around to make sure no one could overhear them. "I saw a man who might be an FBI agent. He was dressed like one. Are the FBI back in Pine Hill?"

Sheriff Valeska stood there silently for a moment, then said, "Even if I knew, Jessica, I couldn't tell you."

Jessica's shoulders dropped. "Is there another mystery?"

Sheriff Valeska paused again before saying, "You, Sophie, and Tony have worked together on other mysteries. Tony's uncle owns the chocolate factory, you know."

Jessica nodded. "Sophie and I are going to take a chocolate-making class there starting tomorrow." She hoped the word *mysteries* and the chocolate factory didn't connect in any way.

Now it was Sheriff Valeska who turned to look around, and Jessica guessed she was also making sure no one could hear what she was about to say. Jessica hoped it was *good* news.

"I can't tell you very much . . ." The sheriff seemed to be

gathering her thoughts and deciding how to say her next words. Finally, she said, "I'd like to ask you to keep your eyes open when you're at the chocolate factory."

"Keep my eyes open? For what?"

"Anything that seems not quite right."

This was starting to feel more like something Sophie would like to be involved in. "What does 'not quite right' mean?" When the sheriff didn't answer, Jessica thought about what could be wrong in a chocolate factory. "A thief?"

Sheriff Valeska shifted her hat farther back on her head. "Someone may not be who they say they are."

"A spy?"

"I can't tell you any more. Now, I have to ask three things of you. One, don't tell anyone else. Two, anyone else means Sophie."

Oh no. She couldn't tell mystery-loving Sophie about a possible mystery in her town?

"We don't know much yet," the sheriff explained. "And Sophie has a way of getting herself in the middle of things."

Sophie did have a way of finding danger. "I won't tell her right now. To protect her."

The sheriff nodded. "The third thing is that if you discover something, don't talk to anyone about it but me. Don't trust anyone else with this. Do you understand?"

Panic surged through Jessica. Not only might there be another mystery in Pine Hill, but she alone could end up right at the center of it. She gulped. "I understand, Sheriff. I won't let you down."

They said good-bye to each other, and Jessica went back to Great Finds where she found her aunt still on the phone, finishing up their reservations for the class. The class still sounded good, but Jessica now wondered what else she was signing up for.

Sophie returned from trash duty. As she reached them, her mother was setting the phone down.

Mrs. Sandoval said, "Class begins tomorrow. The woman on the phone, Erma Clayton, explained that they're teaching the classes around the schedule for their orders. That's why you'll be there Wednesday, Saturday, Monday, and Tuesday instead of four days in a row."

"That's plenty of chocolate for me," Sophie said.

"One important rule is that people in the factory aren't allowed to wear perfume because the scent can get into the chocolate just by being near it and change the taste. The class sounds like fun. Maybe you can bring some chocolate home for us."

Sophie stared suspiciously at her mother. "Who is this person in front of me? We don't have dessert in our house very often, so what you're saying doesn't make sense. Are you telling me that you like chocolate, Mom?"

Her mom smiled. "I may not believe we should have dessert every day, but that doesn't mean I don't like it. If we had some chocolate treats for a week, our family—including Jessica, of course—could take a little break from my no-sugar plan, and I would join you."

Sophie sat on the stool behind the cash register. "I'm twelve years old, and I just learned Mom's shocking secret."

Jessica grinned. "My mother loves chocolate, so I was surprised yours didn't. Now I understand. She loves it too." She glanced over at her aunt, who nodded. "But she doesn't eat it all the time."

Mrs. Sandoval nodded again.

The bell on the door rang as Sheriff Valeska came into the shop. Jessica picked up a feather duster and swept it over the shelves—her least favorite thing to do at Great Finds—but this way she'd have her back to everyone, so the expression on her face couldn't reveal her secret with the sheriff.

Mrs. Sandoval asked, "Mandy, have you caught the guy yet?"

Sophie turned toward her mom. "What guy, Mom? What happened?"

"I'm surprised you haven't heard, Sophie. Someone stole a car that was parked right here on Main Street."

Jessica turned to them with her feather duster in midair. "In Pine Hill?"

The sheriff rubbed her hand over her face. "I wish they hadn't done it. I'm visiting each of the shops on Main Street to make sure no one saw the theft, that nothing suspicious had happened this morning."

"Everything is perfectly normal here, Mandy," Mrs. Sandoval said.

"Well, I set up a checkpoint on the highway leading out of town. We're stopping every car. I don't like doing that because I don't want this to seem like an unfriendly town, but I have to find the stolen car."

More crimes and criminals? If Jessica were alone with the sheriff, she would ask if this could be connected to what she'd asked her to do.

"Right, Jessica?" Sophie said.

Jessica almost jumped out of her skin when she heard her name. She turned around.

Sophie, Aunt April, and Sheriff Valeska all stared at her.

What had they been saying? With Sophie, she never knew. "Um. Right?"

"You'll catch him, Sheriff," Sophie said.

"Unless they escaped with the car before we realized they'd stolen it. But I hope we do, Sophie."

The sheriff left.

Jessica brought the subject back to chocolate to distract her aunt and cousin in case they'd noticed she'd acted strangely around the sheriff. "Aunt April, we'll do our best to bring you samples every day."

Mrs. Sandoval said, "I like that idea. When you're there, you may notice that Sweet Bites Chocolates is in an unusual building. Long before I was born, it was the boathouse for a big country club down at the water's edge. A boathouse sits over the water, and boats are kept in it."

"That sounds like a garage, Aunt April. Are there still boats there?"

"They're long gone. They used to be in the water underneath today's factory. They had parties and weddings where the factory is. The larger, even more elegant building next door burned down." She turned to Sophie. "Before they made chocolate in the boathouse and before you were born, it was a restaurant, and your father and I would go to eat dinner and watch the sun set over the water."

Mrs. Sandoval laughed. "I went there once to talk to a friend who worked in the restaurant. Her office was down a hallway that turned into another hallway and turned a corner and went around that corner and down steps and up steps. It was crazy. You'll have to let me know if they've opened it all up, or if there are still all kinds of odd places there."

It sounded exactly like the type of place where they'd find a mystery. Jessica hoped that wouldn't happen, that she wouldn't learn *anything* interesting to tell the sheriff.

3 A SWEET CLASS

Sophie sat up in bed and rubbed her eyes, trying to wake up. Moving as quietly as she could, she stepped onto the floor and tiptoed over to the bathroom so she could take a shower. Not long after Jessica had come to stay with her for the summer, Sophie had learned her cousin wasn't good at waking up. When Sophie had finished showering, she put on her robe, then slowly opened the bathroom door.

Jessica was sitting up. Without saying a word, she got out of bed and trudged by Sophie into the bathroom. Sophie stepped aside, the door closed behind her, and she heard the water turn on.

As Jessica showered, Sophie got dressed and dried her hair before pulling it back into a ponytail. A short time later, the bathroom door opened and her cousin came out, rubbing her hair with a towel. "My shower helped. I think I'm ready to face the day."

Sophie sat on the end of her bed. "This might be the earliest we've gotten up this summer. It almost—*almost*—makes getting up for school look good."

"This morning was a little easier than school. It involves chocolate." Jessica did a little happy dance, then began drying her hair, which Sophie knew would be followed by her putting on her makeup.

After what seemed like forever, Sophie groaned and flopped backward on the bed. "We're *just* taking a class, Jessica."

Jessica stepped back and checked her reflection in the mirror, then added earrings and a bracelet. "Almost ready. Notice that I'm wearing chocolate brown shorts to celebrate our first day making my favorite treat." She turned to face Sophie. "Let's go."

Sophie rolled off the bed. "I wish you could get ready as quickly as I do." She gestured toward her hair, then to her faded jeans and white T-shirt.

"I've stopped using a lot of my makeup since I came to Pine Hill, but I do like to have it just right."

They went through the living room and into the kitchen to get a bite to eat. Sophie made toast for both of them while Jessica poured juice. When they were seated at the small kitchen table, Sophie said, "I wish we had a mystery. Well, at least part of me wishes we had a mystery."

Jessica coughed and reached for her juice.

"Are you okay?"

After taking another sip of juice, she said, "Fine."

"Aren't you going to say how happy you are that we *don't* have a mystery to work on?"

"Mysteries are interesting when you're in the middle of them, and always seem to end up dangerous, but are better than not doing anything." Jessica got to her feet and took her plate and glass over to the sink, rinsed them off, and put them in the dishwasher. "Today we get to make chocolates."

Sophie finished her toast and took her things to the dishwasher too. "It sounds fun to learn how to make chocolates, but I wish I wanted to eat what we've made."

"Did your mom say what she was going to have us do this afternoon at Great Finds?"

"She only said that she wanted us to come over and help. It could be something interesting, and it could be more dusting."

Sophie grabbed her backpack and Jessica her purse, and they both went out the door, down the steps, and over to the trail that led through the woods.

The cousins followed the trail to Pine Hill, kept going through town and past the resort, then turned left toward the lake where the chocolate factory sat.

They soon approached a building painted a color that Sophie could best describe as "chocolate chip." A big sign with letters that looked like someone had taken bites out of them read, "Sweet Bites Chocolates." The building's large door was painted to look like a box of chocolate and the door handle like a chocolate bar.

Sophie pulled the door open and entered with Jessica right behind her. They stopped just inside the building. A desk to their right was empty, but she thought someone should be sitting there waiting to greet them.

A woman came around the corner in a hurry, panting. She stopped and gave them a big smile. "Hello, ladies. I'm Erma Clayton. I'm so sorry I wasn't here when you came in. I've taken three people back to the classroom area, and you must be two more for me." She sat down in front of her computer.

"Yes, ma'am," Jessica said. "I'm Jessica Ballow, and this is my cousin Sophie Sandoval."

The woman checked her computer screen, made a few clicks, then stood again, grabbing a couple of name tags as she did. She handed one to each of them. "We're happy to have you here for the class."

Sophie pinned her name tag to her shirt, and Jessica did the same.

Still smiling, Mrs. Clayton motioned for them to follow her. They all went down a hall, around a corner, and into a small room with some chairs set up and a screen on the wall. It could have been a classroom in a school anywhere. Sophie felt a bit of nervousness pass through her as she realized this might not be fun, there might not be treats to sample, and they might have to sit in a classroom for days learning how people made chocolates.

Her expression must have given away her thoughts. A man who looked like Tony's dad said, "Come in. Come in. Please find a seat." He watched the two of them walk over and sit down in chairs in the last of the four rows. A man and two women had arrived before them. "And don't worry. We'll only be in this classroom for a little while this morning. Most of the time, you're going to be out in the factory learning how to make chocolates."

Only one more person, an older man, arrived, then the man who'd greeted them walked to the front of the room and began. "I'm Salvatore Donadio. I've only lived in Pine Hill for half a year, but many of you, if not all of you, know my brother who owns Donadio's Deli." Everyone in the class nodded, then glanced at each other, smiling. Tony's dad had a great reputation in the town. Sophie and Jessica had wondered about him when they'd been working on their last mystery and had been glad when he'd checked out okay.

As Mr. Donadio walked across the room, he added, "The next class has twice this number of people signed up, probably because they had more time to plan for it. You're first so we'll learn how to do this together."

He dimmed the lights, returned to the front, and turned on a projector. Pictures of candy flashed onto the screen. Mr. Donadio then told his students the history of chocolate, how it was found in South America and that explorers brought it to Europe where it became very popular, and word about the delicious treat soon spread.

When he'd finished, he said, "Now I'm going to take you on a tour of my beautiful chocolate factory. But first, do you have any questions?"

Sophie raised her hand, and he nodded in her direction.

"Do you only make chocolates here, or do you make other kinds of candy too?"

"Great question! We make more than thirty kinds of chocolate, different flavors, shapes, sizes—"

Sophie felt her heart sink at his words. This would be chocolate and nothing but that. She'd still try to have fun. Even if she didn't learn to love chocolate like Jessica did.

He gestured for the class to follow him, and one by one they went out the door, down the hall, and around another corner. Her mother had been right. This building had so many twists and turns that it was hard to know where she was.

Mr. Donadio stopped in front of a closed door, and his students crowded around him. "This is our storage area, where we keep some of our supplies." He unlocked the door, pushed it open, then stepped aside so they could see into the room.

A wide array of items sat on shelves piled with many different sizes of boxes for chocolates, jars, and cans of all sorts of things that Sophie couldn't even begin to guess what they were used for in making candy. There were pens, pencils, and office paper. Mr. Donadio stepped into the room, picked up a box, and held it up. Sophie could see that it was marked "bubble gum."

"I had what I thought was a great idea," he said. "You can tell me if I was wrong, or if the people who have advised me are wrong." He reached into the box and pulled out a piece of what Sophie could tell was a kind of bubble gum she'd had before. Holding it up, he said, "I thought chocolate-covered bubblegum would be a hit with our customers. What do you think?"

Sophie grimaced. Would that sound good to someone who loved chocolate?

A woman to her right said, "Sal, your company makes wonderful chocolates, but I think that sounds horrible."

Everyone seemed to agree.

Sophie thought his feelings would be hurt, but he just smiled and shrugged. "I'll come up with something new that people love. Chocolate-covered strawberries, those are all over the place, so I don't want to do more of them unless someone really wants them. I want to make something special, different, and quite wonderful."

He next took everyone toward the factory area. As they walked, he said to Sophie and Jessica, "You're friends with Tony, right?"

"Yes, sir," Sophie answered.

"That makes you like family to a Donadio, so please call me Uncle Sal, as Tony does."

"Uncle Sal" stopped at the entrance to the factory. "Here we make delicious chocolates. So that your hands are free, please leave your purses and other belongings behind Mrs. Clayton's desk while we're working."

When they'd done that, he led them into a room around the corner from the lobby. "This is where we keep our finished chocolates at the perfect temperature. You can each choose one."

A sigh went up from almost everyone there.

He put on gloves and picked up the piece of chocolate each person pointed to.

Jessica said, "I'll have anything dark chocolate." When she bit into it, she said, "Yum. Raspberry cream."

Sophie halfheartedly said, "I'll take whichever one you think is best, Uncle Sal." When she took a bite of the light chocolate piece, the orange flavor inside brought a smile to her face. Maybe this wouldn't be bad after all.

When they stepped out of the room, a worker called Uncle Sal over.

Walking away, he said, "Everyone, share your names. I'll be right back."

4 THE FIRST SUSPECT

One of the women in the chocolate-making class—Jessica didn't think she was quite as old as her mom—introduced herself as Emily Foster. "I'm here on vacation. Who could resist a chocolate class?"

A man about her grandfather's age said, "I'm Peter Pleckenpoll." Jessica wondered if she'd be able to remember that. He must have had that problem in the past because he added, "Please call me Mr. P."

Sophie grinned. "That's easy."

A young man with an older woman by his side gave his name as Dylan Hanley. "I'm working in Pine Hill for the summer as part of a college class. This is my mother, Beverly." Turning to the woman at his side, he added, "She's visiting."

"It's a pleasure to meet all of you," Mrs. Hanley said. "I'm enjoying my trip to Pine Hill. Are you from here?"

Jessica opened her mouth to answer, but she continued.

"I'm from Chicago. Dylan grew up there, didn't you, son?" Before he could reply, she said, "Summer isn't bad there, but winter can be cold."

Jessica glanced at Sophie, and her cousin shrugged. They both wanted to say something to be polite but were fairly certain the older woman wouldn't give them a chance. And, as expected, Mrs. Hanley picked up where her last sentence left off.

As she described her trip to Pine Hill in detail, Jessica listened but checked out the people in the class. None of them looked suspicious. Smart criminals would seem innocent though, wouldn't they?

At last Uncle Sal returned, interrupting the woman's story of her travel from the airport, and began his tour with some giant-sized pots to the side of the room. "This is where we keep the chocolate at a perfect melted temperature at all times. If chocolate isn't treated with care, it can get crystals in it and do other strange things, things that don't taste good and might not make a pretty piece of candy."

Jessica said, "We call candy 'sweets' in England."

Uncle Sal nodded. "Yes. My chocolates are sweets when they're sold there."

With a big smile on his face, he led them over to what he called the enrober, a long machine with a belt that carried pieces of candy filling into a shower of liquid chocolate. "We're making my favorite today, chocolate-covered marshmallows. We do them in both dark and milk chocolate, but today we're using milk chocolate."

Jessica would have rather had dark chocolate, but this should still be fun.

"Everyone will have a chance to put the marshmallows we make here on the belt at the beginning and to set the finished pieces on a tray at the end." Still smiling, he warned, "No sampling the finished chocolates."

At everyone's sad expression, he added, "But you can each have a piece of your choice later. Maybe two."

His students laughed.

"You and you,"—he pointed first to Sophie then to Jessica—"can be first on the beginning of the line. Emily and I will go to the end of the line. We only keep perfectly coated pieces of candy. I will teach her what to watch for, then have someone take my place so she can teach them."

Everyone put on plastic gloves. Then the four who were working the line took their positions.

"I hope we can move as fast as we're supposed to," Jessica said to Sophie.

A worker wheeled over a cart with trays of square pieces of marshmallow on it. The man set eight pieces in a row on the end of the belt where the bottoms were then coated with chocolate. They moved down the belt to be showered in a waterfall of chocolate, then slid out of sight into a long, enclosed section, what the man helping them said was the cooling tunnel where the chocolate hardened.

He stepped aside and watched as the two of them each put four pieces of marshmallow in a single row on the belt. Then seconds later, another row. With the third row, he nodded his approval and walked away.

They put row after row on the belt. When a cheer went up, Jessica glanced at the end of the machine. Emily and Uncle Sal were working, so she knew their first chocolates had made it to the end of the line. The rest of their class gathered there to see.

"Whew. This is harder than I realized," Sophie said. "We have to move more quickly, or they won't have as many chocolates made today as they should."

As she reached for more marshmallows, Jessica said, "Yes, it's intense." She lowered her arm, then realized she didn't feel the movement of her bracelet on her wrist. "Sophie, do you see my bracelet? I know I had it when we began."

When Sophie stepped back to check the area, Jessica said, "No, I don't want to mess up this job. Keep moving, but keep your eyes open too."

Jessica leaned back to check the floor as she set the next batch of marshmallows on the belt. Not there. She checked the tray they'd pulled the marshmallows from to see if her bracelet had dropped onto it. No.

A gasp made her turn in Sophie's direction. She followed Sophie's gaze to the belt as it entered the cooling area. A chocolate-coated lump rested beside the covered marshmallows.

Jessica's heart sank to her toes. She whispered, "Uncle Sal will set it aside when it comes out."

Sophie snorted. "And tell everyone in his family." She grabbed four marshmallows and set them on the belt. When Jessica didn't do her half, Sophie grabbed another four and added them to her row.

Jessica felt her face grow hot. "Maybe he won't say anything."

"Are you kidding? Who could resist a story about a chocolate-covered bracelet?"

Jessica stood still. "Tony will think it's funny. Sophie, I'm going to be very embarrassed."

Sophie grabbed more marshmallows. "I need you to keep up with our job right now. We'll come up with a plan, a way to get to the other end of the enrober and be there when it comes out."

"Sorry." She set a row on the belt.

Uncle Sal called out, "Jessica, why don't you take my place here. Mr. Pleckenpoll can work next to Sophie."

Jessica began walking away, but leaned in and said, "If Emily doesn't notice my chocolate-covered jewelry, I might be okay. Think of a diversion."

At the other end of the enrober, Jessica copied Emily's actions by checking the tops and bottoms of each piece of candy to make sure they were covered. Any that weren't or had stuck together were set to the side. All the while, Jessica's nerves stretched tighter and tighter. The time inside the cooling area should end in a minute or two for her bracelet.

Uncle Sal stood near Sophie, and Jessica saw her cousin speaking with him. A few seconds later, he took Sophie's place, and Mr. P. hurried in Jessica's direction, at least he seemed to be hurrying for an old man.

He said, "Emily, I'm here to take over for you."

The woman stepped to the side. "It's all yours. These smell so good that I'm excited about those samples Sal mentioned." She headed toward Uncle Sal as the bracelet rolled out, along with many marshmallows, now completely covered in chocolate. Jessica grabbed it and stuffed it into her pocket as smoothly as she could, hoping no one had seen her. She sneaked a peek at Mr. P.

He raised an eyebrow. "A snack for later?"

Knowing her face had to be bright red, she lifted her bracelet up and barely out of her pocket. "My bracelet fell onto the enrober."

He chuckled. "That could be embarrassing. Your secret is safe with me."

Whew! Mr. P. understood.

Sophie came over to work with Mr. P., so Jessica stepped to the side. Then Uncle Sal left the marshmallow loading area to Dylan and his mother after they'd watched for a minute, and he headed their way.

"Did you get a good idea of what this machine can do?" Uncle Sal asked her, Sophie, and Mr. P.

Jessica glanced at Sophie and saw that her cousin was fighting laughter. Mr. P. was grinning. A bracelet that could pass as dessert probably fit in the category of something Uncle Sal didn't know the machine could do. He took over for Sophie, leaving her and Jessica to watch.

Jessica whispered, "I'm going to go to the restroom to get this out of my pocket before it's had time to melt. Or melt more than it already has."

"I'll walk with you," Sophie replied. "I want to tell you about something I saw."

They told Uncle Sal that they were going to the ladies' room and went on their way.

Once they reached it, Sophie checked under the stall doors to make sure no one was there while Jessica used hot water to rinse off her bracelet.

Sophie said, "Something strange happened right before we left. Mr. P. dropped a chocolate-covered marshmallow and bent over to pick it up."

"So?" Jessica ran a paper towel under the water, then wiped chocolate out of her pocket. The paper towel came out *almost* clean.

"He moved like a young man, much faster than he usually moves."

After checking her hair in the mirror and deciding it was fine, Jessica turned toward Sophie. "Maybe he felt young today."

"When he glanced my direction and saw me watching him, he grabbed his side and made a small moan."

Jessica noted this as something to tell Sheriff Valeska. She'd said to remember anything odd. "I don't know why he'd do that. Keep watching him."

Sophie nodded. "I'm going to. Now, we'd better get back."

When they stepped out the door, Jessica saw a shadow around the corner. It stayed there a moment before moving away. Had someone followed them there?

5 THE FIRST SUSPECT

Back in the factory, Jessica watched everyone as they worked. No one looked suspicious. They all seemed to be who they said they were. But according to the sheriff, one of these people in the class or someone working here could be a spy.

When Jessica had checked her email on Uncle Lucas's computer the night before to see if she'd received anything from her parents who were in another country for her father's work, she'd also searched for information on people who stole secrets from businesses. It was called *industrial espionage*, she'd learned, because it involved a business—or industry—and those people were spying.

So, now she was looking for a spy. Not only that, but she was also a spy herself, because what else could you call someone who was watching people for the sheriff? She was a spy looking for a spy, and the worst part of it all was that she couldn't tell Sophie.

At the end of the class, Uncle Sal gave each of the students a box with four pieces of chocolate in it. Dylan's mother immediately put both of theirs in her purse. Jessica suspected he wasn't going to get a bite of it.

Now she wondered what to do. She was supposed to watch

everyone here and not get in trouble. But what if no one did anything suspicious in class but waited until afterward? How could she catch them? The only way she could think of was to follow them and see if they were who they said they were. That would be easier if Sophie knew what was going on. Jessica would have to be sneaky, and she didn't like that.

As everyone gathered the things they'd brought with them, Jessica pulled Sophie aside, while keeping her eyes on her classmates.

"Sophie, since we don't have a mystery, why don't we get some practice and pretend? Let's follow someone. We can improve our tailing skills."

Sophie's mouth dropped open. "That's the sort of thing I would suggest, but you always try to talk me out of it."

Jessica couldn't argue with the truth. "You're right, but it will give us something to do. And your mom isn't expecting us for a little while, right?"

"Right. Let's follow whoever leaves next."

Sophie grabbed her backpack and Jessica picked up her purse as Emily went out the door. They waited a minute, pretending that they were interested in pictures of chocolates on the wall, before leaving.

By now Emily was at the top of the hill that led down to Sweet Bites Chocolates. Jessica knew they didn't need to hurry though because a thick forest was on both sides of the street, and she'd already passed the old, overgrown road that led to the shore. Unless Emily decided to go through the woods, which seemed unlikely because she wasn't dressed for a hike, she had to continue on the road toward town.

Sophie said, "Let's keep our distance but keep her in sight."

Jessica was glad to have Sophie along. Her cousin knew how to be a detective.

"Do you know anything about her, Jessica? I only know her name."

Jessica had been paying more attention than she usually

would. She'd always liked people, and she was interested in their stories, partly because she enjoyed writing, but this morning she'd tried to hear everything everybody said. "Only that she's visiting Pine Hill right now."

"Well, that's something anyway. I didn't recognize her. But why would someone take a class and stay inside when they came to a place like Pine Hill?

Jessica laughed. "Maybe she's like me and would rather be shopping."

"But she can shop and do inside things like that anywhere. Why here?"

"Excellent question, Sophie. We'll see if we get an answer by following her."

Having reached the top of the hill themselves, they watched Emily take a right turn on the first street she came to. Sophie walked faster. "We'd better speed up." The trees thinned out, and old brick houses started to appear beside the road. Every building in Pine Hill except the chocolate factory and Sophie's house was brick, as far as Jessica could tell.

Most of the town was to the right, including the downtown area, the beach, the marina and, if you walked far enough, Sophie's house. The only place Jessica remembered going to the left was the cemetery. And she hoped she'd never have to go there again.

When they turned onto another road with houses, this time with large trees overhanging the sidewalk, Emily was far ahead of them, but they could still see her.

"Whew! I'm glad she didn't go into one of those houses, or we would have lost her." Sophie did everything in a big way, including a pretend trailing of a pretend suspect. Jessica did hope that Emily was in the clear because she liked her.

"This is kind of fun," Sophie said.

Emily turned right. "I feel like a real detective right now, Jessica. Thank you! I'm not missing mysteries as much. But we'll have to be careful who we follow."

"Does that mean we plan on following more people?"
Having Sophie on board with her spying was a very good thing.

"I'd like to. Maybe tomorrow we can tail one of the other
people in the class."

Jessica laughed. "Maybe Mr. P., but he's old enough that I
don't think he's going to get into trouble."

"I would guess that there are criminals who are young and
some who are very old. But you're right. Mr. P. seems like a nice
guy. I'd like to have him as a grandfather."

Toward the end of the street, Emily stopped. Sophie and
Jessica darted behind one of the trees, which had fortunately
been there as long as the houses had and was big enough around
to hide the two of them. The girls peered around the tree, one of
them on each side.

"She just stopped to tie her shoe," Sophie said. "Now she's
on her way again."

They watched her turn the next corner toward what Jessica
was pretty sure was the marina, the place where all of Pine
Lake's boats were kept.

When they got to the corner, Emily was still ahead of them
and in plain sight. By the time the marina came into view, woods
lined the road again.

"I'm glad Emily's still moving because I don't see anything to
hide behind here, do you, Sophie? She'd see us if we ran toward
the forest."

"Very true. We have to move fast if we need to find a hiding
place."

When they reached the marina, Emily suddenly stopped.
Jessica couldn't tell why until she sat down on a bench, one of
many that were scattered about on Pine Hill's wide sidewalks.
She reached into her bag, pulled out a book, and opened it.

"Soph, we need to find a place to hide and in a hurry. She
could easily look up from her book and see us standing here."

Sophie turned in a circle. Halfway around, she said, "Over
here! Behind this trash can."

"Sophie, anyone who walks by or drives past us is going to think it's crazy for two girls to be crouched behind a trash can."

"Right." She continued around the circle. "Plan B: there's another bench that we passed a minute ago. If we sit on it, we'll be far enough away from Emily that she probably won't notice us, but we'll still be able to keep an eye on her. Better?"

"Much better. And much more comfortable too."

As they sat down on the bench a couple of minutes later, Jessica wished they had brought a book, as Emily had. "She could sit there for hours."

"Tomorrow, we can bring books, and I'll bring a little notebook to write in so we can take notes. What we learn about tailing people could be useful if we ever discover another mystery."

Jessica hoped they weren't in the middle of one right now. If the secret came out, would Sophie ever forgive her for not telling her?

"How much time do we have before we need to be at Great Finds?"

Sophie checked her watch. "We have about twenty-five minutes. I'd like to learn more about Emily today so we can tail someone else tomorrow."

Emily rose to her feet when a boat came in, one that Jessica recognized as belonging to Captain Jack, the man who had taken them fishing once. Smiling from ear to ear, Emily closed her book and put it back in her bag. Then she walked slowly over toward the boat, which was pulling up into its spot at the dock.

Jessica and Sophie got up and walked closer.

A man waved to Emily from the boat. Once it had stopped, he jumped onto the dock. She ran into his arms, and he swung her up in the air. Captain Jack stepped off the boat and tied it up. Just when Jessica thought she and Sophie had gotten away cleanly without Emily noticing them, Captain Jack saw them and waved. He shouted, "Hello, lassies."

Sophie whispered to Jessica, "Pretend we've been out on a walk. Act casual."

They hurried over to his boat.

"What are you lassies up to on this fine summer morning? Any more mysteries?"

Sophie laughed, but Jessica could tell that it wasn't her real, happy laugh.

"We're taking a chocolate class right now," Sophie answered for both of them. "Emily is in it too. Jessica and I had a little bit of time before we had to get over to her mom's shop, so we were walking around."

Jessica bit back a grin. It was the absolute truth. They *were* walking around.

The man with his arm around Emily, said, "You're in the class with my wife?"

Emily nodded. "We had fun today, didn't we, girls?"

"We did. Your husband should have been there too."

He shook his head. "No! I'm here to fish. Emily doesn't like to fish, but she's happy to read a book. I was happy when she found out about the chocolate class because that was an extra special thing for her to do. We both get a vacation that we love."

"Jessica, it's time for us to get over to Mom's shop." To Emily, she added, "My mom owns Great Finds, the antique store on Main Street. If you get tired of reading, you can stop by."

"I may do that."

The girls waved good-bye and hurried away.

6 I SEE YOU

At Great Finds, Sophie stopped in front of the glass window facing the sidewalk. "Look," she said.

"At what?" Jessica asked. "Your mom has quite a few things in the window."

Sophie rolled her eyes. "How many of them could be used to solve a mystery?"

Only one stood out. "The spyglass."

Sophie nodded. "Exactly." She pushed open the door to Great Finds and saw her mother dusting. "That's your least favorite job at Mom's shop, isn't it, Jessica?"

"Yes. But it's easy to do. It seems to go on forever though when I'm doing it."

"Maybe she's already taken care of most of it." She went over to where her mother swept the feather duster over some teacups. "Mom! When did you get the spyglass?" Sophie pointed toward the window.

Mrs. Sandoval smiled widely. "I wondered how long it would take for you to notice. You do have good powers of observation. I can see that's a skill that has helped you solve mysteries. To answer your question, I bought the brass spyglass when I was at an event last spring, and it arrived today. Would you like to see it?"

Sophie didn't even speak up because she was sure her mother already knew the answer. They followed Mrs. Sandoval over to the window, where she took it out and set it in Sophie's hands.

Sophie held up the spyglass and aimed it toward the window. "This is great!" She scanned the street through the lens.

"Mom, the moon is pretty full right now, isn't it?"

"It is. You know your dad loves astronomy, and I remember him saying the other day that it was almost a full moon again."

"So there would be enough light even at night to see through a spyglass. This would be a good night to go camping, wouldn't it?" Sophie smiled brightly at her mother. "The place where we found the briefcase with the feathers has an amazing view of the lake."

"Wouldn't it be just as good to see the moon from your house, Sophie?" Jessica asked.

Sophie shook her head. "It would be more fun to watch the moon from a great spot like that one above Pine Lake."

Her mother chewed on her lip. "It seems safe. You haven't managed to get yourself in the middle of a mystery for weeks." She paused. "There are two of you and that's safer."

Jessica said, "I don't want to go camping, Sophie."

"It's you *and* Jessica or not at all," Mrs. Sandoval said to Sophie.

Sophie groaned and turned to Jessica. "Please?"

"Okay," Jessie agreed, but Sophie could tell she still didn't want to go. "I didn't think I would ever go camping in my whole life."

"Thank you!"

"Sophie, I do have that favor to ask of you," Mrs. Sandoval said. "Remember how I mentioned the choir to you two or three weeks ago?"

Not the choir! Sophie nodded very slowly.

"If you would go and sing—"

"No! Please, Mom, I'm a mystery solver, not a choir singer."

"All I'm asking is that you give it a try. Go once or twice and see if you like it. You have a very pretty voice when you sing at church." Her mother held out her hand.

Sophie stared at it. Then she reached for her mom's hand and shook it. "Deal. I sing twice?"

Her mother nodded.

"And I get to go camping tonight?"

"You aren't far from home when you're there. I think it should be okay. I'll have to see if your father agrees, but I believe he will."

"And we can take the spyglass?" As much as Sophie wanted it, she didn't think her mother would allow that.

"You can take it."

Sophie blinked, not sure she'd heard correctly. Her mother was always very careful with antiques, so why wasn't she worried about this one?

Jessica solved the mystery. "Aunt April, I noticed that the spyglass has a dent in the side. It isn't as perfect as most of the other things you have in your shop."

"Very observant. I bought it thinking that one day I might sell it, but since the spyglass isn't perfect, it isn't as valuable. I've decided to let Sophie use it for a while."

"Really? More than one night?" Sophie held it close to her chest. Then she said, "This has been a day of great things. Uncle Sal let each of us choose a piece of chocolate this morning. And he gave us each a box with four more pieces."

Mrs. Sandoval said, "Uncle Sal? Do you mean Salvatore Donadio?"

Jessica said, "He said that we're friends with Tony, and friends are like family to the Donadios, so we should call him Uncle Sal."

Mrs. Sandoval said, "That's fine. But Sophie, you've always said you did not like chocolate. You do now?"

Sophie tapped the counter as she thought about the answer. "The milk chocolate with the orange filling tasted good. At least, it wasn't bad."

Her mother and Jessica laughed.

Sophie said, "I've had enough chocolate for today. Jessica, let's not take any chocolate tonight. Okay?"

"That's fine with me. I know I get to eat more at the next class."

"It's time to pack for our night." Sophie walked toward the door, her hand securely around the spyglass.

7 IT'S A MYSTERY!

The shop door closed behind Sophie before Jessica could even get there. The last words she heard from her were from her list of things to take that night: ". . . tent, sleeping bags, food for dinner and breakfast, flashlights . . ." Jessica caught up with Sophie about half a block away. She certainly didn't want to waste any time in getting home to pack for this camping trip.

Once they were back at Sophie's house, her cousin packed swiftly. She asked her father to help haul some of their gear to the campsite, and faster than Jessica would have thought possible, they were alone in the woods beside a tent.

"This summer has been full of firsts." Jessica glanced around them. It was beautiful up here in a rustic, old-fashioned way. She and Sophie sat on some lightweight chairs, watching the sun set as they ate dinner. Jessica took a bite of her sandwich and chewed slowly, all the time playing the scene in her mind over and over again of Sheriff Valeska asking her to keep her eyes open at the chocolate factory.

She didn't need to worry here, though. They were a long way from Sweet Bites Chocolates. And the sheriff didn't say anything scary was happening. She said for Jessica to keep her eyes open, so it was probably safe to be in the woods.

Of course, there was the time when she and Sophie had first met, and Sophie had said there were wild animals up here, but Jessica still hadn't seen one. She hoped they were safe from those too. She glanced around as she ate the last bite of her sandwich. Their first mystery had begun with a clue they'd found up here.

The idea of clues sent her thoughts right back to Sweet Bites. There might not be anything strange happening inside that chocolate factory. Sure, there'd been that shadow that went around the corner this morning, but that could have a simple explanation, like one of the people who worked there stopped for a moment.

Jessica swallowed hard. "We're safe. We're safe," she said very low so Sophie wouldn't hear her.

"Are you okay, Jessica?"

"Sure. I'm fine. Absolutely wonderful." She laughed in a way that she hoped sounded real but didn't to her own ears.

A flashlight came on and shined in her direction. "You don't sound okay. Are you nervous about camping?"

Jessica held up her thumb and forefinger a short distance apart. "Maybe a little." She moved her hands so they were about a foot apart. "Maybe more than a little."

"Don't worry. I've camped up here lots of times. We're fine." Sophie took another bite of her sandwich. A minute later, she added, "Turkey sandwiches and watching the sun set over Pine Lake. This is awesome. I brought apples for dessert."

Jessica pointed at her braces, then realized Sophie couldn't see her. "Is mine cut up?"

"Of course. I know it's hard for you to eat apples otherwise." Sophie handed her a plastic bag with the apple in it.

Munching on an apple slice, Jessica realized this place was safe. She only had to worry about possible spies at the chocolate factory. No problem. No problem at all.

Heavy clouds early in the day had moved on, leaving a mostly clear sky. The stars shone overhead, and a full moon cast a bright light onto the lake in front of them, making it seem almost like daytime.

Sophie held up her spyglass and scanned the horizon.

"Is there anything out there?"

"Only water surrounded by pine trees. This is the first time I've used this away from town, and I wanted it to be interesting, maybe even exciting."

"That's a lot to ask for with a lake."

"Especially when we aren't working on a mystery."

Jessica *wasn't* working on a mystery, at least she hoped not. "I think Pine Lake's going to be quiet at night. Can I try the spyglass?"

Sophie handed it to her. "Let me know if you see anything. I'm going to relax and enjoy being out here in nature."

Right, nature. Where was a mall when you needed one? Jessica held up the spyglass and saw the lake through the circle at the end. Motion at the edge of the circle caught her attention, so she shifted it that direction. A little sailboat slowly moved toward the center of the lake.

"Hey Sophie, there's a boat."

"Really? Where?" Sophie reached for the spyglass and held it up, peering through it in the direction Jessica pointed. "There is. It's coming from the far side of the lake. Why would anybody be in a boat at night? That seems kind of risky. What if there was a log or something like that in the water? You wouldn't see it at all."

Jessica could barely make out the boat without the spyglass, and might not have noticed it otherwise. When it slid into the moon's reflection on the water, she could see its sails a little more clearly. "Can I look again?"

"Sure." Sophie handed it back. "A sailboat is so quiet that we wouldn't have known it was there if we weren't camping tonight."

Jessica found the boat again. Then everything went dark. She lowered the spyglass and discovered that a cloud had covered the moon. "I think we're done using this tonight. The clouds made it dark enough that this is hard to see through." *And it's a lot creepier.*

As Jessica listened for anything in the trees and brush around them, the cloud moved off, and the moon reappeared. She returned the spyglass to Sophie who immediately raised it to the view.

"The boat stopped in the middle of the lake. That doesn't make sense."

"Maybe they think the moon is pretty, like we do, and wanted to sit in the moonlight."

Sophie laughed. "That's probably true. You know how I almost always want to be solving a mystery."

Stillness came over their campsite. There was only the sound of crickets in the woods and a light breeze that ruffled her hair. This was actually kind of pleasant, and her spying job at the chocolate factory more like a bad dream.

Suddenly Sophie jumped to her feet. "Jessica! They dropped something over the side of the boat. Then they turned in a circle and started back to shore."

Jessica noticed a second tiny speck on the water coming from near town. "Sophie, over there!" Jessica tugged the spyglass in that direction so Sophie could see it better.

"What is going on? People in two boats want to go out and see the moonlight in the same place?"

Another cloud moved over the moon.

"No!" Sophie cried out. "Move, cloud, move!" She swept her hand to the side as if she could move the cloud that direction. The light began increasing as the cloud moved on. "The first boat is gone. Wait! I see a trail of water behind a boat going back to where I first saw it."

Sophie gave Jessica time with the spyglass. A minute later, Jessica said, "The second boat doesn't have sails. It went right to the spot or very close to where the other boat stopped, and they pulled something onboard. They must have picked up whatever the other boat threw overboard."

"This is very strange."

Knowing Sophie would want to see what was happening, she handed the spyglass back to her.

"Jessica, the first boat went to a part of the lake I don't know very well. It's way on the other side of Pine Hill—beyond that, even." Sophie swung the spyglass to the right. "The second boat isn't going toward the marina either, and that's where all but a few of Pine Lake's boats are kept. Hold it . . . that boat might be going in the direction of the chocolate factory."

"Oh no! There *is* a mystery. If the boat is from there—"

Sophie lowered the spyglass and turned toward Jessica. "What are you saying?"

Jessica needed a quick answer. "That old building feels like a mysterious place with all its wandering hallways."

"Now you're talking. We might have found another mystery." Sophie looked through the spyglass again.

Jessica watched the second boat as it trailed away in the direction of the last place she would want it to go, Sweet Bites Chocolates. Now, instead of having fun making candy, she might have ended up in the middle of a mystery again.

8 THE SECRET'S OUT

Sophie lay in her sleeping bag, zipped all the way up, and stared at the ceiling of their tent. She kept thinking about the boats they had seen, and she couldn't figure out a reasonable explanation for them to be there. It reminded her of watching a foot race when the baton was passed from one person to another, but then it made sense. What would someone drop in a lake at night?

Jessica tossed and turned beside her, so she didn't think she was sleeping either. Sophie rolled onto her side.

"Jessica?" Sophie said in a very low voice so she wouldn't wake her if she had nodded off. "Are you asleep?"

"We have a new mystery. How can I sleep when there's a new mystery? Plus, I'm out here in the woods, practically in the middle of nowhere, in a tent that can't protect me from anything. And I just realized that there isn't any way for me to take a shower when I wake up in the morning, so I don't know if you're going to get cranky Jessica or what."

"Whoa. I know mornings are definitely not your best time of day. Let's fix that problem by my being very quiet and not talking to you until you talk to me in the morning. I'll wait for you to let me know if you're cranky or not."

"That makes sense. Now, about the mystery—"

"The two boats were acting weird. I'll admit that. It seems like a mystery, but I'm not sure what it would be."

Jessica was silent for about a minute, so long that Sophie wondered if she'd fallen asleep after all. Then she spoke. "Sophie, didn't you say you thought the second boat went back toward the chocolate factory?"

"Well, it didn't go toward the marina. You've been there, so you know where that is."

"That's what I thought too," Jessica said in a voice that Sophie would have to call sad. But why would she care?

"There isn't much built on the shore in that area. I guess it's because the space used to be filled with the building Mom talked about."

Jessica was quiet again. Then she said, "Sophie, I need to tell you something now, but I don't want you to be mad at me. Please remember that I couldn't tell you before, and I shouldn't be telling you now, but I'm worried that all of this might be very important."

She paused so long that Sophie wondered if she'd fallen asleep. Then she finally added, "Maybe I should talk to the sheriff first."

"What? After you said the first part, I really want to know what it is that you're talking about."

"Okay. I'm trying to remember exactly what Sheriff Valeska told me, what she asked me to do, and I think I've got it."

"Sheriff Valeska asked *you* to do something? Tell me."

"I'm trying. Wait a second." Jessica took a deep breath then continued, "I think this is close to what she said. 'Jessica, I'd like you to keep your eyes open when you're in the chocolate factory. Let me know if you see anything suspicious. Don't tell anyone else.'"

Sophie wasn't sure what to say. She felt hurt and angry—all of those emotions raced through her in a jumbled mess. "Why didn't she ask me too?"

"Oh, I forgot that part. She said she was worried that you

would get too involved and might get into trouble. And you know that's happened before, Sophie, so it made sense to me. You're a good detective. You would have wanted to dig deeper, and I think she just wanted someone to watch out for anything strange."

"Okay. I guess I can understand. You wouldn't get into the middle of anything."

"Right."

"Did you see anything suspicious at Sweet Bites?"

"Well, I saw a shadow going by at the end of the hall, like someone had been standing there listening. But that didn't have to mean anything."

"I need to keep my eyes open now." Sophie rolled over onto her back. "I think we'd better try to sleep, Jessica. Tomorrow might be a very busy day."

"I had a feeling you would say that."

"The first thing in the morning, we need to get out of here and go see the sheriff."

"Sophie, you know she'll say we don't have any evidence. We don't have any clues for her to follow."

"But I still think she needs to know. What those boats did was strange."

Jessica said, "You're right, Sophie. We do need to tell her. I can't think of a single logical reason for two boats to do what we saw."

———

The next morning, Sophie watched her cousin open her eyes but didn't speak to her.

"I think waking up in a tent is a good thing. I feel fine," Jessica said.

Sophie raised one eyebrow but still didn't say a word.

Jessica unzipped the bag and sat up. "Let's start our day."

Sophie also sat up. "Are you sure?"

"I'm sure. I'm ready to start this mystery. What do we do first, Sophie?"

"First . . ." Sophie let the thought trail off in a mysterious way.

"Yes?"

"First, we eat breakfast."

Jessica pushed Sophie's arm. "I could figure that one out. I remember that you put snack bars in the bag for breakfast, and we have bottles of water. Right?"

As they finished their snack bars, Sophie stood. "Let's get everything packed up here, carry what we can, and get to my house."

———

On the hike back down Cutoff Trail, Sophie said, "Jessica, how would you describe where the second boat came from?"

Jessica took a step to the left so that a bush wouldn't swipe across her leg. "I'm not sure. I remember from the day we were out on the lake fishing earlier this summer that the lake stretches a long way in that direction."

"I've given it a lot of thought, and I think it came from the farthest part of the lake. I suppose it could've gone along the edge of the lake for a while and then cut across, but at that moment it seemed to be coming from over there."

Sophie paused, then added, "I've lived here all my life, but other than going with my parents once when I was a little kid to visit a man who lived in a house over there, I've never been to that part of the lake. I sure wouldn't want to walk that far from town."

"Does the highway even go that way?"

"Sort of. There is no road on the opposite side of the lake from Pine Hill, but the road does go around to the area where we think the boat came from."

They stepped out of the woods and into an open area with a

stream. Sophie took off running and jumped across it. Jessica had always walked across it on the large stones dotting the stream.

Sophie clapped her hands. "You can do it! Getting wet is the worst that can happen."

Jessica took a few steps backward so she could get a running start, took a deep breath, and ran as fast as she could at that stream. When she reached the edge, she pushed off with her feet and sprang across, landing neatly on the other side. "I did it! I did it!"

Grinning, Sophie patted her on the back. "You're getting there. For a city girl, you're doing pretty good."

"You're going to have to visit me in London, England, so I can give you some of my city training."

"Deal. We'll have to see if we can talk Mom and Dad into that."

They continued the short distance to Sophie's house. There they each took showers to wash off their camping grime and were soon ready, but not as soon as Sophie would have liked because Jessica did have to do all of her morning routines.

"Today I can wear perfume since we don't have class. Please remind me not to again tomorrow!"

"Sure." Sophie shrugged. "At least I'll try. I don't wear scented things, so I don't think of it."

They went into the living room. The sound of a door opening behind them caused them to both turn around. Mr. Sandoval came down the hall from his home office.

"Sophie," he said, "I want to make sure you remember that your mother's birthday is tomorrow. I thought we could all go out to dinner."

"Sounds great, Dad."

"In case you've spent your allowance"—he gave her a look that said he assumed she had—"I set some money on your nightstand so you can buy your mom a small gift. Jessica's mom already sent something."

"You've been extra busy with work lately, Dad, haven't you?"

"I have. A large company asked me to review their records. I'll complete the project next week. For now, I'm back to work." He turned toward his office. "I'll see you ladies at dinnertime."

"That's so nice of him," Jessica said after he'd gone into his office and closed the door.

"It's probably because he knows we've had to spend money this summer while we've been solving mysteries." Sophie raced into the bedroom. When she returned, she said, "I may need to check my nightstand every day if Dad's going to set money there."

Jessica laughed. "I doubt that's going to happen very often."

Sophie picked up her backpack and tucked the money into a zipper pocket. "Ready?"

"I am. Let's go tell Sheriff Valeska what happened last night. And let's see if she gives us her usual answer: 'Acting suspicious isn't a crime.'"

9 TELLING THE SHERIFF

When the cousins arrived in town, Sophie slowed down.

"Is something wrong?" Jessica asked her.

"Remember what's happened when we've tried to talk to someone else at the sheriff's office? I think we should only tell the sheriff and come back if she isn't here."

"I agree." Jessica had to tell the sheriff that she'd given away the secret to Sophie, and she hoped she wouldn't be upset.

They made their way to the sheriff's office. Sheriff Valeska was sitting in her chair at her desk. Her secretary, Clare, asked them what they needed. They'd had a little problem with her when she'd first started working here earlier this summer because she hadn't believed kids could solve mysteries. She'd learned from the sheriff that these kids could.

Sophie said, "We have something we need to discuss with the sheriff." Sophie sounded quite professional. Her words reminded Jessica of the way people spoke in some of the old black-and-white detective movies Sophie loved to watch.

The sheriff looked up from her computer, leaned back in her chair, and motioned the two of them over to her desk. "Sit, ladies," she said, pointing at one chair, then another. "What can I help you with today?"

They sat down, and Sophie leaned forward in her chair. "Sheriff, we saw something strange last night."

A puzzled expression crossed the sheriff's face. "Last night? At your house?"

Jessica said, "No, we were camping."

Sophie added, "We went up Cutoff Trail. It was almost the same spot where we found the first clue in our first mystery."

"Okay. Go on. That has a good view over the lake, so I'm curious."

Sophie described what they'd seen with Jessica throwing in a few things now and then that she'd noticed. When they finished, the sheriff was quiet for a few moments. Then she said, "That's very interesting, ladies. You think the second boat went toward the area of the chocolate factory?"

The girls nodded.

"But I remember Sal Donadio mentioning that he didn't have access to the boat storage area, that the area had been closed off years ago, and now it was only accessible through a trapdoor in the floor. He said there wasn't even a ladder there. They had to lower a ladder down through the hole when some plumbing needed to be repaired right after he bought the building."

"But where else would the boat have gone to, Sheriff? It didn't appear to be going in the marina's direction."

"I don't know, Sophie. I would say that maybe they went along the edge of the lake for a while, but I don't know a whole lot of people who would want to make a trip in a rowboat longer than it had to be. That's a lot of work."

"Sheriff . . ." Jessica leaned closer to the sheriff and said in a low voice, "I had to tell Sophie."

Sheriff Valeska glanced around the room. Clare was the only other one there. The sheriff must have decided she needed to tell them something that no one else should know because she said, "Girls, I want to show you something in our storeroom." She pushed back her chair, stood, and walked over to a door that led into a small room to the side of the larger office the sheriff and her deputies shared.

They followed her inside.

The sheriff kept the door open and spoke in a low voice. "Jessica, how much does Sophie know?"

"All of it, Sheriff. It was hard to keep it from her, and I thought that when we saw the boats, it might all connect. I hope you're not upset with me."

A silence stretched so long that Jessica thought the sheriff was angry. Then Sheriff Valeska said, "I'm not upset with you. Disappointed, maybe. But I might have done the same thing. I never should have kept Sophie out of the loop."

Sophie smiled. "Thank you, Sheriff. I thought maybe I'd done something wrong."

"No, Sophie. You tend to leap into things, and I didn't want you to get into danger. I knew Jessica wouldn't do that."

"Now that we've both been told, is there something we can help with, something I can help with?" Sophie asked with more than a little bit of excitement in her voice.

The sheriff gave Sophie a firm look. "Sophie, I don't want you in trouble. Do you understand?"

Sophie nodded. "I do, Sheriff."

The sheriff stood there and continued to give her that look.

"I promise, Sheriff," she added. "I will do my best to stay out of danger."

The sheriff sighed. "That's probably the best I can ask. Be safe, Sophie. And you too, Jessica. Don't let her drag you into anything she shouldn't. Call me first."

Sophie asked. "Did you ever find the stolen car?"

"No. We did not. It's one of the only cars ever stolen in this town, so that's strange too. Please be careful."

Jessica leaned toward the sheriff. "Do you have any more information to give me? You said to keep my eyes open, but I don't know for what."

The sheriff took off her hat and rubbed the top of her head.

"There's the possibility that something odd is going on at the chocolate factory. At least, that's what Sal Donadio thinks. He came up with what he believed was an idea for a new flavor of chocolate, and about a month later another company came out with the exact same thing. He brought me samples of both, and I couldn't tell the difference."

"So, someone is stealing secrets from the chocolate factory? There's a spy?" Jessica asked. She'd been right.

The sheriff laughed. "I wouldn't call it a spy, Jessica. I will say there is the possibility that someone has stolen a single recipe, but it might be a coincidence. Two companies might have thought pineapple with the same secret ingredient would work."

Jessica asked, "Secret ingredient?"

"That's right. Sal isn't saying what it is."

Sophie nodded. "That does make it odd that they taste the same."

Sophie and Jessica left the sheriff's office with her promising to send a patrol car out in the area of the houses at the far end of the lake. She would have them go there a couple of times every night to make sure nothing strange was going on.

Sophie stopped on the sidewalk in front of the building. "I'm frustrated, Jessica."

"The sheriff was nice about everything."

"You're right. But I still think that second boat went to the area around Sweet Bites. The land dips down to the lake there. Then it goes up the hill to the big mansion. There isn't anything else around."

"I think we've done everything we can, Sophie."

"I have an idea."

"Am I going to like this idea?"

"Only one part of it. Let's go sit and talk about it."

Jessica knew where Sophie would go. They were soon sitting on the wooden bench on the sidewalk that her cousin liked to go to when she had to figure something out.

"I'm ready for your plan, Sophie."

Sophie wasted no time. "We need to see if there's a boat under the chocolate factory where boats used to be kept. And if there is one, whether or not it's a rowboat."

"That sounds impossible to me, Sophie."

"Sweet Bites is Tony's uncle's business. We can trust Uncle Sal—at least I hope so—but I don't want to tell him too much."

Jessica thought about it for a few seconds. "We believe he's trustworthy, but he might tell someone who isn't. I think too many people could find out if we asked Uncle Sal about checking under the boathouse."

"We need to bring Tony into this mystery now. If his nephew wanted to explore under there—"

"It would just seem like a kid who's curious. And people don't pay attention to kids all the time, do they? Genius!" Jessica laughed.

As they walked away, Sophie said, "I've been thinking about yesterday. We tailed Emily Foster because you were spying on everyone. Is that right?"

"I was." Jessica held up her hand to stop Sophie from saying more. And hopefully to stop her from getting angry. "But I could have gone by myself. I took you with me because I thought it would be good to have you there."

"So even though I didn't know I was in the middle of a mystery, I *was* in the middle of one. You found the mystery this time."

"Yes. Does that mean you aren't mad at me?"

"I'm working on it. I really am."

10 BRINGING IN TONY

Sophie and Jessica found Tony at Donadio's Deli, as expected. He stood behind the counter making sandwiches for a family.

They got in line behind one other person, then placed their orders for sandwiches. Jessica got a turkey on white, and Sophie a pastrami on rye bread. Sophie caught Tony's eye and gestured with her head toward the table where they would sit. His eyebrows shot up, and he gave a nod. Tony had been in on their last two mysteries, and she knew he would be up for another one.

She and Jessica seated themselves at one of the small tables.

"I'm glad we're here early," Jessica said.

"You're always glad when we're here," her cousin answered.

Jessica felt her face flush. "This time it's because I'm very hungry. That snack bar didn't last very long. Also, since we're here ahead of the lunch crowd, there isn't anyone behind us in line, and Tony can take a few minutes to sit with us."

A few minutes later he brought them their sandwiches, set them down in front of them, and pulled out a chair for himself. He leaned close and spoke in a low voice. "New mystery?"

Sophie laughed. "Maybe we just wanted to say hello to you."

Leaning back in his chair, he watched the two of them "You have your working-on-a-mystery look, Sophie."

Sophie shrugged. "You're right, Tony. Well, maybe there's a mystery. At least I think there's a mystery."

Tony gestured forward with his hand. "Give. What's going on?"

She explained about the boats, and Jessica jumped in to repeat what the sheriff had told her about the chocolate factory. Sophie added the story of their tailing Emily Foster.

Tony gave a low whistle. When he did that, his mother glanced his way. "I'd better hurry. The lunch crowd will arrive soon. You want me to talk to my Uncle Sal?"

"If you can."

"As long as I'm part of the mystery-solving team. My uncle comes in here for lunch every day at about one o'clock." Tony stood. "I never know what he'll order, and sometimes he combines things that are strange together."

Jessica laughed. "We've noticed that at the chocolate factory. He has some crazy ideas."

He leaned forward. "Like?"

"Chocolate-covered bubblegum," Jessica said every word slowly.

Tony grimaced.

"That's what everybody in the class thought. He isn't going to make it now, so he has a big stack of bubblegum in his storage room."

Tony laughed. "That probably means we'll get bubblegum in our stockings this Christmas. And I'm okay with that. I'll ask him when he comes in if we can explore under his factory. Does that sound good?"

"Yes. We'll be over at Great Finds, doing whatever it is Mom needs us to do this afternoon. That was our deal. She pays for the class, and we work." Sophie popped the last bite of her sandwich in her mouth.

Tony straightened. "You don't sound happy about that, Sophie."

She took a sip of her drink, then stood. "I don't mind working there. But right now, I don't think I want to take over the antique store when I'm grown up. You like being here in the deli. Maybe I'll change my mind when I'm older and be glad for all of the time I spent in Mom's shop. But maybe not." Sophie grinned.

"I'll call you at Great Finds this afternoon and let you know what I set up. When do you want to go?"

"I don't want too much time to pass from when we saw the boats to when we get in there."

"Makes sense. I'll ask about this afternoon."

Sophie and Jessica left and went to her mom's shop. When they got there, Mrs. Sandoval put them to work doing Jessica's favorite chore, unpacking boxes. After taking everything out of two boxes and carefully unwrapping each item, Jessica said, "I love this. It's like Christmas! I get to open packages with beautiful things inside, things that are from the past."

"I don't mind in the beginning, but we still have one more box to do. I'm ready to be finished with this. And what I really want is for Tony to call."

At that moment the phone rang. The two of them looked at each other. Mrs. Sandoval answered it, but instead of passing the phone to one of them, she picked up a pen and made some notes on a piece of paper.

Jessica's shoulders dropped. "That can't be him," she said in a low voice to Sophie.

They got back to work unwrapping and started on the last box. When they were almost done, the phone rang again. This time after Mrs. Sandoval answered it, she handed the phone to Sophie. "It's Tony for you."

Sophie took the phone and glanced at her mother, standing nearby. "Hey, Tony. What's up?"

She didn't want her mother to worry about their finding a

possible mystery, so that meant she couldn't say much. She listened as Tony told her the same thing that Sheriff Valeska had, that there was no easy access to the underside of his uncle's building. "Okay."

Mrs. Sandoval picked up one of the pieces they had unwrapped and walked into the back room with it. Sophie whispered, "There must be a way to get into there."

Tony answered. "That's what I said. Uncle Sal told me that the only way he knew was from the lake. All we have to do is swim around the side of the building and underneath the big door that's there. He gave me permission to do that anytime I wanted and said my friends can come with me."

Jessica had gone in a boat with Sophie, and she loved being at the beach, but Sophie didn't know if she could swim. She motioned Jessica closer. "Can you swim?"

Jessica's eyes widened. "Sure."

"Tony, we can do it." She suggested a time and a place to meet in a couple of hours.

Tony agreed, and they hung up.

11 SWIMMING FOR CLUES

A half hour later, the girls left the shop. After a fast trip to Sophie's house, they returned to town with their swimsuits on under their clothes and small towels stuffed into her backpack.

They took the road to the chocolate factory, then right before the factory, the turn to the lake that once led to the long-gone building her mother had told them about.

Tony waited for them on the shore with a ball and an inflated ring. "Uncle Sal doesn't think there is anything under his factory that's worth making an effort to see. He went in there in a boat before he bought the building, and he said it was an old, abandoned place where they used to keep boats. It isn't even connected to the rest of the building anymore, even though it must have been in the past."

All three of them took off their outer clothes and stood in their swim clothes. Sophie's bathing suit was a simple blue one-piece, the style that someone on a swim team would wear. Jessica's was also a one-piece but pink and had a ruffle across one shoulder. Tony wore black swim trunks.

Jessica looked up at the chocolate factory. "I hope no one sees what we're doing. The factory part only has high windows, but the offices have larger windows, and someone could watch us from them."

Tony followed her gaze. "Even if someone saw us go into the water, the windows aren't in a place where they can see us if we stay near the building. "

Sophie said, "Let's play in the water for a while so they'll think that's what we're here to do. Then we'll inch over closer to the building, and they'll assume we're still horsing around."

Sophie tossed the inflated ring toward Jessica, who caught it, and they all went into the water. Jessica leaned on the ring and floated. Sophie and Tony threw the ball.

Just as it started to seem like fun, Sophie realized they were about to go somewhere that was completely unknown and could possibly lead to danger. She threw the ball over Tony's shoulder, and he swam over there. He tossed it a few feet closer to the building, and Sophie swam to get it. Jessica paddled around in a circle that grew ever wider but more toward the direction they needed to go. Foot by foot they grew nearer to the side of the building.

While dogpaddling, Tony glanced up. "I'm sure they can't see us now. You ready to go in there?" He gestured toward the building.

Jessica let go of the inflatable, and Tony dropped the ball inside it. Sophie hoped they would still be there when they came back out. They all swam around the corner of the building and under the old wooden door that covered the lake side. It reminded her of a garage door.

As they dogpaddled in an open area, Tony said, "This isn't what my uncle described. Sure, some of this is old, but half the boards on the little dock in front of us are new wood."

They swam to that dock and climbed up a ladder that went down into the water. At the back, stairs led from the right side of the dock upward to the chocolate factory. The three of them peered over the side of the dock to a rowboat tied up there.

Jessica said, "Okay, Ms. Detective, there's a boat, but it's an old one. I don't think I'd want to be on the lake in it."

Tony pushed on it with his foot, and it rolled from side to side. "She's right. It's floating, but it seems pretty rickety."

Sophie saw a boat that seemed old but sound. "I don't know. If it's dry inside, that makes it a good boat, doesn't it?"

Jessica said, "How could we tell if it had been used?"

"It's empty, so it isn't offering any clues." Sophie turned to check out the large, rustic boathouse. "Let's see if there are any clues in here. Spread out and look for anything unusual."

Tony said, "Your detective team obeys."

Sophie grinned. "Sophie's team. I like that."

Tony checked the back wall to the right of the stairs, Jessica the wall under the stairs, while Sophie stared at the stairs as she decided whether or not she should climb them.

Jessica interrupted her thoughts. "Team leader, this wall has old, cracked paint, so it's been here a while."

Sophie went over to see it. "That may be new wood that they've tried to make appear old. Mom once used paint that does that on something she bought for our house. You know Mom, she wants everything to be old." Walking back toward the stairs, Sophie decided she would try them.

When she stepped onto the first step, Jessica hurried over. "Sophie, what are you doing? Uncle Sal said we could be down here, but he didn't say anything about us going up into the factory."

"Actually, my uncle said we could explore. He didn't say where. Those stairs are in bad shape though."

Sophie went up a few more steps then stopped and studied the next step which had a large, rotten-looking section. She stared up at the top of the stairs. "There's a door. I'd like to see what's beyond it, if we can get inside."

"Uncle Sal made it sound like this area was sealed off years ago."

"You're probably right, Tony. The next step isn't in great shape. I don't think anyone has been here for a long time."

Jessica went to the side of the stairs where Sophie could see her. "They might not be safe! Please come down."

Even she wondered if she should go back down. She did want to see the top though. Sophie gently put first one then the other foot on the broken step. "I think it's okay. I'm standing on this one now. I can keep going."

As she shifted forward to take another step, the wood broke with a crash. When the wall moved swiftly by, she closed her eyes. She landed on her back on the dock. When she opened her eyes, she found wood piled around her and saw the splintered ruins of the staircase above her.

Jessica leaned over her. "Sophie, can you see me?"

"Yes. I'm fine now that I'm not falling anymore."

Tony picked up a piece of wood lying on her and set it to the side.

She took a deep breath, then sat up and rubbed her arm. "Other than a bruised elbow, I'm fine. I am very glad I was only halfway up so I had a short fall." She got to her feet. "I did prove that no one has used those stairs to get to the rowboat from the building."

Tony shook his head. "We might have found an easier way to do that."

Jessica kicked at a splintered piece of wood. "Maybe we should move away from the stairs, in case the whole staircase collapses."

"Good idea." Sophie took a few big steps.

Standing on the dock, Jessica said, "Why would someone repair the dock but not the stairs so they could go from the dock to the building above us?"

Tony walked the dock from side to side. "None of this makes any sense."

A clunk from above their heads made Sophie jump. "Whew. Someone must have dropped something in the factory."

Jessica glanced around nervously. "Sophie, the wood breaking and you falling made a loud crash. If we can hear them upstairs . . ."

Sophie hurried toward the ladder into the water. "We need to leave. Quickly. If there *is* a way in from the factory, someone could be here any second."

They swam back out, found the inflated ring and ball in almost the same place they'd left them, and went back to shore.

As they dried off, Jessica said, "Maybe we should tell Sheriff Valeska." She reached for her shirt and began dressing.

"You know what she'll say." Sophie, with her shirt on over her suit, straightened her shoulders and did her best imitation of the sheriff. "'There is no evidence that a law has been broken. It is private property.'"

Tony held his T-shirt in his hand. "I guess I should tell my uncle that someone repaired the dock. But why would anyone do that?" He pulled on the shirt, then the shorts.

"Tony, we don't know why this happened or who did it. Maybe we should keep it as our secret while we investigate for a few days. His not knowing means he can't act differently around one of his employees, and he can't tell the wrong person about what we found. If he did, that might put him and all of us in danger."

"Our family is very close, and we tend to tell each other things, but I think you're right. Let's wait a few days, a week at the most. By the time the chocolate classes are over next week, we'll have figured it out, or we'll have to tell."

Tugging on her jeans, Sophie said, "Deal."

After Tony had left, Sophie said, "I think we can be positive now: we have another mystery."

"A repaired dock for an old rowboat *is* strange. It does seem to be a mystery."

"We need to be careful."

"I couldn't agree more, Sophie."

"We'll watch carefully every second when we're in the chocolate factory this week. Let's do everything we can to not let the criminals know that we've learned anything about their secrets. We don't know who could be one of the bad guys. Except for Tony's uncle."

"I'm glad someone's in the clear."

12 SHARING SUSPICIONS

Sophie woke to the scent of bacon cooking. Jessica's covers were flipped back, and the shower was running. Moments after the water was turned off, Jessica came out of the bathroom, rubbing her hair with a towel.

"My shower helped, and I think I'm ready to face the day."

Sophie didn't say a word.

Jessica sniffed the air. "Is that bacon I smell?"

Sophie grinned. "That's something that would wake me up too." She scrambled out of bed, grabbed her robe, and slipped it on as she headed for the kitchen. She knew it would take her cousin a while to dry her hair, and her mother might want help with breakfast.

When she opened the kitchen door, Mrs. Sandoval was standing at the stove. She looked up and said, "Good morning. Sophie, please pour orange juice for everyone and set the table. Your dad's home this morning, and I know both you and he love pancakes."

A breakfast of pancakes and bacon was soon ready, a meal that Sophie always loved. Jessica joined them with her hair and makeup perfect and wearing a yellow and white shirt with yellow shorts. Sophie still had her robe on.

When everyone was seated, she asked, "Why the special breakfast, Mom?"

"I haven't gotten to spend time in the morning with you girls for a while, so I thought this would be a good thing to do."

"I feel the same way," Mr. Sandoval said. "What have you been up to?"

Sophie and Jessica glanced at each other. Jessica took a bite of pancake and gave Sophie a look that said it was her job to answer.

"We went swimming yesterday." Sophie bit into a piece of bacon.

After a sip of juice, Jessica added, "And we've been taking the chocolate-making class."

"Dad, we brought chocolates home. You can have some if Mom shares with you."

Smiling, he said, "I'll have to move fast, or they'll be gone."

Mrs. Sandoval leaned over and gave him a kiss on the cheek. "You will have to move very quickly."

"Speaking of chocolate, Aunt April, I noticed that your house is wood outside, and so is the chocolate factory. But everything else I've seen in Pine Hill is made of brick. You know Pine Hill's history well. Do you know why?"

"Jessica, there's a reason for that. The chocolate factory and our house were built by the same builder. He must have preferred wood."

Mr. Sandoval picked up his cup of coffee, stood, and said, "I'll let you solve Pine Hill's past mysteries. I need to get back to my office." He headed for the kitchen door and left.

Mrs. Sandoval stood. "Please come about noon, and you can go to the deli before working. I'll give you money for that, of course. I have a project for you. This may be one you don't like."

With that, she sailed out the door.

Sophie said, "That doesn't make me look forward to this afternoon."

"Me either. But we've already cleaned out her storeroom,

dusted, and unpacked boxes of new things for her shop. Maybe she said that to tease you."

"I guess that's possible. But Mom doesn't usually do that."

After the two of them did the dishes, Sophie went to take a shower and get ready. When she was dressed, she stepped out of her bedroom and found Jessica reading a book in the living room and her mother adding a book to an already tall stack of books that were crowded onto a small table against the wall.

"Mom, what's all that?" Sophie stepped over to the stack. Behind the books lay two, big rolled-up tubes of papers with rubber bands holding them in place and a small, old box.

"The library has decided to have a Pine Hill history room. It was just a meeting room, but now there will also be shelves with things like these. The box is filled with love letters from someone who lived here a long time ago. I found those when I was asked to go in and give values for the items in a house that was going to be sold."

Mrs. Sandoval tapped the rolls of paper with her finger. "One of those is the plans the architect drew for our house. The other is the plans for a large house on the far side of town."

Sophie twisted them and found the one with her address. "Can I open this?"

"Sure. I've never taken the time to truly study the drawings. I doubt you'll find any surprises."

Jessica came over as Sophie rolled out the plans on the dining room table. "Check this out. Here's my room. Correction: our room for the summer." Sophie pointed to that spot on the drawing.

"Sophie, you already know this house inside and out."

Mrs. Sandoval said, "That's what I think too, Jessica. But you know Sophie. She has to look. In addition to the chocolate factory, the man also built the building that was beside it. I think there's a photo of both of them in this old book about Pine Hill."

She went through the stack beside her, pulled out the fattest book, and flipped through it. "Here." She held the book open, and a beautiful building stared out at them. It was like many of the old houses in town, but fancier than any she'd seen with decorations all over it.

"The factory is simpler and reminds me of our house."

"Yes. The builder lived in this house for years." Mrs. Sandoval gathered the stack of books in her arms. "I need to get to the shop."

Sophie stared at the pages in front of her. "I'd like to study these plans."

"Sure. I'll take them next week. See you ladies at lunchtime."

After Mrs. Sandoval had left, Sophie said, "The drawing of the first floor shows everything as it is."

Sophie flipped the page to show the drawing of the second-story.

Jessica circled her finger around one area. "What's this?"

Sophie shrugged. "It's the closet in our guestroom."

"No, I mean in the closet." Jessica tapped the spot on the drawing. "If those lines show the closet, what is this?"

Sophie leaned in closer. "There are dashed lines on the drawing behind that closet, but not behind my parents' closets." She flipped the page back to where it showed her room on the first floor. "And not with my closet. But there are a few tiny dashed lines in my closet, and I know that's . . ." Sophie's jaw dropped, and her eyes slowly rose to meet Jessica's.

"That's my hiding place under a floorboard in the closet. If dashed lines mean there's a secret hiding place"—she flipped back to the closet in the guestroom—"then this might be a larger hiding place. Let's very carefully go over every part of the drawing to see if anything else has those lines."

After studying the attic's drawing, Jessica said, "The attic doesn't have anything like that." Flipping through the stack, she added, "I don't see the basement's drawing here."

"We'll figure that out later. Let's go!" Sophie headed for the staircase.

"I don't have to ask what you're planning to do." Jessica laughed.

Sophie heard Jessica's footsteps on the stairs behind her. Once in the guestroom, Sophie pushed aside hanging clothes and stepped into the closet.

"This is filled with old clothes."

"It's our winter coats and warm clothes," Sophie answered. "When we actually have a guest stay in this room, we clear the closet, but otherwise this is where Mom has us put all of those things." She rubbed her hand over the wall, and a line down the middle stopped her. "Jessica, feel this."

Sophie stepped to the side so Jessica could squeeze into the closet with her.

"There." Sophie gestured toward the area, and Jessica rubbed her hand on it.

"You may have found something, Sophie."

Sophie stepped over to the wall and tapped on it with her knuckles. "It sounds hollow."

"Would you know if something sounded *hollow*?"

"They say that a lot in mystery books. I can only say that it doesn't sound like there's a hard wall there."

"If it opens, there has to be a hinge, and if the only opening is in the middle, then the hinge must be on one of the two corners where the back wall meets the sides. Maybe a flashlight would help, Sophie."

"Good idea. I know there's one downstairs in a kitchen drawer for when the power goes out." Sophie hurried out the door. She returned quickly with a flashlight in her hand and pushed the button to turn it on as she entered the room. Then she stepped into the closet and held it up close to the line in the middle and checked both sides of the wall.

"Excellent idea, Jessica. The left side is solid. The wood there is very tightly put together, but the right side has a slightly wider opening. It's tiny, but it's there." She handed Jessica the flashlight so she could see it too.

"That means either the middle or the side has door hinges, Sophie. Maybe we need to push along both of the openings to see if we can find the right spot to have it open. If there is a door and if it opens that way. Those are really big *ifs*."

Sophie gave the upper corner a push, and the right side of the back of the closet swung back.

"Not anymore."

13 WATCH YOUR STEP

Jessica shined the flashlight into the opening in the back of the closet. A spiral staircase made of stone wound down and into darkness. "I bet we'll find a creepy basement, and I had enough of those with our first mystery. Rats live in basements!" She shuddered.

"Remember this is *my* basement. It's where our washer and dryer are. I've been in my basement hundreds of times, and I know there aren't any rats in it."

"That does make it more appealing. But have you ever seen the other end of this staircase?"

Sophie took the flashlight from Jessica and shined the light all the way around the opening. "No. I haven't. Let's find out where it goes." Sophie took a step toward it.

Jessica put her hand on her arm to stop her. "Maybe we shouldn't go down the stairs alone."

"I think it's safe. No one is down there."

Jessica stepped in front of her. "Let me go first. I'm the guest here, so I won't get in as much trouble as you for exploring without your parents being here." The rough texture of the stones with the mortar in between them gave her something to hold onto as she stepped onto the first step.

As she took a second step, a spiderweb caught in her hair and covered her hand. "Ick! Sophie, there are more spiderwebs here than I have ever seen in my life!"

"I'll get the broom from the kitchen. Maybe we can sweep the air in front of us." Sophie rushed from the closet.

While Jessica waited with webs around her for what seemed like an hour, she hummed her favorite song, a happy one to take her mind off all of the spiders living here who had spun the webs. Sophie returned and passed her the broom. Jessica held it up in front of her and swept down all the webs as she thought, *I won't see any spiders here.* She followed the steps downward as far as the broom had been able to reach, then swept it through the air again to clean another stretch of stairs before continuing.

A voice in the distance behind her said, "Do you see anything?"

"Just more stairs. I'm still going down."

"I guess I'd better follow you."

A scuffling sound came from behind Jessica, and she was glad to know it was Sophie and not a fat rat. Finally, Jessica arrived at the bottom of the stairs. She shined the light in front of her. A room the size of Sophie's bedroom lay before her.

Sophie stepped beside her on the last step.

"There's a desk. It looks like an office, don't you think, Jessica?"

"But why would someone have a hidden office?"

"Well, my dad always says it's hard to get work done with people around. That's why he likes to work from home. Maybe the builder found a way to fix that."

Rolls of drawings like the one that had revealed this staircase were stuffed in one container. A desk, but with a top that slanted at an angle, was off to the side. A long table sat in the center of the room. Sophie walked over to the rolls of papers, pulled one out, and stretched it out on the table. "Bring the flashlight over here, Jessica."

Jessica did as she'd asked and shined the light on the unrolled paper.

"This is for a house on a street where we trailed Emily," Sophie told her. She checked another, then one more. "They're all for houses in Pine Hill."

Jessica took out a set of drawings. "This roll of papers is different, bigger than the others." When she unrolled it and shined the light on it, she said, "It's for the chocolate factory—I mean, the boathouse. Let's see if there's anything usual on it."

Page by page, they flipped through the plans for the building.

"Here." Sophie grabbed the flashlight from Jessica and held the light over it. Then she circled an area with her finger.

Jessica leaned over. "Dashed lines."

Sophie nodded slowly. "We may have found another secret passage." She stood up straight, tucked the flashlight under her arm, and rolled up the papers.

"I think we'll need Tony's help again," Jessica said. "Uncle Sal will have to give us permission to search for it."

"I agree. We'll ask Tony at lunch. I hope he's there today."

Jessica turned in a slow circle. No door was in sight. "I wonder if there's a way to get out of here. I mean, other than the staircase. Shine the light over here on this wall. The left side is the foundation of the house, but the right side should be your basement."

Sophie shined the light as Jessica suggested. "It looks like a solid wall to me. But I have an idea. Jessica, if it was dark in here and light in the basement we might be able to see light coming through a crack. We'd know there's a way out or at least a place we should check to see if it's a way out."

"That sounds like a great idea."

"I'll go out, turn the light on in the basement, and come back here." She handed the flashlight back to Jessica and went back up the steps.

Jessica continued to scan the walls while Sophie was gone but couldn't see anything. This whole place didn't make sense.

When her cousin returned and was safely beside her, Jessica turned off the flashlight, sending them into complete darkness.

After their eyes had adjusted, light trickling under the wall caught their attention. Without speaking, the two of them hurried over and felt around on that wall. Jessica tried pushing, twisting, and turning everything she touched. A snap sounded, and the door swung outward, letting in light from the basement.

Sophie asked, "How did you open it?"

Jessica moved a small piece of wood to the right and left. "I happened to put my hand on the right thing, I guess. The bigger question is why you and your family never noticed that the basement wasn't as big as it should be."

They stepped out into the basement itself.

Sophie said, "We're on the opposite side of the room from where the laundry is done, and that's the only part of it we use very often. And the basement itself is kind of an odd shape. I guess it never seemed strange. This was back in a dark corner."

Turning back to face the once-hidden room, Jessica shined the flashlight toward the ceiling. Two very old-fashioned lights hung there. "I wondered how the builder was able to see and work in here." Jessica stood on a chair so she could see the lights up close. "These are so old-fashioned that they're gas lamps. When the house was first built, I guess it had gas flames for light."

"Come out into the basement, Jessica." When she had, Sophie pushed the newly discovered door shut. "I don't see how to open it from here, so we can close the closet's entrance from upstairs." She turned toward the basement stairs. "I'm surprised at all of this. I checked for secret passages in this house a long time ago."

"Not many people can say that, Sophie."

Sophie laughed. "I spent a lot of time around the fireplace because there are often secret places there, at least in books. But I never checked closets. That surprises me because after reading

The Lion, The Witch and the Wardrobe, you would think I would have immediately checked all the closets. Anyway, I never found anything before today."

As they came up the stairs, Sophie glanced at her watch. "Oh no! Jessica, we have to hurry to get to Great Finds. We'll close the door in the closet later."

They hurried out the door and toward town at a pace somewhere between walking and running. The girls arrived on time but panting.

When they'd caught their breath, they went into the antique shop. Mrs. Sandoval stood at the cash register with a customer, so they went to the other side of the shop and waited. When the customer left, Mrs. Sandoval handed them some money. "Have fun at lunch. I'll have you help me rearrange some things when you come back."

As they left, Jessica said, "That doesn't sound bad to me."

Sophie shrugged. "Me either. Maybe it's something Mom doesn't enjoy."

"Your mother's been very nice to us. We work and she pays us, and we get to have lunch out. I like that."

"You'd like it even if she didn't pay us because she keeps letting us go to the deli. Aren't you getting tired of it?"

"I did for a little while. But then I started having a different sandwich every time I went, or soup. There's so much to choose from that I'm not tired of it anymore. Besides, we usually see Tony there."

When they arrived, they placed their orders. While they waited at a table, Sophie said, "Jessica, we need to share about what we found today with Tony."

"Agreed. I've also been thinking about another way Tony might be able to help us." At Sophie's curious expression, she added, "This must be the most popular place to eat lunch in Pine Hill. He sees many of the people who live here and visit."

Right then, he brought their sandwiches. Glancing around

first, he then leaned close and spoke in a low voice. "Anything new on the mystery?"

Jessica said, "Yes and no. First, I have a question. The other students in the class are suspects. We followed Emily Foster, and she seems okay. I don't think we'll find anything unusual about Dylan, other than the fact that his mother may be driving him a little crazy sometimes."

"Is there anyone else in class?" Tony asked.

Sophie spoke. "Mr. Pleckenpoll. He said we could call him Mr. P."

"Oh yes, the friendly old man. He eats at the deli most days."

"I saw him move more like a young man once, so I'm watching him. Tomorrow we'll follow him."

Tony glanced from Sophie to Jessica. "You've learned something, haven't you?"

"It might be easiest if Tony came to my house tonight so we could show him what we found."

With a serious expression on his face, Tony asked, "What might be easiest? Are you getting me in the middle of a mystery again?"

Jessica hesitated. She'd thought that Tony liked being part of their mysteries. He'd seemed happy when they swam under the boathouse. "Yes, we were. But if you don't want to be involved, we totally understand." She looked nervously over at Sophie, who also wore a concerned expression.

Tony grinned. "Just kidding. I wouldn't want to miss a second of a mystery."

"Not funny." Sophie pushed on his arm. "Do you think you can be at my house at seven o'clock tonight?"

"It will have to be earlier than that. We have a family dinner tonight, and those always last a long time. Could I come over this afternoon after my shift at the deli?"

Jessica thought about it. "We're usually off at about three thirty or four. If you want to come by the shop about then, we can walk to Sophie's house together."

"That's works for me." Tony started toward the counter.

Sophie added. "Come early and help at Great Finds."

He stopped at those words and turned back.

Sophie grinned. "Just kidding. See what happens when you tease me?"

Tony laughed. "I'll see you later."

14 A WAY OUT

When they finished their work for the day a little sooner than expected, Sophie and Jessica waited for Tony outside Great Finds. Sophie took a pad of paper and a pen out of her backpack. "Let's use this time and make a list of possible suspects."

"Everyone in the class, except maybe Emily."

Sophie wrote down the names. "And Mrs. Clayton. I don't want to put Uncle Sal on the list."

"No. I think he's honest. We don't know the names of the people who work there. Some of them seem kind of rough and tough."

"I noticed that too. I'll write 'workers.' We must be missing people because I don't see many real suspects on this list."

"That's true. We usually have suspicious people." Jessica bounced on her toes. "But I'm so glad I don't have to keep the secret from Tony this time. We've brought him into the mystery."

Sophie laughed. "Keep the secret?"

"I may have let a few facts slip in the past."

"A few?"

Jessica blushed. "More than a few, I admit. I'm not good with secrets. I try to be, but sometimes things slip out."

"I have to say that you've done well with everyone but Tony. This summer we've had some big secrets."

As Tony walked up to them, he said, "I have just over an hour before I have to be home."

They started toward Sophie's house at a brisk pace.

"Sophie, you don't have to run. Why don't you tell me about what I'm going to see."

She said, "If I described it, you'd think I'd dreamed it. We'll be there soon."

Jessica panted. "Sooner than usual." She gasped for air. "Can we slow down a little?"

Sophie eased off. But when they could see her house through the trees, she moved faster again.

Once inside, she grabbed the flashlight out of the kitchen drawer. With Tony and Jessica behind her, she hurried upstairs and into the guest room. Pointing at the closet, she said, "In there."

Tony leaned over to see inside the closet. "Winter coats?"

Sophie groaned. "Behind the coats. Here." She handed Tony the flashlight.

The sound of the flashlight turning on came only seconds before he said, "This can't be real!"

Sophie gestured toward the opening. "Let's go downstairs."

He stepped back out. "It's still a real staircase? The stairs go somewhere hidden?"

"That's what I wondered," Jessica answered. "When you see it, everything will make sense. Sort of. I'm still not sure why anyone would work in a basement."

Tony stepped into the closet and started down the stairs with the two girls close behind. At the bottom he paused. "Now I understand what you meant, Jessica. Did you find clues to whose office it was?"

"Mom gave us the clues we needed before we found it. The builder of this house lived here for a while."

"That makes sense. So those are house plans?" He pointed to the rolls of paper.

"Houses. Plus the boathouse."

He turned toward Sophie. "Seriously? Uncle Sal loves history. He's going be thrilled to have the original drawings for the factory."

When silence greeted him, he asked, "What aren't you telling me?"

"Let's show him the drawings, Jessica."

They went over to the table and first spread out the plans for Sophie's house and then for the factory. Shining the light on them, Sophie explained about the closet upstairs and the dashed lines. Then she opened the plans for the factory and showed him similar lines.

"You believe there's a secret passage in the Sweet Bites building?" He laughed. "I don't think that would have been missed all this time."

Sophie didn't say a word; she just gestured toward the stairs they'd come down.

When Tony looked that direction, he said, "You're right. You probably want me to ask Uncle Sal about trying to find this, don't you?"

"But we need to protect him and not say what we're searching for in case it's tied to the mystery. Our mysteries usually become dangerous."

"I know that's a fact." He paused. "I can ask to explore the building."

Sophie said, "I think we should do this when no one else is there."

"He goes to work very early, even on Saturday. He says he likes the quiet. Let's meet at six o'clock."

"Tonight?" Jessica asked with a hopeful tone in her voice.

"Tomorrow morning."

Jessica groaned.

———

Early Saturday morning, they got ready to go. After Jessica had showered, she stood in front of the mirror with her hair combed, but wet. Instead of drying and styling it, then putting on makeup, she pulled her hair back in a ponytail and turned toward the bedroom door. Sophie almost fell on the floor in shock.

Jessica only spoke one word after getting out of bed: "Chocolate." Sophie had assumed that meant her cousin needed a piece of one of her favorite foods to help her wake up, so she'd gone to the kitchen to find the two small boxes of chocolates they'd been given and brought home. They'd eaten a piece out of each box the day before. Both now sat open and empty on the kitchen counter. Her mother wasn't kidding when she said she loved chocolate.

Sophie put some of Jessica's makeup in her cousin's purse. Once she was fully awake, she'd realize her mistake and might be upset. Then Sophie grabbed the page with the dashed lines on it from the roll of plans for the boathouse, folded it, and put it into her backpack. They walked to town in silence.

Tony was waiting in the open doorway of Sweet Bites with a paper sack in his hand when they arrived. "Good morning."

Jessica shook her head from side to side.

"Not a good morning? Is this Jessica every day?"

"Not every day. Mornings aren't her best time," Sophie explained. "Plus, this is the earliest we've had to get up this summer. I think she needs chocolate."

"I brought muffins from Bananas." He held up the bag. "Uncle Sal's back in his office. The door will lock when I close it." He opened the door wider so the girls could enter, then closed it behind them.

Once inside, Tony went straight toward the chocolate storage area, and they followed him. "Let's get Jessica a piece of chocolate and see if that revives her. We can all eat muffins after that."

In the room, Jessica took a deep breath. "I feel better already." She used tongs to take a piece of dark chocolate off a stack and popped it into her mouth. Pure happiness crossed her face. "If you give me a few minutes, I think I'll be fine."

Tony laughed. "You might need for your parents to buy a chocolate factory, Jessica."

"That's an amazingly great idea. I'll tell my mom and dad—when I finally get to see them again," she added with a sad voice.

Back in the entryway, Tony opened the bag of muffins and held it in front of Sophie. "I think I chose good ones for everyone."

"Mine must be the blueberry-banana muffin."

Jessica picked the chocolate chip–banana. "Very wise, Tony. Thank you."

"I now know you like chocolate." He reached into the bag and pulled out the last muffin. "I love Mrs. Bowman's banana-walnut." He crunched the bag into a ball and tossed it into the trash can.

Sophie finished her muffin first and brushed crumbs off her hands.

When Jessica finished her muffin, she seemed to be more herself. She touched her face and hair. "I forgot my makeup, and my hair is like yours, Sophie!"

"I can't help with your hair, but I put your makeup in your purse. What's wrong with my hair?"

"It's perfect on you. But it isn't me. Thanks for bringing my makeup."

Tony said, "You don't need it, you know. You're pretty without makeup."

Jessica smiled from ear to ear. "Thank you. Since you said that, I'll wait to put it on until we're done with our search. We have work to do."

Tony led them down the hall, took a turn at the end, went

down another hallway, up steps to the left, and entered an office. "From the drawings, I think this could be the room."

Sophie tried to spread out the builder's drawing on a woman's desk, but it was too cluttered with papers and other things. She straightened up what she'd accidentally moved, then set the drawing on the floor and kneeled down to review it.

"I brought this because I thought it might give us clues. But studying it here, I'm realizing that all we know is that there are dotted lines on the left side of the building, toward the back, exactly where we are. The wall has been painted many times over the years. I wonder if it's been sealed over and the opening will be impossible to find."

"I'm surprised. You aren't usually so negative, Sophie," Tony said.

Sophie took a deep breath and gave the drawings another glance before speaking. "You're right. Let's find this," she said louder as she rose to her feet.

They checked along the wall, but it was smooth.

Tony said, "I have to agree with you on this one, Sophie. If there used to be a secret passage on this wall, at some point it was painted or boarded over. Let's try another room." The three of them went out the door, down the hall, turned a corner, and turned another corner.

Jessica asked, "Where are you taking us, Tony?"

"I know from experience that all of these turns lead to an office right beside the one we were just in."

When they entered the room, they found three desks inside, but more importantly, decorative panels on all the walls. Sophie said, "This wall has secret panel potential."

"I think it's close to what it was when it was built. My uncle once showed a photo of this room to Nezzy Grant. You know old lady Grant."

Both girls nodded because they knew her very well.

"She remembered that this room was a place for the ladies to rest between dances when they had events here in the boathouse. She said it was very pretty and elegant with chandeliers and velvet chairs."

"It sure doesn't fit that description anymore. But the factory area itself has a little bit of old elegance left. I noticed pretty details on the ceiling. Things like that remind me of older buildings in some of the countries I've lived in."

"Maybe we'll find our secret passage here. I've spent time in this building to know that there's only one other room where it could be."

Each of them took a wall, and they began pushing and tapping.

After a while, Sophie thought she'd found something. "Jessica, listen to this." She rapped on her wall with her knuckles. "Doesn't this sound like it did in that closet?"

Jessica and Tony both hurried over. Sophie tapped along that edge, and then beside it. The sound was very different.

"You're right, Sophie! It's like the closet."

The three of them pushed on and tested the area around the spot with the hollow sound. Suddenly, the panel on the wall popped inward. Sophie grabbed the edge of the opening so she wouldn't fall.

"Who found it?" Sophie turned to Jessica and Tony.

"I think I did," Tony answered. "This area"—he tapped the corner of the rectangle—"moved when I pushed it."

"Good going, Tony." Sophie pushed the panel completely open.

Jessica leaned over to see into the passage. "It's like the other one."

"Except that we don't know where this one goes," Tony added.

Sophie pictured the boat dock with its new wood. "I think we do." She waited to see if Jessica or Tony thought the same thing.

Tony shrugged.

Jessica bounced on her feet. "I know! The dock with the boat! Nothing else makes sense."

"Yes. I don't know why, but the builder decided to create a way out of this room to the boat dock. Maybe he thought secret passages were fun."

Jessica nodded. "I know I do. I'd never seen one before I came to Pine Hill."

Sophie retrieved the flashlight from her backpack, turned it on, and shined it down in the hole.

Spiderwebs on the sides reflected back the light, and Jessica shuddered.

Tony noticed. "You don't like dark, unknown places?"

"That isn't it. I don't like spiderwebs. Sophie's secret staircase was full of webs."

Tony surprised Jessica by not laughing at her. Instead, he said, "I'll go get a broom out of the janitor's closet."

"Thank you, Tony. That's what we did at Sophie's house."

Tony left and was back in a few minutes. Then, broom in hand, he went ahead of them down the stairs, Sophie shining the light from behind him and Jessica following her.

"Don't worry, Jessica. Webs are on some of the side areas, but the passage itself is clean."

Jessica continued down the steps. "That's good and bad. I'm glad there aren't spiderwebs, but that shows us that someone's used this recently."

"Very recently," Tony added.

At the bottom of the circular stone staircase, there was a level area.

Sophie held the flashlight near her watch. "We've been at the factory awhile, so we'd better hurry. Our knowledge of this has to stay a secret. If we don't get out of here soon, someone who comes to work early may see what we're doing."

Tony moved faster. "Uncle Sal will be so surprised when he sees the staircase and this pathway!"

It felt to Jessica like they'd walked forever, but she knew they hadn't walked farther than the building was long. The brick path ended at a wooden wall.

Sophie said, "Step to the side, Tony. Let me shine the light on this wall so we can figure out how this opens because it must open."

"We know it opened a long time ago, but we don't know if it still does. What if someone found the opening, came down here, but couldn't find any way out?" Jessica said, "Or does Sophie the Detective say that it will open?"

"I still think that the rowboat out there in the boathouse is the same one that you and I saw on the lake, Jessica. It came from and returned this direction."

"Wait! There." Tony moved the flashlight in Sophie's hand back where it had just been. "This area with the small piece of wood on it appears worn, as if it's had more use than the rest of the boards." He pushed the small piece of wood to the side, but nothing happened. Sophie pushed it the other direction. Still nothing happened.

Jessica said, "Let me try. This must be the lever that opens it." Jessica stepped up and studied the piece of wood for a moment. "Sophie, shine the light in front of me. There are scratches that make a circle around here." When she had, Jessica reached up, took hold of the piece of wood, and slowly spun it. At the halfway mark, the door swung out. The boat dock lay in front of them and the rowboat beyond.

The three of them stared in silence.

Jessica spoke first. "The door is the wall under the stairs that had the cracked paint."

Sophie said, "Yes. They didn't use the stairs because they had this door."

Jessica turned to Sophie. "So you didn't need to climb them."

"Or fall through them," Tony added.

She rubbed her elbow and winced. "I sometimes wish I hadn't tried."

Jessica stepped outside and examined the lock. "I think I understand how this works. Close the door, and I'll try to open it."

Tony pushed it shut and waited. Scratching and scraping sounds made Sophie wonder if Jessica had really figured it out. Then the door creaked open.

"I did it. That didn't take long."

Sophie checked her watch and said, "No, but all of this took quite a while. Hurry. We need to get all the way up and out of this building before anyone arrives."

They raced back up the stairs and out through the maze of hallways to the main entrance. The factory area was still silent, and all the lights were off in the offices they passed. They went out the door and sat down on the bench in front of the building. They hadn't been there long when Mrs. Clayton drove up to Sweet Bites and parked.

She got out of her car, gave them her usual smile, and said, "Good morning! You're here early. What's the special occasion?"

When Sophie was working on a mystery, she never gave out any extra information to people, in case they later became suspects. Keeping to her method, she simply said, "We wanted to be here early this morning." As Sophie entered the building, she realized that Mrs. Clayton was too nice to be part of their mystery. She should take her off their list of suspects.

15 THE SECOND SUSPECT

Later that morning, Jessica looked up from the chocolate-making demonstration and saw a woman walk by. She seemed nervous, so Jessica asked Sophie, "Who's that?"

"Kelsey Newman," Sophie replied. "She grew up in Pine Hill, went away to college, and came home to take over her parents' flower shop, Buds & Blooms."

Jessica watched as the woman went down the hall and around the corner. It seemed odd that the owner of a flower shop would be in a chocolate factory, but it was a small town. Maybe she had a friend or someone in her family who worked here. But the way Kelsey had glanced over her shoulder as she walked, almost as if she wanted to see if anyone was watching her, made Jessica wonder if something was wrong.

Sophie must have thought the same thing because she whispered in Jessica's ear, "I'm going to follow her."

"I'm coming with you."

To not interrupt their class, Jessica whispered to Emily that they were going to the restroom. She could let Uncle Sal know if he asked. Then they walked away, heading down the hall in the direction Kelsey had gone. When they went around the corner, they found a hallway with closed doors. Continuing down the hallway, she heard raised voices through a closed door, so she and Sophie stopped.

A man's voice said, "Please help," then some other words she couldn't clearly hear.

A woman's voice said, "If I've told you once, I've told you ten times, a hundred times, Kirk, you've gotten yourself mixed up in something serious. Get out."

Sophie whispered, "I'm pretty sure that voice belongs to Kelsey. She has a younger brother named Kirk."

Kirk said several words that were too quiet for Jessica to understand. Then there were scraping sounds, like a chair sliding across the floor.

Sophie hurried down the hall with Jessica behind her. As Sophie pushed on the door to the women's restroom, the office door opened and Kelsey stepped out. The girls quickly darted into the restroom.

Inside the empty room, Jessica asked, "What do you think that was about?"

"It didn't sound good for Kirk."

A couple of minutes later, they went back in class. While they'd been gone, the class had moved back to the enrober to make more chocolate-covered marshmallows. The good news was that it was milk chocolate again, so Sophie stood at the end and waited for the finished marshmallows to come out of the cooling section, eating one she was given with a smile on her face. Jessica might make a chocolate lover out of her yet.

They helped stack all of the new chocolates onto two trays. Uncle Sal gave Jessica one tray and old Mr. Pleckenpoll the other one. It seemed wise to break them up so one person couldn't trip and spill them all on the way to the chocolate storage room, but the old man had so much trouble walking that it appeared like he might fling his half of them on the floor any second. What happened the other day must have been a moment when he felt young. They delivered the trays with no incidents though.

After class, Sophie carefully took off her gloves and dropped them in the trash. Jessica did the same, but not until she'd licked the tip of one finger to get the chocolate off.

"Aren't you getting tired of chocolate yet?"

"I'm a little surprised, but I'm still having fun with it. On the flipside, are you enjoying chocolate more?"

Sophie turned to stare at the chocolate factory's floor. "Yes. I wouldn't mind having a piece or two of chocolate this weekend. I hope that Uncle Sal sends us home with some again."

As they walked toward the front of the building, Uncle Sal stopped them. "I understand that your mother loves chocolate, Sophie."

"I was surprised to find that out because she doesn't let us have dessert very often."

Jessica said, "She wants us to eat healthy."

Uncle Sal smiled widely. "Chocolate can be part of a healthy diet."

Jessica laughed. "I've always thought so."

"She does so much for our town that I'd like to do something for her. I've asked that a box of candy be left at the front desk for your mom. I hope she enjoys every bite. It's an assortment of milk and dark chocolate in different flavors."

"Thank you very much."

He walked on toward the factory floor, calling out to one of his workers, so Sophie and Jessica went on their way.

When they arrived at the front desk, no one was there. "Uncle Sal said that the box of candy would be here, but I don't see anything." Jessica stepped around the corner of the desk and turned in a full circle. "No, wait." A box of chocolates was pushed to the corner of the desk and had been wrapped in what they knew from their tour the first day was the factory's wrapping paper. Sophie joined her behind the desk.

"It was nice of him to wrap it for Mom." Sophie picked up the box.

"What if that box wasn't for her?"

"One box of chocolate would be the same as another. And he

said it would be here at the front. We can wait a minute or two and see if anyone comes with another box, or if Mrs. Clayton returns. Maybe she went home early because it's Saturday."

Sophie sat down in Mrs. Clayton's chair and leaned back in it. "We've already followed Emily, so that leaves Dylan, his mother, and Mr. P. I doubt an old man is our thief. Dylan's mother talks all the time, and that wouldn't be a good quality for a thief, would it?"

They both laughed.

When Jessica turned toward the hallway, she saw someone moving away, another shadowy figure that shouldn't be there. No one had walked across the entry area from the factory or the hall, so this someone had been listening to them. This wouldn't be a good place to discuss the mystery.

Sophie leaned forward. "I probably shouldn't read something on Mrs. Clayton's desk, but this was sitting on top and caught my attention. It might be important. 'Erma, do you know if someone needed something from my desk? I noticed that things weren't the way I left them.' It's signed 'Shelley.'"

Sophie grimaced. "Jessica, I think there was a name sign on the desk I sat at with the factory's drawing this morning. I also think it said 'Shelley.' I'd like to get rid of this note, but that would make what happened even more suspicious if Shelley asked Erma about it later."

Jessica glanced over her shoulder to make sure no one was there. "I hope Erma and Shelley don't tell others. The criminals could start to wonder if someone's after them."

Sophie nodded. When two minutes had passed, Sophie stood, took the box of candy in her hands, and said, "I'd like to get out of here. This must be Mom's box."

Jessica shrugged. "Even if it isn't, they can easily make this box again for whoever was supposed to get it. It's on Mrs. Clayton's desk. If it's her box of chocolates, I don't think she'd mind. She always seems so happy and friendly. Let's go, Sophie."

When they stepped out the doors, no one was in sight except for a gardener working on the flowers in front of the building.

"That delay for the candy cost us time. I guess we're not learning anything more about a class member today," Jessica said. "But Soph, I saw another shadowy figure. I think someone was listening to us."

"It's hard to know who's a friend and who isn't in this mystery."

"I agree."

As they walked, Sophie said, "We might have to start watching the factory when everyone leaves for the day and follow one of them. If we find one who didn't drive to work, that is."

"Soph, I've been thinking about the secret passages. I know you don't like to tell people what we've learned until a mystery is solved, but you should tell your parents what we discovered."

Sophie was silent for a couple of minutes. "Let's keep it a secret for now. The staircase was hidden for a long time, so a few more days won't matter. The two hidden places are so much alike that the bad guys might pick up on a connection to us if Mom or Dad told people about it, and the story got back to them."

"That's a good point, Sophie. Who could resist telling everyone about a secret staircase?" When they could see the resort, Jessica looked up toward the roof. "I wonder if the helicopter is tied into this mystery at all."

"I don't know why it would be, Jessica. Tony's dad said it was a guest arriving. I know better than to ignore anything though. I guess it's possible."

Jessica said, "That day, when we were talking to people in the group of bystanders, I saw someone come out of the side door and go toward the back of the building, walking at a fast pace. He was wearing a suit and had on sunglasses. I thought he might be Agent Dallas of the F.B.I. I even asked the sheriff about him. And that's when she asked me to keep my eyes open at the factory."

Sophie stopped. "And you didn't think this was important to tell me?"

"We didn't have a mystery. All we had was a man in a helicopter."

Sophie groaned. "Are there any other clues that I should know about?"

"I don't think so."

"I would have investigated. His trail may have gone cold."

Jessica rolled her eyes. "You've been reading detective books again, haven't you?"

"Not my usual kind. This one's all about codes and spies. How spies hide things."

"And you're going to use that information how?"

"I may need to know how to write something in a code." Sophie gave Jessica a look that said she shouldn't argue with her.

"I never thought I would solve a mystery, so I won't say we'll never need a code."

Sophie gave a single nod. "Thank you. I like to have all the skills I can, so I'm ready for anything. I learned that the best code seems to be a simple one, at least it would be for our uses. A good one was used by someone almost two thousand years ago in Rome. All he did was move the letter down one, so if I wanted to write the letter *a*, I would use the letter *b*. If I wanted to write the letter *m*, I use the letter *n*, and so on."

"That does sound fun. Are there any others?"

"See? I told you this was interesting. There are so many codes that it's hard for me to even remember them. But I'm working on it. The section about spies might be helpful in a mystery too. When a spy wants to leave something and let another spy know it's there so he or she can pick it up, they call it a 'dead drop.'"

Jessica shivered. "I don't like the word *dead* in there."

"I think they use that because it's not like you handed it to a living person. I've been thinking about places in Pine Hill that I could use for dead drops."

"Because there are so many times when you need to be a spy and hide something from another one?"

"You'll see. This will all come in handy. Maybe not on this mystery, but I'll need to know it sometime."

By now they had reached the edge of the parking lot. Sophie stared at the outside of the building for so long that Jessica wondered if they were going to start attracting attention.

"Soph, we need to move on."

"Maybe we should go inside and wait to see if that man comes through the lobby. You'd remember him, wouldn't you?"

"In a place where most people dress very simply and casually, a man in a suit would stand out. Of course, if he only wore the suit for his helicopter ride and then changed into jeans or something like that, I'm not sure I would recognize him."

Sophie started toward the resort's entrance. "Let's wait in the lobby. Mom's not expecting us for a while."

"But Sophie"—Jessica hurried after her—"what's our reason for being here? Two twelve-year-olds can't sit in a fancy resort's lobby for no reason at all." Jessica had caught up to Sophie, and they were almost to the doorman outside the resort.

Sophie checked the time on her watch. "I would ask if you wanted a milkshake—"

"With our chocolate samples, I've had too many sweets already today."

"I agree. But I remember hearing Mom tell Dad not too long ago that the resort is now serving 'light lunches.' I'm not sure what that means, but it's lunchtime, and I still have money left from my allowance. I wouldn't if Mom didn't keep giving us money for the deli."

"Then let's get lunch."

A "light lunch" turned out to be small things that cost a lot of money. So, instead of that, Sophie and Jessica each got a glass of iced tea, sat in the lobby, and waited.

Jessica glanced around at all the adults coming and going. "We're the only kids here. We can only stay here so long."

"Sip your tea slowly, and we'll go to Great Finds after this."

When they'd almost finished their drinks, they had to tell the waiter that they didn't want anything else when he came to check on them. Jessica said, "I think we're going to need to go soon, Sophie."

"I know." Sophie took a big drink from her tea and started to push it away.

Jessica noticed Mr. Pleckenpoll coming through the doors. "Sophie, there's Mr. P. Maybe we should go say hi to him on our way out." Jessica started to rise to her feet, but Sophie reached out and pushed down on her shoulder, and she sank back into her chair.

Sophie said, "That's Mr. P., all right, but are you noticing anything strange about him?"

"No." She watched him. "Wait! He's moving more quickly than we've seen him do before. In fact, he isn't moving like an old man."

"That's what I thought." When he stepped into an open elevator, Sophie stood. "Let's watch the numbers on the elevator and see what floor he gets off on."

The two of them hurried over to the elevator doors and watched the display until the elevator stopped.

Sophie said, "Five."

They hurried up the stairs that were beside the elevator, racing up toward the fifth floor. By the third floor, Jessica was panting. She felt like she'd climbed a mountain by the time they reached their destination.

Sophie pushed open the door to the fifth floor an inch or so. No one was in the hallway, so she opened it a bit more. Still nothing. Opening it all the way, she stepped out and peered around it.

Jessica whispered, "Anything?"

"No. The elevator moved a lot faster than we did. He's already in his room."

The carpeted hallway stretched before them in both directions. Hotel room doors lined the hallway on each side. A window at the end of the hall let in light, and the elevator sat at the other end. "Sophie, every door's closed."

Sophie started walking down the hall.

"Sophie, what are you doing? Someone might see us. And I don't think we're supposed to be here."

"We need to find out what room he's in."

"What are you proposing? That we knock on every door?" Jessica laughed.

"Not a bad idea."

"I was kidding! What reason could we give for knocking on doors?"

Sophie paused for a moment before speaking. "Maybe we can say we want to tell them about Mom's antique shop. While they're visiting, they could go there."

"Oh, right. Your mother would love that. And I'm saying that in a sarcastic way because she would hate it if we used her shop's name for this. And I don't think the hotel would appreciate it if someone from the town came in and started knocking on doors. It might get your mother in trouble with the resort."

Sophie's shoulders drooped. "You're right. It wasn't my best idea."

Jessica didn't say anything, but she had to agree.

"I guess we'll have to wait here until Mr. P. comes out of his room. Before you say it, I realize that's a bad idea too because someone might want to use the stairs and we can't explain why we're here."

A door halfway down the hall opened. Sophie jumped back into the stairwell, leaving the door open a crack. A man with dark hair peered out the door, looking first to the right and then to the left. Then he stepped out, closed the door, and hurried in their direction. Jessica hoped he was on his way to the elevators, not the stairs. She wanted to do a happy dance when he passed them. When he reached the elevator, he pushed a button, waited until the doors opened, and got on.

When the elevator doors closed, Jessica blew out a big breath. "That was close, Sophie."

"Tell me about it." Sophie turned and started descending the stairs. "We'd better hurry and get over to Great Finds so we can help Mom."

"And eat lunch!"

"That too."

"Let's follow Mr. P. after class on Monday and see if we can figure out his mystery."

"He seems like such a nice old man," Jessica said. "I hope he's not a bad guy."

When they arrived at the front of Great Finds, Sophie and Jessica peered in the window. Sophie said, "Mom is helping one person, and there are two—no, I see three other people waiting. I don't think we should bother her. She's going to be busy for a while. Let's go home and have something to eat there."

As they started toward home, she added, "And maybe we can have a piece of the chocolate in this box."

At Sophie's house, they made peanut butter and jelly sandwiches and sat down to eat them at the kitchen table. After eating a peach for dessert, Sophie opened the wrapping paper on the box of chocolates. A computer-printed note was taped to the box. It read:

Please make sure these end up with the right person.

16 SPARKLING SURPRISE

"Sophie, this box of candy might not have been for your mother," Jessica said as she stared at the note.

"You may be right, but we've already opened it, and if it's a gift for someone, we've ruined it. Maybe we should call the factory and ask Uncle Sal about it."

Jessica nodded. "Very good idea."

Sophie looked up the phone number and dialed the chocolate factory. After five rings she hung up. "Mrs. Clayton must have left for the day, and no one else is answering. We can't return it today. Uncle Sal promised Mom a box of candy, and we have one right here."

"I guess we may as well eat what's inside. He can make a new box for the other person on Monday," Jessica said

Sophie lifted the lid. "Twelve pieces of candy, half dark chocolate and half milk chocolate. I've decided that I like milk chocolate more." Sophie reached for a piece of the lighter brown candy.

"I'm for dark chocolate all the way." Jessica reached for the darker chocolate. "Now the question is, what flavor is it?" Jessica took a little nibble off a corner. Then a slightly larger nibble. "I think this one is orange-filled."

Sophie broke hers in half.

"I wish you wouldn't do that. It makes a pretty piece of chocolate ugly."

Sophie laughed. "And a bite out of the corner doesn't?"

Jessica stared at the piece of chocolate in front of her. "I suppose you're right."

Sophie poked at the filling oozing out of one of her chocolate halves. "It's caramel, I think. You're the chocolate expert. It shouldn't have a red center, should it?"

"Only if Uncle Sal is trying one of his strange combinations again. Caramel and jelly filling is weird." Jessica leaned over to see it.

Sophie stared at the jelly-filled center. "Jessica"—she reached into the gooey center and pulled out something hard—"this isn't jelly." She rolled the hard candy center in her fingers and held it up. A red stone, something that would be in a ring or a necklace, caught the light coming through the kitchen window.

She looked up in time to see Jessica about to take a bigger bite of her piece of chocolate. She shoved her cousin's hand away from her mouth. "Don't eat that!"

Jessica rubbed the spot on her hand where Sophie had pushed her. "Ouch. Why did you do that?"

She held the stone where Jessica could see it. "I'm guessing, but aren't rubies red?"

"Yes! What have we gotten in the middle of this time?" Jessica picked up the piece of chocolate that had been knocked out of her hand and had fallen to the floor. She pulled it in half. "This one only has a normal filling in it. Jewels inside chocolates are a good reason for criminals to be in Pine Hill. I would think that a real ruby this size—if that's what it is—would be worth a lot of money."

Sophie reached for another piece of chocolate, but Jessica put her hand on Sophie's. "Maybe we should leave these all alone."

"I want to see what's in the rest of them, and we already have two of them open."

Jessica stared at the box for so long that Sophie wondered what she was going to do or say. When her cousin reached for a piece of milk chocolate, Sophie knew that Jessica had decided to break them open.

A minute later, a dozen pieces of chocolate, now in half, sat in front of them on the table.

"Only your first piece had the gemstone in it, Sophie. If it is a ruby, it's worth a lot of money."

"It must be real. Why would someone hide a fake gemstone inside a piece of chocolate?"

"Maybe as a surprise for someone?" Jessica said.

"It sure would be a surprise if someone bit into a piece of chocolate and had their teeth hit something hard. I don't think that would be a good idea. If their teeth didn't hit it, they might choke on it. That's a bad idea all around."

"You're right. But if that's the case, then we have somehow stumbled upon some major criminals. Because I have a feeling that this gemstone is worth more money than even you and I can imagine."

Sophie stood. "Let's rinse it off so we can see better what we found." She went across the kitchen, opened the cupboard, and pulled out a fine mesh strainer. "My mom uses this to drain the juice off canned pineapple and other stuff. We won't lose the stone down the drain if we put it in here."

"Great idea."

At the sink, Sophie ran hot water through the strainer. "I want to make sure it doesn't wash away by accident." She removed the gem from the strainer and patted it dry with a kitchen towel. Then she held it up to the sunlight, and it sparkled even more than before.

"That's beautiful! I remember when we went to see the crown jewels in London. They're the jewelry from kings and queens. This is pretty enough to be in a crown. We have to take it to Sheriff Valeska."

"I won't argue with you this time, Jessica. We do need to get this to the sheriff as fast as we can."

She took out a small plastic zipper bag from a drawer and slipped the stone inside. While she did that, Jessica picked up the pieces of chocolate and the box and put them in a larger plastic bag that Sophie stowed in her backpack. With the zipper bag tucked in Sophie's front jeans pocket and the backpack over her shoulders, they went out the door, down the steps, and started on the trail through the woods toward town.

Every once in awhile, Sophie patted that pocket with her right hand. Finally, Jessica asked, "Are you worried you're going to lose it?"

"Yes! I don't want to have to search through the woods to find one red stone. I put it in my pocket because that felt safer." Sophie chewed on her lip. "Jessica, I keep feeling like Sheriff Valeska is going to be upset with us because we have the gemstone, but—"

"Sophie, it isn't our fault. Uncle Sal promised you a box of chocolates. We picked up a box of chocolates. End of story."

"Then let's think about the next step in solving this mystery."

"I don't know if we have a next step, Sophie. The sheriff will say to stay out of it now."

"No, we're inside the chocolate factory. She may need us to keep our eyes open or do something else. She knew something was going on, or she wouldn't have asked you to spy."

"That's what keeps going through my head. But she said it wouldn't be dangerous. Even when she told me to stop watching, she said it wasn't dangerous."

The two of them walked a couple of minutes without saying anything. Then Sophie stopped right in the middle of the trail and turned to Jessica, who barely managed to stop before running into Sophie's back. "We still don't know what's going on. Why would she ask you to spy for her if it didn't matter?"

Jessica tugged on Sophie's arm, and they started moving

forward again on the trail. "Maybe we'll get some answers today. I don't think Sheriff Valeska was expecting us to find a box of chocolates with a gemstone in it."

Sophie stopped again, and this time Jessica did ram into her back.

"Sophie! Stop doing that."

"Sorry. I wondered again if this is a real stone. If it's fake and someone put it in the candy . . ." Sophie shook her head. "That doesn't make any more sense now. Why would anyone hide fake gemstones?" Sophie started on her way again, and Jessica stepped beside her as the path widened nearer to town so she wouldn't hit Sophie if she stopped.

They continued walking and soon could see the town in front of them. Continuing down the sidewalk, they quickly arrived at the sheriff's office. Sophie pushed the door open and entered with Jessica behind her. Sheriff Valeska sat at her desk, working on her computer.

The sheriff looked up, spotted them, and said, "Oh no. What now, Sophie?"

Sophie glanced over her shoulder at the secretary, Clare Morton. She still didn't feel comfortable speaking in front of her. And one of the deputies was working in the back at a filing cabinet. "Sheriff, we have something to show you, but it's kind of a secret. Could we step into one of those rooms?" Sophie gestured with her head toward the room they'd been in the other day.

Sheriff Valeska pushed back from her desk and stood. "Today is busy, so I hope it's important." The sheriff waved her hand at the room's open door. Sophie and Jessica walked in, the sheriff came in behind them and left the door partly open. "What is it, Sophie?"

Sophie glanced around them to make sure no one else was there. Then she reached into her pocket, pulled out the zipper bag with the ruby, and handed it to the sheriff.

Sheriff Valeska stared at the bag, her eyes growing wider and wider as she realized what was inside it. In a serious tone of voice, she slowly said, "Sophie, Jessica, where did you find this?"

17 DANGER!

Chills went down Jessica's spine. She quickly explained to the sheriff about the box of chocolates Uncle Sal had promised them and how Sophie had found the stone in one of the chocolates in the box they'd picked up from the receptionist's desk.

Sophie pulled the pieces and box out of her backpack and handed the bag to Sheriff Valeska. "Do you have any idea why the ruby was in here?"

The sheriff slowly shook her head from side to side, then suddenly nodded up and down as if she'd realized something. "There's a man here in town who I believe can tell us more about this. I thought he was mistaken about what he expected to find in Pine Hill, what he trailed to this area. But"—she rolled her finger over the gemstone, flipping it around in her hand—"I think you've proven his theory to be correct."

She slowly raised her gaze from the ruby and looked at the two of them. "Will anyone suspect one of you when this box of chocolates comes up missing?"

Sophie and Jessica looked at each other, and Jessica said, "Oh no."

Sheriff Valeska said, "I take that as a yes."

Jessica said, "Yes. It's a definite yes. As we told you, Uncle Sal said there would be a box of chocolates sitting there. It was the end of the day, so maybe no one has tried to find them yet."

Sheriff Valeska glanced from one girl to the other and paused, seeming to mull something over. "I'm going to let the two of you in on a secret—"

"Is this more about why you asked me to watch things at the factory?"

The sheriff said, "No, Jessica. That was completely because of the recipe. I felt that Sal Donadio's factory was the least likely place to have danger, and that's the only reason I asked you to watch. Let me go make a phone call. I'll be right back." The sheriff left the room and closed the door behind her.

"What have we accidentally gotten ourselves into, Sophie?"

"I'm not sure, Jessica, but it sounds like it could be something dangerous. Maybe the most dangerous thing we've been in the middle of yet."

"I wish you hadn't said that. We've had so many things happen this summer, scary things, that I don't want this one to be any worse. I don't want there to be another mystery at all."

The sheriff came into the room a few minutes later. "I spoke with that person and learned more. He thinks there's a criminal band working in this area, people who are involved with a gemstone theft ring. He hoped to contact me to make an arrest soon at the chocolate factory because he's become suspicious about things going on there and has been watching the front of the building every night."

"That means that he'll see someone leaving the candy factory with . . ."

The sheriff nodded. "Right, Sophie. With nothing. The box of candy with the ruby inside is gone. I can't stop anyone. I can't arrest anyone. I can't do anything. Someone in this ring must work there, at least one of them must."

"Remember, Sophie, that Uncle Sal says that people who work there can take home chocolate every day. No one would notice if someone had the chocolates. They could normally walk out the front door with them. It should be easy for Uncle Sal to make a new box like this."

"But, Jessica, I think it's pretty likely that someone is going to find out quickly that the gemstone isn't in the box of chocolates they got from the factory. Even if we find a way to leave a new box there, it won't help."

"Yes. And if they're smart, and they probably are, they may already know that someone is watching the front."

Sophie gulped. "And they'll also figure out or at least suspect that Jessica and I have their special box of chocolates. No matter how you look at it, we have a problem."

Jessica said, "But we could go inside the chocolate factory, sneak in, make a new box of chocolates, and put it where this one was."

Sophie nodded. "We picked up this box at the very end of the day, and Mrs. Clayton had already left early, so—"

Jessica jumped in, "So we might be able to get this back on her desk before anyone knows it's missing."

"Girls, I can't let you do that. If you walk in the front door of the candy factory, a hundred people might see you doing that. Even if we ask Sal Donadio to let you in that door on Sunday, people could be nearby and see you. I can't risk your being exposed."

"But, Sheriff, almost anyone would figure out that we have the box of chocolates. Uncle Sal said it was out front, and there were a lot of people around then. Besides"—Sophie grinned —"we don't have to walk in the front door."

"No, we have a better way."

"This I have to hear. The only other entrance into the place is the emergency escape to the roof, which leads to a ladder down the back of the building."

The idea was interesting. "We didn't know about that."

The sheriff said, "But you could still have someone see you on top of the roof. No, I have to protect you girls. You're my responsibility."

Jessica pretended to swim, swinging her arms in the air as though she was cutting through water.

"Swim? There's no way in from the lake. I know that to be a fact."

"Sheriff, I don't know who started that rumor, but it isn't true."

"And you know that because . . .?

Expecting Sheriff Valeska to be none too happy about their earlier trip to the factory, Jessica clenched her teeth.

"We swam there"—Sophie held up one hand when she saw the sheriff about to reprimand her—"with Mr. Donadio giving permission first, and Tony going with us so there was a family member. After I saw the boats on the lake, I wanted to see if there was a boat under the factory."

"And? Was there a boat under the factory?"

"An old rowboat, but we couldn't tell if it had been used."

Jessica said, "But we found a secret passage! We can go from it into the factory."

The sheriff laughed. "I haven't seen that, and I've been in that factory many times."

Jessica nodded. "It's there."

Sheriff Valeska sighed. "I guess we could send a boat to take you underneath the boathouse."

"No, Sheriff! That won't work because people could see it and hear the motor. If we swim tomorrow, it's Sunday, when the factory is closed for the day. No one will know we're there."

"I'm hesitant to tell Sal Donadio that you're doing this because I'm not sure who he trusts and who he might tell. It's private property though—"

"The last time we went, he told Tony that if we wanted to go under there and swim around and have fun, it was no matter to him."

"Then set this up with Tony, and let's do this. I don't see any other way to make it happen." After another hesitation, the sheriff added, "Girls, I need for you to stay away from my office for a while. You're at the chocolate factory almost every day, and people in Pine Hill know that you've solved two mysteries. If they see you coming in and out of here often, they may start to think that you're involved in a mystery again."

Sophie said, "But Sheriff, what if we find an important clue?"

The sheriff sighed. "Let's hope that doesn't happen, Sophie. I don't even want you to call here or for Jessica to send a text message with her phone. I don't have a better solution."

"I do! I read about it in one of my books. It's called a dead drop, a place where we can leave things for each other, but no one else will know they're there."

The sheriff laughed. "Sophie, that sounds like something out of a spy movie. This is Pine Hill."

"But, Sheriff, it would work."

"So where do you suggest we have this dead drop?"

Sophie's mind raced. They needed a place that would be easy to get to but where no one else would think to look. Her favorite bench in town came to mind, the one she always sat on when she wanted to figure things out. "The bench on the sidewalk over by Bananas Bakery. If something were taped underneath it, no one would know it was there."

"I can live with that, Sophie."

"We'll make a chalk mark on the side of the bench's armrest to let you know when there's something for you to pick up."

Sophie thought over the chalk that was in a box of toys from when she was little. "A line made from bright blue chalk."

"That won't be obvious, will it?" Jessica said sarcastically.

"Okay, white chalk. That might look more like dust, so it won't stand out as much."

The sheriff agreed.

"And when you've picked it up, Sheriff, wipe off the chalk mark so we know it's been done. We also need a code so no one else will be able to read the note."

Sheriff Valeska groaned. "Okay. What's the code?"

"I've read about so many good ones." She turned to Jessica.

"Let's use the one I told you about earlier." When Jessica nodded, Sophie described it to the sheriff.

Ten minutes later, Sophie left the sheriff's office, and she marched importantly down the street with her cousin. Sheriff Valeska had put her in charge of what they would do tomorrow afternoon. Well, her, Jessica, and Tony in charge. Her footsteps slowed as she realized that this could land them in the middle of danger.

Jessica said, "Sophie, why are we stopped here?"

Sophie noticed that she was standing in front of Buds & Blooms. "I just realized that we were going into a place tomorrow where someone works who either stole very expensive gemstones or helped someone who did."

"And you just thought of this? I thought of it from the first second that you suggested the idea. But I don't know of any other way to make this work." When a family walked by, she realized they were far from alone here. "There are quite a few people here. Maybe we should head toward home and talk about it there."

"You're right." Sophie gave a glance toward Buds & Blooms. When the owner looked up, Sophie gave a small wave. "I might buy Mom a flower sometime soon. She'd like that."

"Do you think the owner of this business has any connection with the gemstones?"

"I'm not sure of anything anymore. You were a spy who was supposed to find a spy, or at least watch out for one, but now we have a major criminal—or more than one—working in the chocolate factory. I hope that Uncle Sal is wrong about someone stealing his recipes though, because one crime is more than enough."

"Being a secret spy was kind of fun for a little while. But I'm glad we're working on this together now, Sophie."

18 MORE CHOCOLATE

When the girls got back to Sophie's house, they went into the kitchen for a snack. Sophie grabbed a bag of trail mix—a mixture of nuts and dried fruit—out of the cupboard. When she went over to the refrigerator to get juice for them, she stopped and stared at the door.

Jessica took a handful of the trail mix. "Anything wrong?"

Sophie removed a note from the fridge. "We didn't have anything cold for our lunch, so I didn't see this note. Dad is reminding me that we're going to dinner tonight. But I don't remember—"

"Isn't it your mom's birthday today?"

"Oh no! I've been thinking about our mystery, and I didn't think about Mom. That isn't good."

"I've been with you almost all the time, so my guess is that you haven't gotten her a birthday gift or a card, right?"

"Very right. Dad must have left the note for me this morning. We need to hurry back to town so I can find something."

"Maybe you'll see a store and think of a gift you could buy there that your mom would like."

"Mom has so many things because of the store she owns. Her store's where other people want to buy their gifts."

They each ate a handful of trail mix and drank a glass of juice before going to town on their usual path through the woods. Sophie didn't find anything on Main Street that felt like a good gift for her mom. They turned onto another street and came to a corner. She hadn't noticed earlier that the Down Shoppe, an important place in another mystery, was gone and the fishing store, Hook, Line & Sinker, was back there where it should be. Buds & Blooms was across the street.

After crossing the street, Sophie paused at the flower shop's window. "I talked about getting Mom a flower to make her happy, but a whole bunch of flowers might make her very happy. Maybe this is a good birthday present for her. She doesn't buy flowers for herself, other than the ones she plants at our house that she has me weed."

Sophie pulled open the door to the shop and walked inside with Jessica right behind her. Kelsey was helping someone at the counter, so Sophie and Jessica wandered around and looked at the bouquets. There were price tags on a few of them. Sophie leaned over to see one and groaned. "Jessica, I don't think I can afford to get Mom flowers with what Dad gave me for her birthday." She held up the tag for Jessica to see, and her cousin grimaced.

"You may be right. But before we go, let's ask and make sure. Maybe these bouquets are more expensive because of the kind of flowers or something like that."

Sophie chewed on her lip a second, staring at the vases filled with flowers. She still wasn't sure if she should leave or if she should ask. But she could hear her dad's voice telling her, "There's no such thing as a stupid question." When the other customer exited, Kelsey came over. "Can I help you, Sophie?"

Sophie hesitated for a second. "I'm not sure, Kelsey. My mom's birthday is today—"

"And you came here to buy her a gift! That's wonderful. I'm sure I can help you."

"I don't know, Kelsey. This is how much money Dad gave me to buy a gift." Sophie set the money on the counter.

"Are some flowers less expensive than others?" Jessica asked.

"Absolutely. I can make you a beautiful bouquet of flowers, Sophie. Do you need them to be in a vase?"

"Mom has a lot of pretty vases in her store."

Kelsey laughed. "That's partly why the flower bouquets near the entrance are so expensive. They're in antique vases from your mom's shop. Give me about ten minutes, and you can take your flowers with you." Kelsey went into a glass-fronted refrigerator filled with buckets of flowers.

Sophie felt stress ooze out of her. She would have a gift for her mom.

As they walked around the store, waiting for the flower arrangement, something caught Sophie's eye. "Jessica," she said in a low voice, "there are chocolates here."

"I know that lots of times people buy chocolates and flowers together as a gift. My dad has done that for my mom before."

"These aren't just any chocolates. These are from Sweet Bites Chocolates."

Jessica stepped closer. "Sophie, the chocolates are made in this town, so that isn't a surprise."

"But no one else sells them. At least not that I know of, which is strange."

Kelsey stepped out with a pretty bouquet of what Sophie recognized as daisies and carnations, along with other things she couldn't put a name to. She knew her mother would love it because it had an old-fashioned look that reminded her of the things her mother sold in her store. It wasn't too modern.

Kelsey said, "I see you noticed the chocolates that I have there. I'm the only store in Pine Hill that sells them. For some reason the factory wants them to ship to other places and not be sold here." She paused and seemed almost nervous when she added, "My brother Kirk talked me into carrying them here in the store and managed to talk Sal into letting me do it." Then the shadow lifted, and she smiled brightly again, maybe too brightly.

Sophie paid for the flowers Kelsey had wrapped with green paper. Then they went out the door. Standing outside, Sophie said, "Don't you think it's strange that only one store can sell Sweet Bites Chocolates?"

"I think people who visit Pine Hill would love to buy some. It doesn't make sense to me. Do you think it's another clue?"

Sophie turned and studied the building they'd left. "Maybe we should set up surveillance and watch to see who comes and goes."

"Who would we be watching for? People who like chocolate? Or flowers? I don't see how we would learn anything."

"I guess you're right. But something doesn't feel right about this place." Sophie began walking again, and Jessica stepped beside her.

"This time, I agree with you. But we'll have to see if any other clues lead back to Buds & Blooms. Well, any clues other than the owner and her brother having an argument."

Neither of them said anything for a while. Finally, as the shortcut to Sophie's house came into view. Sophie said, "Let's get ready for dinner. Tomorrow we have church. Then adventure."

———

The next morning, Sophie dressed in tan pants and a forest green T-shirt slid into the pew next to Jessica who wore a light pink dress with white sandals. It was Sophie's usual look, but a little dressier for church. She'd worn a dress for dinner last night and didn't want to wear one again today. Jessica loved dressing up for church and everywhere else she could. She'd worn a dress last night too.

Sophie leaned over to her. "I've been thinking about swimming today."

Jessica raised one eyebrow.

Maybe they shouldn't talk about that here. Sophie glanced past Jessica and over to the opposite side of the church. "Dylan and his mother are over there. They're on our unknown list."

Jessica twisted in her seat so she could see the pair. The college student from their class was next to his mother, and she was talking—at least Sophie figured she was talking since her lips were moving.

In a low voice Sophie said, "I'm surprised she doesn't run out of breath. If I blow up a couple of balloons, I start to hurt inside. And she must blow out that amount of air as she speaks."

Jessica agreed. "It is amazing to see. And hear."

"You girls shouldn't speak about anyone that way," Mrs. Sandoval said from beside Sophie.

"Sorry, Mom. Mrs. Hanley seems like a good person. But it's hard to get in a word when she's nearby."

"Still, Sophie. Be kinder. I don't know someone with that name. Who are you talking about?"

Sophie turned again toward the mother and son. "Dylan and his mother are in our chocolate-making class."

"Ah, yes. She came in the store one day this week. It was an afternoon, so it must have been after your class. Very nice woman. Kind. But I have to agree with you. I believe she said more words in the twenty minutes she was in the store than most people say in hours. I asked where she was visiting from. She told me all the places she had lived in her life, and it seems like they moved around a lot when she was young." Mrs. Sandoval smiled.

"I think her son is a little stressed-out."

"Where are you and Jessica going swimming today? I heard you ask her about it."

Sophie gave her best smile but knew it probably didn't look

real. "In the lake. Over by the chocolate factory, I think. We're meeting Tony."

To her relief, the minister walked to the front of the church and up to the pulpit. Sophie knew not to say anything to Jessica during the rest of the service and worked to push the mystery out of her mind for the next hour. Even though they had excitement coming later today.

19 CHOCOLATE-COVERED CLUE

Jessica swam up to the dock where Tony and Sophie already sat waiting. She leaned her elbows on it and looked up at them. "Sophie, you normally plan things very well, so well that we both have plastic bags with things we need taped to our backs including the tape to put them back on for our swim out. But we may have forgotten something."

Sophie stood. "We're here, and no one spotted us yet. I think everything's okay."

Jessica climbed the ladder and stood beside Sophie as Tony rose to his feet. "There's just one thing. We're dripping wet, so we're going to leave a trail of water down the hall."

Sophie put her hand over her mouth and groaned. "You are so right. We know where the bathroom is, so let's go inside the building, run in there to get the paper towels, and dry off. After that, we'll quickly wipe up the floor. That way if there's a security guard, he or she won't spot it."

"That sounds like a plan. It's about the only thing we can do if we want to get this job done today."

"There's one other thing, Tony. Jessica and I know how the chocolates are made because we've been in the class this week, so we're the best chance we've got for fixing this. We'll take the lead on the project."

Tony said, "I'd rather be in the middle of it all, but I see your point. The only thing I know about chocolate is how to eat it."

Jessica peeled the bags off Sophie, and Sophie did the same for her. After Sophie had taken a flashlight out of one, Jessica opened the door slowly.

Sophie whispered, "It wouldn't be good if someone came out this way right now."

When they were sure the passage was empty, Sophie led the way with the flashlight through the passage and up the stairs. Tony pushed the lever, and the panel into the office area opened. Sophie switched off the flashlight and left it on the top stair.

After stepping from the opening into the room, they hurried over to the door, and Sophie slowly opened it. She whispered, "All clear."

Tony whispered back, "We have to hurry. I couldn't figure out a good way to ask if there would be a security guard here today. If there is one, we don't know if that person is going to be passing this way any second."

All three of them jumped when they heard what sounded like something falling off a desk or a shelf from somewhere in the building. They froze in place.

After a minute with no sounds, Sophie whispered, "Dry off in the restroom first. Then meet in the chocolate storage area. Since they keep some of the chocolate boxes and the papers that go around each piece there, along with the chocolates, we'll have everything we need."

Jessica and Tony nodded, then hurried down the hall. Jessica didn't even break the silence in the restroom. She kept thinking about how easily they could be caught.

Sophie whispered, "We dried off so much in the passageway that I don't think we dripped anywhere."

Jessica nodded agreement. She and Sophie hurried down the

hallway, past Mrs. Clayton's desk, and into the factory. They found Tony pacing back and forth in the chocolate storage room.

Sophie took charge. "Jessica, you find all of the chocolates. Tony, you and I will stand guard. Then Jessica and I can put the box of chocolates together."

Sophie was always very organized at times like these. Jessica didn't like it when the door closed and she was alone in here, but having two guards was better than one.

She pulled her phone out of the plastic bag she'd had taped to her back and compared the photos of the chocolates that they'd taken with the pieces on the shelves, choosing those they needed and putting them in paper wrappers in the same size box as the one they'd taken home. She found the first few pieces quickly. It took a little longer to find the others because there were so many that were similar.

Jessica soon knew she'd chosen the exact right chocolates and only needed the final piece. It was the most important one, though, because it would have the ruby inside. Even though there were neat stacks of the many kinds of chocolate with no empty spaces, that piece of chocolate wasn't here. It had been milk chocolate with caramel in the middle and white chocolate lines on top.

Sophie walked in the door, startling Jessica, who clamped her own hand over her mouth so she wouldn't scream. When she saw it was her cousin, she pulled her hand away. "Sophie, don't scare me like that."

"What's taking so long? We need to get out of here as soon as we can."

She pointed at her phone. "I don't see this one." Jessica gestured at the shelves. "Help me find it."

Sophie looked at the phone, then went through the pieces on the shelf. "You're right. I don't see it either."

A voice from behind them said, "What's taking so long?"

Both Sophie and Jessica jumped and squealed.

"Tony Donadio, you are lucky that the door is closed or someone might have heard us." Sophie shook her head.

Jessica gestured to a shelf stacked with chocolates. "Tony, the piece that had the ruby in it doesn't seem to be here. But the milk chocolate with caramel inside looks like it, except it doesn't have white chocolate lines across the top."

"We can add white chocolate to the plain piece," Sophie suggested.

"Sophie, we don't know how to do that."

"I helped Mom decorate a cake once. It looks like it should be pretty simple. But maybe you should grab a few of those pieces of chocolate in case I don't get it right the first time."

Jessica put three onto a paper towel from a roll in there. "Good idea."

"I help decorate some foods at the deli when we're getting ready for parties, and this doesn't look too much different, so I can try too."

Jessica added one more piece of chocolate to the pile in her hand.

"Okay, let's finish this up."

Tony peered out the room's door, waved them on, and they hurried down to the factory, where they found a couple of glass containers and filled them with some of the warm, melted milk chocolate and white chocolate. Using a small knife, Jessica made a slit in the bottom of one piece of candy. Then Sophie opened a second plastic bag and brought out the ruby. Jessica pushed it inside the slit.

"You know, I don't think anyone's going to be able to tell we did this once we've put a little bit of milk chocolate on the bottom. I think this is going to look perfect. We do need for it to dry quickly though."

After Sophie put a small blob of milk chocolate on a piece of plastic, Jessica gently set the piece of chocolate with the ruby inside on top.

Sophie said, "I think if we dip a fork into the white chocolate, we can drizzle it across. It won't be as good as the equipment they've got here, but it will be a lot easier to clean up. Should I go first, Tony?"

Tony said, "If you think you can do it, go ahead. I've never said I was an artist. "

Sophie dipped the ends of the fork into the white chocolate, lifted it, and let some of it drip off. Following the pattern on the photo on Jessica's phone, she swung the fork over the piece of chocolate twice to give it the white chocolate zigzag on top. The first line went perfectly—and then a giant blob fell off the fork.

Sophie groaned. "Let's get the ruby out of here and into another piece of chocolate."

"We should have waited to fix the bottom of the piece of chocolate until we knew we had the top right."

"But then we might mess up the chocolate on top and have to fix the bottom. No, I think we did it in the right order. We have to start over."

Jessica said, "Tony, you get the ruby out of the piece of chocolate, and I'll make a slit in the bottom of another piece."

When that had been done, they sealed the bottom as they had before with new milk chocolate. Then Sophie handed the fork to Tony.

He dipped it into the white chocolate and drizzled it across the chocolate piece and back. All three of them studied the piece of chocolate from different angles. Jessica held her phone up next to it so they could all see it. "What do you think? Is it the same? I mean, exactly the same?"

"Almost," Sophie said. "The one in the picture seems to start on one corner and end on another corner. Tony's version isn't quite on the corner."

"Do you think we have to be that exact?" Tony asked.

Sophie nodded. "When your uncle explained the pieces of chocolate and how you could tell one from another by the pattern on the outside, he said it was important that each be *exactly* the same. That's the word he used. We'd better try one more time." She looked up at the clock. "We've already been here an hour. I hate to try again in case it's a complete disaster. But I think we better."

They did everything as before. When it was time for the white chocolate, Tony asked, "Who should do this one?"

Sophie patted Tony on the shoulder. "You got it way closer than I did, so I say we have you do it."

Tony gave a single nod, and then he went to work. The first line was perfect, but his hand shook, and Jessica could see he was about to freeze up before he swung the fork back to finish it. "You can do it, Tony!" Jessica said.

"Yes, you can," Sophie agreed.

Tony drizzled the white chocolate across the piece, ending in the corner and lifting the fork away so it couldn't drip down the side.

This time when they compared it to the original in the photo, it was the same.

"All right, Tony! Now we need for this to dry somehow, fast. Then put this in the box, wrap it, and get out of here."

Jessica motioned toward the office half of the building. "We passed what I think was a place for workers to have lunch. The chocolate should harden up quickly if we put the piece in the refrigerator in there."

Sophie picked up the plate with the piece of chocolate on it and carefully carried it in that direction.

"While you're gone, I'm going to clean up here so no one will think anything's wrong if they happen to come by."

"I'll help her," Tony said

Jessica set the last piece of the original chocolates on some plastic and crumpled up the paper towel that had somehow gotten a smear of white chocolate on it. "I would normally eat these messed up pieces to get rid of the evidence, but I'm too nervous to eat anything."

The nearby trash can was empty. "The janitor must have already come, so anything we throw in there will stand out.

Tony, I do think we have to eat the chocolate. It's one for each of us, and then we can put the piece we didn't need back in the storage room. It's still perfect."

Jessica popped the candy in her mouth. Her taste buds decided that it was a good time to eat chocolate after all, proving that there was no bad time for chocolate.

She'd have to tell her mother that the next time she saw her, but she couldn't let her know what she'd been doing when she'd figured that out because it might scare her. Being on the other side of the world and having her daughter get into all of these mysteries must have been hard for her. It had been hard for Jessica not to have her nearby when everything had happened with their mysteries this summer.

Tony wiped down their work area. Jessica could tell he was used to cleaning at the deli. The counter and sink sparkled, and the floor was clean. Jessica held on to the paper towel. She'd have to take it back with her. Or maybe she could hide it somewhere in the factory where she could find it the next day and throw it away. Trash didn't mean anything when there was more of it in the trash can.

Footsteps sounded in the hallway. Heart racing, Jessica turned to Tony. She swallowed hard, then whispered, "Sophie wouldn't make that much noise. What do we do?"

The two of them glanced around. Mr. Donadio's big old desk in the corner of the room was the only piece of furniture that wasn't completely open underneath. She tugged on Tony's sleeve, and they both hurried over to it and slid underneath, their knees up near their chins.

Someone entered the room and stopped.

Jessica pictured the place they'd just left. The piece of chocolate they hadn't altered was still sitting out.

The person walked around the room and then got farther and farther away, so he or she must have gone down the hall.

The two of them crawled out from under the desk and peered over the top of it. No one was there. When they stood, Jessica saw that the piece of chocolate was gone. She looked at Tony and back down at the place where the chocolate had been.

He grabbed her by the arm, and they hurried down the hall to the lunchroom where they stepped inside and found Sophie with a scared expression on her face.

Tony said, "You'll—"

Jessica shook her head. Telling Sophie now would only make her more nervous. She and Tony were nervous enough for the group.

He seemed to understand what she was asking, so he said, "Let's get out of here."

"I'm sure it's solid enough now, Sophie. The other pieces of chocolate are in the box. Let's carefully lift the one with the ruby from the sides with a tissue so we don't leave any marks on it." Jessica felt like she was in the middle of an operating room. She carefully picked it up and set it in the empty paper in the box.

"It's perfect." Sophie sighed. "I'm so relieved."

"It's just like one of the boxes of chocolate that they sell."

"Let's take it back to the chocolate room, get a lid on it, wrap it, and put it on Mrs. Clayton's desk where we found the other box. And get out of here!"

Once there, Sophie pulled wrapping paper off a roll, set it down on a small table, then put the box on top. As she began wrapping it, she said, "Jessica, I'm not sure this will be right if I do it. Are you a good wrapper?"

"I love wrapping presents." Jessica stepped over and wrapped it carefully, making sure every fold had a professional look.

Sophie paced around the room. "Hurry!"

"I'm trying. But I want this to be perfect." When Jessica finished, she thought it looked like the first one. "Is it right?"

Sophie nodded. "It's great. Let's go."

With the package in Jessica's hand, the three of them silently went to the door where Tony opened it and motioned for them to follow him. At Mrs. Clayton's desk, Jessica glanced around as she set the box where they'd found the other one. There weren't any shadows nearby.

They hurried down the hall to the office with the secret panel. As the panel closed behind them, Sophie picked up the flashlight and said, "We did it! They'll never know."

Jessica hoped that was true, that the bad guys would never figure out that it had been missing.

Tony took the stairs in a hurry. "Now, let's go!"

Downstairs, they dove into the water and swam out of the boathouse. Jessica was relieved to find everything outside the boathouse as it should be. They swam to the shore and got back into their regular clothes. On the walk to town, Jessica and Tony told Sophie about almost being caught.

Sophie groaned. "We have to be careful. I think we're almost ready to wrap up this mystery, and we don't want anyone to figure out what we've been doing. That could make it hazardous."

20 MYSTERY MAN

On their way to class Monday morning, Jessica said, "I'm looking forward to today's class. I hope we're using dark chocolate today. Saturday's milk chocolate and the piece I ate yesterday were okay—"

"The milk chocolate is more than okay. I really like it. If today is a dark chocolate day, I'll have to see if I like Uncle Sal's version."

"You like chocolate chips, right?"

Sophie wavered her hand from side to side. "Chocolate chip cookies are okay. But I'd just as soon have a plain cookie."

Everything in class was pretty normal. Today they shaped pineapple-flavored centers to prepare them for the enrober. Sophie wondered if this recipe was the one that had been stolen. Correction: that Uncle Sal *thought* had been stolen.

The good news for Sophie was that the chocolates were covered with milk chocolate when the students finished shaping them. Toward the end of class, each student was given a couple of the now chocolate-covered pieces, ones that hadn't come out of the enrober in perfect condition.

The candy tasted great— it did have fruit, after all, one of her favorite things to eat—but she could taste something more than pineapple. She finished it off in a second bite but couldn't figure out the secret ingredient.

When they were about to collect Sophie's backpack and Jessica's purse, Uncle Sal walked up to them. "Are you ladies enjoying the class?"

"I love chocolate, so I'm having a great time," Jessica said.

"I've learned that I like milk chocolate. Probably never as much as Jessica likes dark chocolate, but it's made it more fun."

"It's the first time we've had a class here, and I'm so glad Erma suggested doing it. But any tips you have for making it better are welcome."

"We've had fun, haven't we, Jessica?"

"Yes! We'll think about it, Uncle Sal."

Sophie watched as the last of the other students left through the doors. Right when she thought that maybe she and Jessica could catch up with one and follow them, Uncle Sal asked another question.

"Does everyone else seem to be enjoying the class too? I've noticed you speaking to the others. Have they mentioned anything helpful?"

The door snapped to a close, along with their opportunity to follow someone today. Sophie held back a sigh. "I think everyone's having fun. Don't you, Jessica?"

"Every once in a while, Dylan looks a little like he'd rather be somewhere else."

Uncle Sal looked distressed.

"But I think that's because his mom treats him like a little kid sometimes."

Uncle Sal laughed. "You may be right, Jessica."

As he started to turn toward the hall, Sophie pushed aside their rush to leave so she could ask, "Uncle Sal, your pineapple chocolates are super good. But there's something more than pineapple in them, isn't there?"

Smiling, he said, "Yes. A secret ingredient." He paused. "I've heard about the mysteries you've solved and how you've worked with the sheriff, so I think you can keep a secret."

Sophie glanced in Jessica's direction. "*I can.*"

He leaned closer. "Watermelon."

"Pineapple-watermelon chocolates?" If she hadn't tasted it first, she wouldn't have believed that would be good.

He gave a nod. "People love the taste of them. But they don't think it sounds good." He shrugged. "So I call them Pineapple Delight and don't tell them."

The girls laughed.

Sophie said, "You're right, Uncle Sal. They're delicious!"

Still smiling, he turned and went down the hall.

When they were alone again, Jessica said, "That's a strange combination. Someone would have to steal the recipe to make something that tasted the same and that makes this even more of a mystery. We need to hurry."

Jessica reached into her purse and pulled out her phone. "I don't know why I didn't think of it before, Sophie, but today I'm going to take a picture of Mr. P. as he enters his room. It may not be useful, but maybe we'll learn something about the way he's standing or his clothes or . . . something."

Sophie tapped her forehead with the back of her hand. "I should've thought of that. This mystery has been so strange that I've been thrown off. Did a recipe get stolen or not? And why did Mr. P. walk like a young man?"

"Maybe the chocolate made him feel young again." Jessica tucked her phone into her purse.

"Until then, I wondered why he wasn't walking with a cane. In class, I thought he might fall over any minute, but he walked through the lobby"—they looked at each other—"like a younger man."

"Yes. Who is he?"

"Now that we know where he's staying, we don't have to follow him, but we do have to hurry. Have your phone ready for a picture, Jessica."

Sophie and Jessica calmly walked out the front door and up the street.

"It might seem strange to someone if we run now, but when we're away from the building, follow me, Jessica. I know a shortcut to the resort that I doubt Mr. P. knows about. Let's see if we can beat him there."

They started running, made a turn, cut through the woods for about two minutes, and then down the street through the church's side yard before turning right on a short street with a few houses, and heading up an alley. Jessica was surprised and relieved to see the back of the resort. They both stopped to catch their breath.

Sophie said, "I came with Mom once to deliver a piece of furniture for one of their special, fancy rooms. We used a big elevator near these doors that was for people working here. It wasn't fancy at all."

They stepped through industrial metal doors and entered a hallway that was very plain and clearly not decorated for guests. After going up a back elevator to the fifth floor, they hurried over to the hall with Mr. P.'s room and waited around the corner.

A few minutes after they arrived, he stepped off the elevator and walked down the hall toward his room. Jessica held her phone at the edge of the wall and snapped photos of him. When he paused at his door, they both stepped back quickly. After they heard the sound of the door closing, they peered around the corner again.

"I hope he doesn't spend three hours reading a book or watching TV this afternoon," Jessica said.

"Me too. The good news is that Mom gave us the afternoon off so we can spend as much time here as we need to."

"Yes, but the first person who comes down the hall and turns this corner is going to wonder why two twelve-year-old girls are standing here. They may even call the resort's front desk and ask if we're supposed to be here."

Just like the day before, a man came out Mr. P.'s door about five minutes later. He went to the elevator, got on, and left.

Jessica snapped photos on her phone as he walked away.

"So, his roommate has left. I wonder when he'll leave."

As they waited, Jessica scrolled through the photos on her phone. "Sophie, this is weird. These two men stand the same way and even walk the same way—exactly the same—in these photos. Maybe Mr. P's son is in town with him."

"Let me see."

Jessica handed the phone to Sophie and leaned over her shoulder while she scrolled through the photos again. "Jessica, if the second man had on an old man's wig and makeup, would he look like Mr. P?" Sophie slowly scrolled through the photos one more time.

"Wow! Do you believe that Mr. P. is actually this younger man in a costume?"

"I do. I think we found your spy. He might be involved with the jewels too. The question now is, what do we do about it?"

"The sheriff asked us not to come into the office, so I guess we print out some of the photos on your dad's printer and leave them at the dead drop."

"Maybe when she sees the photos, she will be able to arrest him."

"I'll miss Mr. P. though. He was fun to have around. It's hard to believe he's a bad guy."

"I would guess that the most successful bad guys are the ones who can fool you. And Mr. P. sure fooled us."

21 CODE WORD: SPY

Jessica and Sophie wrote their note to the sheriff, sharing their suspicions. Sophie wanted to say that Mr. P. was definitely a younger man, but Jessica told her that they weren't sure, that the younger man could be his son or some other relative. In the end they decided to write:

Mr. Pleckenpoll from our chocolate class might be in disguise.

Mr. Sandoval had gone to a meeting, so they used his printer to print out four photos, two of the old man and two of the young one.

"To make writing the code faster, Sophie, we should make a chart with the alphabet, then put the code letters beside it."

"That sounds good. It will be harder to make mistakes that way."

Jessica wrote down the alphabet on a sheet of paper. Then she wrote each code letter next to it as Sophie called it out. Their coded message read:

. . .

NS QMFDLFOQPMM GSPN PVS DIPDPMBUF DMBTT NJHIU CF JO EJTHVJTF

"I think our message is clear, Sophie. It's up to the sheriff to do something about it."

"It's frustrating that we can't talk to her to find out what's going on."

"She doesn't tell us everything anyway."

"That's true. We often figure it out on our own, don't we?"

They wrapped the note and the photos they'd printed in a plastic zipper bag in case it rained before Sheriff Valeska picked it up. Sophie got out a roll of tape and slid that into her backpack along with the bag which she sandwiched in between the pages of a book—to hide it if this fell into other hands.

When they arrived at the bench in town and sat down, Jessica glanced around, then said in a low voice, "What's your plan here, Sophie? Should I tie my shoes as a distraction while you stick it under there?"

Sophie unzipped the side pocket of her backpack, took out the tape, then reached into the main compartment and brought out the zipper bag.

As she was setting the backpack on the bench, a bee flew by her hand. She dropped the backpack, and it landed on its side, spilling half of what had been inside.

Jessica knelt in front of the bench to help Sophie gather everything. "Sophie, that was a great idea! No one will suspect what you're doing here."

Sophie said, "It *would* have been a great idea if I'd thought of it."

Jessica laughed. "Accident?" She reached for a snack bar that had slid under the bench as Sophie taped the plastic bag underneath. Jessica found a piece of chalk, now broken in two, and kept that clenched in her hand as they sat back on the bench.

"The item is secured," Sophie said.

Jessica had to fight a giggle. Sometimes Sophie got so into their mysteries that she played the part too well. Right now, Sophie was a spy. "I'm going to mark the bench now, if that works with your plan."

"Perfect."

Jessica reached out in what she hoped was a subtle way and slid the chalk across the bench. "Done. Now what?"

"Now, we go to Great Finds. Maybe Mom will let us go to the deli for lunch. Let's hope the sheriff either walks or drives by and notices the chalk mark."

Jessica said, "Sophie, she didn't even want to do this. I just hope she stops to pick it up."

The two of them walked to Great Finds. Once they were there, Mrs. Sandoval asked them to finish a project before eating. An hour later, they were on their way to the deli—with a stop at the dead drop first.

They raced back to Sophie's favorite bench, Jessica barely keeping up with Sophie. She tugged on her cousin's arm. "You're going to attract a lot more attention running down the sidewalk."

Sophie checked around them. "You're right. It's my first dead drop, and I'm excited to see if it's been picked up."

When they rounded the corner and could see the bench in the distance, Jessica thought there was a new chalk mark at the other end. She realized now that that was the one flaw in their plan. They hadn't told the sheriff how to let them know if she'd left something for them.

As they got closer, the mark became more and more notice-able, to them at least. She thought someone else would see it as a smudge. Sophie led the two of them past the bench and then back around in front of it before they sat down.

"Sophie, the chalk mark I made is gone."

"Yes, and there's a new chalk mark on the other end of the bench. I guess that's how Sheriff Valeska let us know that she's been here."

Sophie reached down, pretending to retie her shoelaces, but Jessica saw her hand swish underneath the bench before sitting up with her shoelaces now secure. "I think it's still there, Jessica. I'm going to set my backpack down, unzip it, and reach under here to peel off the bag. Then I'll slip it into my backpack."

As Sophie set her backpack on the ground, the owner of Buds & Blooms walked by. Instead of smiling at them, she continued on her way without a glance in their direction. Jessica wondered if she'd even noticed that they were there. She was focused on where she was going, and she didn't look very happy about it.

Sophie noticed the same thing. "Jessica, I don't think Kelsey has everything going well in her life right now. She was upset the day she came to the factory to talk to her brother. Maybe he's done something else."

With the florist out of sight, Sophie did as she'd planned. Then she leaned over to see inside her backpack. "Jessica! It's different. What's inside the bag is different."

Jessica said, "Let's get to lunch at the deli and read this. I doubt anyone will pay attention to us, and even if they did, we would only be taking something out of your backpack. And that way, if we find something that belongs with the mystery, we can tell Tony."

Tony wasn't at the deli when they arrived. They chose the table in the back corner, where no one else could see what they were doing, took out the note from the sheriff, and opened it. Using a pen from her purse, Jessica wrote the correct letter over each of the letters in the sheriff's one-line message. Once she had it decoded, it said:

Meet me at the cemetery at four o'clock.

"No! I never wanted to step into that cemetery again!"

Sophie glanced around the room. "Shh, Jessica."

Whispering, Jessica said, "Whoops. Sorry. Sheriff Valeska

must know that we finish at your mom's by three thirty. Four at the latest. I wonder why . . . ?"

"Me too. Why the cemetery? Why couldn't she put her message in another note?"

"I guess we'll find out in a couple of hours. We do need to make sure that we're off duty by three thirty today, though, so that we have plenty of time to get there."

The afternoon went well, or as well as an afternoon can go when you spent a lot of it going up and down a ladder and arranging things on shelves in a basement. But at three o'clock, Mrs. Sandoval said, "Sophie, you remember where Mr. Smith lives, don't you?"

At Sophie's nod, she continued, "I have a delivery for him. He bought one candlestick last year and said he wanted a pair, so he would buy the second one if I ever found one. He knows it's coming and has already paid for it. If you and Jessica want to run it by this afternoon, I'll let you off duty early."

Sophie checked her watch and gave Jessica a thumbs-up. "Sounds good to us, Mom."

Once they had gone out the door with the box in Sophie's hands and Jessica carrying Sophie's backpack, Sophie said, "Mr. Smith lives in the direction of the cemetery, so this is working out perfectly."

Jessica said, "Almost too perfectly. Are you sure your mother isn't involved in this?"

"Positive. She would have warned us to be careful, don't you think?"

"You're right. She's always done that before. The good news is, we're going to get to the cemetery a little bit early. Maybe we can choose a good hiding place and watch the sheriff arrive."

They dropped the box off with Mr. Smith, who lived in a small brick cottage with yellow shutters and had a cute little Chihuahua puppy. Then they continued on their way.

"I've been thinking, Jessica: how do we know that message came from Sheriff Valeska?"

"She used the right code. It had to come from her."

"What if someone found the first note, though, and they figured out the code? It's a code that's been around for a long time, so it might not be too hard for real criminals to figure out."

"That seems unlikely to me. They didn't have time."

"Yes, but if that had happened, we would be stepping into a trap."

The two of them walked along silently. When they were within a few minutes of the cemetery, Jessica said, "If you're right, Sophie, and that's a very big if, then we need to be careful. Being careful is a good idea anyway, especially when we're in the middle of a mystery, which we seem to be standing knee-deep in right now. Do you have a plan?"

"I've been considering it as we've walked. I think we should hide behind one of the larger gravestones and wait for the sheriff."

They arrived at the cemetery and walked under the arch that said Pine Hill Cemetery. This moment always gave Jessica chills. She knew no one was in there, at least no one who could talk to them, but it still gave her the creeps.

Sophie put out her hand to stop her. She surveyed the cemetery, slowly turning her head from left to right. Jessica decided to do the same thing, just to be sure.

"I think it's clear." Sophie pointed across the cemetery. "Let's hide over there behind the largest grave marker we can find. The sheriff is probably going to enter the same way we did, so we'll see her coming." Sophie took a step, stopped, and added, "If she is the one who comes."

They settled behind a gravestone in the shape of an angel. Not long after they got there, someone walked into the cemetery. As the person got closer, Jessica could tell it was a man. He came toward them. Then, when she started to wonder if they would be discovered, he turned and walked in the direction of the old mausoleum. When she saw the side of his face, she had to stifle a gasp with her hand. Jessica looked at Sophie, and her cousin had an expression on her face that she suspected mirrored her own. The younger man from Mr. P.'s room now stood by the side of the mausoleum.

He was far enough away that Jessica felt like she could whisper to Sophie. "He's waiting for something or someone. Sheriff Valeska might be in trouble."

"I agree," Sophie whispered back. "Check your phone to see if we have service here. I'd like to be able to call someone if we need help."

Jessica pulled it out of her purse. "No reception."

"I guess that means we're in a dead zone."

"Ooh. Don't say it that way."

"I had to say it. It was too perfect for this place."

Sheriff Valeska walked into the cemetery and did much as Sophie had done: she paused at the entrance and scanned the area before taking further steps. Sophie should be proud that they'd done the same thing her favorite law enforcement officer had done. Jessica glanced over at Mr. P. and saw that he was also watching the sheriff.

"Jessica, we have to warn her. She may be stepping into a trap."

"What can we do?"

Sophie shouted, "Sheriff, watch out!"

The sheriff darted behind a grave marker and crouched. After a few seconds, she shouted back, "Sophie, what's wrong?"

"It's a trap, Sheriff. That man in the photos we gave you is waiting for you."

The sheriff stood.

"What's she doing?" Sophie asked.

"I have no idea."

Movement from the side caught Jessica's attention. Mr. P. was stepping out into the open. He walked toward the sheriff, but he didn't look menacing, as Jessica had expected. When he shook the sheriff's hand, she and Sophie stood.

"Girls, this man is the reason I asked you to come here. Please meet him."

Sophie said, "Sheriff, we've been in class with him for close to a week. Haven't we?"

She turned to Mr. P. who gave a single nod. "But I'm not who you think I am."

Sophie put her hands on her hips. "If you've been in disguise, why should we believe you? A disguise shows you're hiding the truth."

Sheriff Valeska said, "Because he's an investigator who is in town for a reason."

"The FBI?" Sophie asked

Mr. P. answered, "No, I'm what's known as an insurance investigator. When someone has a large claim—that's the amount of money my company would pay to replace something that was stolen—I'm called in."

The pieces of the puzzle started to fall into place for Sophie. "Were gemstones stolen?"

"Yes. I wasn't certain where they might be. I was working on a tip and a hunch when I came to Pine Hill, but your discovery told me I was definitely in the right place."

"I asked you girls to meet us in a place with few people because we need for this to be in the strictest confidence. I'm going to meet with your parents, Sophie, so I can tell them what's going on. I've kept you safe until now. And I intend to continue doing that. Do *not* investigate anymore."

The new twist on the mystery had Jessica's head in a spin. "So, Mr. Pleckenpoll—I suspect that that isn't your real name—there are more gemstones, aren't there?"

He smiled but didn't answer.

Sophie asked, "You're the one we thought was eavesdropping on us at Sweet Bites, aren't you?"

Mr. P. shook his head. "That wasn't me. I didn't have any idea that you were anything but two kids in a chocolate-making class."

Sophie and Jessica turned to each other. That meant that someone else in the chocolate factory might know that they were detectives.

The sheriff spoke. "Girls, stay away from the investigation. We don't know who we're dealing with, and both of you know what it's like to be caught up in the middle of danger. Especially you, Sophie. And we also want to make sure you do not mess up Mr. Pleckenpoll's investigation. Let him finish his job."

"Okay, Sheriff."

The sheriff asked that she and Jessica leave before them so no one would see them all together.

As they started to walk away, Sophie turned back and asked, "Are you the one who arrived in the helicopter?"

"Yes. It helps me get to the scene more quickly."

Part of the mystery was solved. Then, without a word, they headed for the arch that would lead them out of the cemetery.

Once they'd left the cemetery, Sophie looked around very carefully one more time. Jessica suspected she was making sure no one was watching them. Then Sophie said to Jessica, "You were a spy, and he's a spy. A spy stole the recipe. How many spies can there be in one chocolate factory?"

"We may never know because we're officially out of this mystery. Tomorrow, we're back to being normal kids taking a chocolate-making class."

———

While they were in bed reading that night, a knock sounded on the bedroom door.

"Come in."

Mr. Sandoval opened the door. "Mandy Valeska called. You need to have an adult with you at all times until she wraps this up. Understood?"

"Yes, Dad. We understand."

"Another call came right after that one. Erma Clayton at

Sweet Bites said a piece of equipment needs to be repaired, so your class will begin tomorrow afternoon at 1:00."

Sophie excitedly asked, "We don't have to get up early?"

He grinned. "I thought that might disappoint you."

Sophie glanced over at Jessica. "We'll survive sleeping late, won't we, Jessica?"

Jessica sighed. "The morning's sounding better all the time."

When he'd closed the door, Sophie said, "Maybe we should try to figure out—"

"No, Sophie. The sheriff said we were off the mystery. We know that someone's overheard us speaking, and it doesn't look like it's the good guys. It's time for her to take over."

"I guess you're right. But it's hard to let go. I'll probably lie here trying to figure it out for the next hour."

"Instead of that, dream about chocolate."

22 STICKY SITUATION

The morning began better than the day before. With them out of the mystery and able to sleep in, today perfectly suited Jessica. She planned for it to be calm and fun.

Mrs. Sandoval decided to use some of their extra time by having them vacuum the living room, but after that, they went to the beach and stretched out on the sand. Around noon, they ate sandwiches they'd brought, then put their regular clothes back on and went to Sweet Bites.

When everyone had arrived, Uncle Sal took them one by one into the chocolate room, where each person got to choose a piece of chocolate. Jessica picked one of the milk chocolate caramels rather than her usual dark chocolate. She'd been thinking about the mystery—the one they were supposed to stay out of—so much that that's the kind of chocolate she had on her mind.

They used the enrober again in class today, covering three different flavors of Sweet Bites Chocolates with thick layers of dark chocolate. No jewelry came close to being a sweet treat.

After class, Sophie and Jessica carried the trays of chocolates into the chocolate room. As they used tongs to pick up each piece and set it on the right pile, Jessica noticed that the stack of the candy she'd had that morning was much smaller. She was certain there had been a lot of it when Uncle Sal had selected her piece off the top earlier. Someone must have wanted a whole box of that flavor. Interesting, but probably not important, especially since they weren't working on the mystery anymore. No thinking about clues was allowed.

Sophie was studying the same kind of chocolates. "Jessica, we put white chocolate over one of these. We've been trying to find the exact same piece of chocolate the gemstone was in. Maybe there is no piece of candy like that."

Jessica nodded vigorously. "Yes! What if, just as we did, they insert the stone into one of these caramels, then add white chocolate lines?"

"That's genius." Sophie paused for a minute or two. "This mystery may be coming to an end. If they're concerned that someone is onto them, they may be planning to prepare all of their gemstones for their fence."

"Fence?"

"That's the person who sells stolen things for a thief."

"You have learned a lot from books and movies, Sophie. We better get out of here. People are going to start wondering what's taking so long."

When they stepped out of the room, they found Uncle Sal coming toward them. "Is everything okay? You didn't drop all of the chocolates, did you?"

Sophie answered. "No. Everything's fine." They needed an answer that would throw everyone off in case the criminal was one of the people nearby.

Jessica said, "It smelled so good in there that it was hard to leave."

Everyone around them laughed.

Emily said, "I feel that way every time I step in there. I make myself leave, but if you gave me a cup of hot chocolate and asked me to sit in there and guard the room, I'd be happy to do it." Turning toward Uncle Sal, she said, "I hope you didn't have a large repair bill today for your equipment, Mr. Donadio."

He shook his head. "No. One of my employees opened up the enrober, examined it, and found it was very easy to repair. Two things had come undone and simply had to be reconnected."

"That's good news," Dylan said. "But why did it break in the first place?"

Uncle Sal shook his head again. "That is a mystery."

Jessica and Sophie looked at each other. His mystery probably had something to do with the one they had been investigating.

"No matter. I will see all of you tomorrow for our last class. I must do some paperwork in my office now." He walked away and down the hall.

As everyone went to gather their things on their way out, the missing chocolates kept coming to Jessica's mind. She tugged on Sophie's arm as she reached for her backpack and whispered, "I should have said something earlier, but I knew we shouldn't talk about this. I might have a clue for the mystery we aren't in anymore."

Sophie raised one eyebrow, then she walked over to the side of the room.

Jessica followed her, wondering if she should ignore her thoughts on the mystery. Making a fast decision to tell Sophie, she added, "A lot of those milk chocolates with caramel are gone from the chocolate room."

Sophie took a fast breath. "Wow. If they're used for the jewels, maybe they're getting ready to—"

One of the employees walked by at that moment, so Sophie stopped talking and pretended to be interested in one of the old photographs on the wall.

When they were alone again, Sophie said, "No one's paying attention to us right now, Jessica. Follow me. If anyone asks where we're going, tell them we're going to the restroom or to stop and visit Uncle Sal. We can do either of those things after that, so it isn't a lie."

It made all the sense in the world. But it also meant that this mystery had gone from "stay away" to what might be a full-blown crisis in two seconds. Trying to be casual, something that Jessica wasn't always very good at, she walked down the hall with Sophie. No one stopped them. She wasn't even sure that anyone saw them as they walked away, but she did take a deep breath and calmed down when they turned the corner at the end of the hall, and no one else was in sight.

Sophie put her hand on Jessica's arm and whispered, "Don't say anything."

When they arrived at the storeroom, Jessica became even more curious. The door was slightly open, but Uncle Sal had had to unlock it last week. They pushed it open, didn't find anyone inside, so they entered, and Sophie closed the door behind them.

"Sophie, it may not be safe for us to be here. I think someone's working on something here and will be back soon."

"I know. But let's look around. My guess is that the missing chocolates could be somewhere in here. Maybe someone bought them as you said, but I have a feeling about this. I'd hide them if I were the criminal."

They moved several stacks of empty chocolate boxes.

"There wouldn't be a more perfect place to hide a box of chocolates than in a stack of chocolate boxes, would there?" Jessica said.

They lifted box after empty box. All were light as air, so they were clearly empty. When they had gone through most of the storeroom, Sophie said, "I may have made a mistake. The box of chocolates we took wasn't in here. It was on Mrs. Clayton's desk."

The two of them stared at each other.

Jessica felt like someone had poured a bucket of cold water on her. Mrs. Clayton seemed so very nice. "Do you think it could be her? A new box might be on her desk." The door to the storage area opened, and they heard voices outside.

A man's deep voice said, "I thought I'd left this door open."

Panicked, the girls looked for somewhere to hide, but the room was filled with shelves and not much else.

The same voice, louder this time, said, "You!"

As they whirled around, the door closed again. Sophie and Jessica ran over to it. Jessica turned the knob, rattling it, but it was as she'd thought: locked.

"Jessica, I think we're in trouble. We don't even know who that voice belonged to. But whoever he was, he knows we've been snooping in a place we shouldn't be."

"What now, Sophie?"

"I don't see any tools to help us pry the door open. We do need to find a way to protect ourselves when he comes back. He may bring someone else too."

Fear rushed through Jessica. She had to fight to keep breathing normally. "He *will* be back, won't he?"

"I think so. We gave ourselves away by coming in here. I'm sorry, Jessica."

"It's okay, Sophie. I always knew that there was possible danger with a mystery."

"And if our class hadn't been moved to the afternoon because of the equipment breaking down—" Sophie's eyes widened. "That's it! They needed time this morning, when no one was here, to make the special chocolates."

"But why does it matter if those chocolates are exactly that way? If they needed to get out of here in a hurry, why take the time to do that? Why not just put them in any piece of chocolate?"

Sophie was quiet for a few minutes. "It must be because it's a code to the person the chocolates are going to. Maybe they don't even talk to them, but when chocolates come that have the right pattern on them, the person who receives them knows those pieces are important. That must be the code they always use."

"It all makes sense." She just hoped they'd get to tell the sheriff about it. She walked around the room. "We need a way to protect ourselves since we can't find a way out. We know there isn't a hidden passage in here. We have empty boxes. I guess we could throw a bunch of boxes at somebody and hope it catches them off guard. Maybe we could dart around them and out of here."

"I don't know. That might help. But I don't think it would buy us enough time to actually get away. The front door is going to be locked because Uncle Sal will have left by now."

"And he doesn't know we're here."

"No. The only ones who know we're here are the bad guys. Mom and Dad aren't even expecting us at home for a while." Then Sophie stood up straight and tall, shoulders back. "Let's not be defeated. We can figure a way out of this."

Jessica suspected that Sophie was trying to cheer herself up, but there was nothing wrong in that. "Okay, let's go around the room. There are office supplies, paper and pens. I don't think those will help us."

"Agreed. We've ruled out the boxes. There's gift wrap. And then there are the things left here from Uncle Sal's bad ideas for chocolates. There's bubblegum."

Boxes of bubblegum were neatly stacked on the shelves, enough to make many, many pieces of chocolate-covered bubblegum. Jessica still shuddered at the thought, but this gave her an idea. "Sophie, I don't like spiderwebs, but what if we chewed this gum and made a giant web out of it?"

"Oh my goodness! That's brilliant. If we can make this work, when they step into a web of gum, they'll get stuck. Then, if we move really fast, we can get out of here. Start chewing."

Each of the girls reached for a piece of gum. Then Sophie said, "If you can chew two or three at a time, do it. We have to move quickly because we don't know when they'll be back."

Jessica grabbed a second piece and shoved it into her mouth, chewing slowly on the big wad until it became soft. Around the wad of gum, she said, "This is a little harder to do with braces, but I'm working on it. Sophie, I just realized there's a flaw in my plan."

"What flaw?" Sophie's words could barely be understood around the gum.

"I have to spit this out and handle just-chewed gum."

Sophie sucked in air, then suddenly spit her gum out into her hand. "Please don't make me laugh again with gum stuffed into my mouth." With her fingers, she worked the gooey gum, pulling it into a thin string.

"We need to make sure the door can open so the criminal's whole body comes into the room, not just his feet." She stuck one end of her gum on the shelf at one side of the door and the other end to the shelf at the other, then she stopped. "Jessica, we're going to need something to stand on, so we can get this all the way up to the top shelf. That box of office paper should be sturdy. Can you push it over here by yourself?"

Jessica, still chewing slowly on her giant wad of gum, went over to the box of paper and pushed on the box. It was so heavy that it only moved about a quarter of an inch. She pushed harder the second time, and it went a little bit farther. When she shoved at it with all her might, it moved about a foot. Sophie would probably do better because she was stronger from all the outdoorsy things she did. Pushing it over and over again, Jessica marched it over to Sophie and in front of the beginning of what she hoped would be their lifesaving web of gum.

Sophie stepped onto the box gingerly at first to test it, then stood on it with both feet and stretched the gum up to the corner she'd been trying to reach. She jumped back to the floor and eyed her work. "It's a beginning, but we're going to have to chew a lot of gum for this to work."

Disgusted by the idea of spit-covered gum, Jessica grimaced as she opened her mouth and dropped hers into her hand. Then she continued the web, stretching it right above Sophie's, but from the other side across and then up, so now the web crossed in the middle. She fastened it, after stepping onto their box step stool, to the opposite corner, making an X of sticky gum at the entrance to the room.

Each of the girls popped more gum into her mouth and started chewing as fast as she could. The web grew and grew until it looked like a big pink spiderweb.

"I hope we're done, Sophie, because I don't think I want to chew another piece of gum, especially bubblegum, for the rest of my life."

"Me neither. I'm ready for some real food now."

"You know, at first I thought that box might help trip someone, but—"

"We want them to get stuck in the gum, and that box might stop them before they do that."

The girls pulled the box back away from the door, something that was harder than pushing it had been.

They soon heard voices in the hall.

Sophie whispered, "Let's both crouch over here on the side where the door opens, so when he gets stuck, we can run out behind him more easily."

They did that. And waited. The voices seemed to be arguing outside their door. Jessica picked up a word here and there. *Snoopers. Dangerous.* None of what she heard sounded good for their future. When she heard the key in the lock, her heart beat faster, faster than she'd realized was even possible. She stayed crouched, hoping to be in a position where she could spring out of the room.

Finally, the voices stopped arguing. She hoped that meant that one of the people had gone away. Maybe they would only have one person to stick to the web.

23 THE ESCAPE

When the door opened and someone stepped inside, a man said, "What?" Then, in the half-light from the hallway, Sophie saw arms flailing.

She leapt behind the man, into the hall, and Jessica was right behind her. They raced out the door, down the hall, and around the corner toward Mrs. Clayton's desk. A box of chocolates was sitting on it as Jessica had thought it might be.

Jessica picked it up and ran toward the outside door, pushing on it at a full run, but it didn't open. "Sophie, what do we do?"

Sophie grabbed her arm and pulled her along. "The hidden passage. It's our only way out of here now." They ran down the hall past the storeroom, where they saw a man shouting as he struggled to get up. It wouldn't be long before someone came to help him. When they rounded the next corner, Sophie heard people speaking. She hoped they weren't going to meet anyone on their way to their escape hatch.

The door to the office with the secret panel in it stood open. They rushed inside, closed it, and Sophie hurried over to the wall to unlock the escape hatch.

Jessica opened the box of chocolates she'd tucked under her

arm earlier. "This box isn't wrapped yet. Otherwise, it's exactly what we thought, Sophie. These are the caramels with white chocolate lines on top. This box of candy is probably worth a fortune."

The panel flipped in.

"Hurry! Let's get out of here!" Jessica said.

Sophie said, "No. If we take the chocolates with us, we take the evidence, and the sheriff can't arrest anyone."

Jessica stared down at the box of chocolates in her hand. "We almost left with the only evidence that would put these bad guys in prison." She started to set the box down.

"Wipe off your fingerprints, Jessica. They always do that in the movies. That way when the bad guys pick it up, it will only have their fingerprints."

"Check." Jessica wiped off the box of chocolates with her T-shirt. Then she set it on the desk, using the edge of her shirt as a glove. "There's a phone here. Maybe we should call the sheriff and let her know what's going on. This may be the last day these criminals are even in Pine Hill."

Sophie ran across the room to a chair and dragged it over toward the door, tucking the back of the chair under the doorknob. "I saw this done in a movie. It makes it so that the chair braces against the door, the doorknob can't turn very easily, and the door is hard to push open. Now hurry and call the sheriff. And pray that she is in the office."

Jessica dialed the sheriff, and Clare immediately put her call through. After quickly explaining what was going on, Jessica told her to hurry to catch the criminals in the act. She started to hang up, but then brought the phone back to her ear and added, "Ask Tony where the secret passage is."

Seconds after she'd set the phone down, they were on their way out the escape hatch.

As soon as they were both through, Sophie stopped, only a few steps down now. "Push the panel closed behind you, Jessica."

"If we do that, it's going to be pitch-black in here. We didn't bring a flashlight."

"I'm hoping it will buy us a little bit of time when they come into that room and we aren't there."

"They'll figure it out pretty quickly because there was a chair blocking the door and the chocolates are sitting on the desk." At that moment, the doorknob rattled. Then someone pushed on the door. Jessica slammed the panel closed. "I guess if it buys us a few seconds, Sophie, it's worth it. Walk as fast as you can without falling."

The two of them made their way down the stairs step-by-step, finally finding the level area at the bottom. They hurried along, Sophie rubbing her hand along the wall so she knew where she was.

Jessica pointed toward the end of the walkway. "It's brighter around the door than before."

Light clearly outlined the shape of the door, but before it had been impossible to see where it was. "You're right. I wonder why."

Jessica reached up and turned the lock as she had before, and the door swung open.

They found the big doors to the boathouse open wide and letting sunlight into the space.

"Look at the rowboat, Sophie! They must be ready to escape." Several black bags were stowed in the middle of the boat.

Sophie pushed the door closed behind them and heard it click in place. "We need to hurry! Do we swim out of here?" She could hear voices shouting in the passageway.

Jessica bent over to untie her shoes. "If we're planning to get out of here, we'd better do it in a hurry. We only have seconds before they're standing on the dock beside us, and they don't sound happy."

Jessica now stood barefoot. Sophie kicked off her shoes, and both of them peeled off their outer clothes—leaving only their swimsuits on from earlier—and dove into the water.

Sophie swam as fast as she could underwater, something she didn't do as well as swimming on the surface, and hoped Jessica was swimming as fast or faster.

When Sophie came up for air, she saw that there were four people standing on the dock now, three men and Mrs. Clayton, who no longer had a sweet expression on her face but was instead shouting, "Get them now!"

As Sophie prepared to dive back under the water and swim for her life, Jessica bobbed up beside her. The two of them at the same moment dove again.

She followed the stone piers that supported the boathouse and came up for air again at the outside edge of the boathouse. As she did, she heard the sound of a boat coming at them. Jessica came up for air right beside her.

"If they've brought help in a boat, Jessica, we're sunk."

Jessica nodded. Panting, she said, "We're so close to getting away, but I have to breathe for a couple of minutes before I can go underwater again."

When a boat entered the boathouse, Sophie thought they'd lost the battle. Then she saw the best thing that she'd ever seen in her life: Sheriff Valeska standing on the bridge.

The boat landed at the dock, and officers jumped off. They chased the criminals, who were now trying to make their escape back up the passageway. Sophie and Jessica swam back toward the dock, where the sheriff helped them out of the water.

"Are you girls okay?"

"Yes, ma'am," Sophie said. "But we might not have been if you hadn't arrived. What made you decide to come this way instead of going through the main doors into the chocolate factory?"

The sheriff said, "Tony, you can come out now."

Tony stepped out from the boat's cabin.

"I called him as you said to do, Jessica. He insisted on coming along to show us the hidden door in here."

Tony jumped down from the boat onto the dock, where Jessica and Sophie high-fived him.

Sophie said, "Thank you, Tony and Sheriff Valeska. If Jessica hadn't noticed the phone sitting there, I think we might be toast."

The officers led the criminals back toward the boat, all of them handcuffed now including a mean-looking Mrs. Clayton who said, "I planned everything carefully. Salvatore Donadio was supposed to be too busy with that class to notice our activities. Then you kids signed up for it!"

One man came out in handcuffs with the officer barely touching him, only holding on to the handcuffs themselves. Sophie could see why. The prisoner was covered in bubblegum from the top of his head all the way down to his ankles and shoes. She didn't know how they'd ever get it out of his hair, and his clothes would have to be thrown away.

"I thought that the criminal was going to be Kelsey at Buds & Blooms."

"Why did you think that, Sophie?" the sheriff asked.

"She's the only one who is able to sell the Sweet Bites Chocolates here in town—"

"That isn't any reason to suspect someone as a criminal."

Jessica said, "She's been over here talking to her brother, and he didn't seem happy about something."

"I don't see him here though," Sophie said.

"Just in case," the sheriff said, "we'll bring him and his sister in to ask them some questions."

"You know, Sheriff, if she's the only one selling the chocolates, she's also the only one in town who would be receiving the chocolates with the gemstones inside."

"Which is the one piece of this that we don't have. Any of those chocolates."

Sophie and Jessica looked at each other, grinning.

When the sheriff saw that, she asked, "Do we?"

Sophie nodded. "Yes, we do. There's a box of the chocolates on the desk upstairs where this secret passage begins."

"Did you break them open, though, to see if they had the gemstones inside? That will make them questionable evidence."

"No, they have the same design on them though. And we've learned here at the chocolate factory that the design on top says what's inside. The factory doesn't make that kind of chocolate. It's their milk chocolate with caramel inside. The only time we've ever seen the white chocolate lines on top is when we found the first one with the ruby. The whole box upstairs has those lines on them."

The sheriff gave a low whistle. "It sounds like you may have solved this whole mystery, girls. Do you want to hop on board and have us take you out of here by boat, or walk upstairs and go out the doors? Uncle Sal should be here by now. I called him when we were on our way."

"I think I'm ready to be out of the water," Jessica said

"I agree. I've always like to swim, but for a little while I think I'll stay on land." As they walked away, Sophie added, "And away from bubblegum."

They giggled as they went down the hallway and toward their exit from the building.

24 SAFE & SURPRISED

A short time later, Sophie and Jessica sat in the sheriff's office with Uncle Sal and Sheriff Valeska. The girls had run home quickly for dry clothes, then returned as fast as they could. Neither of them wanted to miss a moment of this time when they would learn the whole story.

"Have you found out anything else?" Sophie asked.

The sheriff tapped her fingers on her desk. "We've learned that Mrs. Clayton isn't who she said she was. Her fingerprints told us what we needed to know. She has masterminded crimes in the past, but there was never enough evidence to convict her and send her to prison."

"Does that mean there is enough evidence this time?"

"Just her standing on that dock with those men, obviously trying to get the two of you, would have been enough to bring her in. The box of chocolate with the gemstones though? That was the clincher. Her fingerprint is inside it, and there is a diamond or ruby in each piece. She's going to go to prison for a very long time. She and all of her henchmen."

The sheriff continued. "The surprise was when one of her men said his only job had been to use the rowboat to pick up the package. He claims he wasn't involved in everything else and hopes to get less punishment by telling what he knows. We finally learned about the boats you saw with the spyglass."

Sophie sat on the edge of her seat. "What did you find out, Sheriff?"

"Remember that stolen car?"

She, Jessica, and Uncle Sal nodded.

Uncle Sal asked, "Did they steal it?"

"No. They usually drove in with the gems but got afraid when they saw my roadblock. They thought I might be after them, so they cleverly used boats to get around it. The man was mad at Erma too because he was sure the police had learned something was wrong when she got greedy and stole the recipe."

"What about Kelsey and Kirk Newman?" Jessica asked. "I don't know him, but she seems like a good person. I guess, though, that people can pretend to be nice. We thought Mrs. Clayton was a sweet lady. She reminded us of Mrs. Bowman at Bananas."

Kelsey and her brother walked into the sheriff's office with one of the deputies right behind them.

The deputy said, "We caught them on their way out of town."

With tears streaming down her face, Kelsey said, "I didn't want to be involved in this. Kirk got into trouble, and I didn't know what else to do but to follow Mrs. Clayton's orders."

Kirk put his arm around his sister's shoulders and pulled her against him for a hug. "It's all my fault. I needed money and borrowed from one of the men at the factory. When they told me I would have to pay back twice as much, I didn't know how I could ever do that."

Kelsey said, "I wish you'd told me, Kirk. Maybe we could have worked it out."

He went on to say, "They gave me another way out. They said chocolate goes well with flowers, so a flower shop would be a perfect place for them to use to send chocolates where they needed to go. They told me that my sister would have to help them, or I would have bigger problems. I didn't understand what they were doing at first."

Still crying, Kelsey wiped her face with the back of her hand and looked at the sheriff. "Kirk told me what they wanted. I couldn't let anything happen to him. We're all each other has now. I never knew or even wanted to know what was in the boxes. I simply gave them to whoever asked for them at the shop."

Sheriff Valeska perked up in her chair. "You didn't mail them? Someone came to pick up the boxes in person?"

Kelsey pulled a chair from over by Clare's desk, and sat down, leaning forward with her face in her hands. Her words were hard to hear as she spoke again. "Sometimes it would be weeks in between. I'd think they weren't going to ask me again, but then a box would be delivered one day. Every time, a man wearing a black hat and a red sweater would come within a couple of hours and say, 'I'm here for the chocolate delivery.'"

"Was it always the same man?" The sheriff asked.

"Yes. Always the same man. There's something about him that seemed more than a little scary."

Sophie said, "Sheriff, since there's a whole box of chocolates, maybe that means that the man is going to pick them up very soon."

"I've already considered that, Sophie. Kelsey, I think we'll be able to have the charges against you lessened if you cooperate with us. You shouldn't have helped the criminals, but you were trying to protect your younger brother. Will you go into your shop and wait for the man to arrive?"

Kelsey let out a deep sigh. "I don't have to go to prison?"

The sheriff said, "I can't promise anything, but I can put in a good word for you. I think that you might get off with probation."

Kelsey put her hand on her chest. "Do I have to be alone when that man comes? Like I said, he's a little on the scary side."

"No. I'll have my deputies, Fred and Hank, in the back room. When the man comes in, hand him the box and let him walk out the door, exactly as you would any other time. Don't speak or act differently. Can you do that?"

"Yes, I promise. What about Kirk, though?"

"Kirk is young enough that he may be able to get off with a similar punishment, but that's not for me to decide. He would have to be careful for a long time."

Kirk said, "I will *never* do anything like this again."

When the brother and sister had left the office accompanied by deputies, Sophie said, "I guess we can wait here until we find out what happened, right, Sheriff?"

The sheriff stared at her. "Isn't there anything you'd rather be doing?"

Jessica laughed. "Are you kidding?"

The sheriff's phone rang, and she picked it up. As she listened to the caller, her eyes focused on Jessica. She said into the phone, "I'll send her out."

Smiling widely, she told Jessica, "There's someone you want to see outside, Jessica."

Jessica's brow furrowed. "Me? Here in Pine Hill?" She stood.

The sheriff said, "Yes, step outside the door."

Jessica headed toward the door, and Sophie followed her, curious to see what was going on. When they were outside, a car pulled into an open parking space up the street. A man stepped out of the driver's side and a woman from the other side.

Jessica yelled and started running towards them. She shouted, "Mom! Dad!"

Sophie stood back and watched them.

Jessica was crying. Her mother and dad stood beside her. Her mother kept hugging Jessica close.

Finally, Jessica called to Sophie, "Come here."

Sophie walked over.

"You haven't seen my parents since you were little."

Sophie smiled at her aunt and uncle. "Jessica's missed you, so I know she's happy to see you."

"We had to come to make sure she was safe. There's been a lot happening in Pine Hill."

Jessica made a snorting sound that was not at all her usual, ladylike thing to do. "So many things."

"I was surprised today when I called my sister and she said I'd find you at the sheriff's office. Are you in trouble, Jessica?"

"Not us, Mom. We do have more to tell you now."

"More? Another mystery?" Her mother looked from Jessica to Sophie.

"Yes. There's only one small piece of it left. Hopefully, that will be solved today."

"Have you seen Mom yet?" Sophie asked.

"We just arrived."

"Let's all go to Great Finds."

When Jessica's parents turned toward their car, Jessica laughed. "We can walk there. Everything in Pine Hill is close enough to walk to."

At Great Finds, Mrs. Sandoval hugged her sister and brother-in-law the moment she saw them. Then she stood back and smiled. "We're so glad you're here! Come. Let me show you around."

Mrs. Sandoval showed everyone around her shop. She even opened the trapdoor in the floor in back to show them the opening to her basement. And she told about how Sophie had discovered it.

Sophie smiled. "That was another mystery."

"It seems we arrived just in time to wrap this one up," Jessica's mother said.

Mrs. Sandoval said, "This one hasn't been dangerous though. Right, Sophie?"

Sophie glanced away.

"Has it, Sophie?" she asked again.

Sophie looked up and at the other side of Great Finds. "Not really, Mom. Maybe not much. Not until today."

The ringing phone saved her from saying more. Mrs. Sandoval gave Sophie a look that said the conversation wasn't over but reached for the phone. "Hello? . . . Yes, Mandy?" She hung up a couple of minutes later. Turning to her sister and brother-in-law, she said, "Our sheriff called to say that Sophie and Jessica have solved another mystery. And she asked if we'd like to learn how it all ended up."

"It only became sticky at the end, right, Sophie?"

Sophie laughed.

Mrs. Sandoval grabbed her purse, saying, "Let's all go." She flipped the sign on the door to "Closed. Be right back." Then everyone filed out of the shop, and she locked the door.

As they walked the short distance to the sheriff's office, a helicopter flew overhead and dropped down to land in the area of the resort. Mr. P., or whatever his name really was, must be leaving now too.

Sophie had one thing she needed to say to wrap up part of the mystery. "When we get home, Mom, we have something to show you about our house."

"Show me?"

"Aunt April, you'll be surprised, but in a good way. And it doesn't involve chocolate."

Mrs. Sandoval shook her head. "Okay, girls. I'm curious."

Inside the sheriff's office, they found Uncle Sal and Kelsey from Buds & Blooms.

After everyone had been introduced and the situation explained to Jessica's parents and Mrs. Sandoval, Sheriff Valeska said, "The man arrived at Buds & Blooms right on time. She handed him the chocolates and he left. We picked him up on the street, so this mystery is over."

Sophie said, "That's great, Sheriff!"

Uncle Sal said, "You two are welcome to come to the next

chocolate class. I want to make it up to you since this one didn't go quite as planned."

Sophie grinned. "I don't know about you, Cousin, but I wouldn't mind another chocolate lesson."

Jessica smiled at her parents. "That would be great. But my mom and dad are here now."

Uncle Sal said, "They're welcome too."

Jessica's mother reached over and took her daughter's hand. "Chocolate? I'd love to come."

Sophie leaned back in her chair. "Now I guess we need to wait for the next mystery."

All three parents groaned at the same moment.

Mrs. Sandoval said, "I hope there *isn't* another one."

Jessica looked at Sophie. "I kind of like our mysteries. I'm not too bad at solving them either, right, Sophie?"

"I think we're both good at solving mysteries now, Jessica."

ONE MORE MYSTERY

While Sophie, Jessica, and Tony were at the Chocolate Factory, they found one more mystery. Who ate the piece of chocolate when Jessica and Tony were hiding?

To use the same code that Sophie and Jessica used, write the alphabet from a to z on a piece of paper. Then, right next to each letter, write the code letter. Beside a, write b. Beside b, write c. Make the whole list and end with an a beside z.

Now, find the answer by decoding this:

VODMF TBM BUF JU XIFO IF TUPQQFE CZ TXFFU CJUFT UP QJDL VQ IJT XBMMFU

Get the answer at shannonlbrown.com/more

WHAT'S NEXT?

For more fun, this Mystery Writing PDF kit is FREE.

Find it at shannonlbrown.com/writeamystery. (*Ages 18 and older only please on this and all links in this ebook. Includes a teacher's guide.*)

ABOUT THE AUTHOR

Shannon Brown loved reading mysteries as a kid. She still does, but now she's excited that she gets to write them too. She enjoys hiking and shopping, and both chocolate and fruit, so parts of her personality are in Sophie and Jessica.

Originally from Alaska, she now lives in Tennessee with her professor husband. She enjoys writing with her adorable calico cat on her lap.

Shannon also writes sweet and clean romances as Cathryn Brown.